❋

# HIDDEN PASSION

Slowly, in disbelief, Ryder turned his head and met her gaze dead center. Up close her eyes were even deeper with color, mossy green flecked with rich, dark brown and shards of pure light. All day he'd been waiting to drown in those eyes, and when she'd stumbled into him, what had he done? Cursed her.

"Wait, I'm sorry." When she swiveled on the stool, he caught her shoulder. "I didn't realize who you were just now," he said swiftly. "I've looked everywhere for you."

She whirled in amazement. "Why? What do you want?"

He saw the quick lift of her chest under the rose shirt, noted the low-cut sweep of her swimsuit under that.

*You*, he thought.

❋

**Also by Leigh Riker**

*Tears of Jade*
*Unforgettable*

Available from HarperPaperbacks

# Morning Rain

## LEIGH RIKER

# HarperPaperbacks

*A Division of HarperCollinsPublishers*

Special edition printing: June 1994

HarperPaperbacks    *A Division of* HarperCollins*Publishers*
10 East 53rd Street, New York, N.Y. 10022

Cover illustration by Diane Sivavec

First printing: August 1991

Printed in the United States of America

HarperPaperbacks and colophon are trademarks of HarperCollins*Publishers*

10  9  8  7  6  5  4  3  2  1

In memory of my grandmother
Anna M. Perry
for love and faith

And with love
for Kimberly Anne Riker
who, from the day of her birth, has given such joy

She rose to his requirement,
      dropped
The playthings of her life
To take the honorable work
Of woman and of wife.

*from* J. 732
*by* Emily Dickinson

＊

＊ *BEFORE....* ＊

＊

*October 1972*

THE SENATOR KNEW how to work a crowd, even one attending a funeral.

Laurel watched him, his dark good looks distinguished by streaks of gray at the temples, shaking hands, smiling—the smile was melancholy—his hand touching a shoulder by way of thanks for some mawkish condolence. Laurel shivered, though the room was overheated. He did everything with style.

The service at Washington Cathedral had been discreet, elegant, tasteful. And attended, or so it had appeared, by half the population of the nation's capital, fifty percent of whom seemed now to be overflowing the senator's suburban Maryland living room. Talking, eating, laughing. Spilling drinks on the watered silk upholstery of Louis XVI chairs, and burning cigarette holes in gleaming mahogany Duncan Phyfe tabletops. Politicking. Yes, Edwin Frasier knew how to work a crowd—even one attending the funeral reception for his beloved elder daughter.

Turning, Laurel slipped into the wide hallway and

across to the dining room, running a practiced eye over the buffet tables. She checked the supply of ice, crystal, and liquid refreshment: wines, liquors, a champagne punch, fresh lemonade—her mother's closely guarded recipe.

Judith Frasier was absent from the gathering. Pale, blond, and carefully composed she had endured the past three days in tight-lipped, dry-eyed silence. Lexa, strong-willed and beautiful, had been the favorite—Judith's pride, and her ultimate despair. Laurel had glimpsed the tears in her mother's eyes at last just before the senator had sent her upstairs to rest, leaving Laurel, still tearless herself, to preside reluctantly as hostess.

How could people eat and laugh when her sister was dead? Feeling dazed, she went out onto the terrace, down the flagstone steps—and into a knot of waiting journalists. As they closed in, her heart began to pound in panic.

"Miss Frasier. How is your mother holding up?"

"She's resting now, but as well as can be expected. Thank you."

"Is it true she's been heavily sedated?"

"What about her drinking, Laurel?"

"The senator, Laurel. He's had his share of problems lately. Do you think public opinion will shift in his favor after this personal tragedy?"

Her palms were damp. "I couldn't say."

When she moved, someone barred her way. "What's your view of the outcry opposing your father's stand on the war? In the *Post* last week Ryder McKendrick wrote that—"

"I won't discuss Mr. McKendrick's article."

In the senator's presence the young newsman's name was an obscenity. A vendetta, he had labeled McKendrick's attack.

Trembling, Laurel took off her tortoiseshell glasses,

then put them back on again. It was like the morning
three days ago in the driving rain outside the campus
clinic, when she had emerged with Lexa's fiancé to be
surrounded by the press. Unlike Lexa, she'd never been
able to banter with them, to feel comfortable as the focus
of their questions.

"Is it true that Lexa's fiancé wasn't the only man in her
life, Laurel, that like the senator—"

Oh God, she thought. Where was Dan Benedict?

"I wouldn't know." Lexa, oh Lexa. Even now they
asked. And still, somehow, she would defend her sister
if she could. Alexandra and Laurel Frasier. The Twins—
their parents had never stopped using capital letters—
always they had been *The Twins* against the world. Only
last summer Lexa, the eldest by just four minutes, had
coaxed Laurel with that very phrase into demonstrating
after Watergate. They'd faced family wrath then, not over
the issue, but for the public display. They'd faced it, as
always, together.

"Maybe the senator's reputation with women served
as a model to—"

"Please, no more." Laurel pushed her way through the
crowd of reporters, as if escaping from a cage. "I can't
answer you. Leave me alone! *Please, leave me alone!*"

Pursued by shame, she ran. They knew about her father's women; everyone must, although Laurel wondered
whether Judith did. But they had no right to pry into
her parents' lives, or hers, or Lexa's; no right to probe
at people's grief. Skimming along the gravel path, she
fled deeper into the garden until she had reached the
safety of the oak tree. Willing her childhood sanctuary
to protect her, she leaned against its gnarled trunk. Her
pulse thundered. Would they follow her?

She could hear Dan Benedict's voice in the background, berating the journalists as he'd done outside the

clinic three days ago. Vultures, her sister's fiancé had called them then. And so they were.

But how had Lexa become that ill so quickly? Laurel wondered. Her sister had caught the sniffles, but the night before her death, she had stayed out until three A.M. and come back to the dorm reeking of stale Coors. In the morning she'd decided to cut her biology lecture, "Just this once."

"Once today, you mean," their roommate, Hilary Chapin, had chimed in from her lower bunk in the three-bed suite. She swung from bed, showing the leggy body that had earned her a small fortune as a part-time model. Hilary's trips to New York for photo sessions were the envy of the campus, more so than her mane of Titian red hair or her mother's legendary wealth, which wasn't nearly as uncommon among Carter College coeds, including the Frasier twins. "Lexa, you know what the senator will say when your semester grades reach Washington. 'One more cut and—'" She made a slicing motion across her throat, grinning.

"I'm not afraid of daddy," Lexa murmured, punching a goosedown pillow around her ears and ending the discussion.

Laurel, struggling to wake up, already felt the vague pressure building in her temples. Lexa *had* often claimed to feel Laurel's childhood aches and pains, and Laurel wondered whether she had been afflicted for once with her sister's hangover.

"I suppose there's a first time for everything," Hilary had commented hours later as she and Laurel hiked across campus to the infirmary, but Laurel hadn't been in the mood for jokes.

"It's not funny, Hil. The nurse on the phone said she's really sick."

"Then it's just the flu. God knows, as soon as we gather

in this place every September, the germs run faster than a guy after Lexa Frasier." Hilary paused. "Where do you think she was last night?"

Laurel shook her head. "One never knows."

"I wonder what Dan makes of that."

"I think he doesn't know," Laurel said. "She calls the wedding the 'hanging in the garden at high noon. Mother and Reverend Haskell presiding.'"

But the mention of Lexa's fiancé had been jolting. Engaged, Laurel thought. During freshman year Hilary and Lexa had conducted a competition for the most male scalps, but this second fall semester everything had changed. For Hilary, too. *Engaged*. Feeling a little left out, Laurel tried the word again. She wasn't used to the idea of Lexa getting married, and now Hilary had joined her.

As they topped the crest of a hill ablaze with New Hampshire autumn color, Hilary drew an envelope from her skirt pocket, and Laurel saw the familiar military logo. She brightened. "Another one? How many times have you read that letter from Chip since this morning?"

"Twenty-one, but who's counting?" Then Hilary's grin faded. "I've developed a morbid fascination with my mail slot. I tell myself that as long as I get something every day, he's still . . ." She trailed off, biting her lip.

Hilary's Navy flier had been in Vietnam for a month, and Laurel was distracted from her own worry over Lexa. "Of course he's okay. Charles Wellington Brewster's coming home with a chest so full of medals he won't be able to stand up straight."

Climbing the clinic steps, Hilary squeezed Laurel's hand. "That's what I like about you, pumpkin. No jealousy. Lexa'd be writing to him behind my back, but you only wish me the best. Her, too. You know, if you'd get your nose out of a book now and then or that drawing pad of yours, you'd have more action than you could handle. We could have a triple wedding ceremony."

"Me?" Laurel made a face. "I'm in no hurry. Besides, I'm shy."

"No kidding."

"Men don't seem to like that." Typically, she shifted the conversation from herself. "I think Dan's shy, too."

"That's not shyness, it's arrogance."

"Oh Hilary, you're too hard on Dan. I don't understand why. He's articulate and bright, he knows where he's going—"

"Laurel, you're quoting the senator."

"Well, Dan *is* his protegé." Ten years older than Lexa and Laurel, a graduate of the senator's summer intern program, and an aide for three years, Dan Benedict was now in Boston, one of Suffolk County's assistant district attorneys, preparing, Laurel felt sure, to begin the political future for which Edwin Frasier had groomed him. "The senator's right," she said. "Dan will make a perfect husband for Lexa."

"Meaning, he'll keep her in line?" Hilary had held open the clinic door. "I wonder."

Now they would never know, Laurel thought as she leaned against the oak tree in her parents' garden. Only too soon the clinic doctor had rendered his incomprehensible diagnosis: Lexa had some hyphenated syndrome that made no sense to Laurel, not even now when she knew what it could do.

There must be some mistake, she'd thought, entering her sister's hospital room. She'd seen Lexa only hours before, but in that time she seemed to have paled and shrunk. Immediately Laurel had wanted to take the disease upon herself, like the phantom hangover that had still pounded in her head.

When she said as much, Lexa's eyes drifted shut. "Your

turn at last. Remember when I got sent home from Miss Hall's school in second grade with stomach pains and you'd just left by ambulance for the hospital with a hot appendix? When you had the chicken pox, but it was me who itched? And when you fell out of our treehouse, my heart—" She gasped and opened her eyes. "Oh God, Laurel, I hurt."

"So do I, Lexie. But you're never really sick. It won't last long."

Tomorrow, Laurel had told herself; tomorrow she'll come home again, and the three of us, Lexa and Hilary and I, will stay up half the night playing bridge. Next weekend Dan will come from Boston to take us all to dinner as he likes to do—flashing credit cards and smiling at Alexandra. To irritate Dan, who's inclined to be priggish, Hilary will read us the good parts from one of Chip's letters. We'll laugh until our sides hurt. Next weekend, tomorrow . . .

Then a nurse had called Laurel into the hall, and Lexa had whispered, "Dear Lord. Don't tell Daddy."

It was only then that Laurel believed the worst might happen. Only then that she'd called the senator. The clinic hadn't been able to reach him, but Laurel knew all his haunts.

How many times had she made such a call? From day school in Bethesda when they were small, from boarding school in Vermont, from the campus of Carter College only last year. Alexandra had been expelled for swearing in chapel; Alexandra was planning to elope with a boy who played folk guitar and smoked funny cigarettes; Alexandra had been arrested for swimming naked in the college president's pond. Senator, I think you'd want to know. But this time, what could she say? Senator, Alexandra's . . . dying.

Dan Benedict reached Carter first. Sitting beside him

in the waiting room, Laurel had looked at the wall clock, feeling hot then chilled. Her own head had pulsed with pain, relentless, excruciating. Twelve-fifteen, the clock said. Where was the senator? The senator could fix anything, she told herself; peccadilloes, the national budget deficit, the arms race, private terrors. God, how she wanted him to fix everything now.

"Dan?" She clutched his arm. "Dan, I'm scared!"

The clock hands had jerked again, but now it was different. She didn't feel the pain. It had vanished, leaving nothing but a strange rushing sound inside her head, as if she were listening to a seashell. Emptiness, such emptiness. Dan's arm came around her shoulders, but the doctor, his steps dragging with fatigue and failure, didn't have to speak; Laurel already knew. She had known in that instant of rushing silence at twelve-sixteen. Alexandra, her twin, her other half, incredibly was dead.

Three days later, in the garden behind the house in Chevy Chase, Laurel lifted her head from the oak tree's gnarled trunk. Her gaze strayed to a nearby salmon-colored aster, still blooming in the cool autumn air, then swept the fading brilliance of yellow chrysanthemums.

She felt so frightened, so alone.

She'd had Hilary until half an hour ago. Then Hilary had left with her mother, "an outlandish woman," Judith insisted, though Laurel liked her very much.

"Poor lamb," Mrs. Harrington had said, standing with her husband and Supreme Court Justice Hulme. "You and Hilary must visit us in Gloucester. Freddy and I will close the house next month. Do find a weekend to come."

Therapy, Laurel thought, but she wished Hilary and her mother were with her now. She wondered whether, back at school, things would seem easier—if Hilary would pull her from grief, or if they'd make each other feel worse. There would be that empty bed in their suite, and Lexa's clothing still hanging in their closet. Or worse, someone else would move in. Worst of all for Laurel would be looking in a mirror. She'd been avoiding that. Wouldn't she see Lexa there instead?

No, she wanted to think, this was only one of Lexa's tricks. She'll wake up. And then: I've never been alone before, not even in our mother's womb.

"Your father's looking for you."

Dan Benedict's strong hands caught Laurel's shoulder from behind, and she started, then relaxed. All day she'd been grateful for his presence. For three days Dan had made the senator's indifference easier to bear. Now he said, "I got rid of those reporters."

"Thank you. I was terrible with them." She threw her hands wide. "I was just standing here contemplating an escape into the tree house." For a moment she'd thought exactly that: of tearing her hose and scuffing her shoes, ripping her new black suit as she shinnied up the huge oak to safety again. But the tree house had been torn down years ago.

"You're getting a bit old to be playing in trees." There was no smile in Dan's tone.

"Not playing," Laurel said, "hiding. Lexa was so much better at all of this. The press and Mother and the senator, even when she thumbed her nose at everyone, Dan, she . . ."

"I know." He turned her into his arms, and for the first time since they'd met in her father's Capitol Hill office when she was thirteen, all arms and legs, she didn't experience the desire to run before she made a fool of herself.

Laurel tipped her head back, showing him hazel eyes magnified by the enormous lenses of her tortoiseshell glasses. She saw a tall man, slightly thin, his shoulders enhanced by careful tailoring. He wore a vested black suit, a white dress shirt of fine cotton—the brand the senator bought, she knew—and an absolutely correct tie. He'd loosened it though, a gesture that touched her. Laurel had never known him to be less than perfectly groomed. He had such serious eyes, she realized, steel blue, and his hair, brown with hints of red, was always neatly parted.

They stood in the loose embrace, not speaking. They didn't know each other well, even after the last three days. Greetings and good-byes mostly. He wasn't at best a talkative man, and in that, she supposed, they were alike. She'd always left the conversation to Alexandra.

"We were to be married in this garden," he said after a silence. "Striped tents over there, a profusion of flowers. She wanted tulips in July . . . and she would have got them, Laurel."

"Yes, she would."

"We had all these plans, the kind of house we wanted, a few more years for me to practice law before—"

"A race for the Senate," Laurel supplied. "You can still do that, Dan."

She never would have expected death to bring such bewilderment to Dan Benedict, who, like the senator, gave the impression of strength, inside and out. Laurel leaned closer to him. Someone else, she had just learned, felt the same confusion she did. She pressed her cheek to his shoulder. And when he murmured, "Yes, I can still do that," she thought her heart would break in sympathy.

Sympathy, and guilt. Dan had loved her sister. But once last year, when they were freshmen, Lexa, who considered the classic deception of twinhood to be a wonderful game, had begged Laurel to pose in her place so she could go to a party with Hilary. Refusing at first— she'd never believed Lexa's assertion that they could trick their parents, either—Laurel had finally relented. Cloaked in her sister's personality that evening, she had dined with this attractive man—and been mildly disappointed when Dan left her at the dormitory with only a chaste good-night kiss. Now she wished she hadn't been able to fool him.

"Dan," she started to say, but he was lifting her chin with a fingertip.

"I hate black on a woman under forty," he said. Then his fingers twined in her hair. "You ought to buy yourself contact lenses. Get rid of these horrid glasses. They make you look like an owl." He removed them, tucking them into his jacket pocket, and staring for long moments into her eyes before, with a groan of anguish, he lowered his head and, to Laurel's astonishment, claimed her mouth.

His kiss was soft, frustrated.

She held still. He seemed to need something from her, to demand it. She felt a vague, pleasant stirring in response before Dan raised his head, ending the kiss. "I'm sorry," he whispered. "God, I'm sorry." His hand, smoothing Laurel's dark hair into place, trembled. "What kind of monster am I, here in the garden with you only an hour after we've buried—"

"It's all right, Dan. I understand." Her mouth felt sensitive from his kiss, and Laurel put a finger to her lips. "I'm sorry, too."

He had only needed human contact, just as she did; it hadn't really been Laurel he was kissing. The sisters looked so much alike, if he didn't look carefully. He wouldn't see now the distance that shyness gave her. He could ignore it, because he must feel as miserable as she did.

Laurel wondered why she didn't mind his using he~ except that she'd played Lexa's favorite game~ identities so many times. It was as if she'~ in to the pose with Dan again to please~

right now she felt closer to Dan Benedict than she'd ever felt to any man. To the senator, Laurel amended.

"There you are. I've been tracking you for fifteen minutes." The sound of her father's voice made Laurel swing around, and Dan released her. The senator, carrying a glass of whiskey, strode across the lawn. "Laurel, we have important guests inside."

"I'm sorry, Senator." They were always important. "I'm coming right in."

Shocked, Laurel realized this was the first time in three days that he'd spoken to her directly. That he was, at last, looking into her face as Dan had—perplexed, grief-stricken, disoriented. He had made all the arrangements to bring Lexa home, planned the cathedral service, managed a graveside eulogy to which Laurel had shut her ears, so as not to break down and disgrace her parents. He had talked with Hilary's mother and Justice Hulme and Dan and hundreds of other people, but not with her.

Laurel wanted to touch him, but held back; maybe now he would reach out to *her*. She needed to cry in his arms, to give him comfort, too. Maybe now . . .

In the next instant she knew it would never happen. And she knew why. He was staring at her, just as Dan had done before he kissed her. Then Edwin Frasier glanced away, into his Kentucky bourbon, his voice thick with grief.

"Why Alexandra?" he said. "Why in God's name did it have to be Lexa?"

## ✳ CHAPTER 1 ✳

✳

NESTLED ON THE green velvet cushion of the library's bay window, Laurel Frasier Benedict stared out over a cooling cup of coffee at the holiday exodus of Boston traffic. Even this normally quiet side street on Beacon Hill was jammed with cars, and it was barely ten o'clock. The Friday morning before Labor Day had made people slightly mad to be out of the city, headed to some over-crowded beach for the last official weekend of summer. All Laurel could say for the day was that it wasn't raining, though a storm was predicted for Sunday. Since that early morning outside the campus clinic after Lexa had died, she'd dreaded rain, dreaded being alone with it.

Laurel sighed and set aside the mug she'd been cradling. She wasn't going anywhere today—unless Hilary had her way. Laurel didn't feel up to acknowledging that Hilary usually did.

Intent on the sounds from across the hall as eight-year-old Ned pulled the last of his belongings together and the dog scrabbled at another bedroom door to be let out, Laurel already felt hollow. She'd felt the same way four-teen years ago when she'd lost Lexa.

She knew she was being maudlin now, missing Ned

13

before he'd left the house; but didn't Dan realize how important their son was to her? What would she do with Ned away at school for nine months?

Laurel frowned. She hadn't needed any media announcements to guess the answer to that. The past two days there'd been tense activity on the three floors of this elegant town house—discussions late into the night and all day, until there seemed to be no break from them. Discussions with Teague Michaels, Dan's probable Senate campaign manager, discussions with local politicos and people from national headquarters, discussions with Edwin Frasier. The senator, she knew, was only slightly less determined than Dan that if Dave Cabell, the incumbent, resigned as a result of Wednesday's coronary occlusion, his own son-in-law would leap into the breach. And Dan would expect Laurel to devote the next two months of her own life to a cause she despised even before he'd taken it up publicly.

The United States Senate. The dream of Daniel Benedict's life had become reality—or at least possible—just forty-eight hours ago.

Laurel couldn't have dreaded it more. The only thing keeping her fear at bay for the moment was the other, stark reality of Ned's leaving.

"The school will be good for him," Dan had argued. "You make such a baby of him."

From Laurel's point of view as a mother, Ned was still close to being just that—a baby, and one she'd gladly coddle while she could.

But Dan's decision had been made long before the news of Dave Cabell's heart attack. Before Laurel could formulate a rational plan to keep her son at home, Ned had been interviewed, then accepted at Dawson Prep. Dan hadn't been swayed by her token protest. After all, in her own family, boarding school was tradition; she and Lexa had been sent away when only a year older than Ned was now. But he seemed so young, and he still needed her.

Maybe that was why Dan wanted him to go away. He'd have her all to himself then. As if he wanted her for anything more than hitting the campaign trail.

Laurel rose from the window seat, where she'd been watching for Dan's chocolate-colored Audi to pull away from the garage underneath the house and park in front to load Ned's luggage. She walked to the wall of shelves across the room and, without thinking, punched a button on the television set. A news update blinked into view and she smiled ruefully. The channel selection had been automatic. Over the last forty-eight hours she had developed a compulsion that amazed her, considering her wariness of publicity.

She might be wary, but she understood the goldfish-bowl existence she'd always known. Her assessment of Dan was as automatic as the news channel she'd chosen. The mobile camera unit had caught him earlier outside the house—his dark brown hair blown by the breeze, his steel blue eyes clear and sharp, his whole bearing suggesting vitality and strength. She had to admit he looked good on television, even better than in person. At forty-three he still had his hair with few touches of gray, all his teeth, that winner's smile—and the taut body of a man ten years younger. The senator had chosen well.

Laurel knew, however, that her speeding pulse resulted not from arousal at the sight of her husband, but from fear. She watched a reporter thrust a microphone under Dan's nose. "Sir, Senator Cabell is in critical condition. How do you see his chances for finishing the race to save his seat?"

"Dave Cabell's a strong man, in more ways than one. We've seen that in his tough stand on arms and defense spending, in last year's budget cut recommendations. I'm sure—" Dan's confident smile zapped the camera lens head-on "—that he'll be on his feet again physically, too, in no time."

"If not," the reporter pressed, "will you step in, Counselor?"

"You're being, at the least, premature." Dan grinned, obviously flattered. "I have faith in Dave Cabell. So should you guys."

"We're not counting him out, but surely your past record as a two-term councilman would pay off with voters."

"Keep watching the news, gentlemen. I'm not going to speculate."

Faintly smiling, Laurel turned off the set. He's good, she thought. Wifely pride made her admit that, but the positive feelings stopped there and so did her smile.

Where did we go wrong? she wondered. Four years after Lexa's death, one year after Laurel finished college, she had married Dan Benedict in a garden ceremony at the house in Chevy Chase. At her mother's request thousands of roses and tulips had been flown in from Holland for the occasion. Laurel walked down the red-carpeted aisle in the lace drift of gown and veil that had been her mother's, wearing her grandmother's pearls and her own clammy skin. The "china doll fragility" of her complexion, noted by the *Washington Post*, had come from nerves— and perhaps, she wondered now, second thoughts?

If so, she hadn't recognized them at the time. She and Dan had started marriage where they'd left off courtship—as each other's longtime habit. From his first telephone call to Laurel at school just weeks after Lexa's death, checking on her well-being, to dinner alone with him because Hilary wouldn't make the third, to a series of holidays spent in Chevy Chase, they'd inexorably moved toward a lifetime together. By the start of her senior year at Carter, Laurel realized they had what once was known as "an understanding." Dan had never actually proposed. One Sunday morning over brunch, he'd taken her hand and said, "I think it would please your parents if we got married at home."

Laurel had felt little resistance. As one of the political Frasiers, she was expected to make a good marriage; certainly she had no blazing career plans to pursue or to set aside. She frowned, remembering for the first time in years Hilary's complaint that she'd been throwing away her art on a man who didn't deserve her. Her art? she thought now. That was a lofty term for a few classes she'd taken in college, a sketchpad full of drawings she'd made in her tree house hideaway years ago. In Laurel's opinion, they weren't terribly good. But Dan's future, she had thought, offered the life she'd always known, even if she hadn't always been comfortable in it. And after the initial closeness they'd experienced at Lexa's death, Laurel welcomed the ongoing sense of familiarity with Dan. When they were together, she felt that Lexa was there, too.

Maybe, she'd thought, with Dan's love and guidance she could become more like Lexa, more the woman Judith and the senator wanted her to be. Then the loss of her sister would stop hurting so desperately. At last she'd cease missing some vital part of herself, cease hearing in her heart the senator's words after the funeral: Why did it have to be Lexa?

Married to Dan, she'd find acceptance and love, and eventually there'd be children. Laurel sighed again. Now she wasn't so sure about their marriage, and though she'd hoped for more babies after Ned . . .

"Mommy?"

Laurel turned at his voice. Ned stood in the library doorway, a vulnerable child with a thatch of his father's deep brown hair and a pair of wide hazel eyes fringed in thick, blunt lashes. He was small for his age and not athletic, though Dan had chosen Dawson partly for its stables where "he'll be able to keep his horse, join the equestrian team, who knows—one day perhaps he'll ride in the Olympics."

Laurel simply hoped that he'd learn to enjoy riding the big black gelding his father had bought two years ago. She couldn't fathom Dan's passion at a distance for horse-flesh when she'd never seen him take the least interest himself in riding. Certainly she had none; but the fact that Dan took their son every Sunday afternoon to the barn where Storm had been stabled until three days ago, kept Laurel from protesting. Otherwise, Dan didn't give Ned much time.

"Yes, darling," she murmured now, "what is it?"

"I've finished packing." He came into the room, and as Laurel held out her arms, he tumbled into them. "Oh, Mommy, I want to stay here. I don't want to go to Dawson, it's so far away. I don't want to ride Storm every day. I won't ever see you again."

The last words came in a broken tone. Laurel's heart turned over. She'd been so preoccupied with her own misgivings that she hadn't gauged the true depth of his. "Darling, hush. It won't be as bad as you're thinking. In fact—" she held him away and forced a smile "—you'll have a wonderful time. It'll be like vacation . . . woods and hills to roam, new friends. And a lovely room, Daddy tells me, with a fireplace just for you—and your room-mate, of course."

"Who will my—my roommate be?"

"Somebody fun, I'm sure. To run and play with, shout and scream when you feel like it, who'll show you how to make water balloons to drop on—" Laurel's gaze jerked upward to Dan, standing at the door. She hadn't heard him come up the stairs. "I was just telling Ned—"

"I know what you were doing." Dan shifted. "Ned, are you ready? The car's waiting. Where are your bags?"

"I'll get them."

Ned scrambled free of her embrace and, not looking at his father, ran past him into the hall.

"He's frightened," Laurel said. "Why can't you make this easier for him? Say something encouraging—"

"You indulge him. He's not a nursing infant, Laurel."

She felt a surge of anger. "So you keep telling me."

He'd always hated seeing her with Ned at the breast, she remembered; had it been jealousy, or resentment that she could love someone else completely? Dan's displeasure had been so blatant, she'd quit nursing when the baby was only four months old.

Ned had been a frail infant, a fragile toddler. Would he be all right away from home? He often had nightmares. Who would hold him when he woke screaming? She remembered her own first days at boarding school. How much more difficult they would have been without Lexa. Ned had been heartbroken for weeks at the prospect of leaving Boston, leaving his best friend, Kip. Would the school be good for him, as Dan insisted, as she'd tried in a show of parental unity to tell him? God, she hoped so. Prayed so. If not, she'd bring him home fast enough no matter whether Dan Benedict was campaigning to be president.

"Don't look mutinous, Laurel." Dan's voice lowered. "I know you think I'm dead wrong, but I'm not. He'll be fine. In a month or two, you'll see."

"In a month or so, maybe you will."

He studied her as if she were a stranger who'd walked into the house. "It doesn't do him any good to hear us quarreling."

"I'm sorry," she said. "You're right." Laurel walked toward him and changed the subject. "I caught you on television a few minutes ago."

"They showed the tape?"

At the leap of interest in his expression, she said, "You looked very impressive."

He smiled. "Vote for me if I run, Mrs. Benedict?"

She tried to smile back. "I'll think about it."

He pulled her into his arms and kissed her. Lightly, perfunctorily. "*If* you run," she murmured as he released her. "Will you, Dan? Teague Michaels hasn't been at the house lately because he likes to beat you at chess."

"He can't beat me in chess," Dan commented, which was true. He turned to see Ned approach, dragging a huge leather suitcase with the sleeve of a shirt caught in the closing. "Off the record," he began, then didn't finish.

Laurel felt the sinking sensation to her toes. After the meetings, and now with the flushed look of anticipation on his face, she hardly needed the answer. She'd tried to want this, too. But she'd always placed it in the distant future, supposed that when the time came, she'd accept it and do her part. Now, she couldn't face a campaign, or its outcome. They would leave this beautiful house in the heart of Boston, which she loved, the home where they'd brought Ned from the hospital. They would move to Washington, near Judith and the senator. And I'll start yearning to build another tree house, Laurel thought. Oh, God.

Silently, she prayed for Dave Cabell.

"Come on, Ned." Dan hoisted the suitcase and two others from the hall. "I can't hold the parking space."

Laurel said, "I wish I were going with you."

Tensing, Dan paused at the head of the stairs. "We've gone over that. Nothing good would come of your hanging around at the school once he's settled. And I've half

a dozen Labor Day speeches to give, which would bore
you to distraction." He'd already been asked to cover for
Dave Cabell.

"Yes, I understand."

He wanted the good-byes to end here. She almost
couldn't manage them. Here was Ned with a tattered
teddy bear under his arm, an ebony plastic soprano recorder tucked in the pocket of his blue linen blazer, and
the totebag of treats she'd packed for the drive to Dawson. Candy bars, apples, roast beef sandwiches, and a
thermos of pineapple juice, Ned's favorite. He was allergic
to oranges—had she put that on his health form? She
fought back tears and the urge to stop him, hold him
fiercely. It had happened too fast. What kind of mother
was she, how could she send—

"Ned, come on!"

"He's hurrying. Go start the car." Laurel ignored the
anger in Dan's eyes as he circled at the bottom of the
flight. In the foyer he stood for a moment as if deciding
whether to respond; then he turned and went out the
door. Laurel whispered, "Give Mommy a kiss, darling,
and a big fat hug."

Ned clutched at her. Cherishing the warmth of his
slight body, she carried him down the flight of stairs.
He'd often been sick as a baby, and the bond they'd
formed was strong, on a level that had nothing to do
with thought. Laurel felt the tears well. It was close to
what she'd shared with Lexa. "Be a good boy, love. I'll
call you tonight."

She held him close a moment longer. Oh God, if she
should ever lose him. A hundred babies couldn't replace
him, and Dan didn't want more. Sometimes she wondered if he had even wanted . . .

She wouldn't finish the thought. Laurel set Ned down
in the foyer. A sudden sound from upstairs, high and

whining, made her smile through the tears she hadn't let him see. "Have you forgotten, Ned?"

"What?"

Laurel whispered in his ear. Let his father wait a minute longer. Ned had been so distraught by the leavetaking that he'd neglected the most important farewell. With a cry he was up the stairs, thin legs pumping and the coattails of his jacket flying. "Pirate! Pirate!"

Suddenly there came a thunder of feet like a small herd of cattle in the house. Down the stairs raced Ned, an enormous blur of white at his heels.

"Ned, be careful, he'll trip you!" Laurel held her breath until the two landed safely at the bottom of the steps. She could hear Dan, impatiently tapping the horn outside.

"Mommy, I think he's feeling sad."

She stared down at the small boy dwarfed by the huge, shaggy-coated and lop-eared dog. That his parents and grandsire had been international champions must have escaped Pirate. The animal was a disgrace—and vastly loved by herself and Ned. She realized Ned was voicing his own dismay; but oddly, Pirate had spent the last three nights across Ned's bed, all four limbs gangling over the side of the mattress and one velvety ear, as always, inside out.

"He's going to miss you, too," Laurel said. "If I can convince Daddy, we'll bring Pirate to visit in a week or two."

"He won't let him come." Ned wrapped his arms around the dog's neck and buried his face in the thick white fur. Then he rose, angrily wiping tear streaks from his face while he looked into the soulful brown eyes that watched his every move. "You be good, Pirate. You can use my bed if you want. Don't let him run in the street, Mommy." He gave Laurel one last look she couldn't read—blame, acceptance?—and was gone at the same instant Dan pounded the car horn.

Pirate collapsed in a heap of belly and legs on the Aubusson rug in the entryway. Snout braced on his front paws, the Great Pyrenees stared at her balefully as Laurel gave one last wave at the departing car.

"Me, too, Pirate," she said. A final glance across the street revealed no reporters, lingering with cameras ready. Until two days ago, she'd hoped never to see another newsman for the rest of her life. Relieved for the moment, she closed the foyer door. "Me, too," Laurel repeated.

Why me? Ryder McKendrick asked himself as he shoved open the glass door to *Newstrend*'s ultramodern reception area of sky blue walls and fudge-brown upholstery. Why the summons at dawn from his editor on the one morning in three weeks when he could have slept late? Then he checked his watch and grinned. It wasn't dawn at all, but nearly noon. His body was still running on foreign time.

He strode past the receptionist at a glass desk flanked by chrome plant containers.

"Hey, you can't go in there without—"

"The dragon lady's expecting me," Ryder called over his shoulder, already through the next door and halfway down the corridor to *Newstrend*'s editorial suite. Playing by somebody else's rules had never gotten him a story, or anything else he wanted.

What could Sara Hennessey want? Her phone call earlier had been irritatingly vague, and Ryder had been just unconscious enough, jet-lagged enough, not to care whether he received her message. He'd rolled over for another two hours' sleep, then couldn't keep his eyes shut. The dim memory of "something important" had finally registered on his reporter's brain.

Glancing into offices and cubicles, he saw gunmetal gray desks and file cabinets, and lots of grimy coffee mugs. *Newstrend* wasn't his usual milieu, but the daily, a tough competitor of the newer *USA Today,* like most papers he'd worked for, concentrated its dazzle in the public areas. Backstage, where everything happened, couldn't have been plainer.

Hennessey's office, except for the few trappings of executive privilege, wasn't much of an improvement.

"Only for you, Sara, my love," he said, pulling off mirrored sunglasses. "What's on your mind that won't wait?"

"Matthew Ryder McKendrick," she murmured, barely glancing up from a sheaf of papers on her desk, "still alive and breathing, I see."

He dropped onto a worn leather chair across from her. "I'm happy to see you, too," he said. "I'd kiss you but—"

"Don't you dare."

Grinning, he contemplated the gleam in her gimlet-dark eyes, noted that the wiry hair cut short had more gray, and that the perpetual frown etched between heavy brows was still in place. Those bony, broad-palmed hands would wield that blue editing pencil, as always, with skill and surprising tenderness.

She set the manuscript aside. Taking a slim black cigar from her drawer, she rolled it in blunt-tipped fingers, testing the aroma. "Cheap," she pronounced, then lit it anyway. "Just got back from Lebanon, did you?"

"Day before yesterday. Hot as hell. The weather, too," he added. "The time change screws me up for a week. After all these years, you'd think I'd adjust automatically when I cross seven time zones."

Hennessey grunted. "Why change now? The rut you're

in may not be comfortable, it may even be dangerous, but it's all yours."

Ryder wanted to squirm. Sara liked to get under his skin, but lately she'd been getting worse. After all these years.

"Don't start," he said.

"The only good reporter to me is a live reporter," she observed. "Mac, Beirut's the best place in the world for an American to get kidnapped or murdered."

"At the least, a sound beating. Don't scold." He opened his arms. "No bruises, Sara, see?"

"This time. Quit trying to get yourself killed." Impatiently, she shrugged out of a wide-lapeled charcoal suit jacket that had seen better days twenty years ago. "Try living again," she said. "Get yourself a woman—"

"I've got a woman. Waiting for me." It was a lie on both counts, but Ryder never blinked.

She took her time, rolling back the cuffs of a white blouse missing its third button. "Yeah, I can imagine. Someone two, three times a month when you can't do without. I'm not talking about down-and-dirty sex to keep the pipes cleaned out. I'm talking about a tie-you-down, make-babies-with-you woman." She waited a fractional second. "Like Maggie."

Shit, now she sounded like his mother. And from either of them, it hurt. He kept silent.

"Six years is a long time," Sara murmured.

"Yeah, and it's going to be longer. Probably forever." He couldn't look her in the eye and stared down at his blue cotton sweater. "If I've learned to live with that, why can't you? She was my wife, dammit. She's dead and buried, and whose fault is that?"

"Tell me," Sara said.

"Mine."

"I doubt that, Mac."

He frowned. Sometimes it didn't seem like six years, it seemed only minutes ago—the four of them, Sara's husband, too, swilling drinks and besting each other's jokes, eating in that little Italian place that Maggie had liked so much. Then again, sometimes it seemed like a century. He figured this sixth anniversary weekend of Maggie's death could turn into one of them.

"Look, Sara, I'd love to hash over old times, but unless you've got business for me, I'm late already."

"For what?" she said.

"Breakfast."

"I thought you had a date waiting." She looked at her watch. Both hands pointed straight up. Sara shrugged. "Well, nice of you to drop by. Sorry you're going to lose out on the Pulitzer again, McKendrick." She tossed the morning *Globe* at Ryder. "Headline, page one. Four columns."

"So? The whole world knows Cabell's in the hospital."

"Latest scuttlebut says he isn't coming out." Sara paused. "I can't imagine Ed Frasier's crying."

"Frasier?" The senator had been retired for four years.

"You've been spending too much time among the Arabs, Mac. His name still makes everybody stand up and sing 'The Star Spangled Banner.' With that shock of white hair, that look of sincerity, he's America's grandfather, with sex. And power, Lord." She laid the cigar in a chunky amber glass ashtray and linked her hands behind her head. "You and I both know, presidents are just temporary guests. Guys like Frasier dig in for the long haul. Thirty years in the Senate, two terms before that in the House, chairman of Armed Services, then Finance. Made his name during the Eisenhower scandals, which you won't remember." Sara smiled as if to say, callow youth. "Television might have been invented for him."

"All right, he's an impressive bastard. Emphasis on the

last word," Ryder said. "So what?"

"He's Daniel Driscoll Benedict's father-in-law."

A chill raced down Ryder's spine. He'd nearly forgotten.

"Daniel D. Benedict," she repeated. "If not exactly to the manor born, he sure as hell married it."

"Frasier wants him in," Ryder surmised.

"Another longterm project."

"You think he'll announce? Even with Frasier behind him," Ryder said, "this guy'd have his work cut out for him. It'd be the same as it was with Jimmy Carter and the presidency. 'Daniel who?' He'd have to shake a lot of hands and log thousands of miles to get himself elected."

"He'll do it." Ryder heard the barely controlled anger. "Unless . . ."

"Oh, no you don't. Investigative journalism? Me?" He dragged a hand through his hair. "Sara, for Chrissake, I'm a photographer these days. You want closeups of him kissing babies, maybe I can spare a couple of hours as a personal favor, but—"

"I don't want a photo album." Pulling a heavy volume from a shelf behind her desk, she slammed it open. "That isn't what I saw here. That isn't what I read in these pages."

His heart thumping, Ryder looked away. "Benedict's run for the Senate isn't Southeast Asia, Hennessey. You know it." Just as she knew that those pictures, dammit, and that text, were off-limits. He had long ago stopped regretting that his only book hadn't won a Pulitzer. Close, it had come so close. But he was better off without it.

"This was gut work, McKendrick. Poetic, inspiring, beautiful—and ugly. I cry like a baby every time I open it."

Which was why he didn't open the book. Ever. "We're

not talking war here, Sara. A political campaign, even with Ed Frasier—"

"Aren't we? Stay home for a change, and look around. I think this country's headed for trouble. With Benedict and Frasier pulling strings at the White House, I know it is."

"What's your axe, Sara? Why ask me to grind it?"

"Goddammit, I want quality! The stuff I see in these—" she shoved the large book closer "—pictures you never forget, the feeling underneath. *Images of Destruction*," she read from the title page, "my God, yes. You went below the surface of that war, McKendrick— caught its people with their souls hanging out. Soldiers, civilians, even the mangy dog begging scraps on the street. That's what I want, right here at home."

Ryder said nothing.

"Mac, you've been fighting the same war over and over on film—and inside yourself—in half a dozen hot spots around the world since those last days in Vietnam, Laos, Cambodia. Trying to make some personal tragedy come out right this time. It's not only Maggie, is it?" She knew him too well, Ryder thought. Sara had survived the loss of her husband, too. "What happened over there?"

He shook his head. "Nothing."

She said, "There's war in your own backyard, Mac, one you can do something about, maybe even a war that has a peaceful end. I need to know what makes Frasier and his son-in-law run so fast, and so far. So does the public."

"Dirt, is that what you want?"

"Investigative reporting," Sara repeated. She leaned over her desk, arms braced on her fingertips. "There isn't a politician who isn't hiding something, somewhere. You know that as well as I do. Hell, since Watergate, everybody knows it. Campaign fund shenanigans, conflicts of interest, influence peddling . . ."

"I'm out of the garbage business: Frasier's doing, re-member?" Ryder grimaced at the memory of the jobs he'd lost because of the senator's influence. One had been at *Capitol,* the other for Sara at *National in the News* after she left the *Post,* taking him with her. His crusading instincts had almost cost him his career. As for his marriage and Nam and . . .

"Sara, Benedict's been practicing law for ten years. Councilman for two terms. Mr. Civic Cleanliness."

"The dirt rubs off. We just can't see it, like the emperor's new clothes. Don't you want another chance at Frasier?"

Ryder tensed. Sara was really on his case this morning. He wondered at her motives, which she didn't seem inclined to reveal.

"Give it a try, McKendrick." She named a figure, double what she'd offered Ryder in the past. "One piece, a profile. If things look promising, we'll run a series."

She meant, if Cabell pulled out of the race, or died. Seeing Ryder's hesitation, she continued, "And don't tell me you're not a writer. I saw the article on aging in our cities for *Time,* and the piece on white-collar crime for *Sunday* magazine. I also remember you from way back, chum. Working your first cub beat for me in Washington right after you and Maggie got married—"

"Sara."

He'd been a rookie then, but he was sure as hell a veteran now. With few illusions. And, he couldn't believe it, he was pushing thirty-nine.

"There's a kill fee," Sara said, "if we can't use the story."

She tossed a folder at him. Ryder leafed through the pictures of Edwin Frasier and his wife, shots of Daniel Benedict leaving the courthouse after winning an acquittal for a client. Then he stopped.

His gaze rested on an even older, grainy photograph

of the senator, his face seamless, his hair thick and only faintly touched by gray. There was a young woman with him, flanked by Dan Benedict, also younger. Their features were indistinct, the photo unclear, creating more of an impression than an image. Ryder simply stared. Dark-haired, mysterious, she carried an aura of sadness in the graceful, swanlike bend of her neck. The picture had been taken at a funeral.

"You people really keep a morgue here, don't you?" Ryder asked, remembering. "This must be fifteen years old."

"Fourteen."

"The senator's daughter," he said. "Something quick and deadly."

"Meningitis." Sara shrugged. "That's the girl's twin in the photo. Now Benedict's wife."

Money, class, breeding, Ryder thought; they stuck out all over, even with the black mourning clothes, gloves, and hat.

He still didn't like it. But Sara was the best editor he knew—keen, insightful, honest. And that article on Frasier's war position, the week before his daughter died, had been only the first. Back from Nam, Ryder had been embittered, depressed over men like Frasier who sent boys to die, who killed women and children. Sara had published the rest of his articles, too—until Frasier intervened.

Nail him, Ryder thought.

Trust her, one part of his mind insisted while another side said, Walk away—there's always Nicaragua. Ryder ignored the fact that he always got sick in Central America. A few weeks on his belly in the jungle, he thought, without a bath, wearing rank fatigues. His pulse running double-time, all the time. Film rotting in the heat and damp. The perfect photo was always the next one. It was the atmosphere he knew, had even thrived on after Nam.

But was Sara right?

"Frasier's daughter," she said. "Much younger there, of course, but she's got the family looks. When she appears with Benedict, there's a quality of distance. As if they aren't much married to each other."

"Jesus, Hennessey."

The last of her limited patience snapped. "What do you want for the rest of your life, Mac—to keep flying around this crazy world taking pictures of men with their intestines in their hands, women weeping over lost husbands, when a story is right here in front of you? What's it gonna be, Mac, this or little kids with soulful eyes—"

He surged to his feet. "Shut up, damn you!"

He could all but hear the rapid tick of his pulse, felt it jumping at the base of his throat.

Sara glanced at the still-open book. "What happened with the kid, Ryder? You've never talked about her."

"I never will," he managed.

He went to the window and leaned his head against the cool glass. "You ought to become a regular on 'Beat the Press.' You've got a real talent for flogging, Sara."

After a moment he could feel her standing just behind him, but she didn't touch him. If she had, he would have jumped out of his skin.

"Take the story, Mac." Her tone was quiet. "One try. If something breaks, and after that you don't want to keep digging—"

"All right, dammit."

"—I'll assign another reporter."

"Photographer," he said. She'd pushed too far. And won. "All right."

She walked him to the door. "I'll have my secretary copy the file on Benedict and Frasier and get it to you by messenger Tuesday. Will you be home by then?"

The old witch. She knew he wasn't going anywhere. "Yeah, I'll be there."

"Mac, you owe this to yourself."

But for some reason he knew Hennessey included herself, too. Ryder shook his head. "No," he said, "I think I owe it to her."

She would assume he'd meant Maggie, and that was fine by him.

Ryder punched the down button for the elevator, waited, then slumped against the back wall of the car during a swift descent to the lobby that took the pit of his stomach into his sneakers. In mirrored glasses, he stared at the ceiling as if it might help him not to feel. But the lump stayed in his throat.

*What happened with the kid?*

He didn't need to see the pictures—the one picture— that could still make him tremble. The images shot through his mind anyway. The happy ones. A child, three, maybe four years old, with dark, hunted eyes. The tiny bones of her arms and legs. The first burst of her smile when he handed her a chocolate bar. *What happened with the kid?*

He could see her on a spring morning when the ruined countryside had managed to look green again, so verdant. Then, he'd imagined her always full of life, and light. Now he wanted to remember her that way. Or not to remember at all.

She couldn't remember.

"Oh, damn." Laurel stepped once more over Pirate's prone form on the den carpet. Where had she put that membership list? The sheet of paper didn't seem to be anywhere, but since Ned's departure, Pirate was everywhere. Laurel gave up and plopped down on the desk chair.

The truth was, she didn't care about the November charity luncheon. When had she cared about any of them? Unlike Judith, she considered them silly affairs and always wondered why she accepted another chairmanship, then another. To her mother, it was an honor, to Laurel, nothing but duty. Why ruin the weekend any further by trying to work out a seating arrangement that would please all the egos involved? Impossible.

Still, she made a last search through the pile of papers on her writing desk. Nothing. Frustrated, she tapped a pencil against a notepad with Dan's name imprinted at the top. She didn't like the way the day was going. She felt worse than Pirate but didn't want to mope around. After a moment the tap became a squiggle on the blank page, then a quick series of lines and circles. Dan would call them doodles, and Laurel supposed the term fit as well as Hilary's calling them art.

But she enjoyed sketching, her own loose term. Within seconds she was staring down at a black-and-white Pirate, nose on paws in canine dejection, his liquid eyes soulful in a furry face. Laurel laughed and flipped the page.

Ned's eyes came all too easily—big, and wounded as he'd looked at her for the last time before he left. Laurel shaded in the delicate jawline, but her joy in the simple activity had disappeared. Depressed now, she tossed her glasses on the desk. With relief, she heard the front doorbell chime.

The sound galvanized Pirate. Yipping and barking, he beat Laurel to the door. "Move, beast." Wrenching the door open, she commanded, "Out—out of the way!" and came face to face with Hilary Chapin.

"Terribly glad to see you, too. What a welcome, dear friend."

"Come in." Laurel grinned, brushing hair from her eyes. "I was talking to this animal, as usual."

"Trying to," Hilary corrected. "And you can't see four inches in front of your face, anyway. Where are your glasses?"

"How did you know I'm not wearing my contacts?"

Hilary waved a hand. "Dan's not home, is he?"

"My God, did you learn that in Logic?"

"Experience." Giving Laurel a hug, she stepped into the foyer, blocking the dog's quick escape effort. Hilary shut the door. "You and I make quite a team. We should play for the Patriots."

Laurel followed her into the living room, with Pirate padding after.

"They *have* left?" Hilary asked, glancing around.

"Almost an hour ago."

"Sorry I'm late. Darn, I wanted to kiss Ned good-bye. And give Daniel a swift kick where it would hurt most." Turning, she gave Laurel a malicious smile.

"Kick me instead," Laurel said, wishing she'd put up more of a fight with Dan. "Ned looked so betrayed."

"Just like his mother, the kid's tougher than he looks." Hilary's gaze swept over Laurel's delicate frame, her green shorts and yellow T-shirt, her scrubbed-clean face and bare feet. She smiled. "I see you've begun the weekend's rebellion without me."

"Rebellion?"

"No makeup, no shoes." Hilary leered. "Probably no underwear, either."

Laurel laughed. "Is it that obvious?"

"On a stringbean figure like mine, no. On you," she said with a grin, "definitely yes."

"That's a stringbean figure worth millions on a runway at the House of Dior."

"For another year or so." Hilary sobered. "I could kill that man, you know. Cheerfully. No remorse at all. I wouldn't care if they sent me to the gas chamber."

"Dan?"

"It's not as if he's spent ten minutes a day with that child since he was born. How much trouble can Ned be to—"

"Hilary, don't."

"And look at you." She eyed the faded T-shirt. "Like a teenager let out of school—boarding school. When I see you like this, looking free again, I just automatically start thinking the *D* word."

"*D* word?"

"Divorce, dear friend."

Laurel's cheeks flushed. She'd awakened one recent morning from a bad dream with tears trickling through her hair onto her pillow. In the dream she'd left Dan— and he was tearing Ned from her arms, taking him away forever.

"I'm a Frasier by birth," she reminded Hilary. "There has never been a divorce in our family. Dan's either."

"How enlightened. Are those words of wisdom from Judith?"

"And the senator."

"Kind of a corollary, I suppose," Hilary said, "to the Frasier-women-don't-need-paid-employment theory."

"Well, they—we don't."

"Someday, pumpkin, you may want to write your own philosophy."

Laurel sighed. "Someday I'll figure out how we've been friends so long when you don't seem to like my husband, my family, or anyone I—"

"I'm crazy about my unofficial nephew. I'll miss Ned as much as you will. And I love it, dear friend, when that stubborn streak of yours finally shows itself. Go ahead, tell me to go to hell." She collapsed on a small Hepplewhite sofa, letting out a soft cry. "My God, isn't there any stuffing in this thing? It's like an instrument of torture."

Laurel laughed, grateful that she'd stopped talking about an awkward subject. Watching the look of mock suffering on Hilary's face, she realized that the years hadn't been unkind. Even tragedy hadn't creased Hilary's flawless skin or dulled the sparkle in her sapphire eyes. Of course, Laurel conceded, success hadn't hurt. Hilary was only now nearing the end of a career in haute couture that had made her a wealthy woman in her own right. And with her mother's money, she had no financial worries at least.

In her favorite armchair Laurel drew her legs up to rest her chin on her knees. "All antiques are uncomfortable," she murmured.

"Then let's not waste another minute here among them," Hilary suggested. "I thought you'd be packed and ready by now."

"I said, I wasn't going."

"I'll give you fifteen minutes."

Laurel smiled at the benevolent expression. "Hilary, I mean it. I can't possibly go to Cape Ann—"

"Why not?"

Laurel bit her bottom lip thoughtfully. The excuse was weak, but it was all she had. "For one thing, every kennel in the Boston area will be filled. What would I do with Pirate?"

"He's supposed to be a watchdog. Let him watch the house for a change."

"He'd admit the first felon who put a foot over the windowsill, and you know it." She tried again. "Besides, I have to call Ned this evening, make certain he's settled."

"Laurel, we do have telephones in Gloucester. And Mother's been nagging me to use the house. Says it gets musty otherwise. She suggests we light a fire tonight, drink mulled wine in front of it, remember the weekends there with her before Freddy died." She paused. "And somebody's bound to throw a party for Labor Day. I could use some laughter. Frankly, so could you."

Hilary had never learned to like Dan, and probably never would. Sometimes Laurel thought this was simply a reaction to the loss in her own life.

One month after Lexa's death, news had come that Chip Brewster was missing in action in Vietnam. He'd never been found, though Hilary was still certain he would be. Glancing up, Laurel caught a rare emotion on her friend's face—a look that the fashion world had never seen. Memory, grief, those sublime days of youth that had been wiped away in a single moment.

"Will you behave yourself if I tag along?" Laurel asked, knowing she was the only person from whom Hilary would tolerate criticism of what was supposedly a free-wheeling social life, or so the gossip columns said at every opportunity. Except for an occasional weekend, the details of which Hilary never provided, Laurel wasn't sure.

"I won't if you won't." Then the smile fell flat. "Oh, all right. Just the two of us, Laurel. We'll giggle and eat too much, get really sunburned before winter, I won't be able to work for a week. We'll remember the good times and forget, oh damn. . . ." She covered her face with long, beautifully tended fingers.

Laurel hadn't counted on this; she was a sucker for anyone's needing her, especially Hilary. "Only the good times," she murmured. "Nothing but those." She stood up and said briskly, "Now, then. Just one problem." Giving Hilary time to compose herself, she glanced at Pirate. "With whom can we leave this monster?"

## ✳ **CHAPTER 2** ✳

✳

"SEBASTIAN NOBLE."

Hilary slung Laurel's suitcase into the car, then straightened with a grin. She had a curiously antagonistic relationship—which she'd never explained—with her mother's Gloucester neighbor, so Laurel felt surprise at the generous offer of the mint-condition MG.

"Sebastian lent you this beautiful machine?"

Laurel leaned against its gleaming red hood, wondering how anyone in his right mind could risk sacrificing such an elegant sports car, knowing how Hilary drove. If he did know. It had always amazed Laurel that Hilary had managed to get a license.

"Not exactly lent. Would you believe, he showed up at my apartment one night last week, dropped the keys into my hand, and said he'd see me at the beach on Saturday."

"What was he doing in New York?"

"Picking up an Aston Martin at the docks. He gets them shipped from Europe. He buys classic wrecks˜over there for a song, then restores them here and makes himself an outrageous profit." Hilary's tone was derogatory.

"I should pile this thing up on the Mass Pike. Imagine, dumping it on me without so much as a phone call beforehand."

She'd answered the door that night with her face slathered in goo, a new beauty mask that a model friend swore by.

"And here I thought you were a natural beauty." Sebastian's normally bland eyes had moved over her, his mouth breaking into a smile.

"I could have killed him," Hilary told Laurel, trying not to think about Sebastian's presumptions. "It would serve him right if I retaliated in kind. Stuffed Pirate into the backseat of this car and drove him to Sebastian's door." She grinned. "Wouldn't he turn blue?"

"Pirate would," Laurel replied. "Dan won't let him in the Audi. He's not the best traveler. He's been known to have training lapses. Besides, Sebastian lives next door to you," she finished, "so what do we do with Pirate?"

Laurel had packed while Hilary dialed most of the area kennels, without success. Now Hilary wiped a perfectly manicured hand across her forehead and said, "Not to worry, love. I'll just phone the last few numbers that were busy before. Have you anything else you want to take?"

"Only my cosmetic case." Resigned to the trip with Hilary at the wheel, Laurel went upstairs.

Ryder leaned on the front doorbell, impatience knotting his stomach. The least he could expect was to throw Benedict off balance a little, not that he'd be the first newsman to demand an interview since Dave Cabell's hospitalization. But by force of habit, if nothing more, he'd damn well be the most thorough. He punched the bell again.

A three-day weekend, and he wasn't going to be able to unwind after all. The assignment already had him. Hell, what was new about working on a holiday? He'd missed them before. Toward the end, Maggie used to say: "Ryder, if you could have sex with a Hasselblad camera, I'd never see you again."

How could he argue? Maggie had only wanted a normal existence. Their marriage working out, children. The same things he'd wanted, once. Everything Ryder couldn't bear to think about now, this weekend included—so why fight it? He was a bonafide workaholic. And damn glad all of a sudden that Sara had reminded him of the fact, no matter what her motives were.

Ryder jabbed Benedict's doorbell again, producing resonant chimes within. Then he heard loud barking from the house. At least the dog acknowledged him, though Benedict's office had been less responsive when he called. "He isn't in right now. I don't know when to expect him. Perhaps not until Tuesday."

There would be no appointment. Go home, McKendrick, he'd told himself. Outline the article you agreed—reluctantly—to do. Keep abreast of developments on Cabell's illness. Stay off the crowded highways, out of crowded restaurants. Polish off a six-pack of Molson. And end up thinking of Maggie.

Ryder's gut had clenched. The hell he would. Not this year. He pushed Benedict's doorbell a fourth time.

Suddenly the front door to the Beacon Hill townhouse was flung open, and Ryder stared into a pair of angry blue eyes. "I'm on the telephone. Couldn't you take your finger off that buzzer for one second and just, please, cram it—"

"Mrs. Benedict?"

He hadn't expected a redhead. Tall and thin in white denims, she sported coral-tipped fingernails, a bright orange cotton sweater. She didn't go with his impressions of Dan Benedict's wife from her long-ago photo: in the grainy picture she'd looked restrained, cool, elegant, lost. People change, he told himself, trying to ignore the continual barking from within. Maybe now she used henna on her hair. "I'd like to speak with Dan. I called the office, but—"

He never got to say the rest, or, reaching for his press card, to identify himself. He heard the low animal growl, saw an immense flash of white that he soon learned was mainly muscle under fur—then something hit him hard in the chest, and he went flying backward into a void of blackness.

"Oh, my God!"

Laurel had heard the sickening sound of the man's skull hitting concrete, and a short moan before he stopped moving.

"He's out cold," Hilary said.

"What should we do? Oh, dear heaven, *Pirate*!"

About to kneel over the stranger who'd been knocked flat on the front walk, Laurel straightened to race into traffic after the dog.

"Let him go," Hilary shouted.

But Ned's plan to keep Pirate safe echoed in her mind, and Laurel kept going.

When she came back, Pirate in tow, Hilary was still bent over the prone form on the sidewalk. The man's mouth was slack, showing the edges of straight white teeth, all intact, but there wasn't a trace of expression on his face.

"Come on," Hilary crooned.

"Let me," Laurel said. She'd had a course in CPR last year at the Junior League and for an instant stared down at the stranger, wondering whether she had the nerve to practice mouth-to-mouth resuscitation on someone she'd never seen before. Then, still panting for breath herself, she dropped to her knees on the sidewalk, oblivious of the abrasive contact on bare skin. With one white-knuckled hand, she held Pirate by the scruff of the neck. "Take him inside, will you? Go on, Hilary, he's too winded to give you any trouble. I chased him for two blocks. Shut him in the powder room next to the kitchen."

With a mother's practiced hand she checked the man's wrist. "His pulse is light but steady."

Hilary gingerly took hold of Pirate's leather collar and pulled. "He really cracked his head when he fell."

Laurel wondered about calling an ambulance. Who was he? Coming downstairs with her cosmetic bag, she had been too late to reach Pirate. She'd seen him fly through the doorway like something out of *Peter Pan*, Nana protecting the children. And now a stranger lay unconscious on the front walk, where only hours ago a small corps of reporters had gathered. Could he be one of them?

For these few moments, she wouldn't let it matter. She passed a hand over his tousled dark blond hair, heavily streaked from summer sun; it felt thick and silky in her fingers. Shouldn't he be coming around by now? He seemed so still, long legs sprawled wide, broad shoulders pressed to the concrete as if someone had nailed him there. Only the long, tanned fingers of his right hand showed any sign of life; as Laurel watched, they twitched.

"Are you all right? Please. Open your eyes."

His lids flickered and he groaned. "What the hell was that?"

After more fluttering, he blinked once and was suddenly staring at her. Laurel looked into a pair of the most beautiful gray eyes she'd ever seen. Even though he hadn't yet brought her into focus, she could see intelligence shimmering there.

And then she felt fear. Did he recognize her? There'd been a time, growing up in the senator's house, when many—if not most—people did. As identical twins, she and Lexa had drawn even more attention. Though it had been years since she'd been photographed in public—the last time was at Lexa's funeral—Laurel remembered all too well her embarrassment and panic at being the target of someone's camera. At her wedding to Dan, she had insisted on a news blackout and refused to meet reporters outside the house.

Now she glanced around. To her intense relief, he wasn't toting a camera.

"Welcome back," she murmured with a smile. And couldn't resist touching his hair again, smoothing it back from his face.

Ryder, flat on his back on the sidewalk, felt the light contact from her hand as if someone had plugged him into a socket. Who was she? He wanted to shake his head to clear it, but he couldn't seem to move. And if he closed his eyes again, the whole world would spin like a carousel. He let his gaze drift over the face above him, and his vision slowly cleared.

There was something about her, he decided. Rich dark hair falling around delicate features tickled his cheek. Again, he felt the sensation clear to his shoes. Her hazel eyes narrowed on him, in concern, he thought at first, then changed his mind. She was nearsighted. Magnificent. It gave her a soft expression—or was it he who was out of focus? When she drew back, he sensed again a familiarity he couldn't explain in the elegant bend of her neck.

"You're beautiful," he said.

"You've hit your head worse than we thought." Her smile grew. "Do you think you could walk if I helped you up?"

But he could only stare back at her; or they kept staring at each other.

"How's the patient?" Carrying several white terrycloth

towels, the redhead who had answered the door before emerged from the house.

"He needs to get in out of the sun. Give me a hand, Hilary."

Ryder frowned. Hilary. People change, and the rich red hair would have photographed darker beneath a mourning veil, but her name didn't sound familiar. He wished he had checked Sara's file more closely that morning. Right now, he couldn't remember much of anything. Puzzled, he allowed himself to be pulled and prodded to his feet; swaying, he felt so dizzy that both women, flanking him, had to take most of his weight.

The stairs proved hard going. By the time they eased him onto a leather sofa in the den, which was closest to the front door, beads of cold sweat misted Ryder's forehead. He was afraid he might be sick.

"I think I'm bleeding."

He tried to put a hand to his head, but his arm wouldn't cooperate.

"Lie back. Don't worry about the furniture. It'll clean." After a pause during which he felt slim fingers gently probing through his hair, she said, "It's not much, I think. Only a small bump that's oozing slightly. Hilary, let me have those towels."

She placed one on the arm of the sofa. His neck wouldn't hold his head up, anyway. Ryder flopped back like a rag doll, panting from the exertion of getting up the stairs and through the door into the coolness of the house. Dazedly, he thought: God, a newshound's golden opportunity. I'm settled in Dan Benedict's inner sanctum, and I scarcely know my own name.

As she bent to him, he inhaled the scent of jasmine, sweet and clean and light, and closed his eyes. . . .

\*　　　　　\*　　　　　\*

"Is he still breathing?"

Laurel laughed softly. "Of course he's breathing. But perhaps I should wake him in a minute. I think I read that, with possible concussion—"

"Why don't we simply look at him for a while?" Hilary's question stopped the brushing motion of a hand near his cheek as Laurel rearranged the towel beneath his head. "I'm enjoying the scenery. Why don't you?" At Laurel's astonished look, she added, "He was certainly watching you not long ago."

"Watching me? Don't be ridiculous." Remembering those intelligent gray eyes, Laurel pulled her hand back. "If he was staring at anyone, it would be you."

Hilary muttered something about being blind to one's own assets before she said, "You know what you need, my dear friend?" Her tone carried through the silent room. "And don't shut me up, because it needs saying. You ought to shake off the shackles, find yourself a stunning male—" the pause was long enough, her glance meaningful enough, to let Laurel know she meant the stranger on her sofa "—and spend the rest of this weekend with your firm little backside nestled in a nice, soft mattress."

As Hilary breezed into the kitchen, leaving Laurel with the sleeping stranger in the den, she herself began to wonder about the weekend. Perhaps Laurel was right; they shouldn't go to Gloucester. If she didn't feel quite so keenly the need to escape the rat race of her career for a few days . . .

But she did. Skimming a finger over the Yellow Pages for yet another Boston kennel, she had a quick, unpleasant mental impression of Sebastian Noble; dark, mocking. She tucked the phone between her ear and shoulder.

Dialing, she recalled her first encounter with him last

spring, when she had traveled to Gloucester for a restful weekend—so she'd hoped.

At six A.M. the first morning she'd been wakened by a sudden shrilling of metal against metal, as if someone had drawn extraordinarily long fingernails down a particularly chalky board. With her nerves in spasms, Hilary sat up in the front bedroom of her mother's summer house, perched above the gray Atlantic, and cursed. "What maniac could be working before the sun's up?"

She climbed from the warmth of feather comforters and soft sheets to peer out the side windows in the direction of the grating, metallic sound. Her mother's newest neighbor, Hilary quickly surmised. The garage doors—it had once been called a car barn, and had four stalls—were standing open, a cacophony of sound radiating into the quiet surroundings. Not even the thick canopy of trees between his house and hers could mute the noise.

Hilary flung open the window and leaned out, shouting.

"Shut up!"

In answer, she heard an electric saw's high-pitched whine.

"Shut up before I call the police!"

Hilary was back in bed, the covers over her head, before she became aware of silence. Good. In the stillness, she grinned to herself, then punched the pillow and flopped back onto the mattress.

She didn't realize that someone was in the room until he made the announcement. "You're Hilary Chapin."

Heart thumping, she jerked upright again to face a man she'd never seen before: He was tall, and his biceps bunched as he wielded a long wrench in both hands. He had nearly black hair, and eyes to match. She saw straight dark brows, prominent bones, and a long, unsmiling mouth. He wasn't really handsome, but utterly compelling. And, just now, frightening.

"Get out of my room," she said.

She watched the steel implement in his fingers, which he drew along its surface almost thoughtfully. He knew her name; did he mean to hurt her? To step closer and swing the heavy tool at her skull? In her business she'd had her share of obscene phone calls, known more than her share of strange personalities since Chip had gone. You couldn't appear in national magazines, half clothed, without expecting the occasional weird reaction.

"Don't look so shocked. You left the back door unlatched," he said. "You must have been expecting me."

Then she realized, still staring at the wrench, where he'd come from. The silence had begun when he crossed from his yard to hers. "I expect an introduction."

But he only observed, "You've got your mother's eyes."

Her mother, now Mrs. Justice Hulme. Her mother, the traitor. Some warning she'd given her daughter. For the first time since the wedding a year ago, Hilary resented Myra's third marriage, four years after Freddy's death, to a Supreme Court justice she'd met at Lexa's funeral. Myra would be here otherwise, for protection, she reasoned, forgetting how much she liked her stepfather, Everett Hulme. Instead she was alone, and all but naked in a white gauze nightgown. She yanked the sheets up over her breasts, not that he'd been staring at them; his gaze was fixed on her face.

"You're too skinny," he pronounced.

"Thank you so much for that lovely compliment. I have to be," she said. "The camera adds fifteen pounds."

"Well, I'm not a camera. In my opinion you could use some weight."

Hilary let out a sound of annoyance, wrapping the sheets around her and stumbling from bed. She felt at a disadvantage, not embarrassed—her body, her face were her fortune—yet somehow, the word made her skin creep, she felt compromised. His tone just then had been . . . sultry, intimate.

"I don't care what you think. I asked you to leave this house. I didn't hear the doorbell, or a knock. I don't even know who you are."

For the first time, he faltered. "I assumed Myra had mentioned me."

Myra had, but Hilary wouldn't give him the satisfaction of saying so. She had him off balance now and sensed she was better off that way.

Her mother's allusion to "that nice young man who's moved in next door" didn't go with the powerful-chested, T-shirted male standing near her bed. What had happened to Myra's capacity for judgment?

Of course, she probably hadn't seen beyond the muscles to the gleam of dark skin with the sheen of sweat, even the smear of black grease over his upper lip like a badly drawn moustache. Hilary would have laughed at such blatant masculinity if he hadn't been looking at her so intently.

"Sebastian Noble." He introduced himself. "I'm sorry about the pounding. I've got a deadline on a car to deliver in Bryn Mawr. A demanding client who's not about to accept less than perfection."

"You fix cars? Here, in Gloucester?"

"I do restorations. 'Vintage automobiles for discriminating investors.' I've only been in business seven months, but already turning a profit. Enough to buy granola at least, and pay the electric bill. What do you think of that?"

The question seemed surprisingly serious, considering the smile that suddenly curved his mouth. Hilary said, "I think you should change your business hours. Try opening at ten or eleven o'clock."

"Then I'd be keeping you up until the middle of the night." He looked pleased at the prospect, his dark gaze and tone making something more of it.

Hilary turned her back, the swath of sheet trailing behind her as she headed into the hall. She felt better when she wasn't watching those dark eyes, when she couldn't see the heavy wrench.

"Not if I make a call to Town Hall, you wouldn't. Mr. Noble—" she circled in the bathroom doorway—"there are zoning regulations in this town and—"

"I wouldn't chip my fingernail polish if I were you, dialing the local authorities. Noble Classics is legal, all permits properly applied for and granted." He studied her, gaze wandering over the length of Hilary's exposed legs, back to her bared shoulders, and the sheet like a Roman toga around her, to the hard look in her eyes. "Friends in high places," he murmured, shifting the wrench to one hand and reaching out the other index finger to touch her hair. Hilary's body jolted as if battered by the heavy steel in his grasp.

"I don't give a damn for your well-placed friends, or your permits. You keep the sounds of early morning labor to a whisper, or I will call the police."

"Closest thing to a cop around here is the Fish and Wildlife man. Somehow," Sebastian said, "I don't think he'd care about my hammering dents out of a 1942 Nash 600."

"Get your hand off me."

Freeing her hair, which he'd been sifting through his fingers, Hilary stepped backward into the bathroom, wondering whether she shouldn't have run downstairs instead. He was wrong about the police, of course. She wondered whether he was a compulsive liar. Then he surprised her by saying, "I'm sorry I woke you. Especially on Sunday morning after a heavy Saturday night. A raw egg works wonders in a Bloody Mary, for hangover."

"I haven't got a hangover!"

Not a bad one, anyway, Hilary thought. She'd simply come in late, after three o'clock, after a shipboard cocktail party that had turned into dinner on land in Rockport, then dancing, drinks, and more drinks. But how would he know?

Feeling the color rise in her face, she turned her back. "Do I have to ask again for you to leave?"

His amused voice drifted past the doorway. "I know when I'm not wanted." And then from the stair landing, "Unless you'd like me to wash your back?"

The slam of the bathroom door had nearly warped the frame. She'd been relieved to have him go then, and she was still relieved, every time Sebastian bid her good-bye. If only, Hilary thought now, she could prevent him from saying hello in the first place. . . .

"Oh, hello . . . yes." She had been startled from her reverie by someone answering the telephone at the kennel in Brookline. Dwelling on Sebastian, she'd given it more than twenty rings. "I'm wondering whether you have room, possibly, for one last boarder." She paused. "Well, large, actually. A Pyrenees, but very well mannered," Hilary lied. "Have you? That's wonderful!"

Or was it? She hung up, thinking that every weekend in Gloucester Sebastian magically appeared, seeming to intuit the very moment of her arrival. Suddenly he would sweep through the back door without a knock, depositing on the kitchen table a string bag full of citrus fruit or vegetables. "Too much cholesterol in your diet, Hilary. Not enough fiber." And when she asked, incensed, how he would know what she ate, he'd say blandly, "Dining with the yachting crowd? What else would they serve but red meat, or lobster?"

Still, she had the feeling he watched all her comings and goings. Certainly he knew when she rose in the morning and went to bed at night. Sebastian hadn't disturbed her sleep since that first dawn. Not with his metallic poundings, anyway.

A glorified car mechanic. What had made him settle in the seaside village, far from the port of New York and not that close to Boston? And why had he shown up at her door that night not long ago, leaving his car with her and saying, "See you on the weekend, Hilary. You're welcome."

"For what?"

She'd stood, hands planted on her hips, in the apartment doorway. The stiffening beauty mask was still on her face. "For providing you free transportation over Labor Day." Then he'd bounded down the stairs without a backward glance, denying her the chance to say she wasn't going to the shore.

Well, why not go? She wouldn't let Sebastian chase her away. With Laurel's company, and the prospect of a party or two for backup, she'd escape the growing dissatisfaction she felt at these end years of modeling, the yearning for something more, something new; she'd escape the wondering, worrying about Chip. She might even stay an extra day or two.

Even if the weekend meant another run-in with Sebastian Noble.

Opening his eyes to blinding afternoon sun, Ryder felt as if he'd lost most of a day. He shut them again at the painful, dull throb in their sockets, at the pulse of nausea in the pit of his stomach.

"How are you feeling?"

Her low voice startled him. Carefully, he sat up and looked into hazel eyes, then smiled weakly. Everything about him felt weak. "Not so sure I'm glad to be alive," he said at last.

"I didn't think an ambulance would be necessary, but

will you let us drive you to the hospital? An X ray might be wise."

He began to shake his head, then thought better of it. "God." Ryder slouched lower on the sofa, letting his skull rest against the back. "I'll be okay. I'll just rest another minute."

"I do think you should get checked."

"I've taken harder falls, just never been hit by a Mack truck before."

She smiled. "I'm sorry. That was Pirate. He thinks he owns the place."

Ryder took another survey of the slender woman standing near the sofa, her hands clasped together. She looked nervous, fretful—like a bad interview.

"Benedict's dog," he said. All his words seemed to come slowly. "The other woman, you called her Hilary . . ."

He could see her fingers tighten, the knuckles turn white.

"A friend," she said. "A friend of the family."

So the redhead wasn't Benedict's wife, Frasier's daughter.

"And you?"

She looked away. "I'm . . . a friend, too."

"Quite a few friends gathering," he said. "Why? Because of the political climate?" Ryder struggled upright, fighting a gentler wave of nausea. He needed to see her reaction as it formed.

It took a moment too long, and surprised him when it came. "There have been a lot of reporters around the house today." Glancing at a newspaper on the end table, she swallowed. "We—Hilary and I—have been helping to drive them off." She looked at him. "Dan has already left for the weekend."

"His wife, too?"

". . . Yes."

This time Ryder frowned at the hesitation. Why would there be guests in an empty house?

She was frowning, too. "Hilary and I . . . she promised to . . . she's been trying to make arrangements for the dog, since we won't be staying after all. A change of plan after Dan decided to go away . . . because of the commotion."

Ryder was glad that he'd taken a soft approach and had left his camera in the car, his notebook, too. His duty as a news photographer was to record a moment for other people; yet he wanted to keep this one for himself. Even if he could have thought of them, he didn't want to ask the hard questions. He sensed she wouldn't answer them anyway.

Instead, he focused on the wedding band she wore, and felt a stab of disappointment. Married. "That's a handsome ring," he said. "Uncluttered, classy."

"Thank you, I . . ." She broke off, then began again. "My husband had good taste."

"Had?"

"He picked this ring when we were married ten years ago." She swallowed. "I mean, I'm . . . I'm a widow now."

"I'm a widower myself," Ryder said, relief flooding through him. Then he added, "Since you've spent your day picking me up off the sidewalk, reviving me, I think we should introduce ourselves. I'm—"

"Just tell me your first name."

Some devil seemed to be goading her, but he was damned if he knew what it might be. Maybe her husband had recently died, and she was still in mourning, not ready to even be friends with another man. First names only? He could have smiled. Or maybe she just didn't like his looks. Then why did she keep staring at him, at his mouth and eyes?

"We're not in a singles bar here," he finally said. When she said nothing to that, he answered reluctantly with the truth. "Matthew," he said. "My first name is Matthew."

Something hovered in the air between them. Something tantalizing and dangerous that made every nerve in his reporter's body hum.

"I'm . . . Alexandra," she said at last.

It wasn't what he expected from her.

"Alexandra." He had a nearly uncontrollable impulse to touch her, to unclasp her hands, still twining together. "That's too many syllables. What's the diminutive? Are you called Alex or—"

"No."

He tried teasing. "Nothing? Not even Princess? That's a very royal sounding name for your parents to have stuck on a little girl."

Her face paled, and she opened her mouth as if to explain, then closed it and again said nothing.

"I've got Pirate a kennel!" Hilary made the announcement as she sailed back into the room to find them staring at each other in a sharply defined square of sunlight. "Gloucester, here we come!"

"I'm not sure we should leave just yet, Hilary." Troubled hazel eyes sought out her friend. "I thought perhaps we'd give . . . Matthew a lift to Mass General to make sure he's all right."

"I'm fine."

Immediately, he wondered why he'd said it. Wondered why he didn't linger, playing the invalid awhile to see what developed, wondered why he wanted to keep looking at this slim, cool woman who'd insisted they remain strangers.

"Then we're on our way," Hilary said.

As he pushed slowly to his feet, Ryder had a distinct sense of missed trains, of proverbial ships passing in the night. But his mind wasn't that fuzzy. He knew damn well it wasn't his nature to let her go with that.

## CHAPTER 3

DAN BENEDICT'S GAZE followed the liquid flow of horse and rider over the high jump: a clean, leggy lift of animal and woman; lush female stretched along the chestnut gelding's neck as they rose, airborne, together, small, strong hands laced through leather reins, urging massive equine power; the two of them against the late summer sun, becoming one, gliding, at last, safely over the white rail fence. It was then that he began to breathe again, cupping his hands and shouting.

"Beautiful!"

It isn't like watching Ned, he thought. With Ned, he never tasted fear, like ashes, in his mouth. When she raced for the next jump, he glimpsed the shine of blue-black hair from beneath her jaunty cap. One fall, that's all it would take. A mental lapse on her part, a quick refusal by the thoroughbred.

Dan mistrusted horses. Half the reason he'd bought Storm for Ned two years ago was that he'd hoped to cure his own fears. A thousand pounds of horseflesh, he thought; why didn't she have Ned's reticence around the huge animals?

Heart in his mouth, Dan watched as she soared over

55

the last, and highest, fence, daylight clearly showing beneath the big gelding's hooves. He'd worried about that size and power, thinking the horse too large for her; but he'd been told by the trainer, her coach, that it was more a matter of breeding and disposition. Respecting the man's opinion, he still hoped so. In six years, the big chestnut hadn't let him down. That was something, Dan thought, but not enough. He wanted guarantees.

After all, he'd married Laurel, hadn't he?

Dan pushed the thought away. Still, he'd been foolish, stealing this weekend for himself. The speechmaking had been mainly fiction; the only scheduled stop, in Lincoln, he'd canceled. It had been assumed that Cabell's ill health was the reason, which Dan hadn't corrected. Foolish, though. Dangerous. And worth every subterfuge.

Watching the horse and rider wheel at the end of the long, narrow field, Dan tried to ease his frown. If he didn't control himself, he'd get a migraine. But impatience boiled in him. He wanted to stable the horse, leave without cooling him down, take her home.

The ground seemed to shake as she thundered up to the rails, bringing the horse to a dancing stop. "Get down here," he said.

With a laugh she hooked a leg over the saddle and slid to the ground, into his embrace. "I think he's going to win a blue at the show next month," she said. As if in agreement, the chestnut blew air through his nostrils, then shook a reddish gold mane, like a woman freeing her hair of tangles. "Look, Fool's Gold knows we're talking about him. Don't you, beauty?"

"He knows I'm jealous, getting more so." He turned her. "Kiss me, and show him who's first."

Lightly her tongue ran over his lower lip before she pulled away. "He's got to be hot-walked, Dan. Sorry, but for now, my darling, you'll have to take second place."

She knew how to drive him crazy. Dan waited gloomily while she walked the horse of which he'd become as resentful as a husband with a new baby in the house. He'd been jealous of Laurel, too, with Ned. Jealous, Dan remembered, because his son had the wrong mother.

When at last Maria walked toward him from the barn, alone, Dan was still lost in memory, and sorrow. She'd lost their babies, all of them, and then nearly lost her life, trying to give him more.

It had been the easiest thing in the world for his wife to conceive and carry to term; it should be easy for women of Maria's culture, Latin, fertile . . . but a dangerous feat now, so the doctors said, for the woman he loved. And next Tuesday, it would become impossible.

Maria stepped between his legs, wound her arms around his neck. "May I have that kiss now?"

He bent his head, molding her body to his and letting her feel how much he'd been wanting her. The desperation in his kiss was not only physical. When they drew apart, Maria looked serious. "You're worried, aren't you, about—"

"You on that treacherous animal."

He felt her withdrawal. "Dan, let's not quarrel in the time we have." She eased away from him, walking to her side of the station wagon. "I won't give up Fool's Gold or my riding, competing either." Opening the door, she looked at him across the rooftop. "Just as you won't give up your wife . . . and child."

He stood for a moment, amazed. Why had she tried to bring up a subject they'd agreed to ignore—Laurel, and Ned? Was it to avoid the issue of her surgery? He heard Maria say from inside the car, "Let's go home, shall we?"

"Yes," Dan said, "home," meaning exactly that.

\*       \*       \*

Seated on white wicker in the yellow-splashed sun room of Hilary's Gloucester house, Laurel stared at the Saturday morning paper.

"Are you planning to waste this glorious day?" Hilary asked, barely pausing in the hall. Laurel had a glimpse of flying shirttails, dusty rose, and the briefest scrap of plum-with-pink bikini. "It's already noon. Let's get going before the sun's down."

Laurel straightened the stack of other newspapers. "Maybe I'll read for a while. You go ahead. I'll meet you at the beach later."

"Oh, no you don't." Hilary dropped a woven beach bag to the hardwood floor and leaned against the door frame. Over one shoulder she carried a camera.

"You're not using that on me," Laurel said.

"All right, if that's all that's keeping you—"

"Or any of the others." Hilary owned at least five cameras.

She sighed. "You know me too well. But I'm not setting foot outside without you, dear friend. You seem determined to hibernate, and winter's coming soon enough."

Laurel glanced down at her borrowed suit, high French cut with a low, scooped front and ridiculously thin straps holding everything together, more or less. She'd never worn electric blue in her life. "I don't suppose you've got anything less, well, revealing?" Her stomach wasn't flat enough after Ned; she had a small mole showing on her exposed cleavage. "I need a cover, at least. Do you have another shirt?"

"Take mine. And leave those newspapers here."

Electric blue and dull pink. Hilary raced down the hallway, returning with a soft, worn blue man's T-shirt, which she drew over her head and skinned down her narrow body. She looked sensational. Laurel didn't ask who belonged to the underwear. For all she knew, it was Chip Brewster's. Hilary was already dragging her toward the front door.

When they'd reached the shore, Hilary said, "If he's running—and Dan Benedict's been running since he was born—you'll know soon enough. You can't tell me you're looking forward to the limelight."

"No," Laurel admitted with a sigh as she spread her oversized beach towel next to Hilary's.

Suntan lotion in hand, Hilary paused. "Have you ever thought of telling that man you're married to that you'd like some say in your own life? Just as a change of pace, I mean."

Laurel winced, visibly. "I've known Dan's goals since the day I met him. I can hardly object to them now. Besides, he hasn't announced. Cabell's still in the race."

"For how long?"

"Until he wins, I hope." She lay back and closed her eyes. The sun felt wonderful, hot and close; Laurel soon felt her muscles begin to relax. But in the silence she sensed Hilary's question, which she'd voiced more than once before.

*Why did you marry him?*

"He's a good man, Hilary. You don't see Dan's better qualities. He's also the father of my child."

"Of that we can all be sure."

Laurel lay silent. Why hadn't she said, "I married him because I love him"? But she hadn't felt love yesterday when he took Ned away to school, and resentment still simmered in her veins. The trade-off had been Dan's promise not to send Ned to summer camp, and Laurel's hope that, in Ned's absence, Dan would miss him, too, and decide to spend more time with their son. But it seemed to Laurel their marriage was becoming a series of bargains, more business deal than intimate relationship. She sighed. Frankly, Hilary wasn't the only one who'd thought the *D* word yesterday.

Or was she only feeling blue today because of Dave Cabell's illness, bringing media hype so close to her, too suddenly? And yesterday, oh Lord, yesterday she'd lied to a total stranger just to protect her privacy.

What was she really afraid of?

More obligations? Or Dan's expectation—and the senator's and Judith's—that "a politician needs a strong woman behind him"? But Hilary had a point. What did Laurel need for herself? She thought of the upcoming charity luncheon and could have groaned. Menus, speakers, seating plans, a thousand tedious telephone calls. "Your mother always found plenty to do at home," her father had said, "as a helpmeet to me, Laurel, in my career." And in the next breath, "As Dan's wife, Lexa would have done the same."

*Frasier women don't work.*

Laurel rolled over. She'd been brainwashed all her life, and to consider anything different made her stomach clench. If Lexa had wanted drawing lessons, say, wouldn't she have managed them somehow? Without Dan or the senator batting an eye?

Why can't I be more like her? If Dan gets the opportunity to run for office, why can't I be happy for him? she asked herself.

Shielding her eyes from the sun, Laurel sat up. No use wondering, she thought, and rummaged in her totebag for a pen and pad. If she couldn't doze, she might as well work on that damn luncheon program.

With brisk strokes she jotted down speaker candidates, then reminder notes to herself: check with the florist, the caterer—could they offer a vegetarian entree as an alternate luncheon choice? Idly she doodled on the pad.

"What are you drawing?"

"I'm not—" Laurel glanced down and found that she'd been sketching in the margins, making a picture frame of sorts around her notes.

Hilary said, "A flapper girl in a cloche hat."

"The luncheon theme's The Roaring Twenties. Next year's to be the Thirties and after that," she said, "on and on until the turn of the century."

"The Depression? Hitler?" Hilary snorted. "How cheerful." She leaned closer. "But you've caught just the right attitude here, the bow mouth and a shell-like ear, that long neck and narrow shoulder—I can almost see the gown she'd wear—and all in a few strokes."

"It's rather stylized," Laurel murmured doubtfully.

"It's perfect. Do something with it."

"Like what?" Then the idea flashed through her mind. "The luncheon program cover, maybe? We're to have crisp decor, white linens with silver-and-black tableware. The only touch of color will be the centerpiece flowers, chrysanthemums and asters."

Hilary snatched the pad from her. "Do this in pen and ink. It'll be perfect."

"Maybe one splash of bright yellow," Laurel said, "here, in the bow on her hat."

"Right at the nape of that long, elegant neck ... wonderful. That's free advice from an old clothes horse." Hilary hugged her. "Do it, Laurel. Who's in charge of programs?"

"One of Judith's older friends." Laurel grinned. "Eighty-five if she's a day. She must have been a flapper herself once."

"Then she'll love it." Hilary straightened. "Come on, I'll buy you a drink to celebrate. After that, who knows?"

"Hil, you promised a quiet three days, sun and conversation." Last night they had stayed up late, drinking a little too much wine and talking—carefully—around sensitive issues.

Her friend's famous sapphire eyes darkened now. "It's not the good times we remember, though, is it? I think Myra's advice was wrong."

Thinking of Chip Brewster, Laurel also remembered Lexa. Then a surprising vision replaced them: pewter gray eyes, and dark golden hair streaked from sun.

"I've fried sufficiently for one day," Hilary said. "Come on, let's take our peeling pink noses over to the Yardarm for happy hour."

Laurel got up. He'd been attractive, with that air of competence that came close to being ruthless. Always shy, she envied him that. Yet experience had etched the hard planes of his face, had carved not only laugh lines at the edges of his mouth and the corners of those intelligent gray eyes.

"Laurel. . . ."

It had been just one of those encounters people have, she thought, harmless, a few minutes or an hour on the train, on the shuttle to Washington, perhaps. Briefer than that. And silly to even think about. She was a married woman. She shook out her towel and smiled to herself. Who else but Laurel Frasier Benedict would indulge in a ten-minute flirtation, most of which had probably been in her own mind?

She said to Hilary, "Let's go."

Her weekend mission was to keep Hilary's memory of Chip Brewster under control—and to suppress her own misgivings about Ned's first days at boarding school, about Dan. Besides, the bar would undoubtedly have a television set, and a news update.

Slumped on a stool at the beachside bar where a baseball game blared from the overhead TV, Ryder smoked a cigarette and nursed a second martini.

After leaving Benedict's house he'd spent yesterday in his apartment, a clutter of rooms that hadn't changed in six years—Sara's point, he conceded—and he hadn't accomplished one thing, not even a lead-in for his profile of Dan Benedict. He'd kept thinking of a soft, husky voice and warm hazel eyes, and how with every question he'd put to her, he'd seemed to know less about her, not more.

That was the newshound in him, not the man. The other feelings she aroused in him were strong, basic ones he hadn't felt so keenly for a long time. Sara's point, too.

After a tossing, rumpled night, Ryder had left for Gloucester. With only a first name to go on, he thanked Fate that Hilary had said where they were going.

He'd find her. The town wasn't all that big. Upon arrival he'd tramped the beach, but she hadn't been in the crowd. Then he had driven aimlessly down one lane, up the next, without any luck.

Maybe she and the redhead had driven on, looking for weekend parties in other coastal towns. A widow, she'd told him. He remembered Hilary's enthusiasm for their trip. The merry widow?

But hadn't he seen the haunted look in her eyes? Well, what had made him think she wanted to ease her sorrows with him? Maybe she simply knew a bad risk when she met one, as Maggie should have before it was too late. Maggie. Oh Christ.

Ryder cupped his hands around the sweating glass in front of him. Hell, what good did being sorry do? Six years ago tomorrow, he thought. He didn't need another drink, but he sure wanted one. Tomorrow he'd want the whole bottle, forget the ice and the glass.

He ordered again, muttering instructions that he knew the barkeep wouldn't follow. The shoreside bar had filled, doors to rafters, in the hour he'd been sitting here.

When a third someone slid onto the red plastic seat beside him, Ryder didn't bother to look up. All day he'd been searching for the scent of jasmine, sweet and mild, that irritated him now. His mind was playing tricks on him, he could swear that—

"Goddammit."

A heavy totebag had nudged him, making Ryder spill liquor on the bar, and that flower scent assailed his nostrils again. A slender hand braced a delicate female weight against his bare forearm, and heat flashed through his body.

Immediately, she recoiled. "I'm terribly sorry, I lost my balance."

The voice. Slowly, in disbelief, Ryder turned his head and met her gaze, dead center. Up close her eyes were even deeper with color, mossy green flecked with rich, dark brown and shards of pure light. All day he'd been waiting to drown in those eyes, and when she'd stumbled into him, what had he done? Cursed her. Apology on the tip of his tongue, Ryder watched as recognition came, then shock.

"Wait, I'm sorry." When she swiveled on the stool, he caught her shoulder. "I didn't realize who you were just now," he said swiftly. "I've looked everywhere for you."

"You're following me," she accused. And then he saw fear. He dropped his hand.

"Yes." The bar noise swelled around them, drowning the word. "Yes, I am."

"Why?" He saw the quick lift of her chest beneath the rose shirt, noted the low-cut sweep of swimsuit under that. "What do you want?"

*You*, he thought.

"Just to talk," he said. She turned aside and Ryder reached out, not quite touching her again. "Alexandra . . ."

"Well, hello there," someone said.

Looking up, he encountered an unruly mass of dark red hair and sparkling eyes, their color belonging in a museum's gem collection. She was smiling, as if at some personal victory.

"Hello yourself, Red."

"Hilary, I think we should—"

"Have those drinks now," came the quick reply. She waved toward the bartender and commanded, "Vodka with bitters, please. Two."

Over his shoulder Ryder said, "Hilary, would you like my place?"

"I'm happy on my feet, love," she said, when they'd been served. "You stay right next to the lady." After one sip, her gaze began to roam again. "Oh my God, there's Rick . . . would you mind, darlings? I must say hello. I haven't seen him since Mother dragged me here for the summer three years ago."

With the mumbled explanation that Rick Darcy was the best dancer she'd ever known, Hilary disappeared into the crowd.

Beside him, panic seemed to get swallowed with as much effort as the vodka. "I knew it," he heard after a silence. "Damn you, Chip Brewster."

No explanation followed the statement. Elbows resting lightly on the rim of the bar, she cradled her glass in slender hands and stared at anything but him. Ryder tried to settle into a companionable silence. Neither ploy worked. The longer they sat, the more aware of each other they became.

Finally, she said, "How's your head today?"

"Still on my shoulders." He smoothed the back of his hair, as if to prove the lump was gone. "No, really, it's fine." He grinned. "But we've got to stop meeting like this."

"We've got to stop meeting at all."

She took a breath, her eyes avoiding his. He moved

their glasses, and twin rings of wetness reflected in the bar's polished surface, intersecting. They made a curiously intimate image.

Ryder cleared his throat. "Listen, why don't we—"

She cleared hers at the same time. "Listen, there's something I must tell you. Yesterday I said that I'm—"

She didn't get the next words out. Hilary's arm came around her shoulder, disrupting the pattern she'd been idly drawing in the wet rings on the bartop. "Pumpkin, I have the most smashing invitation. Rick's giving a wonderful Labor Day party two days early. He owns this tiny little gem of an island just off the coast, and we're both inv—"

She turned on the stool and slipped her arms around Hilary's waist. "Please don't do this to yourself."

"I tried, last night, pumpkin. I know I promised. But sometimes. . . ."

Dark, silken hair swung in a negative motion. "Go on, then. But I'm not coming along to watch. I'll wait for you at the house."

Her tone hardened. "We're not coeds at Carter College now, you know. My pleasures, dear friend, are mine for the choosing—"

"But Hilary, you keep making the wrong choices. Please don't ask me to endorse them."

"Why not?" she said. "I've been tolerating yours for years."

Before the insult had registered, Hilary was gone.

After a long moment Ryder heard from the stool next to his, "Maybe the gossip columns are right about her after all." He watched the jerky movement of her fingers, altering the wet design on the bartop. "Not true," she corrected herself in the next breath. "I've known her all my life practically."

"I've got a friend like that," Ryder said. He smiled

faintly, thinking of Sara Hennessey. "No illusions."

"As you must have heard just then, there are very few—on either side."

"Then let's see if we can find some new ones." He thought of Maggie, and the memories he didn't want to touch tonight. "Together."

"Are you trying to pick me up?" The words seemed to stick in her throat.

"All the way from Boston to Gloucester," he said. "You have to admire my persistence. And you have to admit, that was a pretty desperate ploy—cracking my head on Benedict's sidewalk—to meet you."

She couldn't help smiling. "Pretty desperate."

"Come on, no threat," he said. "We'll make some good conversation." The now-familiar wariness showed in her eyes. "Maybe drink a little wine, and find some good food, why not? Nothing else." Unless you want it, too, Ryder added to himself.

An hour ago he'd have given that possibility a million-to-one chance.

"I can't, really, I—"

"What will you do tonight? By yourself, alone?" Ryder watched her teeth worry her bottom lip. He thought how soft it looked, how warm. "Besides, you had something to tell me."

"Just dinner, then," she agreed at last.

She slid off the stool, graceful as a schoolgirl, then hesitated. "My treat," Ryder said. He tossed some bills on the bar and saw that, in the water near their glasses, she'd traced one clear, clean letter *L* with a single, ornate gothic *M*, artfully entwined, as if they were lovers' limbs.

*L*, he thought, not *A* for Alexandra.

And his newsman's brain clicked into gear. He wanted conversation all right. He wanted the truth.

## CHAPTER 4

WITH THE TINES of her fork Laurel scrawled a design on the oilcloth that covered the small, square table in the casual restaurant where they'd been sitting for two hours. Laurel, who'd spent most of that time wondering how to correct her false identity, couldn't eat another bite.

"Mind if I finish that?" he gestured at her still-full plate.

"Please do."

"What are you drawing?"

She raised her gaze to his face. "Drawing?"

He swallowed. "It's a habit of yours, I've noticed."

She stared down at the faint lines on the red-and-white plastic. What if she simply wrote her full name there and let him read it? After a moment's study she said, "I think it's a bouquet."

"Roses? Peonies? Chrysanthemums?"

Laurel thought of the garden at her parents' house and the last blooms of autumn, dusky gold and burgundy and pallid yellow, when Lexa had died. "It's impressionistic. Geraniums, perhaps," she said, "because of the red."

He wiped his mouth with a napkin and tipped his chair back on its rear legs. "Are you an artist?"

"No."

He looked exasperated by her closemouthed attitude. "Well, did you ever want to be?"

"No. I mean, I'm not sure. I don't remember." She felt light-headed from too much wine and not enough food. "What about you?"

"I'm getting close to what I want to be—the best damned photojournalist in the world." At the words Laurel turned startled eyes on him. He grinned. "Or so I tell myself, and a few gullible editors."

Laurel's stomach churned. A reporter. That had been her first assumption; she should have trusted her instincts.

"Actually," he went on, "at one point I planned on discovering new planets, basing myself on the moon. Then I wanted to play pro basketball, if not hockey. I wasn't tall enough for one, not tough enough for the other. That was followed at eighteen by a heartfelt desire to hold the world's beer chugging record."

She managed a smile at his teasing tone but glanced toward the exit. "Who do you work for?"

"I free-lance." He went on, "It pays well enough if you're able to do without sleep and food, and to be in three corners of the globe simultaneously." He added, "No, really, it's not a bad living, and has its compensations as long as you're . . . single."

She said nothing.

"Among the perks are being my own boss, which I find essential. Knowing what's going on in the world before everybody else does, if I'm lucky." He focused on the center of the table. "And ultimately, there's the satisfaction of seeing a great photograph come out of the developing tray."

Laurel tried not to let him see how shaken she was. "Would I have seen your work?"

"Probably. I've done a few things for *Sunday* magazine.

*Time* carried a piece of mine last month. And *Newstrend* picks up my stuff. In fact, my next—"

"What about *Capitol*? Or *National in the News*?" Her weightlessness gave way to dread. There was more than one photojournalist in the world, she kept thinking.

His gaze sharpened. "Nothing for a long while."

"Why not? They're good magazines."

"Depends on your bias," he said. "Ours didn't agree."

The tines of her fork dug deeper into the oilcloth. Or did he mean that the senator hadn't agreed? She suppressed an urge to bolt from the restaurant.

"Do you travel with your work?"

"About two-thirds of my time's spent overseas, yes. At this point my apartment in Cambridge is nothing more than a crash pad between assignments. There's always a little war somewhere," he said. "Unfortunately. There always was."

"Southeast Asia?"

"Yeah." His gaze was intent now. "What are we playing here, Trivial Pursuit?" He tipped his chair upright, and leaned his forearms on the table. "Listen, I think we need to start over, get a few things straight on both sides. For one thing, my name isn't Matthew." Laurel's heart lurched. "I mean, that's really my first name, but I haven't used it since I finished college. Call me Ryder—that's my middle name—which I use professionally." He held out his hand palm up in which to place hers. She ignored it. "Ryder McKendrick."

Ryder McKendrick. Laurel began to perspire. Like other men, he'd come back from Vietnam angry, frustrated by a useless war he'd fought with a pen and a camera, not a gun; but unlike many others, Ryder McKendrick had found a platform, eloquent and harmful, from which to speak out against Edwin Frasier and the rest of the war's hawks. Against her father. For over a year Ryder had hammered in print at those on Capitol Hill whose voting endorsed napalm and jet bombers like the one Chip Brewster had piloted. He'd even done a book, she remembered now...*Destruction*. Hadn't the title been something like that?

Then Edwin Frasier, she recalled, had wreaked his own havoc. She wondered how long her father's enemy would stay seated at the same table with her if he did know exactly who she was.

If she ran now, he would guess. She could tell by looking at him that his newsman's instincts were already in high gear.

"Your turn," he said. "Where are you from? I hear the South in your voice, but in two hours that's about all I've learned. What do you do? You don't know whether you ever wanted to become an artist, yet you see with an artist's eye..."

In the midst of her fear that he would expose her, Laurel felt astonished. "I don't, that's only..." Doodling.

"False modesty," he said. "Where's your home?"

"Maryland." How long would it take him to connect her with politics? There wasn't much else in town. "And you?"

"Pennsylvania. Claremont. Population 37,000. My dad's a CPA, Mom teaches violin—which I managed to put aside at the age of twelve. In her spare time these days she's making a harpsichord from some complicated kit. Dad flies gas-engine model planes on weekends." Ryder grinned. "I've got one sibling, nine cousins, two living grandparents." After a pause, he added, "Your turn again."

Laurel's heart sank. He'd been so open with her, and all she'd done was lie; the worst part of this was that she actually liked him.

"I... have one sister. When I was a child, I had a tree

house," she admitted, "where I spent most of my summers until I was thirteen. That is, when I wasn't away at camp or traveling with the . . ." She'd almost said "the senator." "With my parents. I'd shinny up the old oak in our garden, tuck myself away in the tree house in its branches with a thermos of lemonade and a pile of books. Sometimes I never wanted to come down." She gave him a rueful smile. "Reading's still my favorite thing to do on a hot summer day or a cold winter night. No longer in a tree house, though."

"You'd sketch there, too," Ryder surmised.

"Why, yes, but nothing very good."

He let her self-deprecation pass. "So you left your tree house, and got married." He tore a paper napkin into some origami concept, a kamikaze plane, perhaps. His movements were controlled violence. "What about this husband of yours? You said you're a widow." He waited, not looking at her. When she didn't answer he said, "You're not a widow, are you?"

She couldn't avoid glancing at the band on her ring finger. His gaze followed hers. He saw too much.

"Divorced?" he pressed.

"No."

The bits of paper lifted, floated, fell, as Ryder swept his hand over the table. Still looking at the ring, he frowned. "Where is he, then? Back home—taking care of the kids?"

"I said I'm a widow. He . . . he died of a heart attack."

"So you're not cheating on a husband here. Then you're only cheating me." His eyes met hers. "Come on, lady. Talk."

"You've had enough." Too much.

Why wouldn't he stop? She couldn't keep telling lies. Yet here she was, across the table from a tough reporter who probably carried a grudge against the senator who certainly carried one against him; she was sitting with a dangerous man. The senator and Dan would kill her if they knew.

Laurel knew she ought to leave. But she had no wallet on her—like Judith, she rarely carried money—not even a quarter to call a cab. Hilary's house was miles away on the other side of Gloucester. She glanced out the window. It was nearly dark and getting foggy. If she left the restaurant, his growing suspicions would be proved without a word. And walking all that way . . . ? Alone? What if he followed her?

What did he want of her? His coming to Gloucester was anything but chance or coincidence. Again, fear struck her. A story. If he really didn't know who she was, he might be using her for background, as a secondary source. He wouldn't need to know her as Dan's wife for that.

"Can we please go now?" Laurel said. "I'd like to leave."

As she pushed back her chair, Ryder caught her wrist. "Wait a minute. What's going on? There's a story here, I can smell it."

Panic seized her. Wrenching free, she knocked over her coffee cup. A brown stain pooled on the oilcloth. "The only story is an invasion of privacy—mine, by having dinner with a . . . a *reporter*."

Looking stunned, Ryder gestured for their check. She had spoken the word with the same vehemence as *assassin*. And Laurel, wanting to run, forced herself instead to walk out of the restaurant like the coward she was.

Outside the restaurant, in the gathering darkness she hadn't seen his face, but sensed his scowl as he muttered, "I'll drive you home."

Neither of them said another word, except for Laurel's curt directions as they wound through the narrow streets, then climbed the winding hills toward Hilary's villa. She had opened her door while the compact sedan was still rolling. "Thank you," she murmured, "for dinner . . . and everything."

"Why don't you just say what you mean, again?"

He had left her standing in the drive, freed at last from that accusing, magnetic gray gaze. She only wished she could have paid for her own dinner.

Trying to put him out of her mind, she had telephoned Dawson.

"Oh, Mommy, I was afraid you wouldn't call again." Ned's voice quavered.

"I promised I would. I'm at Aunt Hilary's, darling, and just back from dinner. How are you?"

She heard a flood of unhappiness. His roommate still hadn't arrived, he was alone in the room, and outside, strange night birds called. He'd never heard such noises on Beacon Hill.

"Ned, you won't be happy at school if you don't try to like it there. Tell me more about the campus, the buildings and lawns, and is Storm's stall as grand as Daddy said?"

"Dad didn't tell me." Ned pounced on the last question. "He didn't say much all the way here. He turned on the tape deck and told me to go to sleep, or read my Hardy Boys book."

Silently, Laurel swore. She'd asked Dan to make things easier. She should have gone along with them, insisted on it. Enduring Dan's speech-making weekend would have been healthier than setting herself up as a target for Ryder McKendrick's poison pen. At last she said, "Your father was probably just thinking about business, Ned."

But Laurel's own first, unhappy memories of boarding school rushed through her mind. She'd heard noises too; she'd cried herself to sleep. But she'd had Lexa there for comfort, and when Hilary had come banging in with her Vuitton luggage as their third roommate. . . .

Ned will be all right, she told herself when she'd hung up after further reassurance; but she guessed, with a fresh surge of anger at Dan, that he hadn't even kissed Ned good-bye. "I'm not his friend, Laurel," he'd said once, "I'm his father," as if the two were mutually exclusive.

Were they, really? Certainly she'd grown up in a similar atmosphere. Laurel had more than one memory of the senator, shaking hands with her and Lexa, in their boarding school dormitory, or at some airport before they left for summer camp in Switzerland or France.

She had married a man just like her father. Would Lexa have worked as hard to keep her marriage intact? If Lexa were alive, she thought, I wouldn't be married to Dan.

Laurel's head began to ache. She walked through the rooms, wishing Hilary would come home so they could talk.

Turning toward the stairs, she glanced out the window at the murky night; the fog she had first noticed at the restaurant had rolled in off the ocean and covered the area now like an early snowfall. In spite of herself, she wondered how soon Ryder would be safely home. He'd certainly left fast enough. With a dismissive shake of her head, she started up to bed.

The front door knocker banged abruptly. Hilary, she assumed, and didn't stop to think before answering.

On the porch stood Ryder McKendrick who announced, "This fog's all the way to Boston. I'd end up wrapped around a light pole or in a ditch." His gray eyes were ringed with fatigue, his dark gold hair rumpled. "I need a place to sleep for a couple of hours."

"This isn't my house." Trapped, Laurel realized her heart was drumming. She hadn't wanted to tell him she was alone. Then she took a closer look and knew she was being ridiculous; he looked ready to lose consciousness in the doorway. "Hilary isn't back yet," she admitted. "Why don't you try—"

"I've tried every motel and rooming house in town. Where the hell d'you think I've been for the last hour? It's a holiday weekend, remember." Ryder's look was grave, pleading. "Listen, I'm sorry I lost my temper. But do you really think she'd mind if I borrowed the sofa for a few hours? You won't even have to see me again. I'll leave at first light."

"The sofas are loveseats. You'd be uncomfortable."

"At the moment," he murmured, "I could sleep on nails."

Laurel felt her resolve weakening. They'd had enough wine at dinner to make driving to Boston even more hazardous in the fog; story or not, she didn't want to be responsible for another accident. His head must still be hurting from yesterday, for which she felt to blame. The same tug of compassion that had let Hilary convince her to come to Gloucester in the first place—because Hilary needed her—made Laurel step back against her better judgment and open the door completely.

"There's an extra room made up at the top of the stairs. Bathroom across the hall." She decided she must be insane.

He was halfway up the flight, not looking back. "Goodnight, then." His steps dragged. "Thanks."

Finishing a second cup of coffee the next morning, Laurel avoided Ryder's gaze. Too aware of him in the house all night, she hadn't slept well. At dawn he hadn't left; fog still covered everything, and Hilary had yet to come home.

"I can't imagine where she's gone," Laurel muttered, setting her cup down. "She should have called by now."

"She's a big girl," Ryder remarked, "but obviously without your manners. Don't worry, she'll find her way home when she wants to."

His casual acceptance of Hilary's absence made Laurel shudder. "But we heard there were so many accidents on the road."

"Minus one," he said with a smile. "Thanks again for taking me in last night. I know you didn't want to."

The fog would lift soon, she told herself. He would be gone within the hour, with no more information to use against her. And she'd have no more looking into that teasing gray gaze.

"You needed the rest," she said.

"Now you sound like somebody's mother." Ryder helped himself to more fluffy scrambled eggs, redolent of chives and cheese. "Do you have children?"

Laurel tensed. "No."

Ah, what tangled webs we weave when first we practice to deceive. The old rhyme didn't calm the pulsing of her heart. What if he tried to get at Ned?

In the silence, they finished eating. As Laurel picked up his dish to clear the table, Ryder's hand stopped her. "Why are you afraid of me?"

"I'm not afraid," she lied. Again.

She took their plates to the sink and turned on the hot water full blast so that she didn't hear Ryder behind her.

"You're not good at lying." When his hands came to rest on her shoulders, she stiffened in shock. "For some reason you've got a well-established fear of the press. Now you can either tell me what's bothering you—I can't help what I do for a living—and we can talk it out, or you can go right on acting paranoid every time I ask a simple question. But my God," he said, "I thought we had things in common, I even thought . . . Ah, hell."

As his hands slipped from her shoulders, Laurel found

she was shaking. What was she to believe? As a newsman, he knew just how to probe for information. She'd seen that last night.

Yet when he touched her this morning, she felt the same weightlessness inside her she'd felt then, the same soaring of her spirit—and couldn't blame it on too much wine or too little food. That left her with only the look in his eyes to blame for making her want to be with him, to trust him.

"I'm sorry, I'm ... feeling touchy, that's all."

"Yeah, sure. Forget it."

"I just don't like to talk about myself."

"So I gathered."

Ryder lifted his eyebrows. He'd been continually bewildered by her refusal to talk, and last night at the restaurant he'd been surprisingly hurt by her outburst against him as a journalist, as if his taking her to dinner hid something criminal, devious on his part. All he'd wanted was to know the truth about her. Anger had felt more comfortable than hurt, and he'd left her at Hilary's door; but his headlights hadn't cut through the fog, and after five minutes on the road, he'd been lost in a huge ball of cotton. Calmer by then, he'd realized that, if he wanted to learn anything about her, he had to go back. But this morning she seemed scarcely less reluctant to tell him about herself.

What was she hiding? It was as if she were two different people, one cool and distanced, the other—the woman he liked—warm and open.

"There's one more cup of coffee in the pot," she said. "Would you like it?"

"Why not? Maybe by the time I finish it, I'll have learned something about you other than your first name." If Alexandra really was her first name, he thought, remembering the letter *L* she'd drawn on the bartop. Ryder eased down at the table, letting her pour, and said, "Tell me about your husband."

"I'd rather not—"

"Talk about him," Ryder finished for her, this time without an edge to his voice. The silence stretched. She dried their plates, putting them on the shelf with a clatter. He stood at the kitchen window, staring out at the gray morning. "The fog's dissipating, but I think it'll rain. Sky's getting ugly. Not a great day for the beach," he said.

Laurel had the impression from his tone that his thoughts were very far from holiday celebrations. His broad shoulders slumped, pulling at the green plaid cotton shirt he wore, which clung to the muscles on either side of his spine, and she felt a stir of unwelcome response deep inside.

"What's your friend do? Hilary?"

She hung the dish towel to dry as he turned. "Don't you recognize the face?"

"That kind of face, huh?" Laurel saw the intelligence, the curiosity in his eyes that was so much a part of Ryder McKendrick's appeal. She saw the instant he made the connection in his mind. "Hilary Chapin, right? I knew I'd seen her somewhere. But she's got a different persona out of camera range. Yesterday . . ."

Laurel didn't know how much to tell Ryder; she didn't want to be unfair to her closest friend, but recalling Hilary's restlessness the day before, and her continued absence this morning, she sighed.

"Yesterday she was hurting, not angry. Sometimes she remembers too much. . . ."

"Remembers what?"

"Someone she loved . . . a man she still loves." She gnawed at her lower lip, drawing his attention to her mouth. "When we were in school, he . . . was in Vietnam as a Navy pilot. In 1972 he got shot down. He's been listed as MIA ever since."

Ryder winced. "He, and twenty-four hundred other men."

"Hilary's never quite recovered. Not knowing is worse than if he'd been killed outright, I think. That guy yesterday at the Yardarm, the one giving the party she wanted me to go to?" When Ryder nodded, Laurel said, "He hasn't a chance against Chip Brewster. No one does." She finished lamely, "I don't know what to do for her."

Ryder shoved his hands in his pants pockets. "There's nothing you can do." For a long time he just stood there, unmoving, not speaking, as if he'd forgotten she was in the room.

"My wife," he said at last, "died six years ago . . . six years ago tonight. It's never an easy weekend for me, either."

Laurel softened. "If you want to talk about it, I'm a very good listener."

"You must be," he said, "you're a hell of a lousy talker."

She wanted to listen. She didn't want him to go, not only because she'd be left behind to fret over Dan and Ned, over Hilary, and every telecast about Dave Cabell. She wanted to listen, then to tell him everything she'd kept from him about herself. Laurel followed him into the living room, where he stood looking out the front window at the haze of fog, just lifting from the ground.

Ryder's tone was hoarse. "My wife's name was Maggie. She had short blond hair and true blue eyes. She went swimming alone that Sunday before Labor Day. Today. Just before sundown, where there were no lifeguards. The sky looked very much like this, I remember. The wind was rising, too."

"Oh, God," she said, as if she knew what he would say next. But she shouldn't sympathize, Ryder thought. He'd been alone that night for good reason. He hadn't wanted to break away for the holiday; he'd had a layout to finish, which was overdue. He'd given Maggie a hell of a time before he agreed to make the trip to the cottage at the Cape. Tears, shouts, recriminations, threats—the worst one of all. Nine years after he'd come back from Nam, he'd finally broken her, and to this day he could still see her face, the shock and the pain.

Maggie had left the house and hadn't come back. She's just licking her wounds, he'd thought, hauling out his paperwork; she'll eat dinner somewhere, have a drink, then come home. She'd make up first, as she always did, and he would let her. He didn't know then that Maggie had done her final pleading with him.

At ten o'clock, shoving the layout aside, he'd begun to worry. By midnight he was at the police barracks.

"Ryder, what happened?" Laurel's husky voice, full of concern, pulled him back.

"The next day, in midmorning, she washed up with the debris from the storm on the beach below ours."

"Oh, dear God. I'm sorry."

At one-thirty in the afternoon, Ryder identified the corpse as Margaret McKendrick. Nausea, grief, tears— none of that would come. He was a widower at thirty-three, and the only thing left of a good marriage gone bad was his overwhelming guilt.

Guilt he could feel. Ryder simply added it to what he'd brought back from Vietnam. He wondered whether the woman behind him now wasn't right to keep him at an emotional distance.

"Did you . . . were you the one to find her?" she asked.

He shook his head. "No, but I deserved to. Because it was my fault."

Laurel took a few steps so she could see his face. "But she drowned, you weren't even there—"

"I should have been," he said, "only I never was, for her. Not after . . . oh, hell."

He took a deep breath, letting it out slowly. "Six years," he murmured. "I thought I was going to kick it this time. Coming to Gloucester, seeing you." He looked up. "Not as a dodge, but because I really want to know you. I did from the first, on Beacon Hill. That kind of instant chemistry hasn't happened to me in a long time. I don't know what it means yet, except that I'm attracted to you," Ryder said. "I'm not even sure that's a good thing for either of us."

*I know it's not,* Laurel thought.

"No," she said. "I think this is . . . crazy."

"Crazy good, or crazy bad?"

His gray gaze held her captive; she'd never dreamed he was vulnerable, too. His eyes were somber, his mouth faintly smiling. She wouldn't hurt him for the world.

"I'm not sure either," she murmured.

He stood too close.

"What would make us sure, do you think?"

"A fresh pot of coffee," Laurel suggested, and he laughed softly.

"Still afraid of me?" But he didn't wait for her answer. He walked past her to the front door. "Do you get the *Globe* here? I'd like a weather forecast."

"Yes, but it was soggy this morning and fell apart. I threw it out."

Her pulse jumped when he turned on the television set.

The first thing she saw was Dave Cabell's face, and Laurel's heart turned over in alarm. Only the essentials seeped through, freezing her.

"Another heart attack," Ryder said. "The second in three days."

And she couldn't keep from asking, "Isn't that unusual?

He's in a hospital, surely they could prevent—"

"The first seventy-two hours are always critical." He gave her an odd look. "Multiple attacks aren't uncommon. They must have told you that when your husband—"

"His was very sudden. Massive. He . . . didn't make it to the hospital."

The room tilted, and Ryder's voice seemed to be coming from far off. Another attack, critical this time. Poor Dave, but if the worst happened, if Dan . . .

"Hey, are you all right? I didn't mean to . . . Where are you going?" Ryder asked.

She didn't answer. She couldn't face the news, couldn't face him either, or herself. The lies she'd told. Turning from his touch, she found the strength this time to run.

Laurel skidded down the steep embankment behind the rambling, shingled house, not trusting the rickety wooden stairs that Hilary's stepfather had installed years ago. Below, fronting the vastness of a pewter sea frothed with whitecaps, lay a broad strip of coarse sand, Hilary's private beach, and a meandering expanse of dunes. Here, Laurel and Hilary as girls had sunbathed away the hot afternoons of August, the last warm weekends of autumn.

After Lexa had died, they'd come here, she remembered. And when the news had reached them about Chip.

Now Ryder caught her at the bottom of the bluff. "Don't," he murmured. "I'm sorry about your husband. I shouldn't have brought up Maggie either, oh God, sweetheart, don't."

"Ryder—"

But he didn't seem to want talking now. He'd tried talking, and it hadn't worked. He'd wanted the truth, and she wouldn't give it to him. Ryder hauled her closer, into his arms, and kissed her.

## ❋ CHAPTER 5 ❋

❋

His mouth, soft and hot, sent a flood of feeling through her, that sense again of soaring, of wanting to fly. Laurel stayed still, arms at her sides, willing to allow the kiss, unable to break it. She wanted to give in, but felt like a traitor, betraying her husband with a man she barely knew. Wanted too much to know better.

"No," she said when he moved closer.

"Oh yes," he answered and tilted his head to shift the angle of the kiss. "My God, you know it's yes."

His eyes were dark and somber, like the sea. The fog was gone, but the weather had turned nasty, with gusting wind and heavy clouds scudding low over the ocean, its once blue-green surface now an ever-darkening blend of grays.

Her heart beat heavily. Could she tell him now that she'd been lying to him since they'd met?

"No," she repeated, drawing back, "no."

Ryder peered into her eyes. Her lashes were stuck together, more black satin, like her hair. Her cheeks were damp, radiant from the light mist that had started to fall. Radiant from his kisses. Gently he asked, "Why not?"

She shook her head, looking down. Dan, she thought,

and Ned. All the obligations of her life. Her wedding
band dug into her finger as she clenched a fist against the
pain. She couldn't betray her marriage, the commitment
she believed in. It wasn't right to want something you
couldn't have, from a man who could destroy you with
a few well-chosen words. And what words he'd have, if
she surrendered to the heat that kept throbbing in her.

"Is it because of Maggie?" His voice shook. "What I
told you?"

"Oh, Ryder, no." She couldn't let him think that.

"What, then?"

When she tried to move away, his hand closed on the
crook of her elbow, and he turned her to him again. The
wind whipped their hair, Laurel's a black silk lash and
Ryder's all flying, molten gold ribbons.

Just seconds ago, in his arms, she'd felt free, soaring,
as she had the first time she'd glimpsed his beautiful gray
eyes; as she had only once before in her life, in childhood.

She'd been eight years old then, Ned's age. One summer day, Laurel remembered, she'd scaled the giant oak
to the tree house high in its branches. *Look, Lexie, watch
me. I'm going to fly..*

*Jump*, Lexa shouted. *Jump*.

So she had jumped, she'd flown—and learned a painful
lesson.

"Sweetheart?" Ryder said. "Alexandra . . ."

What could she tell him now that wouldn't make him
hate her? Blinded by a wet black curtain of hair, she pulled
away. The rain came harder now, no longer a mist but
warm and slanting. She loped along the beach, not knowing where she was going, not caring, hearing Ryder's soft
footsteps in the sand behind her. When he was gone,
she'd be alone, afraid, remembering in the rain.

His fingers grasped the back of her cotton T-top,
grazed the seat of her white shorts, and defeated by one

flash of desire when he touched her, she sank onto the sand. The coarse grains bit into her flesh. Ryder knelt in front of her. They had reached the low shelter of a sprawling dune, and here the wind cut less sharply, the rain drove more finely.

"You want me, too," he said.

Ryder reached for her, pulling Laurel to her knees. Their bodies touched, patellae and thighs and the jut of hipbones. She couldn't move or make a sound. Her breasts flattened against the thud of his heart as he pressed his lips to the dewy wetness of her hair. Even there, she felt the heat of his mouth. "Alex—"

And she moaned. Jump, Lexa had said. Jump, she imagined her saying now. Lexa wouldn't pause to consider consequences if things went wrong. Let him print the story in the *Enquirer* if he wants to, she would say. By then I'll have had the feelings first. That's what Lexa would have done.

And as if Laurel were again part of their adolescent deception, she knew what she would do. Didn't he know her already not as herself, Laurel, but as Alexandra? She'd told the lie to protect her privacy, but had that been the only reason? No, she realized. Because now it wouldn't be Laurel holding back, as she always did; now it would be Lexa who dared as she always had—who gave her mouth to his, who opened to their kiss, Lexa who risked everything for these first sharp shafts of pleasure that pierced her body and made her greedy for more.

"See?" he whispered, shaken. "See?"

Ryder took the kiss deeper, then deeper still, and touched her breast. God, he'd never wanted any woman this much. He wasn't going to make it back to the house, and judging—he felt sudden triumph—by her glazed eyes, neither would she. She was fumbling with the buttons of his shirt. Dragging at the damp fabric, she cast it aside, then ran her wet hands down his bared torso.

Again, he covered her drugged smile of delight with his mouth. There was only one thing left in his mind as her skin seemed to slide under his wet hands. Even her mouth slipped under his, the rain an aphrodisiac.

He couldn't bother with her clothes. Ryder drew her down on top of him, his lower back and hips landing on the sodden shirt in the sand. He tunneled his hands under her top and ran his fingers lightly over her breasts, raising the nipples, hard as stones beneath the red-striped cotton. He heard her moan compete with his. He stripped only the white shorts down her rain-slick legs, and a wisp of panty with them.

"Ryder—" her voice came weakly "—what if people . . ."

"There's no one around."

A storm, the private beach—but he wouldn't have cared if there'd been a crowd. Still, he rolled her over until he shielded her from view. Rain pelted his shoulder blades, rivered down the valley of his spine. She used the pads of her fingers to stroke him there, lightly, sliding the water's slickness over his naked skin. Her clothes felt damp and hot; he was glad he'd shed his shirt, her bottoms.

Laurel had ceased thinking of the grains of sand against her clothes, the backs of her legs. She'd ceased worrying about tomorrow, or the next hour when things might go wrong again. For now, with Ryder's face above her, his gray eyes dark with pleasure, his mouth coming down again to hers, everything seemed right.

"You'd better move," he said, lips against her throat. "Slide up a little, so you're on my shirt." He positioned her, all the while nuzzling beneath her ear, sending wild shivers down Laurel's back and between her shoulders. Then, "Do this for me, will you?" His fingers tangled in the wet black satin of her hair. "I don't have my hands free."

Tentatively at first, Laurel's hands dropped to his fly, while he rested on his elbows, holding his hips away from her. When she touched him Ryder groaned. His lips left hers to move lower, trailing heat as Laurel closed her eyes against the slanting rain. Ryder kissed her through the wet T-top, first one breast and then the other, until she cried out at the pleasure sweeping through her body. "Oh, that, God, it's—"

"Good," he whispered. "I knew it would be, sweet-heart. So good."

The pleasure raced, intensifying, making its own demands now. He freed himself, lifted and paused above her for an instant, then drove into her for the first time. It was, he told himself, gasping into the sweetness of her mouth, the beginning of a universe.

The world had slipped away, Laurel thought as she trudged with Ryder back up the embankment to the house. Her bare feet—she carried her shoes—slid in the sand and mud, and her clothes were soaked and dirty, but she felt like singing. Her hand firmly clasped in his, she wouldn't think that those precious moments on the beach had been both beginning, and end.

"Who's first for the shower?" he asked.

"You," she said. "I'll make coffee and find us something to eat."

She was glad he hadn't suggested they share the bath-room. Now that they were away from the beach, she felt shy again, uncertain. Yet the new throb of pleasure lingered.

When he came downstairs, wearing fresh jeans and a loose knit eggshell-colored sweater, his hair dark from his shower and his skin smelling of soap, Laurel went into his arms. His scent, and the full-bodied aroma of coffee brewing, filled her with contentment. She'd never felt this way before, never with Dan. How much could be wrung from a few hours together?

Laurel slipped from his embrace. "I'd better shower," she said.

She finished in record time, reappearing in gray slacks and a yellow sweater. "Are you ready for coffee?"

He spanned her waist from behind, his mouth pressing the tender place beneath her earlobe. "Ready for you," he said. "See how glib you make me?"

She shivered and almost spilled the coffee. "Caffeine first."

"Not trying to get rid of me again, are you?"

Would he stay, then? "No, of course not."

They lingered over second cups, and Ryder smiled at her across the table. "I like you that way." When Laurel glanced down at herself, he lifted her chin to look into her eyes. "The glasses," he said. "They're sexy." Then he leaned over the table and kissed her. It was a light kiss, lips barely touching, but fire flared inside her.

They talked of inconsequential things, laughing often and seeking each other's eyes while Laurel thought, amazed at herself, we're lovers, which seemed just as trite as her acknowledgment of pleasure and made her smile. If only she'd feel so charitable about her behavior on Tuesday, in Boston, she thought, when she was facing Dan again. She couldn't pretend to be Lexa then, not even to herself.

Ryder touched her cheek with one finger and she looked, startled, into his eyes. "You're far away, and not happy anymore."

"Just thinking."

"About your husband," he guessed, too accurately.

"There hasn't been anyone else for you until today, has there?"

"No," she said.

Laurel rose and took their cups to the sink. Ryder was right behind her again.

"Don't feel guilty," he said, "that you're still alive."

Her pulse skipped. She could have sworn he'd said, *still a lie.*

"How long ago did he die?"

"Just a few months ago," she said. "Do you think we could stop this? I really can't—"

He turned her to face him, but she couldn't meet his gaze. "I want to know who you are, what you are. I want to know what makes you happy and what makes you sad. I want to—"

"I . . . I can't tell you any more."

His hands dropped. "All right," he said. "Then don't tell me anything. I won't stop feeling the way I do about you, though. Sweetheart, maybe you don't want to believe this, but in forty-eight hours I've fallen head over tail for a woman who hasn't even told me her last name."

Ryder's heart was in his eyes, and she couldn't answer what she saw there. "I think you're confusing hormones," she began, "with—"

"Like hell I am." His gray eyes had clouded. "Don't you know yet that anything is possible in this world? Anything you can imagine, sweetheart, and a shitload of things you can't. Some of them . . ." He stopped, his face pale beneath his tan.

"Ryder—"

"Some of them are even good."

He busied himself lighting a cigarette, then blew out a stream of smoke. She noticed his hands were shaking.

"Do you want me to go?" he asked and crushed out the cigarette he'd just lit. "I mean, hell, maybe this is just too soon for you. I've been alone for six years. A few women have come and gone in my life since Maggie died, but no one who meant anything. I didn't want them to. Then I saw you, and the world started spinning like a pinwheel, full of color again." He held up a hand. "No, let me finish. Maybe you haven't had enough time, and I shouldn't have pushed things today but—"

She gave him the truth at last. "Today was one of the most special times of my life, Ryder."

"Then let's not put an end to it," he said.

She would have told him then; she was sure she could have before they went any further, but he folded her in his arms and said, "It takes time, sweetheart. We'll go slow, I promise. In a year or so, your husband's death won't seem so—"

"It's not his death!" Laurel managed to say. "It . . . it was our marriage. I couldn't say we were happy."

His embrace tightened. "I'm sorry. No," he said fiercely, "I only wish I were. You make me selfish, today I—"

"Today, oh God, with you—"

"Me, too," he said on a sigh of relief. "Hush, sweetheart. Me, too." Then Ryder's mouth covered hers, and she was lost again. Lost in pleasure, and in lies.

Just when he'd found his way home again, Dan Benedict told himself, he was thrust out into the darkness. Sunday always came too soon. Tomorrow he planned to grab the bonus hours of Monday like gold, in both fists. Not only home, he thought as he stretched his body full length on the wide bed, but treasure.

In Maria he'd found the mother lode, he thought, watching her walk across the bedroom toward the connecting bath. In ten years she hadn't bored him; hadn't stopped sharing herself, always in new and different ways.

"You didn't see me for the wall of law books in your office," she always teased. But he'd noticed Maria her first morning on the job, three months after he'd married Laurel—and sold his political soul to Edwin Frasier.

In that moment, he'd risked his marriage, the senator's promises, his own reputation. "Are you free for lunch, Maria? There's a delightful place nearby. Salads and quiche, they fix a truly aristocratic eggplant parmigiana."

He'd thought she was Italian. Dan remembered his surprise at discovering Maria's Puerto Rican heritage. It reminded him too clearly of his beginnings, of the stench of garbage in hallways, of three tiny rooms after you'd climbed halfway to the moon—and the smell of cheap alcohol, sprinkled like rosewater around the place. His father, in T-shirt and beer belly, was always snoring on the broken-down sofa. The shouts in Spanish from the courtyard had never roused him.

"You know, we're not all on welfare," Maria had said. They'd been sitting at one of the umbrella tables in the outdoor restaurant, picking from each other's plates and talking as if they'd known one another for a decade, not half a morning. "My brother's a cop," she'd added. "And my kid sister's in college at B.U. We live in a real house, Mr. Benedict, with doors on the rooms and a bathroom that's not across the hall."

By then he already loved that smile, her full lower lip, the dark, dancing eyes that teased yet promised. Dan wanted to leap up from the table, drag her by the hand to the nearest hotel, and wipe the smile from her mouth with his. He wanted to see her mouth, her whole body slack with passion, her eyes dazed and needing.

"You're lucky," he'd said instead. "We had to share with five other families."

He had been twenty-one years old and in law school before he had the luxury of his own room and bath, and the privacy to take a shower that lasted more than two minutes without someone banging at the door.

"Did you live on welfare?" she wanted to know.

"Most of the time."

He'd wiped the smile away after all, but not as he'd intended. Nor had he intended to tell her so much about himself. Even Laurel didn't know many details of his background. He supposed—knew—that the senator did, but at least he had the good grace never to mention Dan's past. The senator spoke only of the future.

"I'm never going back there," Dan had murmured, shoving aside his lunch and reaching for her hand.

"I wouldn't think you'd have to."

Maria's eyes drifted over the three-piece suit and silk tie, the gleam of gold cuff links at his wrists. He was glad he didn't own a wedding band, sorry that he'd irrevocably linked his life to Laurel Frasier's when he was at that moment falling helplessly in love with someone else.

Office gossip traveled fast; by the end of that afternoon, everyone at Dobbs, Fairfield had learned of their lunch together, and Maria had discovered that Dan Benedict was a married man.

For a month she had barely looked his way. Dan sent roses for her birthday in November and a slender gold chain with a locket at Christmas. The locket held a picture of himself. By then, he'd been beyond caution.

"For God's sake, Benedict," said one of the senior partners, "the girl's looking for a meal ticket, nothing else."

Dan had spent the next two Saturday afternoons in the park across from Maria's home before he'd dared to approach her. She'd been riding a bicycle along the path, coming toward him. When she was nearly past, she'd seen the sign propped on the bench at his side, roughly lettered with marking pen on a shirt cardboard he'd found in the metal trash basket: CONTRIBUTE TO CHARITY. GIVE ME YOUR HEART, MARIA.

The bike screeched to a halt. "Oh, Dan, you crazy man."

He pulled her from the seat, into his arms, and crushed his mouth on hers. He'd seen acceptance in those eyes, defeat and joy. And tears. "I mean it. I adore you, every inch, I want—"

"I want a husband, Dan. You're already married," she said. "Ambitious, too. You won't divorce her."

"Well, I . . ." Edwin Frasier would crucify him if he left Laurel.

"You won't divorce her," Maria repeated, placing her fingers over his lips. "So what can I hope for, Dan?"

"I don't know." His eyes were grave. "Me. I don't know what else."

"I want children." To his surprise, she'd teased that her Latin heritage was showing. "Lots of them," she said.

"We'll have them, then."

Remembering the promise of ten years ago, Dan shifted on the mattress in the bedroom of the house he'd bought her. Her answer had changed both their lives, forever. "I love you. I must be crazy, too . . . but, Danny, I love you."

He rolled over, sighing. The sheets carried the scent of their lovemaking, and he buried his face in her pillow, inhaling her. God, damn, hell. What was he going to do?

Ten years had seen a lot of changes. All but one, Dan acknowledged. And that, Maria had prophesied. He hadn't divorced his wife, and now, now he couldn't think of it. Not when the realization of all the years, from Washington's slums to assistant D.A. to law partner to city councilman, might—at last—come true. Impatient with himself, he got off the bed and padded naked to the television.

He'd spent more time in front of this screen, or the larger console set in the den, this weekend than Maria had any notion of, including a furtive five minutes the night before while Maria telephoned her ailing mother in Boston. He'd plugged into a small Walkman during his morning jog alone—and his heart sped up with the reports.

Cabell's condition deteriorated by the hour. He was on a respirator. His family had been called to the bedside. The doctors were no longer cautiously optimistic.

How could he relish such news? But dammit, it wasn't his fault that Cabell smoked four packs a day or—

"Turn that thing off."

Maria emerged from their dressing closet, wearing a short silk robe with Japanese motifs that suited her Latin coloring.

"I thought we'd agreed that your life beyond this house would stay off-limits," she said. "Now you've brought it through the door yourself. Shall we talk about this?" She gestured at the set. "You've been sneaking looks for two days." She came toward him. "Or would you rather just fall into bed again?"

He thought he would simply take the whipping and be done with it. She was entitled to hold the lash. What had he given her in all these years? This house, that animal she rode like a centaur, some clothes and money. All material things. His love, yes, but not his name. Not his children. God, never his children, though they'd tried. "Sex has never been the only thing with us, Maria."

"Sometimes I wish it were."

He caught her arm. "You're upset about Tuesday," he told her, "not about Dave Cabell. Let's talk about that if we have to talk away the rest of our time together."

Maria's face whitened. "Dan, please."

"Please what? Pretend I'm not half crazy, too, about

the thought of you going under the knife?" He saw her flinch. "Knowing that the only sensible damn solution is going to break your heart—"

She tore from his grasp. "We made the decision, Dan. Together." She had miscarried half a dozen times, nearly bled to death the last, six months ago. "I'm not afraid of a pair of inch-long scars on my belly." She raised dark, bruised-looking eyes to his. "I just hate knowing there won't be another chance, that she . . . that *she* has all of you from now on. Your ring, your name, your son," she said. "Oh God, I didn't want to do this. I promised myself I wouldn't. I hate whining."

He pulled her to him. "I'll be with you on Tuesday morning, Maria. Don't you think it would tear at me, not being there?"

"I'm not a child." She always said the same thing, jumping that infernal horse over one lethal fence after another. "I can manage," she said. "I do it all the time."

She'd never reminded him before of his other life, and of how infrequently he managed to invade hers. When she tugged, he let her go. Dan watched her fuss with a small collection of glass paperweights that she kept on the table by their bed. "What does *she* think of all this?" Maria finally asked. "More to the point, what does Edwin Frasier think?"

"I haven't talked to him since Friday."

"Then he must be ringing your telephone off the desk by now."

"If he is, I don't care."

"Liar," she said softly.

"Maria . . ." He went after her. "This has nothing to do with us. David Cabell's in the hospital, that's *all*. Nobody's said he isn't finishing his campaign, there's been no announcement by his staff or mine."

"Tell me there won't be."

The words were out before he stopped to think. "Tell me you don't still want a child." Her swift intake of breath, the filling of her eyes made him ashamed. "No, Christ, I'm sorry. I didn't mean that. Maria, they're just both dreams of a lifetime, that's all I meant, and—"

"Only one of them can come true."

She began to cry. He hated tears; they always reminded him of his mother. She'd shed so many tears over his father that they'd worn her out. Dan had heard most of them late at night, an undertone to the street noise thrown, like stones, against the windows. "Don't, Maria, please. I've never seen you cry." The sound of her sobs racked him clear through. "Please," he begged.

"I'm afraid," she mourned, "and I've never been afraid before, with you."

"I'm not going to let anything hurt us. I won't."

She raised her arms to his neck, drawing him toward her. He could see that she didn't believe him, but he didn't know how to convince her when his own stomach had clenched into a tight knot. As he lowered his mouth to hers, she said, "This is the last time we'll simply have each other. I feel it, Dan. Love me like the first time . . . love me." He pressed her into the mattress.

Later, lying in the dark, Dan nearly convinced himself that she was only worried about the operation. In time, the sorrow would lessen. He'd spend more weekends with her, somehow. Laurel didn't need him half so much, he thought. Maybe I can . . .

No, not now. Next year, perhaps. Damn, he sounded like the typical cheating husband. Always planning to leave his wife, never doing it. But if he got his shot at the Senate, when his position became secure . . .

Easing his arm from beneath Maria's sleeping form, he got up and walked through the spacious rooms of the sprawling house into the den. Sound asleep now, she wouldn't hear. He switched on the large-screen TV. Checking his watch, he saw that it was just past nine o'clock. Hell, there wouldn't be news until—

Christ. In the ten-year-old picture, Cabell's campaigner's grin was intact, a macabre counterpoint to the announcer's voice.

". . . died tonight in Massachusetts General Hospital of complications following two major coronaries within three days. Details at eleven."

His own heart hammered. He'd waited for this chance, deserved it. Had paid for it with his life. But he wouldn't wake her now, dammit. He wouldn't allow these last precious moments of their privacy to be spoiled. Let them look for him, from Alaska to Florida. Even Laurel, he—

The sound behind him made Dan freeze. He heard Maria step into the den, a soft rustle of silk with each step until she stood beside him. He caught the subtle scent of violets before he heard the resignation in her voice.

"Tell me now, Danny, that you aren't going to run."

## ✳ CHAPTER 6 ✳

✳

WITH ANXIOUS EYES, Laurel scanned the Copley Plaza ballroom for the third time in as many minutes. Where was Dan? Not among the clot of admirers by the podium, not with Teague Michaels across the room. She gnawed at her bottom lip. It was fifteen minutes past twelve; the press conference to announce Dan's candidacy had been scheduled for noon. If the thing had to be done, why not do it on time?

Laurel turned and stared out one of the enormous windows that rose to the high ceiling. She realized that she hadn't been looking for her husband so much as for Ryder McKendrick. What made her think—pray—he wouldn't come? How could she have been so stupid in Gloucester, so reckless and indiscreet?

After the beach and the storm, Hilary still hadn't come back. That night they'd had the old house to themselves, the wind moaning, soft rain against the windows. Ryder's hard body pressing into hers. Laurel closed her eyes against the night's remembered pleasure.

On Monday morning they'd awakened to more rain, "a blessing," Ryder whispered. Rolling, he dragged her onto him, smoothing his hands down her spine and the backs of her thighs. He pulled Laurel's head down. "Pretend it's raining all over the world. Let's stay here forever."

If only they could have stayed. She'd felt undone by pleasure, soft and pliant. Then she learned what had happened during the night. Dave Cabell, dead. She had watched the television coverage the next morning in stunned silence until Ryder said, "He was a good senator."

"What do you think will happen now?"

He laughed shortly. "Your friend Benedict will offer himself, in the spirit of sacrifice."

Laurel had expected to strangle at any instant, and the same feeling came to her now, in the Copley Plaza ballroom. Ryder was a newsman, first and last. Sharp, incisive, with no qualms about going for the jugular. He'd done it, with the senator. He might just do it again. Only this time, the spilled blood would be hers.

Laurel fought down panic as she heard her name being called. The voice wasn't the one she expected—feared—but she didn't welcome Teague Michaels, either.

"Dan wants you to say a few words about Cabell. Think you can handle it off the cuff, or should I jot down a few deathless phrases?"

Laurel turned to stare at him. "Considering the circumstances, I find your choice of words in bad taste."

Teague grinned, showing the gap between his square front teeth. He was a short man, blunt and square all over, no more than an inch taller than Laurel. His blue eyes, which were light enough to appear colorless in the glare from the windows, met hers on a level. Laurel dropped her gaze, taking in another of Teague's badly chosen suits, straight off a department store rack—bargain basement, she decided.

"Laurel, you find *me* in bad taste," he said, still smiling.

"I can just see your feet, propped on a desk in Washington."

The acid tone wasn't her usual, but Teague Michaels provoked Laurel. She had mistrusted him from the instant Dan introduced them, or soon after; he'd made a clumsy pass at her, which she'd never forgiven. He was, in her opinion, without class—the worst indictment of character, according to her mother. That the senator, and Dan, not only tolerated Michaels but respected his judgment, baffled Laurel as much as it irritated her. To Laurel, even worse than the man was the fact that he brought out such sarcasm in her.

"Shoes off," she finished, "a hole in one sock—"

"And getting my job done." His smile was gone. Laurel had to admit that Teague Michaels could probably get Dan elected. Which only made her spirits sink lower than her opinion of him. Teague watched the play of emotions on her face for a moment before he said, "Just see that you do your job, little lady." He emphasized the last words. "You ought to listen to your husband. Treat me better. He says, 'Be nice to Laurel, Teague,' and I'm nice to Laurel. Why don't you give it a try?"

Her answer was a frosty smile.

"Okay, forget Be Kind to Campaign Managers week. I'll be so damn busy I won't notice." He leaned closer. "Now listen, here's what I want you to say—a few words about Cabell's being a great guy, how you feel sympathy for his widow and kids. I think there's three of 'em."

"Four," Laurel corrected. "He had two sons, two daughters." One of the girls, she remembered, was coming out in December; Laurel was co-chairperson of the cotillion committee.

Teague's thick, sand-colored eyebrows rose. "Well. Breeding shows, so they've always told me." The colorless eyes slid over her. "Though I've always wondered myself what's underneath that reserved show of manners and good taste."

"Why wonder? You wouldn't understand."

His hand at the small of her back, Michaels began steering her toward the podium. Laurel tried not to flinch from his touch.

"Remember," Teague muttered in her ear, "head up, back straight, put a smile on your face, and look at the audience when it's your turn to speak. Otherwise, the devoted wife expression will do just fi—" He broke off, glancing across the room. "Kee-rist, what have I done to deserve this? Beirut for him, I'd think, San Salvador, anywhere but this ballroom."

He didn't have to say the name. Laurel followed Teague Michaels's gaze and lost the rhythm of her heartbeat. "Oh, God," she whispered without thinking as her gaze collided with a pair of intelligent gray eyes.

"Ryder McKendrick," Teague said. "We agree on something, Laurel."

Ryder leaned a shoulder against the wall by the double doors to the ballroom, trying to order his thoughts. He'd thought for one instant that the slender woman in the fluid, salmon-colored shirtwaist must be a mirage, the product of his overstimulated libido after twenty-four hours without her.

On Monday afternoon he'd left her waiting for Hilary at the house in Gloucester. "I'm sorry, sweetheart. We've got a lot of talking to do, but this story won't wait." He had kissed her good-bye with a promise to call that night.

"Maybe you shouldn't."

"What do you mean, shouldn't?" His eyes reminded her of the pleasures they'd shared. "I'm a 'hated journalist.' If nothing else, remember, I'm persistent."

He'd ignored his first stirrings of unease. Then from

his apartment in Cambridge, Ryder had tried to telephone her in Gloucester.

Hilary's response had been a choked, "Alexandra?"

Quickly, he'd identified himself. No, she hadn't given him the number. Actually, Ryder had memorized it from the kitchen telephone dial. "Can you tell me where to reach her?"

"I'm sorry, but—oh Lord, Alexandra."

He'd been talking to a dead line when he realized that she knew him only as Matthew. Trying a second time, a third, he'd gotten no answer at all.

And now, Ryder thought, here she was—Alexandra—walking with that regal posture past the white damask-covered table to the speaker's podium at the end. She'd left her glasses somewhere. Ryder frowned. A family friend? But few extra guests were in the large room. Not even Senator Frasier had shown up, or his wife. This was a gathering, mainly, of the press corps.

Ryder cursed himself. Benedict had come into the room, and she was standing in the circle of his arm, smiling unsteadily and nodding as he spoke. Then her head bowed, and Ryder knew. He knew. He'd seen that posture before, in the grainy photo in Sara's file at *Newstrend*, her hair covered by a mourning veil, eyes shadowed.

There were thousands of women with dark hair, he tried to tell himself, even with that particular bend of the neck at certain moments, but only one of them lived in a specific Beacon Hill town house, and only one was married to Dan Benedict.

When her eyes lifted, meeting his, he knew what she must be seeing on his face: confusion, shock, the truth. After all, she was Benedict's wife. He tried to push it down, but anger rose in him, as strong and obvious as the attraction he'd felt to her. No wonder Hilary had gasped. Alexandra wasn't her name. "I don't like to talk about myself," she'd said. But why had she picked him?

Well, hell, he'd picked her up in a bar, hadn't he? Ryder fumbled with the recorder slung around his neck. Some journalist, he told himself. Last weekend he hadn't seen— hadn't wanted to see—what was right in front of him.

Well, here she is, he thought, and my God, look who she is. The surviving Frasier twin. A chill ran down his spine as he jabbed a finger at the button to start the tape. He rapidly checked the film and settings on the Nikon, the Rolleiflex, too. If Benedict only knew, Ryder thought bitterly as Dan stepped up to the podium microphone, where his wife had spent her holiday.

Where was a tree house refuge when she needed one? Laurel glanced toward the ballroom doors. Ryder stood pressed against the wall next to them, arms folded over his chest, one foot crossed over the other ankle. The casual pose couldn't disguise his frown before he turned slightly, putting his profile to the podium, his back toward Laurel. She deserved the snub, of course. My God, what had she been thinking of?

Laurel steeled herself for the first barrage of camera flashes as Dan, at the nearby microphone, began to speak.

She kept losing the train of thought in Dan's speech, which seemed itself hypocritical. Laurel knew that Dan had respected Dave, even liked him, but it was Dave Cabell's death that could catapult her husband to national prominence. All Laurel could think of was how she could speak when her turn came. Speak, with Ryder in the room.

She applauded as loudly as anyone else when Dan finished, his arms raised high and clasped above his head in premature victory. Strength, dignity, honesty emanated from him in waves. Then he turned, and drew her to him, kissing her for the cameras. She heard people laugh, and realized that she'd made some clever comment of endorsement, though she couldn't recall what it was. Dan pushed her gently to the podium, adjusting the microphone to her shorter stature, and, leaning close, added a last statement: "Now we bring on my secret campaign weapon—my wife, Laurel Frasier Benedict."

She could have kicked him for reminding this roomful of people—Ryder—that she was related to Edwin Frasier. Laurel's mind went blank. She hated public speaking. Hated having to say a word while her entire being was centered on the man at one side of the ballroom, two expensive-looking cameras slung around his neck on leather straps, crisscrossed like bandoliers.

Swallowing, she raised her head, looking straight at the throng of reporters with pens poised above notepads, mikes held aloft to catch her words. "Mary Cabell is a dear friend of mine. I've known her for more than a decade. I remember when her children were no older than my son is now . . . and today, I grieve with her."

Laurel finished five minutes later. By then she'd grown accustomed to the constant interruption of camera flashes, the buzz of whispered conversation in the room. She stepped away from the microphone to a blast of applause.

Then the press closed in.

"Is it true, Dan, that Mrs. Cabell wanted the junior senator's slot for herself in January?"

"No," he said and only that.

But Laurel knew that last night a grief-stricken Mary Cabell had been comforted, cajoled, then bullied from any thought of running for her dead husband's Senate seat. She would instead, it had been agreed in the presence of Dan and half a dozen prominent party figures, complete Dave's term—and then gracefully retire.

"That leaves Jack Sommers, and maybe three others."

"All good Democrats. That's what the primary's for."

"What about Jay Heron?"

"He's welcome to run. Whether or not a Republican can win . . ." Dan let the phrase trail away as several reporters laughed. Laurel could almost feel the senator's presence. She knew how quickly other opposition would be cut to size. She also saw Ryder, watching her.

Then someone called out: "Laurel, wouldn't the senator love to have seen this day?"

"I'm sure he would, but he's in Hong Kong until Friday." Laurel used the moment of camaraderie for cover. "I need some air," she whispered to Dan. Ignoring several more questions, she pushed her way through the group of journalists.

She should have known she'd be followed and by whom, but she'd hoped to get outside. In the center of the ballroom he caught her, one hand on her shoulder easily turning her around.

"Ah, the widow Benedict, I presume."

Laurel didn't dare react; dozens of other newsmen were watching keenly. "Ryder—"

His tone was hard, accusing. "I tried to call you last night."

Speechless, her heart thudding, she stared at his blue shirt and regimental tie. He'd dressed for the occasion: a navy wool blazer with brass buttons, a pair of charcoal gray flannel pants that exactly matched the color of his pain-filled eyes.

"It took me until twenty minutes ago to figure out why Hilary sounded so odd on the phone. As if she were covering for you, as if—"

"Oh God, please let me—"

"Explain?" He laughed, bitterly. "How do you explain posing as a dead woman?"

"Ryder, I made a mistake."

"We both made a mistake," he said. "Too bad it felt so good."

She flinched, and glanced away.

"Alexandra." He shook his head. "I couldn't seem to think of you by that name, not even when we..." He broke off. "The name doesn't suit you. She was your sister, wasn't she?"

"Yes."

"Look at me," he demanded, "look at me so I can remember you, not her. Laurel," he murmured for the first time, then said it again. "Laurel. That's a softer name—but you're not soft, are you, sweetheart?"

"Please." She wanted to force her apology on him, but knew he wouldn't take it. Just as she'd known he would hate her when he learned the truth.

"My God, everything about you was an illusion."

"Not everything. Please, Ryder, don't make a scene." Teague Michaels, in conversation with Dan, had turned to look. "We're being watched," she said, but Ryder wouldn't relent.

"Oh, I'd love to make a scene," he said between his teeth. "What if I just stride to that microphone, brush your husband aside, and tell these people a few things about you that they'd be only too happy to share with the voters of Massachusetts?"

Laurel blanched.

"Let's see," he said, "first, the small deception when your dog knocked me flat. Just visiting, you said, a friend of the family. And the coy pretense that you wouldn't let me stay overnight in Gloucester because no one else was home—as if you cared. And, oh yes, let's not forget that business in the rain, half-naked on the sand with—"

"Tell them, then!" Her hands clenched into small fists. "Go on," she said, shaking. "Get it over with."

"No. I don't think so. Not this fast." He took several steps away from her, then stopped. She would have sworn she heard regret in his tone. "My God, do you know how I felt when I realized . . ." But he looked her over with hard, experienced eyes. "No, on second thought, I will have your explanation. I haven't heard a good dirty story in a long time. Even if I am the punchline."

"That's not true." Laurel swallowed. Glancing away, she encountered Dan's questioning gaze. "But I can't tell you what is true, here."

The double doors to the ballroom had opened, and waiters pushed trolleys laden with champagne and liquor bottles toward the long table at the podium.

"The candidate's kicking off with no expense spared," Ryder said, then looked at the fringe of reporters hovering near. "All right. Meet me on the mezzanine. What are you drinking?"

"A glass of wine, white . . . whatever's driest."

"Five minutes."

His gaze made it clear that he thought the drink too classy for her. Ryder strode away, mingling with the throng of reporters until she'd left the room.

Laurel didn't look behind her. What could she say to him? She'd been caught in the lies, as she'd fully expected she would be. She couldn't risk the scene he might still make.

She rushed into the hotel lobby, getting a blurred impression on her way of rich wood paneling, gilded ceilings, mosaic floors, and marble-topped tables beneath Waterford crystal chandeliers. She kept walking until Dan's fingers closed around her upper arm.

"Where the devil are you going?"

She had difficulty bringing him into focus. "I told you, I need a breath of air."

"You're not some fainting Southern belle laced too tightly into her corset. I saw you talking to McKendrick. What did he want?"

She shook her head, hoping he couldn't feel her trembling. "Nothing, he . . . a quote for his story, that's all."

"I hope you didn't give him one."

"The senator trained us—me—better than that."

"Ed'll be furious when he knows that bastard's been hanging around."

"Dan, what would you expect? Any privacy we had disappeared completely in there—" she pointed toward the ballroom "—when you announced your candidacy. You knew that. Ryder McKendrick's no different from any other reporter."

"Are you defending him? He's hurt your family before, Laurel. He won't think twice about hurting us. He's not the same as the rest. He's on a crusade. Muckraking yellow journalist . . ." His voice lowered. "I don't want him around," he insisted. "Around you. I'm thinking how wise I was to send Ned off to school, out of harm's way."

"Yes. I think so, too."

Dan's expression softened. "Do you?" He took her shoulders, pulling Laurel closer. "Smile. We're being stared at by camera eyes."

They'd been pursued, of course. From now on, they always would be. She let herself be held, knowing he did it for appearance's sake. "You make too much of Ry—McKendrick, Dan. I only . . . fielded a few harmless questions. He didn't learn a thing."

Now she was lying to her husband. Laurel closed her eyes, leaning against him. He had a different smell from Ryder's. She didn't want to think it, but it came nevertheless. Not as male. She felt her heart begin to pound in remembrance, in panic.

"Dan, I really do need some air." She needed to be alone. "You go inside. They'll want more pictures, won't they?"

"And Teague needs my itinerary for tomorrow, yes. Remember, I'll be in Chicago."

Laurel nodded, though she hadn't remembered until now. It would be a one-day trip, the sort of hiatus that normally allowed her and Ned to shed their shoes and wear old clothes to dinner, to gorge on frozen deep-fried chicken nuked in the microwave oven, on tortilla chips and soda. But this time Ned was away, and he'd taken her sense of fun with him.

If he hadn't left for school, she'd have stayed at home last weekend, or taken Ned with her to Hilary's in Gloucester. Suddenly she envisioned Ryder, leaving the ballroom with their drinks, already searching for her.

She didn't know which was worse, to stay and have Ryder make that scene after all, or to run out on him.

"Laurel? You really are looking faint," Dan said.

"I'll be fine." Kissing his cheek, she slipped away and headed for the lobby exit. Her heels clicked loudly on the polished floor. "Don't worry about me. Please don't worry."

But she could feel him watching, knew the instant he turned away, so as not to be stared at as if they'd been quarreling. Outside the hotel she gulped in great breaths of air, then hailed the limousine Dan had rented to bring them to the hotel for his announcement.

She'd been right to leave, right not to face Ryder and those damning gray eyes. What good would it have done when he already knew the truth?

There was only one question in Laurel's mind: What would he do with it?

## CHAPTER 7 ✻

"I'M COMING, I'M coming!"

At nine-thirty the following morning, to the funky beat of Tower of Power from the library stereo, Laurel dashed down the stairs as the doorbell chimed again. "Just a minute!"

On the landing she dodged a pile of Dan's dress shirts waiting to be sent to the laundry, then a pair of his running shoes that needed new soles—and as usual when the bell rang so insistently, the white blur of Pirate's body tumbling with her toward the front door. "Damn," she muttered, not quite missing the dog's last maneuver across her path. She lunged, in a tangle of legs and fur and her own long-skirted caftan, for the doorknob.

In a beige windbreaker and khaki pants, Ryder McKendrick stood on the porch, his finger poised over the bell. At the incessant barking he stepped back. "Pirate, no!" Laurel cried.

"Aren't you going to give the command for attack?"

"He doesn't know any."

"You could have fooled me."

Laurel forced the dog to sit by exerting pressure on his collar. "Stay," she said, though Pirate rarely obeyed.

He'd flunked obedience training twice. Dan regularly threatened to get rid of him, but Laurel hadn't found the heart to try classes once more. She had the feeling of tampering with his spirit.

"Maybe he doesn't like the music," Ryder said. "Does he bite?"

"No. I'm sorry he bowled you over the other day. He gets carried away."

"I can understand that." His gaze was frosty. "Sometimes I get carried away myself."

The day of reckoning, Laurel thought as Pirate growled low in his throat. "Lie down," she ordered, and to her astonishment the dog padded meekly up the stairs to the library. "He loves Tower of Power," she said.

"Whose choice was that, at nine in the morning? His?"

"Mine."

He studied her. "I'm surprised. I'd have expected to hear George Winston at the piano or a little Beethoven."

"Only when Dan is home," she said.

"But then I'm also surprised your husband doesn't own a Doberman."

Ryder took a step, then another. What did he want? she wondered. What good would her explanation do now? She'd had enough trouble explaining her flight yesterday to Dan.

Still angry, he had left for Chicago this morning without a word. Yet late last night she had heard the low rumble of his voice on the den phone talking to someone else. Had he called Ned to share his announcement? No, it wasn't like him to be that . . . involved with their son.

Unhappiness pierced her. Then Laurel became aware that Ryder was staring at her, intently, that she was wearing nothing underneath her red paisley caftan.

"May I come in?" Not waiting for her answer, Ryder

pushed into the foyer and shut the door. "I have a message for your husband."

"Dan's out of town for the day, he—"

"Took the first flight from Logan, I know where he is." He kept walking, and Laurel kept backing up until she bumped into the open double doors to the living room. "Tell him this for me," Ryder said. "I don't like threats before I've had my first cup of coffee. Teague Michaels—and Benedict—won't get rid of me unless I want to be got rid of!"

"Teague came to your house this morning?"

"To my apartment, yes."

Laurel was shocked. "Dan wouldn't send Teague to threaten you, Ryder."

"I think he would."

"You're wrong, then. About a number of things."

"About your *mistake*?" He seized her face in his hands, and demanded: "Where were you yesterday? You think I liked being stuck with a drink in each hand—"

"You're hurting me!"

"I hope so, lady. I sure as hell hope so."

He let her go and took several deep, uneven breaths. "I spilled my guts to you about Maggie, thinking you'd understand because you . . . because you'd lost a husband not long ago. I believed you, so much that I could take a chance again on a woman after six goddamn years . . ."

He turned away.

"Ryder, I'm—"

"Sorry? Don't say it. Sorry for what?" He started toward the front door. "The false sympathy, or the phony passion?"

"That wasn't pretense. I wanted y—"

Turning, he shook his head. "You didn't want me. You conned me."

"No more than you did me," she said, "conducting your research."

"You? I didn't even know who the hell you were, though I should have." Recognition dawned in his eyes. "But you knew who I was, didn't you?"

She dropped her gaze. "Yes. I knew."

"When?"

"At the restaurant where we had dinner. At the house here, before, I suspected. I hoped it wasn't true that you were a newsman. Then it was worse, you were the newsman who'd gone after my father."

"So," he said, "the lies about yourself. More lies, I should say." Ryder shoved his hands in his pockets. "Is that how you entertain yourselves, you and Hilary, every weekend? Take off for the beach, attract some sucker at the bar, take him home for a couple of rolls in the hay? Why not," he went on, "hell, you'll never see him again ... or was Gloucester supposed to pay me back for your father?"

If she'd been near enough, she would have slapped him. But Laurel was afraid to get any closer. His eyes flashed with temper, and a large part of her knew he had the right to be angry, to be hurt. He didn't have the right to abuse her.

"You're correct in this much, I've lived with the press in my back pocket all my life. As you've seen, I don't like your kind very much. They—you—have hurt my father and my sister and, through them, me. If you weren't researching a story about Dan, then what—"

"But I was," he admitted. "Be warned, I still am. That's not why I came after you, though."

"Well, whatever your reason, I didn't ask you to drive to Gloucester. I didn't beg you to take me to dinner or to stay the night—"

"You begged me to take you, period."

Laurel's cheeks heated as he walked closer. She said stiffly, "I am not a promiscuous woman. I've never done anything remotely like that before."

"In these precarious times, I'm glad to hear that." He inclined his head in acknowledgment. "Was your sister?"

"Was she what?"

"A little looser in the morals department."

"I think you'd better leave my house, Mr. McKendrick!"

"Hey—" He grabbed her arm on the upswing. "All right, take it easy. I'm sorry. Forget your sister for the moment. But you must have known," Ryder said, releasing her, "that I'd meet up with you again, especially when Dave Cabell died. That if he did I'd attend the press conference yesterday." At her stricken look he said, "Why'd you do it, then?"

But she only shook her head. How could she tell him that she'd used Lexa's reasoning to get what she, Laurel, really wanted?

"What are you going to do?" she asked.

He frowned. "About what?"

"Me." Laurel swallowed. "Will you write about me? For *Newstrend* or *Sunday* magazine—'the sordid truth about the candidate's wife'?"

"That strikes me more as a subject for the tabloids. I don't write for the tabloids." Then he added, "And I'd have to write about myself, too, wouldn't I?"

"Yes."

"Then I don't think I will," he said. "My mother wouldn't like it." He trailed a finger down her cheek. "Laurel, Christ. Okay, so we were attracted to each other, maybe both a little lonely. I might understand Gloucester, but why did you tell me here, after your dog had jumped me on the front walk, that you were just a friend of the family? You didn't know for sure who I was then."

"I sensed you were looking for Dan."

"And that was enough?"

"More than enough," she admitted. "I hate being in the spotlight. Yesterday at Dan's announcement I dreaded making that speech. I break out in sweats before, have palpitations . . . being photographed, taped has always seemed a violation to me, like being robbed." She worried her bottom lip. "When we were little, Lexa loved the attention. The camera was another friend to her, but I . . ." She shrugged, unable to explain the shyness that had always plagued her and finished weakly, "She was so . . . so very pretty."

"But you were identical twins. I'd bet my darkroom that the camera's just as kind to you, Laurel."

"That's what Hilary always says. She's an amateur photographer."

With her admission his eyes had cleared. She watched a smile lift the corners of his mouth. "You know something? You've just let me see inside Laurel Frasier Benedict. You don't know how it felt last weekend, your shutting doors in my face."

"They should never have been opened." She turned, intending to put distance between them, but at the front door he had her trapped. His darkening gaze mesmerized her. "Ryder, I don't want to have an affair with you."

"Ah, but I want to have one with you."

Tower of Power's album had ended. His words seemed louder in the silence. Laurel had never believed in timely interruptions, but when the telephone rang, she gave thanks for this one. Ryder's body was too close, too warm.

"Take your call," he murmured. "I'll be around. Keeping an eye on Benedict . . . and you."

The phone shrilled again. Laurel stood, barely hearing it, watching him leave. The door was wide open when she realized her error. She'd completely forgotten the dog.

Pirate, scenting fresh air, had scrambled from his sleepy perch somewhere upstairs, flown down the steps, hit the Aubusson carpet in the foyer running, and made a straight line for freedom. Fortunately this time, Ryder was at the bottom of the outside steps. Pirate bounded past, ears flapping in the breeze, his white tail a plume.

"Catch him!" Laurel cried. "He's panic-stricken in traffic!"

"Get the telephone," Ryder shouted back. She had the briefest impression of him, windbreaker flying as he ran. Laurel sprinted for the den.

"Mrs. Benedict?"

Gasping, "Yes," she leaned against the wall and waited for the caller to identify himself. The stern, authoritarian voice belonged to Ned's new headmaster. Laurel's blood chilled as he told her what was wrong.

"An accident?" Her voice rose. "What sort of accident?" Vaguely she heard the front door close, and Pirate ambled past. "Dear God, no."

She felt the color bleach from her face, and the room started whirling, as if the past were flying into the present. There must be some mistake, she'd said when the infirmary called about Lexa, there must be. . . .

She opened her mouth, but no sound came out.

The telephone was pried from her fingers, and she felt the pressure of a hand, easing her head onto a solid shoulder. Ryder's voice. "Hello, this is a friend of Mrs. Benedict's. I think you'd better give me the information."

As a reporter he knew how to act in a crisis; Laurel sagged against him.

As if it had been yesterday, she could smell the antiseptic hallway of the campus clinic. Lexa, dead . . .

She watched Ryder start to scribble something on

Dan's notepad by the phone, then tear off the top sheet and set it aside. "Give me the route numbers, I'll find it," he said, but she had no idea what he was talking about.

She didn't realize he'd hung up until Ryder's hands at her shoulders held her off. "He's going to be all right, Laurel. Do you hear me?"

She nodded, though the words didn't register. Terrible, she thought. There had been no way to make it better.

"All right then, put something on." Ryder's gaze swept over her. "Just a skirt," he suggested, "and a blouse. You can run a comb through your hair in the car. The head-master will meet us at the infirmary."

In a daze Laurel glided toward the stairs. She didn't question his going with her to the school; she couldn't have made the trip alone.

When she came downstairs Ryder set aside a small silver-framed photograph he'd been examining with a frown. Laurel barely recognized it as one of Ned, with Storm. She allowed Ryder to close the house, shutting Pirate with his food dish and water in the kitchen, then lead her outside. At the end of the walk, he stopped.

"You do have a car somewhere? Mine's in the shop, having a new clutch put in. I took a cab."

Laurel fumbled through her purse. Thank God Dan hadn't taken the car to the airport. Handing Ryder her key ring, she waited for him to back the sleek Audi 5000S from the garage.

Heading through heavy traffic toward the Mass Pike, Ryder maneuvered the luxury sedan with the same skill he'd shown at the wheel of his own car, an aging import. "This is quite an automobile," he said.

"But you expected my husband to drive a sinister black Daimler?"

Ryder flashed a smile. "A Continental, perhaps. At least a Mercedes. Or no, a Cadillac."

"Never a Cadillac," Laurel demurred. "The senator says that, except for stretch limos, they're nouveau riche."

"The senator's a snob, huh?"

"Don't print it."

Their smiles met, then Laurel's, weaker, faded. Ryder asked, "How do you know about Daimlers?"

"From a friend of a friend," Laurel replied, knowing that he was trying to distract her from thoughts of Ned. Wouldn't Hilary grimace at her calling Sebastian Noble any such thing? "He restores classic automobiles."

On Monday in Gloucester—had it only been two days ago?—Sebastian had knocked at Hilary's door. She had returned his MG on Friday but hadn't left his keys in the ignition. "She thought it safer to keep them until you were home," Laurel explained. She'd added that she was a friend, and that Hilary was out, "at a party on an island off the coast. Rick Darcy's, I think that was the name. Shall I tell her you stopped by?"

"I doubt she'd be impressed."

Just when Laurel had wondered at Sebastian's sour turn of mood on hearing of Hilary's prolonged absence—when she'd been wondering whether to confide her own worry—he'd surprised her by offering Laurel a ride to Boston.

Laurel would have smiled at the remembrance of a surprisingly pleasant trip home, but she couldn't concentrate on her brief meeting with Sebastian Noble last weekend. Or on Hilary who, according to Ryder's telephone call on Monday night, was home again, in Gloucester.

"Your sister died at school, didn't she?" Ryder asked, breaking their silence, "of something quick and brutal."

"Waterhouse-Friderichsen syndrome," Laurel said. "A killer in less than twenty-four hours. I guess that's why I overreacted about Ned a while ago."

"Would you like me to tell you what's happened?"

Ryder asked and waited for her nod. "He fell from his horse. Nothing broken," he assured her, "but a possible concussion. They'll take X rays to be sure."

Why had Dan insisted on buying him the horse? Storm was much too powerful for a slightly built eight-year-old child to handle. "I can't help but worry about him," she murmured, feeling, as she always did about Dan, that she was defending herself.

Ryder passed a slow-moving van. "You're his mother, aren't you? Mothers have the God-given right to fret about their children. I think it's in the maternal bylaws somewhere."

She watched him smile, but couldn't answer it.

"I broke my arm once," she said almost to herself. "I was high up in a tree—"

"The oak behind your house, the one with the fortress in it," he guessed, "where you went to read or draw."

"Yes." She was touched that he'd remembered, that he would try to temper her anxiety over Ned.

"You really ought to do something with that talent now."

Laurel looked at him blankly.

"I saw the sketches you made of Pirate and your boy— wasn't it?—on the notepad when I was on the phone in the den. They're very good."

"Oh, those were just . . . doodles."

He snorted. "Are you telling me I have bad taste?"

Laurel opened her hands and smoothed her skirt with both palms. "No," she murmured, pleased. "From what I've seen, you have excellent taste."

"Then take the compliment."

The pleasure continued to flood through her, making her feel guilty. Ned was hurt, and here she was thinking about her sketches. But she wished she could show Ryder the design for the charity luncheon program: she'd been working at it off and on since Gloucester.

"Go for it," he said when she'd explained what she wanted to do. There'd be no money in it, but the senator and Dan couldn't object if there wasn't; and she'd have the satisfaction of seeing her work on all those luncheon programs.

Ryder murmured, "You have to validate yourself."

They were on the Mass Pike now and, with a keen eye out for state troopers, he was keeping a steady seventy-miles-per-hour pace toward the exit at Auburn, fifty miles away.

"I'll send the cover design out tomorrow," Laurel said.

"I'll want an autographed copy." He grinned at her. "Not bad for a kid who broke an arm falling out of a tree."

"I didn't fall," Laurel said, "I jumped."

"What did you think, you could fly?"

"I was sure I could. And my sister said jump, so I did." Laurel grinned now at the memory. "I sailed off that branch, and cracked my arm in four places. I don't know which was worse, the pain, then the itching cast—or the senator's anger."

"Anger?" Ryder frowned. "What about your mother?"

"Oh, the inconvenience set her back, I think." Judith's interrupted ladies' bridge club luncheon that day, as well as the long hours of sitting with a traumatized child, had made Laurel feel guilty for making a mess of her mother's routine. "Mother avoids unpleasantness when she can. If the senator had been in town that day . . ."

Ryder's voice was taut. "And what did he say when he showed up?"

"To stay on the ground, where I belonged."

Ryder passed an eighteen-wheeler on the upgrade. "That's what Benedict wants, too, isn't it?"

Embarrassed that she'd given the impression of being

some miserable unfortunate ironically surrounded by luxuries that couldn't take the place of love, Laurel didn't answer.

"Tell me about *your* parents," she said.

"Mine? My mother's an authentic stereotype." Ryder grinned, though he didn't shift his gaze from the windshield. Traffic was heavy, with the usual incessant lane changing. "I happen to like stereotypes. Mom with the capital letter. She's a pillowy person," he said, "always glad to hold you when the world's not going right, someone you could talk to without an appointment." Seeing Laurel flinch, he finished, "My mother and dad are still like lovebirds after forty years of marriage, even though she calls him the most aggravating man on earth, and except for one glaring flaw in her character, she's absurdly close to being perfect."

"What's the flaw?"

"She wants grandchildren." He said it flatly. "It's my habit to telephone home every Sunday afternoon, when she doesn't call me, and every Sunday afternoon she reminds me of it."

"You're not an only child," she remembered.

"No," he said, "but my kid sister lives in Denver. Tracy and Joe have decided not to have a family. She's a stock analyst, very into her career, and kids would get in the way, quote, unquote."

"Which only makes your mother more determined with you," Laurel surmised.

"I'm the oldest—but not a chance." He frowned at the road ahead. "I wouldn't bring a kid into this world. Not because of interference."

Laurel sat very still. Had Maggie's death hardened him so? Or was it something else, something he wouldn't talk about at all?

After a pause, Ryder said, "I don't hold parenthood

against anybody else. How old's your boy? He looks like you."

"He turned eight this summer." Laurel remembered his examining the picture from the den. "He resembles his father more. He has Dan's hair, his look of concentration. And," she added thoughtfully, "my sister's eyes."

Ryder looked at her oddly. "No brothers or sisters for him?"

Laurel sighed. "I'd love another baby, but Dan's not good at taking the backseat to other people."

"Is that why Ned's at boarding school in the second grade?"

"Third," she corrected and then, "His father wants him to have all the advantages."

"What about his mother?"

"I want him to have advantages, too."

Ryder said softly, "Don't do that, Laurel. You're shutting off again." He glanced at her. "It's not only to lock me out. And don't you suppose Ned wants someone to cuddle him when he's ill, when he's fallen off his horse, when he's flunked his math test for the second time—when he's hit a home run and feels on top of the world?"

Yes, her heart cried, though he wasn't inclined to hit home runs. "Do you think I wanted him to go away? But Ryder, this will be a frantic few months for Dan and me, with the campaign—"

"Not good enough. If you'd rather have Ned at home, why not have him there?"

"I went away to school, too. Everyone in my family does." Facing the windshield, Laurel straightened in her seat. "How much farther to Dawson?" she said.

During his lunch break, Dan Benedict drummed his fingers on the desktop in his Chicago hotel room. The meetings with an important Dobbs, Fairfield client would last longer than expected, far past dinner if they hoped to work out a settlement, and he'd have to stay the night. Cursing, Dan slammed down the telephone receiver, then immediately picked it up again and waited for the operator.

"I'm trying to get Shelby, Massachusetts," he said. "This is the third attempt. Will you please—"

The calls had been disconnected twice by the other party, the switchboard informed him.

"Well, try again."

He could hear her voice this time, weak and thin.

"Maria!"

"Dan, I want to sleep."

He tightened his grip on the receiver. "Are you all right? I've been crazy, wondering."

"I'll be fine," she said.

"You're not alone, are you?"

"My sister was here yesterday. She had to go back to Boston. She's got three kids." It seemed an accusation.

"Maria," he crooned, "I want to be there, but—"

"No, I understand."

"The announcement," he said, "was a nightmare. I couldn't keep my thoughts together. All I could think was, is Maria okay? I looked at my watch a thousand times, wanting to cut everything short and bolt from the Copley Plaza."

Her breath caught. "Danny, I'm sorry for what I said to you last weekend."

"I've already forgotten."

"And your—Laurel looked lovely in the news photos. She'll be an asset to your campaign."

"That's what she was raised for."

He hated her sincerity; he'd rather have her jealousy, like last weekend when she'd raged at him. This Maria frightened him.

"I don't want to talk about Laurel or the campaign. I want to know how you are. Was it bad, darling? I—"

"It's done, Danny."

She was trying to close out the pain, not physical but emotional. The necessary tubal ligation would leave only slight scars, but her heart would take longer to heal. Only, dammit, he didn't care that there wouldn't be babies. Didn't she know that?

"Nothing's changed for us," he said. "Not because of the operation, or my campaign. Nothing," Dan insisted.

"Everything's still the same, even though it's different?"

Her tone alarmed him; she sounded like a mother, soothing an injured child. "Maria," he began.

"I need to rest, Danny."

She hung up before his lips could form a plea.


By the time Laurel and Ryder had reached Dawson, Ned was out of the infirmary and back in his dormitory room. Hurrying from the clinic, where they'd first stopped, a much-relieved Laurel led the way across the broad front lawn of the campus.

She hadn't seen the school before; now, she thought it similar to Carter, where she and Lexa and Hilary had spent the better part of two happy autumns. A first blaze of color was already lighting the trees with scarlet and rust, and even the buildings reminded her of Carter: stalwart, square, sandstone-faced with leaded windows. She wasn't thinking quite so much of Lexa now. The headmaster's assurance that Ned would survive his accident "except for the temporary damage to his pride" had made her spirits lighten.

When they'd climbed the dormitory steps, she asked Ryder, "Would you like to come up with me?"

"You'd better go alone." He turned away as soon as he'd opened the door for her.

"I may be a while," she said.

"Take your time. Patience is one of my best qualities . . . as a journalist."

Laurel didn't examine his tone, but she felt Ryder's resentment of Dan, and the reality of her life. But my life is Ned, she thought as she stepped into his room, not a few days over a holiday weekend, not a stranger with some unexplained sadness in his past. It's Ned, lying half asleep on his bed with a Tonka truck jammed beneath his chin as if it were a teddy bear. He'd slept with his toys, stuffed or metallic, from infancy.

She almost hated to disturb him; he looked so tranquil. Then the straight line of his mouth lifted as his eyes flew open. "Mommy!"

"I wish I could have been here sooner." Laurel dropped down on his bed, gathering him to her. "Were you frightened?"

"At first I was. Tom and I were riding in the woods, then this big branch came out of nowhere and smacked me, right here." He pulled back, showing Laurel the swelling, now turning purple, on his forehead. He'd been facing away from her when she came in, and she couldn't keep from reacting.

"Lord. Does it hurt, baby?"

"It's okay. I saw funny lights," Ned answered. "Then everything went dark, Mommy, and I fell off." He looked at her soberly. "Storm got away. Do you think Dad will be mad?"

Laurel took a breath. "It wasn't your fault, Ned." Why did he always expect Dan's irritation to be directed toward him? Probably, she answered herself in the same instant, because it mostly was. It was a burden for an adult to bear, let alone an eight-year-old boy.

Brushing away the quick tears from Ned's hazel eyes, she said, "Someone from the school will find your horse.

I'm sure he isn't hurt, or lost. He probably stopped some-where to crop grass."

Ned giggled. "He always wants to eat."

Laurel poked his tummy. "Just like a little boy I know."

"I'm pretty hungry now," he confessed, "only the doc-tor said I shouldn't eat. I might throw up. I got a con— con—"

"Concussion. Nothing to fret about, or they wouldn't have let you come home today." Ned could be a terrible worrywart, and Laurel was glad to learn that the doctor had explained.

"My brain has a bruise, too," Ned told her. He lay back against his pillows, dropping the yellow metal truck on which he'd been lying to the floor. "Can I go home with you? Really?"

She could have groaned at her poor choice of words a moment ago. Ned hung on every syllable, and would make the literal interpretation.

"Ned, you've only been away six days. Didn't we agree on a proper trial?"

Her glance swept the freshly painted blue walls, twin white dressers and bedside tables, the pair of beds with brightly patterned sheets, cars and trucks and airplanes in primary colors.

"It's not as good as my real room, Mommy." He wasn't smiling now. "I'm never going to like it here."

She felt frustrated. "I don't suppose you will, with that attitude. Ned, I'm surprised. And disappointed."

Irritated with herself, too, she rose and walked to the window. Ryder was nowhere in sight. Had he gone to the car to wait? At the clinic he'd held back, too, waiting in the lobby while Laurel spoke with the headmaster and the doctor. Of course. She'd arrived with an attractive man not her husband. She hadn't been thinking clearly, but thank heaven Ryder had. How would she have explained his presence?

"Are you mad at me now?"

Laurel turned from the window, finding Ned on his knees in bed, his gaze wide and questioning. "I'm never 'mad' at you."

"Angry," Ned corrected himself. "Mad means crazy. That's what Dad said."

"Well, he's right."

"He's always right, isn't he?"

Laurel felt her throat tighten. "Nobody's right all the time, Ned."

"He acts like he is."

"Daddy tries to set an example for you, so you'll grow up to be a good father someday yourself."

"Why does he have to look mad, though—angry—just because he's telling me something?"

She didn't have an answer. "I don't know. Maybe it's enough for you simply to realize that his way is different from yours, or mine. And that . . ." She paused, wondering whether she believed what she was saying. "And that he loves you."

Ned was silent. Then, "Will he be a senator like Grandpa? I saw the story in the newspaper. The headmaster said my father would be famous."

She forced a smile. "Just like Grandpa, if he wins the election in November."

"Will I have to call him senator, then?"

"No, of course not."

"Why do you? With Grandpa?"

"Just habit, Ned." The only one she felt comfortable with. "My sister, your Aunt Lexa, always called him Daddy, though."

"Which did he like better?"

*My God, why did it have to be Lexa?* "Better?" Laurel's

breath caught. "We were both his daughters, so—"

"Mommy, don't be silly!"

Realizing that she'd misunderstood, she flushed. "I think he liked Lexa to call him Daddy and he liked for me to call him the senator."

She stayed with Ned until twilight. Standing up to leave just before five o'clock, Laurel carried the box containing the Sorry game they'd played back to Ned's closet.

"I wish I didn't have to go. But Daddy's coming back late tonight. Or if not, he'll call. I wouldn't want him to worry, so I'll have to be home."

"When will you come back?"

"Next weekend. No, the one after." She'd remembered a fund-raising banquet for Saturday. "We'll all come."

Ned looked doubtful. "I'd rather go with you now."

Laurel clenched her hands. "I'm sorry, you can't. That's also a school policy, Ned." Fighting the urge to pack his clothes and take him with her, she gathered her handbag and sunglasses. "Otherwise, every new boy would want to run home. Is there anyone on your floor, your roommate, too, who hasn't felt a little homesick this first week?"

"No," he admitted.

Laurel leaned down to him, and he planted a damp kiss on her cheek. "Besides, darling, you're making new friends."

"I don't have any friends. Except for Kip, and he's at home in Cambridge."

Laurel's pulse skittered. "But you went riding this morning with—"

"Tom's not my friend," Ned said doggedly. He drew away from her, as if she'd betrayed him. "He . . . he made me fall. He made me hit the tree. Tom smacked Storm to make him run, so I'd get hurt."

\*       \*       \*

"Do you think he was telling the truth?"

Laurel spoke quietly as Ryder, holding the double leather reins to Storm's bridle, hot-walked the horse around the stableyard. While Laurel was with Ned, Ryder and a young groom had searched for the animal. He'd finally been located, trailing his reins, at the edge of the wooded reservation, only yards from the highway. Leading Storm home, Ryder had volunteered to cool him down.

Now he repeated, "Telling the truth? I wouldn't know. He's your child."

"And not given to lying," she conceded. "In fact, if anything, Ned's usually quite literal."

"Then I'd guess what he said is true."

"But why would another child want to hurt him?"

"I don't know."

He was being deliberately uncommunicative, and Laurel couldn't imagine why. Ryder's gaze had been sharp when she first told him of Ned's accusation. Then he'd retreated into short answers. "Perhaps I ought to talk to him again," she said.

"Laurel, I can only walk this horse for so long."

"I'm sorry. Ryder, you've been wonderful, pulling me together this morning and driving up here, abandoning your own plans...." Then Laurel canceled her earlier conviction that Ryder was right about keeping a low profile. Besides, he'd already been seen by the stableboy. "Would you come with me, just for a few minutes?" she asked. "Talk to Ned? Sometimes, like most children, he tries to play on his mother's sympathies—I'm aware of that—but if you..."

Ryder jerked the horse to a halt and stared at Laurel over Storm's back. "Let's get one thing clear," he said. "I don't want to meet your son."

**❋**

**❋ *CHAPTER 8* ❋**

**❋**

RYDER LET HIMSELF into the apartment, dropping his key ring onto a scarred walnut table in the narrow foyer. Like Laurel with her talent, he ought to do something with the place, but since Maggie's death, he'd thought the hell with it.

Ryder wandered down the long hall toward the living room. Maggie had rented the apartment while he was in Vietnam. Maybe that had been part of their problem. The separateness of her choosing a home in which he'd had no say, of his looking every day at death half the world away. The connections simply hadn't fit together after that. After . . . Nam.

He pulled a door shut on his left as he passed by. The large bedroom just off the foyer, with an adjoining bath, had been a maid's room long ago, Maggie'd told him. She'd hoped it would be a nursery. Instead, the bathroom was now a darkroom, and the bedroom was cluttered with cartons: Maggie's clothing, Maggie's life.

She'd had no family. An only child, she'd lost her parents during high school. "Building again," she'd said, "from the ground up, with you, my love." They'd planned to have four kids, a station wagon, maybe a big dog with no manners. Then he'd turned the dream into a nightmare.

But everything, Ryder told himself, was terror in those days—protest, assassination, violence, then coming home to a wife turned activist at Harvard graduate school, finding that he'd left himself behind in a steaming jungle, in screams and fire.

Oh, hell. What good, thinking about the past? Maggie was dead. And so was, well, all innocence. The hairs at the nape of his neck prickled. Strange, but he'd looked into that photograph on Benedict's desk this morning and seen a glimpse of purity again. It had set his heart racing. A dark-haired child, delicately boned, with Laurel's hazel eyes. Her sister's eyes, she had insisted; why couldn't she see that they were hers, only younger, that was all. Ryder didn't want to look into such eyes again and see his own guilt.

He glanced into the kitchen on his way past. An open box of Sugar Crisp had been left on the counter, with coffee-stained cups and yesterday's soft-boiled eggs congealed on a plate. It would take three weeks to fill the unused dishwasher by himself; Ryder stored their wedding china in it instead.

The telephone rang as he reached the living room, which interrupted the long central hallway and was situated crosswise, giving the layout the shape of a crucifix. Rooting through a pile of mail and manila folders on the oak sideboard, he picked up the receiver, half hoping to hear Laurel. He'd apologize for his rudeness at the school. It wasn't her fault he avoided children. "Hello. McKendrick."

"Good piece by Parker in the *Globe* on Benedict's announcement," came the husky tone that in a man would be called a whiskey voice. Ryder knew in this case it wasn't. More likely, from too many cigars. "What have you got, Mac?"

"An appointment tomorrow morning at Benedict's office." He was already dreading it. "Eleven o'clock. And how are you, Sara?"

She laughed. "No more polite than the rest of you peeping toms who get paid for snooping into other people's lives. What did he say?"

"Michaels did the talking." Ryder's teeth clenched. "Actually, it was a warning. No repeats of my little thrust-and-parry with Senator Frasier. I told him that if they had nothing to hide, Benedict shouldn't object to a full hour with me taking notes and pictures. For a start."

"Bravo."

Ryder didn't feel triumphant. He wondered how he was going to sit across from Dan Benedict for sixty minutes without giving in to the urge to rearrange the candidate's photogenic face. Pure male jealousy. And wrong. He had no right to it, or her. "Look, Sara, maybe I shouldn't pursue this."

"Ryder McKendrick. Some tough war correspondent."

The tone had him glancing toward the bookshelves opposite the sideboard where he was standing. His gaze passed over the ivory walls, the windows at either end of the large room—they'd knocked out the dining room wall to make one huge space, high-ceilinged and washed now with fading daylight. He had taken the draperies to the cleaners several years ago, then forgotten to pick them up. Ryder's eyes settled on the lowest shelf, and the tall, slim spine of a book he knew too well.

*Images of Destruction.* It wasn't a pretty book, not coffee table fare. His publisher had considered the title grim, but for Ryder nothing else would do. It was the way he'd seen the war. Images, nearly a hundred of his photographs: his best photographs still. He didn't apologize for the pictures, no matter how unpleasant. Wasted bodies, wasted faces. Old and young. It wasn't a pretty book, but it told a story no one else would tell. It had won him prizes, very nearly the Pulitzer, as Sara pointed out at every opportunity, and a terrible portion of his soul lay entombed between its covers.

He felt coldness seep through him, and turned away. Today he'd come close to that tragedy again. Too close. And Laurel had sensed his disintegration. He'd given her a bad time, refusing to meet her son. Now, Ryder resolutely pushed the rudeness away, and his lingering impression of those war-torn images. "Don't scold me again, Sara. I've had a hell of a day, one you wouldn't believe."

"Try me."

Ryder winced, wondering what the reaction would be if he confided to Sara Hennessey, the toughest editor he'd ever known, with not a gullible bone in her body, that he had just spent his day with Dan Benedict's wife. That he'd gone to her house not only to give Dan a message, but to see her; that he'd spent the cab ride home from her place trying—after her parting words—to talk himself out of caring for her.

"Not a prayer," Ryder answered. He flipped open the manila folder Sara had sent, and looked into Benedict's earnest expression. "Okay, Hennessey. No cattle prods. I'll do your dirty work."

Ryder turned over several sheets of biographical data on the candidate. He found himself staring at the same haunting, badly focused picture of Laurel Frasier in mourning that he'd first seen in Sara's office. The slender bend of her neck, the slim black dress. She wasn't grieving only for her twin sister, then or now. What did she need? Her fingers reached for the senator's sleeve—seeking solace? Or something more?

"What's the angle you'll use?" Sara asked.

"I haven't got one."

It was a truthful answer—he still hadn't the vaguest notion how he wanted to approach Benedict—but Sara muttered, "Dissembler."

"Trade secret, then. How's that?"

"Better. But not as good as the article I'll expect from you, McKendrick. Friday morning."

"If my creative juices flow," he cautioned, closing the file.

"Ten A.M., Mac. Daydreaming's for poets. You're a hard-nosed reporter, remember?" Sara dropped the receiver into its cradle without saying good-bye.

Ryder let the telephone fall into place, not quite a slam, and reached for the bottle of Stolichnaya on the cluttered sideboard. How could he do his job? He poured himself a tumblerful. What would he learn about Benedict—that he was dishonest, crafty, given to betraying his own mother? That he made a poor husband, and possibly, a worse father? Ryder snorted in disgust. Conjecture on his part, but because of Laurel he knew which he'd rather find out about Daniel Benedict; and what would he do with that?

Nothing, if she had her way. The sensible way. Ryder slumped down on the beige sofa, and pressed the vodka glass against his forehead. She was right. What in hell did he need with a married woman?

A married woman, with a lousy self-image. She'd been so pleased when he encouraged her drawing, as if few people in her life had ever praised her.

Then he'd rejected her child.

After that, they'd driven back to Boston without speaking, and Ryder had kicked himself all the way home. He'd wanted to see her again. But Laurel said, "I told you, I'm not that kind of woman."

And he'd seen images of Gloucester that last, rainy weekend. Already it seemed years ago that he'd held her, stroked her.

When he pressed her, sitting in Dan's Audi on Beacon Hill, she'd said, "Last weekend I missed my little boy." Her gaze held challenge. "And yes, I was fretting over a marriage that I'm no longer sure I want—I meant it when I said we weren't happy—and I suppose I was frustrated that I'm feeling I need more in my life. But the only way," she told him, "that I could spend that night in Gloucester with you was to . . . yes, to pose as a dead woman."

"Laurel."

"I don't think my sister was the amoral person you implied she might be." She held up a hand when he would have stopped her. "But she did have—at the time—more of a social life, more poise and, I suppose, daring. When we were girls, we did what all twins do—traded identities to fool our parents, our friends, and once, even Dan. It was a game, one she liked more than I did, one she felt more certain we could get away with, and not hurt anyone." She bowed her head, showing him that elegant bend of her neck. "I'm more sorry than I can say—because I think I did hurt you—but that's what I was doing in Gloucester. Pretending to be someone else." She lifted her troubled gaze to his. "It won't happen again."

"Don't kid yourself."

She touched the door handle.

"Is that what you were doing when you drew our initials on the wet bartop? You told me your name was Alexandra, but you made an *M*—for Matthew, because I'd gone along with your little game to see where it would lead—and then you made an *L*. An *L*," Ryder repeated, "not an *A* for Alexandra."

Stunned, Laurel had shaken her head in disbelief. "We

called my sister Lexa. I don't remember drawing anything."

"That's my point," he said. "You did it without thinking. And I doubt you'd have absently put down anyone else's name. You'd have written the truth."

Considering her fear of the press, he supposed part of the blame for her pretense belonged to him.

"I never knew your sister." When Laurel pushed down on the door handle, he reached across and took her hand. "The woman I made love to in Gloucester, in the rain, that soft, warm, giving woman—no matter what you called yourself—was you. And it was right, Laurel." She stared at their hands, his thumb making slow circles on her skin. Then she pulled away.

"I can do without the cheap analysis," she said and reached for the door handle again.

"Can you?" He'd followed her from the garage. "I think you've been doing without too much for a helluva long time—"

"I think you're projecting your own problems onto me!"

"And I think our most unconscious thoughts and actions are the most revealing."

"What does that mean?"

"That you may have a point about me, but in Gloucester you took the right steps. Maybe for the wrong reasons, but you took them. And you should keep on taking them, taking what you want for yourself, not for someone else."

At her front door she'd whirled on him. "Don't you tell me what I need. You may think a cheap affair is just fine, but I don't. I'm ashamed of what we did in Gloucester, and I want you to leave me alone." Fumbling for her key, she had her back to him. Ryder saw her hand shaking. "You can take your choice—whether that's Lexa talking or me, Laurel Frasier Benedict."

When he turned her to face him, she held the key between them like a switchblade. He hadn't even glanced around to see that they were alone on the Beacon Hill street. Frustration drove him. He dragged her to him, and the key punched into his belly like a well-aimed fist. He had planted the kiss on her mouth before she could resist.

In the dim light of his Cambridge apartment, Ryder let his head fall back against the sofa cushion and closed his eyes. He'd been tough on her but God, she was probably right. He had a few rules, and staying away from married women had always been one of them.

If Sara Hennessey knew . . .

And then there was the boy he couldn't even bear to look at. He kept seeing the fine bones, the solemn eyes from the picture on Benedict's desk. Then the image altered, and he was seeing something else, something he didn't want to see, something worse. He opened his eyes, but the impression remained and his heart began to pound. Oh God, now he could feel it: that thin body cradled on his lap, the small head resting beneath his chin, on his chest against the khaki bush shirt he'd always worn, the wispy silk strands of hair as black as jet under his palm, stroking, caring. Oh Christ, it wasn't Ned Benedict in his thoughts now.

And he couldn't stop thinking.

Papa-san, she'd called him: she'd been as small as a two-year-old, though they—the nuns at the orphanage—said she was probably older than that by a year or more, and stunted by malnutrition. Or had it been from the pounding of mortar fire disturbing sleep, from the loss of both parents and a brother? Those wide black eyes had asked for someone to trust again. Papa-san.

The first time he saw her, he had fallen like bricks. Even

now, he could scarcely believe that she hadn't come back with him.

He tried to push them back, but the thoughts kept coming, the memories. On a bright spring morning he held her up, high on his shoulders, the whole world looking new again and clean, the guns silent for once, his friend Ham taking pictures. "Honey," Ryder had written Maggie, "I've got the sweetest little girl for us."

Ngoc Hoa: he let himself form the name as he hadn't done in years. He had teased her that her name meant Cherry Blossom.

It was growing dark now, but Ryder didn't light the lamps. He sat in the stillness, remembering what he didn't want to, remembering, because of Ned Benedict. And Laurel's fear for him today.

It's such a small thing, he thought; it will get better.

Papa-san, you take me home with you?

That's a promise, he had told her.

In USA, no bombs?

No more bombs, Cherry Blossom.

Ryder shuddered in the darkness. Ngoc Hoa, I should have been a soldier, for you I could have been a soldier. I hated the guns, but I would have killed them all.

He took a deep breath, then another. He laced his hands behind his head and blinked at the ceiling. A long crack ran from the spot where the dining room archway had once been to the living room window behind him. Maybe, he told himself, we ruined this apartment, too. Structural defects—he and Maggie, tearing down the walls to save their damaged lives. It hadn't worked, and he shouldn't make the same mistake again.

A married woman, he told himself. A married woman with a child. A married woman with one child, who wanted more . . . when he knew he could never look at a child with love in his heart again.

Ngoc Hoa, precious flower. Oh God, where are you now? She'd been so small, Ryder thought, like Ned; such a tiny thing to occupy so large a space inside him. Ah, Hoa, Cherry Blossom. You could have saved us all.

## CHAPTER 9

"HELP!"

Hilary Chapin, precariously perched on a kitchen chair, reached for the wafer-thin Sèvres porcelain cup and saucer on the top shelf—and missed. Losing her balance, she grazed the cabinet door on the way past, then the tile floor rushed up to meet her. A loud outcry of pain and the sound of shattering glass preceded utter silence.

Then nothingness ended in the slam of a door somewhere, and a pair of dark eyes looked into hers. They weren't Chip's eyes, was Hilary's first thought, not blue and clear as the Mediterranean, where she'd sailed with her mother and Freddy—but nearly black. And furious.

"What's wrong with you, up on that damn rickety chair like some old maid dusting china? You're hardly the domestic type." Then he demanded, "What hurts, where?"

"My ass," Hilary replied. "And my ears." They were ringing because of him. "Where did you learn those beautiful manners, Sebastian?"

The glare turned into a grin with astonishing speed.

"From the countess, of course. Isn't that what you expected me to say? I mean, how else would a commoner become acceptable in polite society?"

"Go to hell."

Agony flared in Hilary's right ankle, but she shrugged off Sebastian's touch and managed to stand.

"You don't approve of the countess?"

"Myra's never mentioned her. I doubt she exists."

Sebastian's grin broadened. "Why would I make her up?"

"To irritate me."

"That's pretty egotistical, Hilary, even for a cover girl."

"Go to bloody hell."

"You said that," he reminded her, "without the colorful adjective," and followed Hilary at a cautious distance as she limped from the kitchen through broken china into the sun room. Sinking down onto a cushioned chair, she released her breath slowly through her teeth. She hurt far worse, all over, than she was willing to admit to Sebastian.

"Can I get you anything?"

"No!" Hilary snapped because he'd said something nice. "Go home, Sebastian."

He dropped into the chair opposite, his dark eyes steady on her face. "I think not. It isn't every Wednesday that I hear screams from next door and the sound effects of World War Three. I'll just stay a moment—"

"Hoping to see me pass out, I suppose?"

"Paranoia becomes you, my love."

Hilary's eyes flashed at the endearment. "Haven't you got anything better to do than gloat over a tiny accident in my kitchen? Pounding on some hapless piece of metal, perhaps?"

"And have you stick your head out the window? I've had enough yelling for one hour," Sebastian murmured.

Hilary gritted her teeth. "You do this on purpose."

"Do what?"

"Sit around all day thinking up statements that will set my blood boiling."

"I'd dearly love to see your blood boil, Hilary. But alas, as they say in polite company, that privilege is given only to the likes of—as one example—Rich Darcy."

Hilary tensed. "You know Rick?"

"Does that surprise you too much? As a matter of fact, I met him in this very room during one of your mother's Saturday evening . . . blasts."

She smiled thinly. "If you were invited, Mother must have been feeling kindly toward the masses."

"Myra adores me," Sebastian corrected.

"My mother may have money," Hilary murmured, "but she always did have rotten taste."

Sebastian stared at his hands, clasped between his spread thighs. As usual, she noted, his fingernails were embedded with grime, though he must have washed his face. His tanned features were clean for a change, and his black hair was glossy, if in need of a trimming.

"You've got lousy taste yourself. Worse," he muttered at last. "Otherwise, why spend the weekend with Darcy and those wild friends of his, sailing and drinking, snorting—"

"There weren't any drugs."

"No taste, and naive as well. You didn't see the coke, that doesn't mean it wasn't there. Or a lot of other scheduled substances that the Coast Guard would like to know about. My opinion of your character, and your ability to survive—" he glanced toward the kitchen "—keeps shifting lower, Hilary."

"I don't give a damn for your opinion! And it's none of your business what I do with—"

"Did you sleep with him?"

Hilary was on her feet seconds before the pain shot through her ankle. "Get out of this house."

"Answer me."

She wasn't used to seeing such intensity in his eyes. Other than the first moment she'd seen Sebastian, Hilary had never glimpsed more than that bland smile, mocking her, or at most, the occasional coolness that rendered his eyes like black ice. Now, they were lasers going through her.

"You're getting quite the reputation in Gloucester," he said.

"Sebastian, nobody has a 'reputation' these days."

But he went on, "I thought it my duty as a good neighbor to point out that men like Darcy enjoy boasting. Not that I've heard directly—"

"Get out," Hilary repeated, pushing him toward the back door. To her amazement Sebastian went. It would have been simple enough to resist; he was far stronger than she, his muscles rippling under her fingers as Hilary nudged at his spine. At the door he said, without turning around, "You ought to be more careful, Hilary." She saw him glance behind him at the broken porcelain on the floor. "Twenty-nine percent of all accidents involving temporary disability happen in the home."

He left her wondering whether he'd been talking about the cup and saucer, or her own—supposedly bad—behavior.

"He made up the statistic, I'd bet my broken back on that." Laurel heard the complaint by telephone later that night. But Laurel said she didn't think Sebastian was a liar.

"He's a pretty bright guy. In fact, he's pretty, period."

"Oh, and his list of champions grows with each passing day. My mother," Hilary groaned, "and now, my best friend."

The weekend before, and Sebastian's easy conversation

on the way to Boston, came back to Laurel. She had liked him. Unfortunately, Hilary remembered Ryder, too, which gave her the opportunity to switch topics.

"Speaking of men, the one I left you with at the Yard-arm, in particular..." Hilary's pain-dulled voice came alive again. "I think he called here Monday night. But it was weird, scary, so I didn't recognize his voice in time. Laurel, he asked for Alexandra. I was so shocked I nearly fainted. And I thought you said his name was Matthew, not—"

"I told him I was Alexandra, to throw him off the track."

Hilary sighed relief. "But why would he say he was—"

"Ryder McKendrick." Laurel paused, then added as if it explained everything, "He's a journalist."

"A journalist," Hilary repeated.

Laurel reminded her about the senator and Ryder, years ago during the war. "And yet, I liked him. I do like him," she amended, then drew a breath. "I went to dinner with him that night after you left, and—oh God, Hil, I can't believe what happened. It was what Lexa would have done without making excuses to anybody, including herself, without waking up to guilt. But I—"

"You went to bed with him?"

"You make that sound worse than it seems to me."

"My dear friend, a weekend affair needn't slash your life to pieces. It takes more than that." Hilary paused, and Laurel heard a grunt of pain as she shifted position. She also heard hints of Chip Brewster. "I'll tell you something else. It's about time."

"Lexa claimed she lost her virginity at thirteen," Laurel said. "True or not, she beat me by light-years. I was in a hotel room in Bermuda, honeymooning with Dan, before a man touched me below the waist."

"That must have been exciting, with Daniel," Hilary murmured, "and part of the problem now."

Laurel sighed. "Dan didn't drag me to the altar. I wanted to be married. I still want to be married. I wanted a baby, I'd have more if Dan would agree. And I want to be faithful to him. I'm not about to complicate my life when the campaign's just underway by—"

"Oh, spare me. Are you really going on the trail for that man to make him look better to the voters than he is? Just so Dan Benedict can fulfill some power dream that he shares with Edwin Frasier?"

"Hilary, does it occur to you that I may be attracted to Ryder McKendrick—" her voice faltered with the name "—*because* he's writing about Dan? Perhaps, unconsciously, I want to wound Dan because we've been having a few difficulties. Well, that's certainly occurred to me, and I will not upset Ned's life, or mine, or betray my husband, whether you like him or not, for a man I barely know."

"Is that all he was, then? Part of the weekend revolution? A one-nighter?"

Laurel shook her head. Then, realizing that Hilary couldn't see the answer, she said, "No. But I need to convince myself he was. It's already a mess, isn't it? And more. There's something . . . unsettled about Ryder, something I can't get to. . . ." She trailed off, not knowing how to explain. "I was right," she said after a moment. "It never should have started, but at least it should have ended on Monday, before Dan's announcement."

Laurel found herself explaining about Ryder's interception of her afterward, of her flight from the hotel lobby, and then, of Dan's anger. "Poor Ned," Hilary sympathized when Laurel paused after telling how Ryder had shown up this morning on her doorstep, and then about the trip to Dawson. "We've had bad luck today, haven't we? I'll send him something."

"Hilary, no more trains. Just a card, or a coloring book."

"We'll see. Tell me more," Hilary pleaded. "So Ryder went with you, and then?"

In her mind Laurel was riding once more through the green countryside from Dawson, keeping carefully to her side of the front seat. They were nearly in Boston before Ryder spoke. "Ned. Is that for your father, by any chance?"

"Yes. Edwin Eliot Frasier Benedict."

"Why not Dan, Junior?" And then, "No, I can guess the answer to that. Your husband would rather have pleased another ego."

"He thought it would honor my father, if that's what you mean."

"Close enough."

Laurel straightened. "What are you trying to do, find a seamy angle for some yellow journalistic smear of my husband?" Her pulse sped. "Quit trying to draw me into argument. I won't help you dig dirt."

For one instant Laurel had thought he would stop the Audi in the passing lane of the Mass Pike. "What do you think I am?" Ryder glided to the far right lane and accelerated. "What in hell makes you think that every time I open my mouth to ask you a question, I'm working an in-depth interview on your private life? Because I asked about your kid's name? For your information, whatever I learn about Benedict isn't going to come from his loving wife!"

Laurel had subsided into a huffy, near-tears silence. But he was right, in a way. She'd been nothing except fearful of his intentions. Perhaps he'd simply been trying to smooth over his earlier rejection of Ned but couldn't quite manage it. "Ryder, I was jumping to conclusions.

I'm sorry, too, that you had to get involved today when I know—"

"I didn't have to get involved, okay?"

At seventy-five miles per hour he nudged up to the car in front of Dan's Audi, and Laurel had decided that the wiser course was to keep quiet the rest of the way home.

"And then what?" Hilary's voice drew her back.

"I told him I wouldn't see him again."

She could still see his eyes, dark with frustration; she could still taste his kiss. Laurel wished, for one moment, that she didn't have Dan to worry about, or Ned—Ned, whom she adored with all her heart—or Ryder's influence on the campaign.

"You're walling off your own emotions," Hilary pointed out. "I could see on your front walk after he'd been knocked silly that—"

"What do you want from me? I've got a real life here, not some fantasy from a book or a movie."

"Laurel, I want you to make your own choices, to be happy and productive, not to go on wasting yourself—your ability to love, the flair you have with a pencil on paper or a palette of colors and a canvas—just to please Dan Benedict, or your parents!" Ryder had said much the same thing, Laurel thought as Hilary finished, "I want you to stop trying to be Lexa."

❋

❋ *CHAPTER 10* ❋

❋

RYDER HAD LONG ago learned to trust his instincts—professional, if not personal. Standing just inside the lobby of the Sheraton Boston Hotel on Saturday night, he photographed guests arriving for Dan Benedict's fund-raiser banquet—$500 a plate—and recalled part of an old saying: Beware of the man who travels by limousine. Seeing Edwin Frasier step from the dark Mercedes, he didn't need to remember the rest.

In the sudden explosion of camera flashes, the senator raised both arms above his head, making a *V* of his fingers and blessing the crowd with his famous smile. With those white teeth, smooth-shaven cheeks, shrewd blue eyes, and his immaculately tailored tuxedo, he looked half his age. Sweeping into the lobby on a wave of greetings from the press, most of whom adored him, and always had, he was a crowd-pleaser, all right. "Make way for a winner, gentlemen."

"Make way for the candidate!"

Turning his head as the phalanx of press, aides, and the bodyguard passed him, Ryder encountered the man of the hour. Benedict's arm was protectively around his wife's bare shoulders. If you could Xerox a smile, Ryder

149

told himself, he was looking at a perfect copy: Edwin Frasier's campaign grin superimposed on his son-in-law's appealing face.

Ryder assessed Benedict. Thin enough to look magnificent on television, he had the kind of lean good looks that sent women voters to the polls in droves. And Laurel at his side wouldn't hurt the male vote.

Ryder let his gaze stray, taking in the gown she wore: black velvet skirt, drinking up light from the overhead chandeliers, snowy white bodice made of lace. The neck was square and low-cut, the sleeves long and slim. She'd drawn her hair up, sleek and shiny, a cascade of dark curls softening the effect. She looked elegant, refined, desirable.

He tried not to see the careful smile on her lips. A smile that died as her eyes met his.

Stepping back, he collided with Sara Hennessey, who'd been standing near him, taking notes. "I'm reminded," she murmured, "of the entrances of kings. I can hardly wait for the banquet."

"Rubber chicken."

Sara closed the leather-covered pad, then smoothed one hand over a favorite slink of narrow Fortuny mushroom pleats; she wore the classic thirties gown, inherited from her mother, at every opportunity. It didn't quite go with the skinny black cigar she drew from her evening bag, Ryder decided with a smile. She said, "Then you don't know the senator as well as you think. He'd never allow standard banquet fare, Mac. Style is his middle name."

Ryder could think of several others that might suit. "You assume Frasier's paying tonight."

"I assume he'll be paying every night, one way or another, until the election."

"Maybe." He hadn't had the impression, though, that Benedict was simply a stooge. Carbon copy smile aside, he'd proved a tough opponent during their interview—the day after the trip to Dawson—and the first reaction from his office on the published profile yesterday was that of extreme displeasure. Ryder guessed there would be more. "Maybe tonight they'll take in a cool million in pledges, Sara."

"Isn't that the point of this?"

They went into the banquet hall, where Ryder clung to the fringes of the room. He'd worn a dark suit and rep tie, but in the huge roomful of richly gowned women, of uniformly black-and-white-tuxedoed men, he felt like a kid at a grownup party. Only a handful of press had been allowed to attend. It didn't help that Sara immediately abandoned him for a cluster of women, all of whom looked conservative, and wealthy.

She fits right in, he thought with affection. No matter the kicking and screaming against the establishment, she was really one of them. They even forgave her the cigar.

Leaving his cameras behind, Ryder wandered toward the cash bar—the Establishment version of Bring Your Own Bottle—knowing that she wouldn't introduce him. Because he wouldn't want her to. Paying for his drink, he smiled slightly. At some point the senator separated style from basic economics.

Making the scotch last, he studied strangers, then Laurel, at the other side of the banquet hall, deep in conversation with Teague Michaels, whose hand brushed frequently against her skin. Ryder watched her frown. He'd seen it before; during Benedict's announcement, when Michaels had walked her to the podium with that same hand pressing her spine. He'd had the impression then too, that Laurel wanted to cringe away from the touch.

He decided, in spite of their last good-bye and his own resolution thereafter, to rescue her. Ryder signaled the bartender for another round. Walking slowly through the room, threading his way among the white-clothed tables and an army of waiters placing fruit cups on service plates, he stopped in front of Teague and Laurel.

"I thought we'd have that drink now."

Michaels frowned. "We're conducting a private conversation, McKendrick. No reporters."

Still holding their two drinks, Ryder raised both arms, as if being frisked. "No camera. No tape recorders, and not a scrap of paper on me."

"No invitation, either. How'd you get in here tonight?"

"With the first lady of journalism."

Michaels glanced around the banquet hall, finding Sara. "I think I'll have a word with her, then." He walked away.

Laurel said, "Dan's not happy about your piece on him in *Newstrend* yesterday."

"What did you think of it?"

"Teague was just telling me how angry the senator is, too."

Ryder's tone hardened. "I said, what about you?"

"I thought it was well written, clean, and concise. Impeccably researched."

He grinned. "I'm a good newsman. I always double-check my sources."

"And never go to print without a backup."

"Let's drink, then, to responsible . . . reporting." Ryder handed her the wineglass. "White," he said, "and very dry. I hope it's not too cheap."

She took a sip. "It's good, thank you."

"Laurel—"

"I can't talk to you," she said. "You shouldn't have come over."

"You saw me when you came in, didn't you? Were you glad?"

"Glad?" She looked at him over the rim of the glass. "It's your job."

Ryder tossed back the last of his drink. He'd been trying not to think about her since Dawson on Wednesday, had nearly convinced himself in three days that he'd succeeded. Then Laurel had walked through the lobby doors on Benedict's arm, and none of his cautions to himself mattered any longer. "I'm not working at the moment," he said.

"You're always working."

He felt his temper rise. That again. "Let's take a walk. Outside, away from here."

"You must be joking."

When she turned, he caught her arm. Under his fingers, the fine white lace of her sleeve felt like cobwebs.

He saw alarm in her eyes.

"One weekend that shouldn't have been," she murmured. "Why don't you leave it at that before we both regret it? Teague's staring. He'll speak to Dan."

"What a dutiful creature you are," Ryder said after a pause. "What's the matter, Laurel? Afraid to feel something without Benedict or the sen—"

Suddenly, he was standing alone. Cursing himself, Ryder watched her walk through the crowd.

"A lovely woman."

He turned his head to find Sara Hennessey nodding in Laurel's direction. "No wonder her men are so protective. Michaels just advised me to keep you on a short leash, words to that effect."

"Screw that. What do you know about her, Sara?"

She looked back at him. "She doesn't like publicity, though she's had plenty of it. The senator's daughters were twins, as you know. Peas in a pod. Alexandra died when they were just about nineteen. She was fun-loving and, some said, irresponsible. The senator always put her high jinks down to youthful spirits. He spoiled her silly."

"And Laurel?"

"Serious, a good student, an obedient child. But I doubt that, in such a flamboyant household, she was ever the favorite."

"Where did Benedict come in?"

"I keep telling you, Mac, to stay home and open your eyes. Dan Benedict was Alexandra's fiancé at the time of her death."

Ryder received the old news like a body blow to his gut. In the aftermath of that first article against Frasier, and a series of overseas postings to the Paris peace talks by Sara probably meant to keep him out of trouble, he'd all but forgotten. My God, had she married Benedict as a stand-in for her sister? Or did he simply want to see it that way?

"So he was Laurel's solace at the funeral," he said, remembering the haunting photograph in Sara's file. "And comfort turned to . . . affection, love, then marriage?"

Sara's gaze searched his. "I'm not sure about love, though the rest is probably close enough to the truth."

"That quality of distance," Ryder murmured.

"Yes."

"The senator seems to dote on her." He watched Laurel reach the entryway to the banquet hall, slipping between her husband and her father. When she glanced into the senator's face, she seemed to draw his smile from deep inside. Then Ryder saw that Frasier wasn't looking at his daughter; he was looking over Laurel's head at the Democratic congressman from Ryder's district. And his last resolution to stand clear of Laurel Frasier Benedict vanished at the look on her face.

"Are you planning to interview the candidate's wife?" Sara asked.

"In a way," Ryder said.

Feeling as if she were the main course at a banquet for cannibals, Laurel pushed rare roast beef around on her plate. Her father's public rejection of her still hurt, though perhaps no one else had sensed it. She seized upon the possibility. No one else had lived for years with the blank stare above his grin that told her so clearly, ever since Lexa's death, that the senator resented her very existence.

Why let it matter now? She was Dan's wife, Ned's mother.

Laurel used her fork to gingerly shove aside a glazed pile of string beans. The lemon butter had already congealed over them. The speeches were beginning, before dessert. She shifted to one side so a waiter could remove her still-full plate from the table and looked at her lap as half a dozen camera flashes exploded around the hall. Had one of them, earlier, caught her with Ryder?

"Dan's going to take care of McKendrick for you," Teague had whispered in her ear during the salad course. But what did he mean?

Absently, she spooned blancmange into her mouth, shuddering at the dessert's too-sweet raspberry sauce. She scarcely heard the man at the podium. All week, ever since the day at Dawson when Ned was hurt, she'd been sure she was right not to see Ryder McKendrick again. It would be foolish, dangerous. And despite Hilary's contention that she should change her life, if she tried, with Ryder, they'd both be hurt; and whatever sorrows he was already carrying inside would become that much worse. Her own life would seem all the more difficult.

Then tonight she'd welcomed the sight of him. Her

gaze wandered from the head table and the boring speeches—nothing more than a Madison Avenue pitch for money when you reduced the words to a single thought—to clash with Ryder's the length of the banquet hall. How long had he been staring at her? How long had Dan been watching?

She turned her head to find him frowning so slightly that only she must see it. "Don't worry," he murmured. "The press—McKendrick—won't hurt you. I'll see to that."

Laurel's pulse accelerated. My God, why did Ryder stay? She tore her gaze from his to the speaker who was introducing her father.

"Senator Edwin Frasier, ladies and gentlemen..."

Ryder shifted his weight in the straight chair, tilting back on its rear legs and rifling his inside jacket pocket for cigarettes. Frasier was just starting to roll.

Bullshit artist, but he'd have them opening their wallets. There'd be campaign promises, hints of political payoffs in exchange for generous pledges, the continual reminder of Benedict's relationship to the illustrious Edwin Frasier, whose name, and very famous face, epitomized the role of U.S. senator.

Did nobody remember his hawk's stance on a bitter war? Wasn't there someone else here who saw through the smiles to the conniving politician underneath?

Apparently not.

"Let us win the primary battle and the next and the next. With your mandate, my dear friends, and with Dan Benedict's talents, we *will* win them... and keep on winning!" The senator raised his arms again to thunderous applause and stepped down from the podium.

Ryder didn't watch Dan Benedict shaking hands, clasping his father-in-law's shoulder. He didn't see him at the microphone or hear him begin to speak in less histrionic fashion than Edwin Frasier. Ten minutes later, blowing smoke toward the ceiling, Ryder noted that the checkbooks had begun to appear as Benedict finished. The race was on. But Ryder's attention wasn't focused on Dan Benedict.

". . . and thanks to my beautiful wife, Laurel Frasier Benedict, for the years of faith and preparation for this moment." Ryder wondered whether anybody else saw her flinch; he'd never heard Benedict use her first name alone.

"She'd like to bolt," Sara whispered beside him, following Ryder's look.

"What do you suppose makes a woman put herself through an experience she's had before, and hated?"

Sara didn't get to answer.

Someone said, "McKendrick," and Ryder glanced up at the commanding tone.

"It better be good, Michaels, interrupting the candidate's first formal speech of the campaign just as I was about to write a check in the amount of my article fee from yesterday."

"Frasier wants to see you."

The chair legs thumped down on the floor. Ryder stubbed out the cigarette in his empty coffee cup. The banquet hadn't been rubber chicken after all, but he'd barely tasted the food. He rose to his feet.

"I'll be right back, Sara."

He followed Michaels into the hall. Beware of the man who rides in a limousine, he thought, and then the rest came to him. Ryder wasn't sure, but it sounded like Mencken: He has too much to lose.

***

## ❋ CHAPTER 11 ❋

❋

LAUREL STEPPED OUT of her black silk peau de soie evening sandals and wriggled her toes. Then she took the pins from her hair, letting it fall. Yawning as she pulled a hairbrush through the tangled strands, she didn't glance into the bedroom mirror. Unlike Lexa, she had never been fond of mirrors, and didn't want to see the dark circles under her eyes now. It had been a long night, tedious and tense at the same time, and she couldn't wait to fall into bed.

She'd like to shut out the lights, yank the covers over her head, and sleep for a week—as if she could. Dan already had her scheduled for dozens of speeches within the next ten days. Her nerves were jumping at the thought. How would she make it through the next eight weeks of public speaking, surrounded by cameras and questions?

Tossing the hairbrush aside, she determined to think about Dan's campaign tomorrow. Things always seemed clearer in the morning. Taking a batiste nightgown from a drawer, she could hear him coming up the stairs. He'd offered to feed the dog a midnight snack so Laurel's dress wouldn't get soiled.

"Thank you," she said as he came into the room.

Dan didn't answer her weary smile. He hadn't said much on the way home, except: "The senator's good at playing one of the people. I realize I'm not. I'll have to work hard to make them like me enough to vote for me." Though he'd lapsed then into silence, the brief confidence had made her feel closer to him. Laurel believed he would woo the public, not as easily as the senator, or as quickly, but in the end just as well.

Now he stripped off his evening tie, then tore the pearl studs from his dress shirt, throwing them on the bureau. A hundred dollars he paid for that shirt, Laurel thought, and it's becoming a rag, which made her certain that he was furious about something. Dan cared for his belongings like a shepherd tending a precious flock. The way he would care for his constituents, she admitted.

But tonight he had cut short his speech. She'd thought then it was to encourage pledges before the audience grew restive. But who had summoned Ryder McKendrick from the banquet hall, and why? He'd left with Teague, but Teague was only a messenger.

Alarm swept through her. "Dan, what is it?"

Next she heard the sibilant hiss of his zipper. "You looked wonderful tonight," he said, as if she'd defied him instead of looking her best. "I want you every inch the candidate's wife," he'd said that morning. "An asset, just as you've always been."

She hadn't found that complimentary, either. She never did when he reminded her of her background. Still, she'd complied.

"Then what have I done?" Laurel asked.

He turned, naked, showing her a finely tuned body, the bedroom light glinting through the smattering of dark hairs on his chest.

"Come here," he said.

"I haven't taken off my dress yet."

"I don't want you to take it off."

Holding the seafoam green nightgown, she walked toward him, heart thumping.

"You're a beautiful woman, Laurel. I used to think you were plainer than . . ." He stopped, his gaze running over her in the long sweep of formal black velvet and white lace. "No, but you aren't plain at all." His eyes darkened as he took the batiste from her hands and threw it aside. "Apparently I'm not the only one to think so."

Slowly, Dan drew the lace bodice of her dress down one shoulder. "Your friend—" he pressed his mouth to her skin "—seems to think you're a vision. His word. I saw you talking with him," Dan said. "That's the second time. He didn't look—again—as if he were asking for a quote."

Laurel felt her pulse race faster. She couldn't pretend to misunderstand. "No, he wasn't."

"What, then?"

"Just idle conversation. Weather, the banquet menu. Why would he tell you I was a, what did you say, *vision*?"

"I thought you might be able to answer that."

"I can't," she said.

He raised his head. "Well, you had better, lest I deal with Mr. McKendrick more harshly than he—presumably—deserves."

Laurel tried to move away, but he was too quick. What did he know? Not of the weekend in Gloucester, not about the day at Ned's school. Perhaps only that Ryder had come to the house after Dan's announcement? It would be enough.

"Dan, he must have wanted to throw you off base. He was probably getting back at you for not liking his article. It really was a good piece, not unfair."

She shouldn't have said that. His eyes narrowed.

"McKendrick seems to have won you over, Laurel. I can't help wondering why, and how."

"He hasn't won me over. But the trouble with the senator happened years ago. The war's over, people have changed. Even Ryder McKendrick."

"He's using you," Dan said, "to get at me."

Her pulse skipped; she'd had much the same thought not long ago at the Copley Plaza. Even tonight, hadn't she accused Ryder of playing reporter when he'd drawn her away from Teague? But hearing the same thing from Dan made it seem worse.

"You obviously think that no one would want to talk with me just for myself. Because I'm—"

"A desirable woman?"

She couldn't breathe properly. "I meant as a . . . friend, someone interesting."

He laughed. "You and Ryder McKendrick? Friends?" Dan's gaze slipped over her again. "So he's not looking for a quote, is he? Well, he wasn't looking at you like a man who wants to be pals, either."

She tried again to free herself. "Dan, I can't help it if he tried to anger you tonight by saying I looked nice."

"He didn't say you looked nice. He said—"

"Stop it, stop this!" Laurel's eyes darkened. "I'm sorry you can't believe me. I don't know what else to say."

"I didn't say I don't believe you," he corrected. "I only wonder if I should. There's a difference, I think." He drew back, letting her go, and sat on the edge of the bed.

"Why don't you try to convince me, Laurel?"

With the question, sultry and caressing, he swept a hand from her bared shoulder to the curve of her hip in soft dark velvet, pulling her near. She stood stock still, breathing fast and light, her pulse hammering like a drum.

His hand at her breast gently kneaded. "Well, he's got

an eye at least. I can't fault the photographer's professional assessment."

Laurel closed her eyes against his smile, fighting the reactions he wanted. But she felt his touch everywhere, fingering the froths of white at her sleeves, sliding under the neckline of her gown to the cleft between her breasts. When she opened her eyes, keeping them lowered, she saw the effect she was having on him.

"I can't very well hide my concurrence, either," Dan said as her gaze, embarrassed, flew upward. "Physically."

This is a court of law, Laurel thought, I'm being tried, found guilty, without a jury of my peers. Then why did she feel a stronger reaction to him than she'd ever felt before? In the beginning, when she had hoped that he could love her, she'd tried and tried to feel like this, but she never had, until—

"Oh God, Dan."

He slipped the dress from her other shoulder, and she stood pinned between his thighs, black velvet drifting over his nakedness. Wondering why she felt guilty for responding to her husband.

"Tell me you need me."

"Yes, I do. Yes."

Then she realized he had a right to mistrust her, that the guilt came not from Dan, but from Gloucester, and Ryder McKendrick. She laid her cheek against Dan's hair, felt his fingers at her back, drawing down the long zipper, then peeling the dress to her waist. Quivering, Laurel could barely stand. He held her with one hand at her hipbone, cupping its sleekness in his palm while he reached out with the other hand to switch off the lamp, plunging the room into a blackness as rich as the gown itself, plunging them both into thick, dark intimacies.

This is my husband, she chanted silently; he is my husband.

He rolled her onto the mattress. "I told him, and I'll tell you," he said fiercely. "You're mine. I won't lose you to Ryder McKendrick or anyone else."

"Dan," Laurel cried, holding him close and tight as he moved above her. But fear clutched at her with all the strength of his embrace. "Oh, Dan." Because she knew he still didn't believe her—and why should he when, as soon as she closed her eyes, she saw another man?

"I'm sorry, Laurel. Jesus."

Dan rolled onto his back, throwing one arm across his eyes. He'd gone at her like some crazed animal, and hated himself for it. Where had such passion come from?

Maria, he thought. They hadn't seen each other since her operation, and he didn't know when he'd be able to break away for a night in Shelby.

He began to review his schedule. There were only ten days until the primary. He had Jack Sommers, the strongest Democratic contender, to jump over before the real work began, work that could turn him into a United States senator.

If not . . . if he didn't win . . .

Dan lowered his arm to stroke a finger along his jaw. The faint pockmarks could have been acne scars, but they weren't. Dan had sworn, on his own blood, that he'd never end up like his father.

Was it too much, dammit, to ask that things go smoothly now? That Laurel play the role for which she'd been trained all her life? And Maria . . .

Dammit to hell, couldn't even the woman he loved be happy for him? He sat up in bed. Maria, his soft, willing Maria, was becoming as much a stranger to him as his wife, his son. Nothing about Ned, about his marriage, seemed right to him, nothing except Laurel's untapped usefulness in the campaign.

"Dan?"

No, he thought angrily, it wasn't too much to ask. "I talked with your father tonight," he said, "at length." He felt an odd, misplaced tension as he often did with her. "Do you know what he told me?"

"I can't imagine." The hopeful tone had dulled, and she sat up beside him.

"He saw McKendrick's article in *Newstrend* yesterday, of course."

"And didn't like it."

"It seems no one else shares your generous opinion. As usual, McKendrick's after something—something he isn't going to get. I run a clean campaign, Laurel. There's nothing he can find to use against me, no matter how he digs." Dan paused, knowing he lied. There was one thing. One person. The knowledge only strengthened his conviction that Edwin Frasier had been right. "The senator gave me some advice, however. He said perhaps we ought not to push McKendrick away, but to keep the enemy close, the better to stay on our toes."

"I don't consider Ryder McKendrick your enemy."

"But I do, and if the tough-minded journalist wants the inside story of this run for the Senate, he's going to have it. At the same time, I'll be getting what I want."

Laurel paled. She knew that Dan wasn't afraid of Ryder McKendrick's professionalism, just as he wasn't remembering the media battle against Edwin Frasier over Vietnam, either.

"Is there any good reason why we shouldn't expose ourselves to Mr. McKendrick's close-up lens, his inquiring pen?" he asked.

She said nothing.

"Is there *any* reason, Laurel?"

The words seemed torn from her. "Dan, why not admit that you want him close because you want to watch—"

"There is only one reason for any of this." His gaze sharpened. "I am going to win this election." Dan clutched at her bare upper arms to emphasize the point before he smiled. "And you, Laurel, not to mention Ryder McKendrick, are going to help me."

## CHAPTER 12

" 'THIS IS THE toughest race I've ever run,' Dan Benedict says, but he isn't training for the Boston Marathon, which he's entered and finished twice. He is talking about his unexpected run for the U.S. Senate...."

Laurel tossed the issue of *Newstrend* aside with her discarded notes for the speech she was to give within the next half hour. Nerves had made concentration impossible. She'd reread Ryder's latest article, the second in the series—the first since Dan had invited him to follow the campaign—hoping to regain her equilibrium. "Familiar to the residents of Beantown, but considered by some to be an elitist, Benedict faces an uphill battle in the rest of the state." The piece was solid, with only a tinge of subjective disapproval. Even Dan hadn't been able to find specific fault with it. Or with her.

Laurel got up from the chintz-upholstered armchair in the hotel suite—today was Springfield—and briefly assessed her appearance again in the dresser mirror. This campaign was making her vain. She'd brushed her hair three times, reapplied lipstick twice. The clean lines of her gray suit, white blouse, and softly knotted tie of navy and burgundy silk, were flawless; she'd put on fresh white hose after finding a narrow run in another pair. She gathered her black patent leather handbag containing aspirin, cough drops, linen handkerchief. And the letter she'd received from Judith's friend that morning. The rejection of her Flapper Girl design for the charity luncheon program cover still smarted, but Laurel couldn't think about that now. There'd be time for disappointment after her speech. Instead she thought: my notes!

She tucked the stack of four-by-six index cards she'd left on the coffee table into her handbag. Why was Dan throwing her to the lions by herself so soon?

"Laurel, we've got one week to make the primary vote. No second chances. You'll be fine." He had smiled reassuringly before he left. "Despite the fact that you dislike speaking, you haven't made a mistake yet. I leave you in Springfield without a qualm. I'll lend you Teague."

"But Dan—"

"I'll see you in Framingham on Thursday."

Still, the prospect of speaking to so many people without Dan's presence nearby made Laurel want to flee. Today wouldn't be like yesterday afternoon, chatting with forty women at a coffee hour in Fall River; on Monday at least she had relaxed a little, and been herself. People only wanted to see her smile, to ask where she'd bought her dress or shoes. But in the next few minutes she'd be mouthing Teague Michaels's speech, and Dan's politics. And hoping not to faint.

Closing the door, Laurel stepped into the hall and pushed the down button for the elevator. God, she'd give anything not to face five hundred strange faces; she'd never spoken to such a large group before. What could she tell them that would make a difference at the polls next Tuesday? Besides, she thought on the way down, the policies in her speech weren't hers.

Laurel stood for a moment after the elevator doors

glided open, noting through the corridor windows that outside it was raining heavily, which struck her as a bad omen. Rain always did. Except once, she thought, in Gloucester, then immediately pushed the thought away.

"Smile, it's no worse than the Christians getting thrown into the arena—thumbs up, thumbs down."

Laurel stepped forward, absurdly glad to hear Ryder McKendrick making a joke. "My sentiments precisely."

"You'll only be on for ten or fifteen minutes, not long enough for the end of the world."

Laurel grinned. "We live in a time of push-button diplomacy."

"You'll do fine."

Still nervous, she wasn't that certain, but after thanking Ryder, she turned her back, unable even to wonder why he was in Springfield when Dan was on the road to Worcester. Entering the meeting room, she was unreasonably grateful that Dan had also left his campaign manager behind. Teague Michaels was at the microphone, testing the sound level.

Everything worked, Laurel thought with a groan; no mechanical difficulty would save her today.

Teague warmed up the group with his standard repertoire of political jokes, segued into glowing praise of Dan, and then—much too soon—introduced her.

"...my pleasure to give you the candidate's gracious wife, Laurel Frasier Benedict. Let's hear it for Ed Frasier's daughter!"

Laurel smiled stiffly, wanting to kick him as she usually did for demeaning her in the guise of praise. Glancing around the room, she couldn't find Ryder, whose smile would have meant a great deal just then if she couldn't welcome it any other time without feeling guilty. At the podium she arranged the cards in front of her and tried to remember what she wanted to say.

"Good afternoon. I suppose, today, that's a euphemism." She gestured toward the high windows to one side of the room where gusts of rain could be seen sweeping against the glass. Thunder rumbled overhead as if on cue, and the ladies dutifully laughed. "I do hope, however, that we can make this a positive day by joining together in support of Dan Benedict for the U.S. Senate.

"That this would not be a new experience for me, to become once again part of the exciting political and social scene in our nation's capital—the closest I've ever known to a hometown as my father served the people of Massachusetts there for more than thirty years—is not to downplay the significance of that experience." Laurel's voice was quavering less now. "Yet when my husband first approached me with the notion of running, at the very difficult time of Dave Cabell's illness, I had mixed feelings. I love Boston, the home we've made there, and the many friends we cherish.

"But the sacrifice of uprooting our family, of leaving friends behind, is balanced by the opportunity Dan will have to effect change for the many rather than the few."

With growing confidence Laurel moved into the body of her speech, sensing that she had the audience with her. She outlined Dan's program for his first term, stressing the need for quality public education, and decrying the recent upswing in unemployment among factory workers replaced by technology. She mentioned retraining programs, then much-needed support systems for the elderly. She touched on foreign policy, considered one of Dan's weaker points, assuring her audience that, although he wasn't widely traveled abroad, his policies were sound and not inflammatory to world peace. Finishing with a brief statement on the importance of federal aid to state and local government, Laurel brought the twenty-minute speech to a close.

"I believe that the country, and, specifically, the Commonwealth of Massachusetts, needs Dan Benedict in Washington. He is a man who cares. A man who takes his stand and draws others to his side. I join him in his determination to win a seat in the U.S. Senate, as will our eight-year-old son, Ned, with a glad heart. Dan Benedict is a man who, with our help and all of yours, can guide and direct this great country—as Edwin Frasier did before him—for the good of humanity. Thank you."

Laurel stepped down to healthy applause, taking her place at the long table where other, local speakers sat. Though she'd made it through without fainting and had managed to relax sufficiently to make her points, her knees were still weak. The words Teague Michaels had written for her threatened to stick in her throat every time she used them. They made her feel like a second-rate cheerleader.

Her gaze skimmed the room again as the session was thrown open to questions. After a dozen rote responses, she decided it was just as well Ryder hadn't been in the audience. The long discourse on school budgets by the woman at the microphone would have proved too much; with Ryder watching, Laurel might have given in to one of the laughing fits that used to seize Lexa in public.

"God, can they be serious?" Behind the senator's back her sister would pull faces, somehow never getting caught. "Boring, boring."

". . . and I wonder what Mrs. Benedict would say to that," the woman finished.

Oh Lord, she hadn't heard the question. "I'm sorry, could you clarify?"

The Springfield coordinator for Dan's campaign, serving as moderator, rephrased it: something about the quality of public education being threatened, the population getting older, the tax base eroding.

Aware that she'd have to speak against her own beliefs, Laurel came to her feet. "That's a difficult issue, one that affects all of us."

"All of us, Mrs. Benedict?" The woman leaned into the microphone. "Isn't your child boarding at Dawson Prep? I find it hard to believe that Dan Benedict cares for public education when it's not good enough for his son. And what of the rest of us who can't afford fancy private schools?"

Damn him, Laurel thought. Dan was already being criticized as much as praised for his connection to the senator, and now, charges of nepotism had been joined by the school issue, which was further proof of elitism. "I assure you that public education is one of my husband's highest priorities. He has been a member of the school board in our district for the past two years, and while Ned attended grammar school in the neighborhood I was active in the PTA, which I served as vice president last term. We've sent Ned away because of the campaign."

"Are you saying your boy won't attend Dawson if your husband goes to Washington?"

This time Laurel answered from the heart. "Personally I would like to see Ned closer to home, a part of the public system wherever we settle, but—"

"Isn't it true, Mrs. Benedict, that you are a product of boarding schools? I remember your sister being expel—"

"My sister, Lexa, enjoyed high spirits." Laurel smiled coldly. "And you're right, she was expelled from Miss Hall's Academy, but reinstated. Our parents were then traveling a great deal, as my father was chairman of the Armed Services Committee, so it was only natural that Lexa and I be sent away to school where our studies would not be interrupted. You'll also remember that my sister died when only nineteen." Facing the woman down, Laurel felt her blood boil. "As for our son, when Dan and I can make the decision about his education, our very first consideration will be the public schools closest to us."

To Laurel's relief, Teague seized the microphone. "Thank you, ladies, and the few gentlemen who have joined us. Mrs. Benedict has another speech to give. I'm sorry, we must cut this short."

With Teague running interference, Laurel left the crowd for the auditorium's rear entrance. There were cries of "Wait!" and "Mrs. Benedict, an autograph?" Reflected bursts of camera lights flashed against the walls. But other than the need for escape, all that registered in Laurel's mind was Ryder McKendrick, leaning against the wall by the door to the parking lot. As she swept past into the safety of the waiting Lincoln Continental, he murmured, "What percentage of that crap do you really believe?"

Ryder leaned against the headboard of his hotel room bed in Springfield that night, smoking and blowing perfect rings at the ceiling. He didn't know what to believe. Except that Laurel meant to avoid him, and that she was having a hard time of it.

No more than I am, trying not to mind, he added silently. He had come into the campaign with no illusions, knowing that this time Sara was wrong; Laurel was very much married to Dan Benedict. Teague Michaels watched Ryder like a bloodhound, and the first negative sentence he wrote about Dan Benedict might be his last. Hell, he shouldn't have opened his mouth to Benedict at the banquet and, goaded by his own feelings, put his foot in.

"Your wife's a vision in that lace and velvet. I didn't have the chance to tell her so tonight."

"You won't get the chance. I'll tell you once, Mc-Kendrick—"

"Look, I've had all the warnings and dire predictions tonight that I'm going to take. You tell Michaels—"

"Gentlemen, gentlemen."

They both glanced up, eyes angry, at Edwin Frasier's approach. Ryder stepped back without intending to. There was no denying the senator's presence.

"Your reporting continues to verge upon the fictional, Mr. McKendrick." He held out his hand. "Most recently, in *Newstrend*."

The grip was forceful, making Ryder return the pressure. A couple of strobe lights went off. "I'm not writing fantasy, Senator. I never was."

"A pity. Judith tells me you're nearly as amusing as Doonesbury."

"I doubt you find that amusing, either."

The senator released Ryder's hand. "I don't find the welfare of this nation a matter for glib jokes, or back-stabbing."

"Neither do I."

Dan Benedict ended the silence he'd been keeping since the senator's intervention. "Find yourself another story, McKendrick. And another woman to stare at."

"Dan, take it easy." The senator was smiling; he'd been smiling all along.

But Benedict continued, "We have laws in this country for people like you, men who decide to smear innocent—"

"I'm aware of the law, Counselor. It's called the First Amendment."

Not looking back, he had walked away, straight through the crowded room, past the campaign table, and to the Sheraton lobby, collecting Sara on the way.

Ryder dragged on his cigarette. What had prompted

Benedict later to reverse himself? he wondered now. His invitation to join the campaign, as "a chronicler of our crusade," still didn't sit right. Even if it were true that Benedict had nothing to hide, why show it so willingly to Ryder McKendrick? The senator had had a strong say in all of this, that much he would bet on, heavily.

Was he pulling Laurel's strings, too?

Ryder crushed his cigarette in the ashtray balanced on his stomach, and blew out a last trail of smoke. He ought to quit, but now didn't seem to be the time. To quit smoking, or the campaign. He was wound too tight, with no other release. Sara, hounding him for copy. Benedict, leaving him with Michaels for the day, saying, "Nothing pressing in Worcester, why not take a few shots of Laurel? Maybe your readers would like the feminine angle." His gut burning now because she'd snubbed him today after smiling at him. Well, what did he expect, encouraging her before the speech, then tearing it apart afterward because she wouldn't smile at him a second time? He felt like a cat with a tin can tied to its tail.

Dumping the ashtray onto the night stand, he swung off the bed. But hell, he was here, wasn't he? And so was Laurel. Down the hall, on the same floor, with Benedict safely out of town. Ryder glanced at his watch.

A minute later he was rapping on her door.

He had knocked again when the bolt was suddenly released, and her face appeared in a slight gap between the door and the frame. She'd left the security chain on. Ryder leaned a shoulder against the wall, facing her, and smiled.

"Hi."

"It's after midnight. What do you want?"

"Dangerous question."

She was wearing a long dressing gown of royal blue silk, and underneath it he glimpsed a matching nightie.

Her hair was loose, and furrowed, as if she'd been dragging her fingers through it. "I know what time it is. You weren't asleep."

She held up a thin stack of index cards in embarrassment. "Lord, could you hear me inside, talking to myself to get ready for tomorrow? I must have sounded insane."

"You didn't sound it this afternoon."

"No, I believe you used another term." Crap, he'd said.

"I was talking content, not delivery."

Surprised, she smiled. "You listened, then?"

"I was in the back hall, but the doors were open." He held up a bottle. "I've brought you a nightcap. Ask me in. We'll talk speech making."

Shaking her head, she said, "I can't ask you—"

"What will the neighbors say if you don't?" He measured the blue robe with his gaze. "What will Michaels think if he sees us here?"

"The worst, undoubtedly, but I'm not inviting you in. I'm not dressed."

"I've seen you in less," Ryder pointed out.

"A gentleman wouldn't remind me."

Wagging the bottle, he said, "I'm not a gentleman. I'm a journalist."

Color rose in her cheeks. "I never drink with reporters after midnight. Besides, I need a clear head tomorrow."

"Downstairs for coffee, then," he said, pushing away from the wall to the door's opening. "Get dressed, and meet me in the lounge. And don't stand me up this time."

"I don't drink coffee either after midnight."

"With reporters?"

She looked exasperated. "With anybody. Or alone. Caffeine keeps me awake, and I'm not in a very good mood right now, so good n—"

"Why so grouchy?"

She sighed. "If you must know, I had a ... rejection today."

"Forget my opinion," he said. "Your speech was otherwise well received."

He watched her teeth sink into her lower lip and felt a familiar flare of heat. "No, I meant a rejection on some ... artwork of mine ... that program cover I mentioned." Disappointment had thickened her voice.

"May I see?"

"The cover's in Boston. Only the letter is here."

"Let me read it."

With another sigh she disappeared, then came back, holding out a single sheet of paper through the slim gap in the door. He leaned against the frame to read. The letter was curt, without encouragement. After a moment he said, "I don't know much about design, but I've seen your sketches and I'd be happy to run the cover or anything else past Sara Hennessey at *Newstrend*. She knows everybody. I'm sure she could steer you in the right direction."

He caught the flash of interest in her eyes before she quickly banked it.

"That's kind of you, but I don't want ..." She didn't finish.

"To be obligated to me?"

She nodded. "Besides," she said ruefully, "I've more than enough to keep me busy these days. The cover was only to alleviate boredom before Dan—"

"Laurel, Jesus."

"All my life I've had my parents and my husband guiding me. If I'm ever inclined to pursue a career, in art or anything else, I ... I'll do it on my own." The letter was snatched back through the door opening. "And I believe we agreed that day at Dawson, the night of Dan's fundraiser, to forget—"

"I have a photographic memory. Indelible," he said. "I won't forget Dawson or Gloucester or the last five minutes." Ryder wedged his knee between the door and the frame; his pants leg brushed against the silk dressing gown. "Take the chain off this door, and let me in." Then he forced his tone to soften. "Please, just for a minute. You need to talk about the let—"

"No."

"Laurel, you're making me crazy."

"You're making yourself crazy. I've told you—"

The elevator doors slid open halfway along the hall, and a middle-aged couple stepped out, laughing. They began walking in Ryder's direction. He backed away from Laurel's door and said, "I'm not giving up. You've got to talk to me sometime. I'm a reporter, remember."

"And like all reporters, pushy." Then Laurel gently closed the door in his face.

In Framingham on Thursday Laurel sat on the hotel room sofa across from Dan, who was finishing his plate of poached egg on English muffin. It had become their habit to have breakfast together at six A.M., during which Dan discussed changes in their schedules for the day and briefed Laurel, sometimes with Teague's help, on sensitive issues.

"What's your itinerary for today?" Dan asked without looking at it.

Laurel knew the printed form by heart.

"An early morning visit with the editor of the local paper. Informal, a few pictures. Hopefully, a good write-up tomorrow." She grimaced, remembering Ryder's face when she'd shut the door on him two nights ago. But when she had to deal with the press officially, she'd found she could force the charm; it didn't come without effort, but she had learned the lesson at Judith's knee.

"After the newspaper chat," she continued, "I'll be driven to a nearby suburb for coffee with three dozen women in a private home." The paper cups would be inscribed in red, white, and blue: Dan's Our Man. "Coffee will be followed by stops at a senior citizens' community for tea and cookies, at a school for retarded children, and the burn unit of the hospital. I'll have luncheon with campaign workers at a local restaurant, simple and unassuming. And, of course, interrupted by the public—a 'spontaneous' opportunity to shake hands and ask for votes."

"You do it charmingly," Dan said with a smile. "Teague says you're becoming the favorite, and I should concede."

"I know too much about being a senator. You're welcome to the job."

Her own was tough enough. In the afternoon Laurel would appear on a women's television show where "I'll talk about Ned, and mention Pirate, and discuss the woes and joys of living in Boston. After that three more coffee hours—" she'd be jangled long before dinner if she took more than a sip at each "—and oh yes, there's a reception sponsored by the League of Women Voters at the end of the afternoon."

She wouldn't need to concentrate on Judith's commands: Keep the line moving; don't ask questions. "Hello, nice to meet you, glad you could come." But it had been easier for Lexa, who wanted to finish and pursue her own plans; Laurel always held things up, getting involved in people, and conversation.

"You'll be exhausted by dinnertime," Dan said.

"No more than you."

She sat back on the sofa, realizing that Dan's schedule was even more grueling. While he finished his coffee and added notations to his printed itinerary, she studied road maps of the area they'd be touring separately, familiarizing herself with pronunciation and geography.

"Well," he said finally. "You're set for today. I'd better get moving myself. Teague's got a driver coming for you in twenty minutes. He'll be with me today. You'll be all right? You were wonderful, he told me, in Springfield. I'll send him back for Friday."

"Nothing too ominous, I'll be fine." She had survived.

Dan kissed her lightly on the cheek. "I'll just make one call then," he said, and disappeared into the bedroom instead of using the sitting room extension.

Laurel wasn't an eavesdropper, and political maneuvering had been too much a part of her early life to appeal now. She was used to conversations behind closed doors. But this one seemed different. She heard low murmurings, long pauses and sudden, intense replies that couldn't quite be heard through the door. It wasn't the first time he'd done this. Who was on the line? It wasn't the voice Dan used with Teague. It didn't sound like politics.

"I've got to leave you on your own for the weekend, Laurel," Dan announced, coming from the bedroom.

"But we're supposed to meet the governor on Saturday."

He loaded his briefcase. "He's canceled. We'll do it next week."

"Then what—"

"You can handle tomorrow here. I'll meet you in Lexington on Monday."

"We were to spend Sunday with Ned," she reminded him. Squeezing in the visit, Laurel thought, after two or three local speeches.

"Something's come up. He'll understand. We can go another time, I'll have Teague free up an afternoon."

"He'll be counting on us, Dan. We haven't been to Dawson since you dropped him off two weeks ago."

"You were there when he fell from his horse, remember?"

"That wasn't exactly a visit. And you weren't there."

His tone sharpened. "Laurel, I'm sorry. This can't be helped."

"What can't be helped?"

He slammed the briefcase shut. "Do I have to remind you that we've got a primary election on Tuesday? And I'm running behind the opposition? Do I have to point out that we've had only ten days to campaign and that Jack Sommers is doing a hell of a lot better than I am in the Third District?"

"No. Nor do you have to patronize me."

Fuming, she stood and took her bag from the sofa, stuffing her note cards into a side pocket, then snapping it shut. On the night of the fund-raiser she'd made a commitment to the campaign, and again, to this marriage. She'd turned her back on Ryder McKendrick. If Dan had been jealous enough to let her see it, there must be something left for them.

In Springfield her determination to keep clear of Ryder had only strengthened when he'd knocked at her door and she'd sent him away. She'd even buried the brief dream of that program cover design, or anything after it. But now, she felt fresh disappointment over the visit with Ned, and vague suspicion. What had come up that Dan needed to hide from her in sarcasm? A lot more, she thought, than the much-needed, but lagging, labor vote.

"I'm not patronizing." He slipped into his suit coat. "But while I'm gone," he said lightly and much to her surprise, "you'll be free after Friday. Why not spend a day or two with Hilary?"

Hilary sat up in bed, wincing. "I can't come back to New York," she repeated into the telephone, then paused for the irate response. "I don't know when. A week or so. My back—"

She listened while she tapped one fingernail against a tooth. "I don't care about the bookings. I know all about the bookings, and I can't do a thing right now. How could I stand under those lights? I've been flat on my ass for the last nine days—"

Garbled shouting came through the wires. Hilary held the phone away from her ear. "Then cancel the whole week! I can't help losing the money, either. No, and not the cover of *Cosmo*."

At the burst of profanity, Hilary slammed the receiver back into its cradle. The hell with bookings. She was sick of modeling, sick of the people in it, including herself.

She had half a mind to quit right now, and take off for Africa with her cameras. Then she smiled. It would be even better to see Laurel.

According to the first, more pleasant phone call of the day, Laurel was coming for the weekend; and the house looked a shambles. Hilary sat up straighter, gritting her teeth. The injury hadn't been serious,—only slow to mend. But Sebastian had insisted she see a doctor the morning after she'd fallen from the chair.

At Hilary's protest he'd said, "Why don't you let me take care of you for a couple of hours?"

"I've been taking care of myself for years, Sebastian."

"This won't kill you."

He'd gently lowered her onto the passenger seat of an absurdly small car. Yet the black leather interior was roomy, and she stretched out her legs with a sigh. Hilary realized that she was sitting quite comfortably on the left-hand side as Sebastian slid behind the steering wheel on the right.

"What is this thing?" she asked to distract herself from pain. "A Dinky model with a working engine?"

"Myra loves it," he said, turning on the fuel pump switch. A red light glowed on the woodgrain dashboard. "It's English, of course. Relatively rare. A Riley Elf, almost twenty years old. The countess says—"

"You told me the countess never rides in anything less than a Bentley, and, preferably, a Rolls."

Sebastian flicked the ignition key, and the small engine throbbed, deep and throaty. He grinned. "She makes the exception for me."

"There's a lot of that going around these days."

"What?"

"Younger men, menopausal women. Preferably with money."

Sebastian eased the right-hand gearshift into reverse. He didn't speak until he'd backed the car from his driveway and started down the narrow street. "I hope it's broken."

"What?"

"Your back."

He was six years younger than Hilary, and God knew how many more the junior of his countess, whom Hilary had yet to glimpse. In the week and a half since her accident, she'd been forced by proximity to catalogue Sebastian's comings and goings next door as he seemed always to notice hers. Mostly, Hilary had to admit, he worked. He got up early and never shut off the lights in his garage until after midnight. When did he see the mysterious countess?

To Hilary's irritation, she had in mind various images of the woman—all well aged and wealthier than Myra. Sebastian was insecure enough about his own lack of riches to choose just such a woman as compensation.

He'd driven Hilary to the hospital without another word. Though she conceded that Sebastian's mood had warmed during the week, and every morning he'd—But she didn't want to waste time thinking about Sebastian's kindnesses, or his love life; she wouldn't waste another minute on him.

With a grunt of pain, she slipped from bed and headed slowly, gingerly, for the shower. Hot water helped.

Finished in the bathroom, she limped out to the aroma of fresh coffee brewing. It wasn't an unfamiliar bouquet over the past nine days, and for some reason made her spirits lift. When she entered the kitchen, Sebastian was just sliding eggs and bacon onto two plates at the table, pouring hot, dark coffee into ceramic mugs. "I didn't know whether you'd want me using the bone china cups that were nearly the cause of your demise."

"Don't you ever knock?"

"When Myra's in residence, we never observe the more tedious amenities."

"I am not my mother. Or the countess."

He slid into place opposite her, grinning. "I always knock at the Countess's. She has a butler, understand. And a couple of, what do you call them, footmen?"

Hilary dug into the steaming plate of food. She never knew whether he was teasing her, or being serious. Either way, he irritated her. Even his grin, open and boyish, couldn't be trusted. Hilary stared into her coffee. For a moment she saw another smile, another pair of eyes. Pure and blue, loving her. They'd been so perfectly matched, she and Chip; they'd had such plans. Suddenly she resented Sebastian Noble's being in her kitchen, making himself at home, and depression seeped through her as it had Labor Day weekend when she'd arrived with Laurel.

"What's the matter, Hilary?"

"Nothing." She glanced up. "You."

"Go on, I'm fascinated by the subject."

"It isn't all you make it out to be, Sebastian." Across

the raspberry jam, yellow butter, and Myra's Belleek salt and pepper shakers, Hilary glared at him. She wasn't about to be drawn into a painful discussion of Chip Brewster. "Having pots of money, servants, half a dozen different homes around the world . . ."

"I didn't say it was."

But Hilary couldn't stop now. "Where did you come from? Why move to Gloucester of all places to hammer on old cars? You must have a home somewhere, somebody—"

"Baltimore." He'd said it without intonation, so that it seemed a foreign word. "Did you ever see the Hitchcock film, *Marnie*? Those row houses with the white marble steps to scrub every day, two blocks from the water?"

She visualized the place, far removed from butlers and footmen. She could almost hear the cry of gulls wheeling overhead, smell the stench of fish that men would reek of, coming home to their shabby quarters.

"Was your father a seaman?"

"No."

"Then what did he do?"

"He didn't have to do anything," Sebastian said. "He didn't have to leave my mother either. But he was of the old school, you see. A man who owned up to his 'responsibilities,' no matter how distasteful. He provided for us . . . me. My mother wouldn't take a penny from him. He used to call her now and then from . . ." Sebastian stopped. "From wherever he was, and she'd end up crying. I always wanted to . . . well, never mind. I was just a kid."

Hilary sat immobilized, fear tumbling through her veins. Why had she asked? She didn't want to know about him. She didn't want to feel sympathy or anything else for Sebastian Noble. Now she had an image, too real, of him as a boy: streetwise, tough. A pair of dark, intense eyes in a thin, compelling face; straight dark hair falling over his forehead. Fatherless, and bitter. He had offered too much of himself.

Sebastian must have agreed. Suddenly he flashed her a smile and said, "Well, I'm not a kid anymore. I don't have to go back to Baltimore, which is why I'm here, in Gloucester. To stay," he added. "Aren't you glad?"

"Sebastian, that guileless expression and those steamy eyes may work on Myra, who's susceptible, apparently, to your curious charm but not on me. Never on me."

"The countess says—"

"And stop throwing that woman in my face! I don't care how many lovers you take, if you spend all night servicing them! I don't care about you."

"Well."

"Well what?"

"I see I've got my work cut out for me."

Sebastian rose from the table, carrying his dishes to the sink and emptying his coffee cup. Hilary watched the movement of his shoulder muscles under the blue T-shirt he wore. "What work?"

For a moment he didn't answer. Then Sebastian turned. "Oh, I'm putting a Morgan back together for a guy in Pittsburgh. I guess I'd better get to it. You'll be okay on your own?"

"I'm fine," she said, "but—"

"Sure you are."

Hilary could have screamed. He could affect the blandest expression of anyone she'd ever known; it troubled her now, though she couldn't say why. She was usually happy enough to get rid of him. But she sensed that she had hurt him. It was one thing to banter with Sebastian Noble, quite another to want him bleeding. Sebastian started for the kitchen door.

"Who was he, Hilary?"

"Who was who . . . whom?"

"The bastard that turned you sour. Was it a man?" he asked. "Or do you simply like the look of your own face on a magazine cover too much?"

Without waiting for an answer, he closed the door behind him. And left her choking on her coffee.

As usual, he'd had the last word.

## ❋ CHAPTER 13 ❋

❋

"HE WAS TWICE the human being you are. And he didn't sour me." Hilary spoke to Sebastian's back as he bent over the innards of a foreign car in the end bay of his garage. "He disappeared."

It had taken her hours to work up a reply to Sebastian's parting statement at the house, most of the afternoon while she dusted furniture, swept floors, changed sheets for Laurel's arrival. Long, laborious hours with sweat running down her face from the effort of staying on her feet. Finished, she had still wanted nothing more than to wish Sebastian Noble a hot afterlife. The painful walk across the lawn had been worth it.

As he straightened from the car, Sebastian was speechless.

"His name was Chip Brewster, and he piloted a Navy F-4 Phantom over Vietnam. We were engaged to be married. On November 7, 1972, his jet fighter was brought down . . . he's been officially missing in action ever since."

"Hilary, I'm sorry."

"In a pig's eye you are." Her glance flicked over him, sweat-dampened dark hair to grease-smeared face and striking black eyes to the car dirt streaking down his bare chest. She'd never seen him clean; she'd rarely known him to be civil. He'd probably never been within fifty miles of Baltimore. "Why would you care? How old were you then, Sebastian? What were you doing that day? Kicking a football across a vacant field? Sitting in junior high school English class?"

"You know how old I was. Six months shy of thirteen. I already had a job washing cars in my landlord's service station. My mother needed the income."

She was surprised enough to back down slightly. "When did you go to school?"

"Until I was twelve." Long dark lashes veiled the irritation in his eyes as Sebastian stared at the cement floor between them. "So there you are. An illiterate for a neighbor. What will the good people of Gloucester think of that?"

"The countess?"

She had thought he might smile, but he didn't. She'd thought he was joking, but he wasn't.

"There isn't any countess," Sebastian said.

"But—"

"I invented her to annoy you." He turned back to the car he'd been working on.

"You said your father sent money for you. Why couldn't you finish school?"

"His money was in trust for me. I didn't—couldn't—use it until I was of age. For college, he thought. Instead, I bought this place because I wouldn't give him..." He broke off, looking around at her. "Forget it. Why should you care? Hadn't you better run home and start calling everyone you know? Tell them that Sebastian Noble wouldn't know Shakespeare from Mark Twain?" He gave the screwdriver in his hand a vicious twist somewhere deep in the car's engine. "Don't forget though, I can sign my name."

"On inflated bills of sale?" Hilary ventured closer, wondering why she stayed. They always argued, and his tone now was tight as a leaf spring. He wanted a fight. So did she. "Hunks of metal that anybody in his right mind would sell for scrap. You know what you are, Sebastian?"

"Tell me."

"A con artist, a huckster."

"There are a lot of con artists in this world. Must be room for one more." His tone had turned breezy, which should have warned her. "After all, you seem to make a good living in the field."

Hilary took a breath. "Damn you to hell."

"Probably."

"Get your head out of that piece of junk while I'm talking!" She had put a hand on his grimy forearm before she stopped to think. Sebastian came to his full height in one easy motion, and stared at the whiteness of her skin against his dark tan. Hilary snatched her hand back. "You think I'm frivolous? You think I'm rich and spoiled and useless? You think it was a huge joke, don't you, inventing a countess for a lover—"

"I never said she was my lover."

"Inventing her as a slap in the face then, to Myra and all the other people in this town who've taken you for one of them . . . my God, why? Maybe you did grow up in a slum—"

His gaze met hers. "It wasn't a slum."

"Genteel poverty, then. I don't care what you call it. But don't you dare look down your uneducated nose at my mother or her friends or me! I work as hard as you do, Sebastian Noble—ten, twelve hours a day under blazing lights, performing like a monkey, not able to move as I please or stop or take a drink when I want . . . twelve hours, despising every one of them. I don't need the job, though, do I? Why keep at it, then, you ask?" She glared into his mild expression, wanting to slap his face. "Because otherwise I'd have time to think. And on the other side of that camera, where I'd much rather be, I'd have time to feel. And I don't care to remind myself that being born to money, going to the finest schools and spending my holidays on yachts in the Med, riding in Rollses and Bentleys and Mercedes, never kept me from losing all I wanted!"

"Brewster," he said.

"Yes. Charles Wellington Brewster, who would have made me happy." Hilary glanced into his eyes. "I would have made him happy, too. Money and all its privileges will never buy me that, Sebastian. Or you."

"I didn't say it would."

"Then why do you goad me with white lies about your countess?"

Sebastian's gaze clouded. "Maybe because you're always so haughty and self-satisfied."

He plunged back inside the dismantled engine, as if to end the conversation and their argument. Hilary felt confused. "Did you really make her up?" she asked after a moment.

"Total fabrication."

"That's a big word for someone with a sixth-grade education." Or had he made that up, too, like his statistics? Illiteracy might be just another of them.

"Seventy-five cents," Sebastian murmured. With a hammer, he clashed on an outcropping of metal that could have been a radiator—though Hilary wasn't certain—then said quietly, "Would you really like it better? Being on the opposite end of the camera?"

"Yes, if I had any guts. I'd give up modeling tomorrow,

grab my Leica and a satchel full of lenses and . . . tip off the edge of the earth."

Sebastian wiped his hands on a greasy red rag that couldn't have helped much. With a sigh, he stood straight and looked at her. "That's all for today."

It was one of his typically oblique comments, delivered with a peacemaking smile. Did he mean his work or . . . ? Hilary swallowed, feeling oddly panicked. "What—what kind of car is this?" She didn't like the look in his eye.

"I told you, a Morgan Plus 4, drophead coupe. It's a 1958, but only twenty thousand miles on the odometer. Body's made of wood." He glanced at it, then back at Hilary, thoughtfully. "I always wondered what it would be like, playing photographer. Talk about hucksters. That's some job, isn't it? Snapping pictures of beautiful women all day."

"It's just a job, Sebastian." He had this broad streak of naiveté, a product, she supposed, of his beginnings like the envy of money, of other people's roles. Hers, apparently. "They see me—see models, I mean—as nothing more than raw material. Most of them have wild, creative egos. I—any fashion subject, that is—must be just a different type of still life."

"That isn't what I've heard. They use the camera, don't they? To seduce. Inconceivable that they wouldn't. The temptation would be too great."

"Temptation?" Her pulse jumped.

"To make love through the lens. It's a barrier, but at the same time, a license." He closed the distance between them. "They talk to you, don't they, in near whispers while they work?"

"Sebastian, you've been taken in by the *Playboy* mystique."

He smiled. "I'm too young, remember? I missed the

Me Generation, most of it, anyway."

"Obviously not all."

Why didn't she move? He was in front of her, all the blandness missing from his expression just when she needed it. "What do they say, Hilary?" Sebastian framed her face at a distance between both hands, as if he were an artist. "'Smile, move a little. Softer, yes, that's nice. Good. Raise your chin, darling...'"

"Stop it." She couldn't seem to breathe right.

"No, that's not the look I want. Give me something abandoned, let your eyes go wide... the mouth should be parted, you're waiting... you want it..."

"Sebastian," Hilary said helplessly.

"Baby, you want it." His hands fell, and she was folded in his arms. Instantly she forgot the argument, his constant insults. She forgot how dirty his hands always seemed; ignored the grease on his bare chest, pressing into hers. The awareness of oil, musk, and flesh made her dizzy. Then in slow motion his mouth came down on hers, and the long kiss took her breath, her strength.

"Oh, my God."

When Hilary pulled away his deep-set eyes seemed to mirror her surprise at such sensation passing between them. He didn't try to hold her. He only said, "You liked that. Didn't you?"

"No!" She didn't think to turn around and run; her legs felt wooden, heavy. She kept backing up, amazed when she didn't stumble over some broken fender or discarded battery, and fall. Her heart thundered. "Don't ever pull a stunt like that again, you hear me?"

"You're hungry." Sebastian's voice, soft and pleading, followed her. "You don't know it, Hilary, but you are."

"Stay away from me," she said. "You made that up, the same way you invent everything else."

\*          \*          \*

Laurel tried to imagine that she was somewhere else. The civic auditorium, small and hot and overcrowded, made her crave air-conditioning, a quiet hotel room, a soft bed. Disturbed by Dan's last-minute change of plan for the weekend, she hadn't slept well the previous night.

Today had been a marathon of public appearances: a street-corner rally, a luncheon speech to city government officials, two coffee hours, and an emotionally wrenching thirty minutes with out-of-work, and desperate, mill workers. And the day wasn't over. She had to deliver Dan's message to this stuffy room filled with senior citizens.

Not having worn her contacts, Laurel adjusted her glasses—her eyes this morning had felt as if sandpaper were beneath the lids—and spoke into the microphone, which hadn't been fixed to her height. She kept straining her neck, leaning closer. The sound transmission rose and fell. She wondered whether anybody knew what she was saying; certainly Laurel didn't. But then, as always, they were Teague's words, Dan's campaign propaganda.

*How much of that do you believe?* A fraction, she thought. She'd rather paint pictures for these people, stark black enamel instead of urban crime statistics, a sky blue wash for the innocence of childhood, hard orange light a metaphor for battered cities. If she could paint all that, perhaps she'd reach them.

Then it wouldn't be Dan's message, but her own.

The notion startled her. Laurel pushed at the tortoise-shell frame of her glasses with an index finger, gaze running quickly over the page on the podium in front of her. She'd lost her place.

". . . but this issue, um, the cuts in Social Security proposed by the present administration, mean severe deprivation to the senior citizens of this country."

She didn't like what came next. Dan's proposal meant

another reduction in Medicare instead. What would happen to half the people in this room when they could no longer visit a physician without counting the cost beforehand?

Laurel turned the pages of her prepared speech facedown and removed her glasses. Despite her commitment to Dan's campaign, she couldn't keep saying things she didn't believe.

"I realize the necessity of compromise. But when I look around this room, I see real people, not statistics. I see former schoolteachers, physicians, bus drivers, and homemakers. Dan Benedict's future constituents comprise a true cross section of society—from the wealth of Brookline to the poverty of South Boston and the more rural pockets of hopelessness—and though Social Security reductions may be changed under Dan's proposal to a less threatening 'freeze' for the short term, I would hope to see medical benefits untouched over the long term."

She caught Teague's eye, and his frown. Dan might wring her neck on Monday in Lexington, but for now she heard applause and smiled. They were clapping for her words, her feeling for them. The sensation was heady. For the first time Laurel understood why the senator had spent his life in this courtship dance with the voters.

As she stepped down, the crowd surged to its feet, and Laurel was quickly surrounded.

"Mrs. Benedict, God bless you."

"My son says that by the next century there won't be no Medicare."

"Laurel—" an elderly woman clutched her sleeve. "My sister in Worcester, she's sick with diabetes, last summer she lost her sight. Without her Medic—"

Teague Michaels imposed his squat form between Laurel and the voters. "Ladies, gentlemen, I'm sorry but the candidate's wife has other obligations. Dan has your interests at heart, I assure you. Sorry, let us through." Under his breath, he muttered, "Dammit, where's Security?"

It had been a hell of a day, Teague thought. First, Dan taking off at noon, leaving him to explain the cancellation of two engagements in the Framingham area. Then moments ago, during Laurel's speech, he'd had a confrontation with Ryder McKendrick, which had also proved disastrous.

"Where's Benedict gone to?"

"The press of business," Michaels had answered.

Shrewd gray eyes had wandered from Teague's glowering expression to Laurel at the podium. "I thought the only thing of consequence just now was getting himself elected. Seems strange that before the Tuesday primary—"

"You writing again, McKendrick? Or just poking your nose in where it don't belong?"

Ryder smiled, as if he realized that Teague's grammar lapsed when he got angry. "One's part of the other, isn't it? You know, Michaels, the candidate's been giving me the slip. I caught him in Pittsfield after Worcester, before Framingham, but now he's gone again." Ryder paused. "Like a thief in the night."

For Teague, the press was like a constant toothache. He swore to himself, then pointed at Laurel. "Why don't you let Dan worry about last-minute campaign adjustments and just enjoy the little lady's speech?" He'd nodded toward the rapt audience. "She's got them, doesn't she?" Laurel's skills were improving, and she didn't seem as nervous. "Take a few notes. You might come up with something better than your usual thinly veiled lies."

"Benedict hasn't accused me of lying since I joined this campaign. I wouldn't either if I were you."

McKendrick had leaned against the wall, not speaking for the rest of Laurel's presentation, in which she had violated the first law of campaigning for her husband: she had expressed her own opinion. The deviation, judging by the smile that tugged at his mouth, hadn't been lost on Ryder McKendrick.

Dragging her through the crush of voters toward the rear doors of the civic auditorium, Teague silently cursed again. He could see the headlines now.

He hurried her along the hallway. But at least today one thing had turned out right. McKendrick's attention had been captured by the speech, not the woman. When it came to a choice between Laurel Benedict and a good story under McKendrick's byline, there was no competition. Which only worked in his favor, Teague thought. The same as it did with Dan, who wanted to get elected far more than he wanted to please his wife.

"Take a breather," Teague ordered, slowing their pace at last. Thank God the auditorium acoustics had been poor, and Laurel had fidgeted with the mike. Maybe enough people had missed her little declaration of independence.

A liberal. The senator would kill her; Dan would, too.

Spotting several people behind them in the hall, Michaels urged Laurel into an empty office. "They'll be looking for you. We don't need a question-and-answer session today. Not after—"

"Don't lecture. I said what I wanted to say."

"You had what you were supposed to say right in front of you."

Bracing her hands on the desk, she looked down at them. "You needn't tell me how angry he's going to be. It's occurred to me already."

"He should be. It's not your place to make policy."

She glanced around. "And what is my place, Teague?"

His tone was overly patient. "As the wife of the candidate, you—"

"I meant the senator," she said.

"Frasier? But why—"

"Because he taught me better political manners than to step on his toes in public. Dan's, too, of course."

Michaels walked toward her. Amazement widened his eyes. He hadn't seen Laurel as a thoughtful woman until now. "Relax. We can get a spot in the papers, use McKendrick—"

She turned, smiling. "I doubt that."

The movement had brought her up close to him, and Teague let his hands glide over the firm, smooth skin of her upper arms. Laurel recoiled when he touched her but didn't step away.

"You and Dan may think that Ryder McKendrick's for sale, and even the senator says so, but I don't think it's true."

"We'll see." This wasn't the direction he wanted these few moments of privacy to take. "Let's forget politics," he suggested. "Take a couple of hours to unwind over drinks and dinner. We'll formulate a rebuttal to any unpleasantness from the press about today."

"I'm leaving for Gloucester in an hour."

She tried to draw away, but he tightened his hold, and her hazel eyes turned darker, rich brown overtaking green. He wondered whether she felt fear of him; the possibility excited him. Laurel Frasier Benedict, he thought, child of privilege, the refined woman who always condescended to him. She'd fight, but he'd win. He wanted to laugh, exultant that Dan had left town today, left Laurel for his other, secret life.

Few people other than Teague knew about Maria. The result was a tighter partnership: Teague, promoting Dan's political possibilities; Teague, handling the day-to-day business of Maria. It was Teague Michaels who kept the accounts, made the investments, issued the checks.

Teague Michaels who knew about the house in Shelby, about the horse stabled nearby, the station wagon and clothing bills, and exactly how much was spent each month for food, utilities, maintenance. Dan Benedict's weakness was Teague Michaels's strength.

Dan was going to Washington, all right; but by God, so was he. Teague Michaels, with his rumpled suits and stubborn cowlick. Smart as the devil, though. How could Dan object, if he ever knew, to Teague . . . and Laurel?

"Let me go," she said, but he only smiled into her darkened eyes.

"It's been a long day, Laurel. Tense." He forced her closer, one hand clamped behind her neck. He drew her head up toward him and back, and her mouth opened. "You don't want to do that," he said, knowing she would scream. "Haven't we got headlines enough?"

Her pulse thumped under his hand. "If you don't let me go, I guess not."

Teague's mouth was a whisper away from hers when a hard voice spoke from the doorway. "Excuse me."

Ryder McKendrick's gaze ran over them, and Laurel took in a deep gulp of air. Moving away from Michaels, she murmured, "Thank you."

"What for?" Ryder said.

What did she expect, when she hadn't spoken four words to him since Springfield? Head down, moments later Laurel sped along the corridor, her heart pounding because of Teague, telling herself that she would have stopped him on her own, that she was only looking for the ladies' room now. What had she expected from Ryder? A classic rescue?

"Laurel."

She heard his footsteps, following as he had that morning in Gloucester to the beach. Then he swung her around, gently. "What happened back there? That wasn't a political discussion."

She kept her gaze averted. "No."

"I came to tell Michaels—and you—that the car is waiting out front. Your husband's security people are on the verge of panic, but I figured the two missing principals must be together, so—"

"Always the consummate newshound, aren't you?"

"What's that supposed to mean?"

"That if I'm with Teague Michaels, alone in an abandoned office, we must be—" She broke off, then began again. What else would he think of her, with that harsh question, What for? "That I must be giving out more ... phony passion."

"I didn't think that," Ryder murmured. "Actually, I envisioned you deep in some cover-up conspiracy for the newspapers ... me. Speaking of which, that was a pretty impassioned speech you made back there." He gestured toward the auditorium as Laurel looked at him. He was smiling slightly.

"Thank you."

"You're more than welcome."

Pride surged through her. "I believe every word of what I said, Ryder."

"I'm glad."

"I shocked myself," she admitted when his smile broadened to reach his eyes.

"I'm glad again."

She smiled back, shakily, then took a deep breath. "Well, you said the car's waiting. I'm on my way to Hilary's."

Ryder sobered. "Laurel, did he hurt you?"

She saw more than quick anger in his eyes. "No, but it's not the first time he's touched me. Once before, soon after we met, he—he—"

She was trembling, and couldn't go on.

"Weeks," he said through his teeth, "two goddamn weeks of this. I've had enough. Come on," he added, "let's get rid of Michaels and the limo. I'm driving you to Gloucester."

✳

✳ *CHAPTER 14* ✳

✳

IT HADN'T BEEN easy. Getting away from Teague as well as Dan's security men took some doing. First one, then the other. "I'll take the limousine to the hotel, Teague," Laurel had said as he began to climb into the rear seat. "Alone." He had stared at her, unwilling to provoke a scene. "I'll send the car back for you while I'm packing."

The limo had been on its way to the civic auditorium again when Laurel stepped from the elevator into the hotel lobby. Outside, Ryder waited with his car.

"Not your usual mode of transportation these days," he'd said, "but it ought to get you there."

"Let's go. I dismissed Dan's guards for the night. Told them I planned to go straight to bed after dinner in my room. I'll phone from Hilary's."

She'd tell Teague that she'd rented a car, wanting the drive to herself. He could hardly object, even if the security men would. Laurel leaned into the surprising comfort of Ryder's front seat and let the low hum of the Datsun's engine lull her into sleep. They were pulling into Hilary's drive before she awoke to the smell of the sea more than an hour later, embarrassed.

"I'm sorry. I make a dreadful traveling companion."

"Only when you're snoring."

"I don't snore!" But she should have stayed awake to prepare herself for Gloucester. Being here with Ryder threatened to bring all the memories of a rainy weekend to life again. "I don't, do I?"

He laughed, taking her bags from the car just as Hilary burst from the house, preventing his reply. "Welcome! I've been watching the road for hours."

"We were held up a little," Laurel explained.

Hilary gave her a quick kiss, then turned to Ryder in surprise, kissing him heartily on both cheeks. "I'm so glad you could come, too, McKendrick."

Laurel's throat tightened. "Ryder kindly offered to play chauffeur."

"I've got to start back," he added, and shot her an apologetic glance.

"Nonsense. I've cooked for the entire Supreme Court, some recipe of Myra's—a favorite of the justice's—that I neglected to cut down. Please stay for dinner." She linked an arm through Ryder's, both of his laden with luggage so that he was helpless. "We'll convince you to stay the night after you've eaten."

In the kitchen, where Laurel and Ryder had once shared coffee and intimate midnight meals, she produced spicy conch chowder, an enticing green salad full of late summer vegetables, and fresh-baked bread. "And for dessert," Hilary announced, "one of Myra's neighbors' homemade apple pies."

Chattering all the while, she placed big wedges on delicate china plates. Her cheeks were flushed, her eyes sparkling, but Laurel had the impression it wasn't all excitement. Hilary had virtually exploded out the front door when they arrived.

Laurel decided to probe a little. "How's your back?" she asked, stirring cream into her coffee. "I detect only a slight limp, but over the phone you'd have had me believe you were ready for traction."

Hilary grinned. "Actually, cleaning up this place for your visit seemed to get the kinks out. I think I've been lying around too much."

"You needed the vacation."

"Yes, but I think it's back to the grind on Monday. And I'd rather not have the same incentive for another rest. Or the same company."

At that instant, the back door swung open and Sebastian Noble strode into the kitchen. Laurel came to her feet.

"Sebastian! How wonderful to see you."

He crossed to her, leaning to kiss her cheek. "We're honored, the humble folk of Gloucester. I've got used to seeing you on television in a mob of strangers—limousines and microphones, the candidate at your side. . . ."

His inquisitive glance met Ryder's.

"Nice." Hilary focused on the silver coffee spoon in her hand, as if studying her reflection upside down. "Now say good night to the adults and toddle back home like a good boy, Sebastian."

The rudeness astonished Laurel. Hilary's face was pale, Sebastian's full of sudden color.

She smiled at Sebastian. "I don't believe you've met Ryder." Laurel placed a hand on his sleeve. "Ryder McKendrick, Sebastian Noble. Ryder's a newsman, covering Dan's campaign, and my part in it," she explained. "Sebastian restores classic automobiles."

"For fun and profit," Sebastian said, shaking hands. "You wouldn't be a foreign correspondent, would you? I think I remember the byline."

"Yeah, I covered the mess in Nam. A few places since. But you wouldn't have been out of kindergarten then."

Sebastian laughed. "I'm not as young as I look." He

glanced at Hilary. "Or as dim-witted."

"Classic cars," Ryder repeated, much to Laurel's relief. She liked Sebastian, and Hilary; it pained her to see them snipe at each other. "What have you got in stock?"

"I seem to be specializing in English cars recently. I've been working on a Morgan—" he shot another look at Hilary "—from the wood up, but you might be interested in the '53 Jag that's waiting for a buyer."

"Not an XK 120?"

"In show condition."

"May I see it?"

"Of course. In fact . . ." Sebastian looked speculative. "I'm wondering if you might lend me a bit of expertise, take a few shots for me if you've got a camera handy. I've been meaning to place the ads but haven't got round to it."

Ryder grinned. "My stuff's in the car. Ladies, if you'll excuse us . . ."

The door shut behind them. Hilary turned the spoon over several times, then laid it soundlessly on her saucer. Outside, Laurel heard the quick burst of Ryder's laughter, carrying through the dark. "Hilary, what's wrong?"

"My back's kicking up a little."

Laurel leaned over the table, bending her head to look into Hilary's downcast face. "This is me, remember? Your old roommate who's suffered with you through everything from tonsillitis to an F in Western Civ to—"

"Death itself."

"Hilary. It's Sebastian Noble, isn't it? You've . . . quarreled."

"I wouldn't waste my time."

Laurel watched Hilary rise, scattering silverware to the floor. Stacking plates to help, Laurel said gently, "What was the fight about?"

"That man—that odious man—never knocks, you

know that? He simply flings open my door, any time of the day or night, and walks in, uninvited. I don't want him around. The next time he tries that, so help me I'll find a shotgun. Myra's got everything else stashed here, there must be a stray weapon or two."

"Hilary, calm down." Laurel took the dishes to the sink. "Now sit, and tell me. Everything. You're not leaving this kitchen until you do."

Sighing, Hilary sat down. "All right. He—does this sound properly outraged?—he attacked me. He's not the pussycat you think. He's gauche and insufferable. For ten days I haven't had a second's peace."

"He made a pass at you!"

"Yes, he made a pass. Clumsy, of course. What else from someone who probably shaves once a week?"

Laurel bit her lip against the smile. "Well, well. Perhaps there's hope after all."

"You can't possibly think that I have any romantic interest . . . Laurel, I despise him."

"I'll shut up if you'll give me the lurid details. Where, when, how?"

Hilary groaned. "I'd rather hear about you, and Ryder McKendrick, mild-mannered reporter for a great metropolitan newspaper? I have the feeling he slips into phone booths and becomes someone else entirely."

Her pulse jumping, Laurel said, "Superman?"

"Wishful thinking, perhaps. But Laurel, he has the look of someone who's been straining at the leash too long. Is Dan making his life a hell?" she asked. "Or are you?"

What was she trying to do to him? Dan had been in Shelby four hours, but the feeling of having just arrived wouldn't leave him. He felt as if he'd rung the doorbell minutes before, as if he hadn't dared to use his key because he couldn't trust his welcome.

In fact, he'd slipped into the house, wanting to surprise her. He'd found Maria humming to herself as she fixed a meatloaf for dinner.

"I didn't expect you this soon," she'd said. "You should have called."

"You know I was in Framingham with the campaign. I can't call every ten minutes. I couldn't give you a time. We—I—had a dinner last evening, and a couple of whistlestops this morning." He felt uneasy at the coolness in her eyes.

"Dinner with whom?"

Dan watched her crack eggs into a bowl. "A congressman and his wife. Strictly business." He smiled, forgetting that she had her back turned. "Strictly boring."

"Did Laurel think so?"

He froze, the grin disappearing. "We aren't going around about that again, are we?" Dan let his hands span her narrow waist. "Can't you offer me dinner first? I tried to get you earlier, before my first campaign stop, but you were already out." He didn't mention politicking on the way from Framingham.

"I'm trying to find a job. I want money of my own, Dan." Maria looked into his face as she turned in his arms. "Some control over what happens to me."

"Christ almighty, that's ridiculous! I don't come here looking for a damned career woman." He hauled her closer. "And I don't want to be tested on my feelings just now." He had drawn her, silent, toward their bedroom. "Take those off—" he'd gestured at the cotton top and jeans "—and let me see what I've been missing for too long."

I've missed you, too, he wanted to hear her say. She hadn't. And like the welcome she hadn't given, their lovemaking had lacked something.

"Let's talk in the kitchen," she'd said afterward.

He'd always kept his professional life, his marriage, apart from what they shared; but tonight, Maria wanted to know about the campaign, about Laurel again.

"Watch the late news if you want to know," he finally said. "Dammit, Maria, this weekend wasn't easy to arrange, and I'll have to campaign all day tomorrow plus half of Sunday." He'd left Laurel with his afternoon speech making today, and stolen the hours that belonged to Ned from Sunday. "Let's at least keep what we have for ourselves."

"Does it ever occur to you that I might not want to be a convenience?" She smiled slightly to soften the words. "I thought we'd run over to the stable after we eat, if you don't mind. I haven't worked Gold at all this week."

Angry, he wouldn't ask about the job she'd mentioned.

"Of course I mind. If you're so damn preoccupied, why not put that horse up for sale?"

Maria only smiled again. "Everybody needs a hobby for weekends."

Later, Dan followed her in misery to the station wagon, to the stables, and under bright floodlights, watched her take the cursed jumps one at a time, perfectly; terrified as always, he clutched the wooden rail of the fence and prayed. But she'd become a beautiful rider to watch, even for him.

"Ned has such fear," he told her when they were driving home. "I keep hoping he'll outgrow it, but he never does."

"Storm is a calm mount, Dan. I wouldn't worry." As a favor to Dan, she had selected the horse herself and overseen Storm's initial move to Brookline. "I'm sure Ned has capable teachers."

"They don't seem to do much good."

The flat statement closed the topic. But when had his

son, Laurel's son, begun to creep into their conversations?

"Forget Ned. I love you, Maria." There was no answer. "I need you."

Turning into the driveway, she said, "Why? I see you all the time now, nearly every night. Looking so competent, and in control. Smiling at the cameras. Always ready with the right word. Your arm around Laurel." Maria shrugged again. "I wonder why you'd think you need me, Dan. I can only deliver a single vote."

"I'd love you even if you didn't." He tried to make her smile. "Even if you campaigned against me."

His tone said the notion was inconceivable, and he saw the corner of her mouth lift at his teasing. "I'd never campaign against you," Maria said. "I do want you to win. I wish I could help you. Tuesday's the primary, isn't it? You'll be at some hotel in Boston, in a fancy suite with half a dozen television sets blaring the returns."

"No, we've decided to stay at home."

"There'll be a victory speech at headquarters then, a party for your campaign workers." Stopping the car, she turned dark eyes to his. "And I'll be here, watching. Missing you, as I do, wondering when I'll see you again, except on television."

"Next week," he said rashly, and then, "Damn, Laurel's been nagging me to visit Ned. I'll get out of it," Dan decided.

She shook her head. "He needs you, too. A little boy needs his father. No," she said, getting out of the car. "You go to—which is his school?"

"Dawson."

"You go to Dawson then."

He sighed. Normally adept at bending others to his will, he wondered why he couldn't break her mood. What had she said on the telephone that day? *Everything's still the same, even though it's different.* "Maria, it's not as if we're close. He won't allow it."

"Maybe you don't try very hard, Dan." Her voice was soft, defeated. "I wish I could help," she repeated. "Somehow."


"Thanks for the help."

Sebastian held the back door for Ryder as they rejoined the two women, who were still sitting at the kitchen table.

"All the ad work done?" Laurel looked up with a smile at Ryder, burdened with equipment.

"Well, we could have used a few daylight shots." He turned to Hilary. "Didn't Sebastian tell me that you have photographic aspirations? Why not take a roll of film for him tomorrow?"

"I don't think I can."

Hilary wouldn't elaborate. Offering fresh coffee laced with brandy, she ushered everyone into the parlor, where a cozy fire burned. The night had become chill along the coast, and the reflected glow of flames warmed the room.

Laurel tucked her legs beneath her on one of the facing suede-covered sofas to avoid the clutter of photographic gear on the floor, and Ryder's leather bag. "I could just stay here," she said, "out of the hustle of campaigning." She stifled a yawn. "Hasn't it been good to get away, Hilary?"

"Good, but not long enough."

"Spoken like a true, overworked international media wonder."

Ryder grinned at Sebastian's taunt. He picked up a current magazine from the coffee table, the cover photo of Hilary uppermost. "Well, she is."

Sebastian ignored it. "I'm well aware of that."

"Hilary's planning to chuck her career." Laurel lifted her mug of coffee and brandy in salute. "Take a year off and spend her fortune on cameras, jet away to the Dark Continent."

Ryder's gaze sought Hilary's. "Is that true?"

"As true as daydreams get, I suppose."

"Why just a daydream?"

Sebastian answered, lazily inspecting his coffee. "How would we all survive without her face in at least three magazines every month?"

"Sebastian, shut up."

"At least you've given up telling me to go home."

"Go home," Hilary said, but he merely smiled and held out his cup.

"Got any more of that brandy? I buy only the cheap stuff."

Laurel laughed, not imagining he was serious. "As long as we seem to be escaping the troublesome present... what are your dreams, Sebastian?"

"Ladies first."

Laurel didn't hesitate. "To lie in the sun for a year and not have to make another tedious speech. To read until my eyes fall out, to draw when I feel like it. Have a baby."

Sebastian's speculative gaze went to Ryder.

"Don't look at me. I'm not planning to have a baby."

Laurel was the only one who knew he wasn't joking. "Ryder wants to be the best photojournalist in the world." He sat next to her on the loveseat, and his arm so casually touching hers brought too many memories to mind. His anti-child statement seemed the least of them just now. Laurel looked away. "Sebastian?"

"To go on restoring classic automobiles until the happy day when some fabulously wealthy woman—" he glanced at Hilary "—like the countess comes to buy one of them. And in the bargain, gets me."

Hilary groaned. "Sebastian, go to hell."

"I think I'm in the middle of a rehearsal for *Who's Afraid of Virginia Woolf,*" Ryder said to Laurel. She drew away from him, her body sensitized to the light touch of his shirt sleeve against her arm. That rainy night here in Gloucester, with Hilary gone, they'd come downstairs to eat and Ryder had drawn her down onto this sofa, the suede against her bare skin and. . . .

"They're crazy about each other," she said. "Hilary and Sebastian."

"I could tell." His gaze rested on the magazine between them. Then Laurel realized what she was doing. Trying to suppress her memories, she had rummaged in her purse, found a pencil nub, and was idly sketching in the margin of a page. Shutting out the background noise of Sebastian's squabble with Hilary, making things worse for Laurel, Ryder leaned closer. His fingers brushed hers. "It looks like . . . a bouquet of geraniums."

Was he remembering, too? The evening they'd shared dinner while she drew stylized flowers on oilcloth, and tried to find a way to tell him she was Dan's wife?

"Take this." Ryder took a tablet of paper from his camera case. "Try them."

Laurel looked toward Hilary and Sebastian, who were engaged in a mock argument, or so she wanted to think, about vintage versus new automobiles. "The classiest car in the world, Sebastian, is the DeNobili X7, absolutely classic elegance, with a hell of a monster under the hood. My stepfather owned one."

"Absolutely classic crap," Sebastian muttered.

"Are you kidding? Ferrari wishes he could design a twelve-cylinder like that."

"Somebody, someday, I hope to God, will wipe DeNobili's face—and that car—right off the track."

The vehemence of his statement and the flash of dark, hooded eyes made the room go still. "Well," Hilary said, and then nothing more.

Even Laurel's memories and the awareness of the man only inches from her had been interrupted. Her hand moved faster on the blank sheet of paper, her movements swift and light, until Ryder pulled the sketch away.

He handed it across to Sebastian on the other sofa.

"Sensational." She'd drawn them closer together than they were, as close as she and Ryder, with Sebastian leaning into Hilary's shoulder and her head falling slightly back against him. In his expression was tenderness and wonder; in Hilary's, trust and contentment, neither of which had been visible in a thousand magazine photographs since Chip Brewster's disappearance.

"Laurel, you're in danger of becoming a romantic."

As Hilary reached for the pencil sketch, Sebastian snatched it up, and rose to his feet. Before she could retreat, he had leaned down and planted a swift kiss on her lips. "Have another brandy for me, my friends. I'm off to get this in the safe before—"

"Sebastian Noble! Come back here!"

"I'm keeping it. Thanks, Laurel. Good night, all."

Laurel and Ryder were still laughing when Hilary came back into the house, having pursued Sebastian halfway across the lawn, and slammed the door. "Didn't I tell you?" she demanded of Laurel. "That man ought to be locked up."

"But he has such fun at your expense," Ryder pointed out. "Though I wonder why that reaction to DeNobili's X7? The man's reputation is unassailable."

"Sheer ego," Hilary said. "He probably thinks he could build a better one himself."

Laurel felt too weary from the day's speech making, and too lazy by the fire to participate. Her memories and Ryder's nearness had drained her. She shifted position, nestling into the corner of the sofa, and listened to the deep murmur of his voice as the conversation, over yet another brandy, eased back into the subject of photography. He hadn't been satisfied with Hilary's off-putting remarks about her dream.

Soon he had her engrossed in a discussion of filters, f-stops, depth of field—whatever that was—and the relative merits of various lenses. "Slap a 135mm telephoto, or better yet, say, a 75–150mm zoom on that baby, you'd get a hell of a take," Ryder insisted. "Almost unlimited versatility. Split-second framing, focusing. Red, I'm telling you, those wildlife shots would jump at you."

"Would," Hilary said with a smile.

"Well, if you ever want to get off the merry-go-round for that year in Africa, I know a guy who used to be with AP during Laos. He kind of dropped out after that and runs a small preserve now, mostly big cats, not far from Nairobi."

"That sounds wonderful."

Ryder didn't miss the sudden light in her eyes. "Let me know when you're ready. I'll give him a call."

"Thanks."

Laurel had been lost in her own world: on the next sheet of blank paper from Ryder's pad, she'd started another sketch. Taking time for shadings and light this time, she drew a face, his face. Then he stood up, stretching, and she couldn't finish, she wouldn't get his smile right.

"I'd better start driving," he said, and she felt instantly bereft.

"You're a lovely man, McKendrick." Hilary rose from the other sofa. "What would entice you to stay? How about a terrific book full of wonderful close-up Stieglitz faces?"

"Just a fresh cup of black coffee, I think. To counteract the brandy so I don't fall asleep at the wheel."

"I meant for the night." She smiled while Laurel recalled their first night here when Ryder had come back in the fog. The sky now was clear and crisp. "There are plenty of spare rooms. You may have your choice—" her gaze skipped to Laurel "—of arrangements."

"I'm sure not."

Discussing wide-angle lenses and various speeds of film, he followed Hilary to the kitchen and returned, sipping at a mug of steaming coffee. He set it on an end table to pack his battered leather bag, but forgot the pad of paper he'd lent Laurel, who tucked it out of sight. She'd return it after she'd completed the sketch of him.

Ryder looked at her. "I'll see you in Lexington. Walk me to the car?"

She hesitated, but only for a moment. Or had Hilary, with a last good-bye to Ryder, shut her outside with him? The air was cold and blowing; she could smell winter coming. On the porch Laurel shivered.

"Here, take my jacket."

She wrapped herself in it, breathing his scent and telling herself she'd been a fool to let him drive her here tonight. She smelled lime and faint musk with a hint of good tobacco. Here, of all places. Ryder shifted from one foot to the other.

"I don't want to go, Laurel."

"I can't ask you to stay."

"You'd like me to," he said.

She couldn't break the hold of his gaze and admitted, "Yes. I'm afraid I would."

That quickly she was backed against the house, Ryder's hands running lightly down the jacket lapels, his knuckles grazing her breasts. When his head lowered, she moaned, "Ryder, don't."

"Have pity, dammit. All night, for weeks, I haven't thought of anything but you."

She felt the pressure of him, his heat as he leaned into her and took his mouth from her earlobe down her throat to the collar of her blouse. Her head fell back, and Laurel shuddered, thinking how preferable his touch was to that of Teague Michaels. It seemed to cleanse her, but she didn't stop her protest, because she thought of Dan, too. "Please . . ."

Ryder only raised his head, his mouth seeking hers at last. The air was cold around them, his body so warm, his kiss as it had been one rainy morning. Hearing the crash of surf in the distance now, she held on for long moments. "Nobody's waiting inside," he whispered. "Hilary's gone upstairs."

She smiled against his brandy-flavored mouth. "Discreet if not tactful."

"Come out to the car, please, Laurel."

"No," she managed.

"Then down to the beach."

"I can't!"

She'd gone before, and could still feel the grains of sand against her skin, the rain against her hair. His mouth, so warm and tempting. *Jump, Laurel, jump.* As a child she'd broken an arm; as a woman she had nearly broken her heart, and perhaps his, too. But she had learned something. She couldn't hide behind Lexa again, just as she couldn't betray Dan, or her own strong sense of loyalty.

Ryder and Hilary were right; she needed something for her own. But Ryder McKendrick—and perhaps losing her marriage instead of saving it? No, she decided, and on Sunday she'd borrow a car to visit Ned by herself.

An affair with Ryder might not be cheap or, as Laurel suspected, lightly taken by either of them, but it would be irresponsible. It was something Lexa might do, but never Laurel Frasier Benedict.

So when Ryder touched her cheek, she shook her head. "I can't," she said again.

"You can," he corrected. "You just won't."

He kissed her, hard, then drew slowly away, his lips the last to leave off touching. For a moment, he stood assessing her features, the effect he'd had on her. "I hope you have the same dreams tonight that I'm going to have."

He'd walked nearly to his car before Laurel called out in a shaky voice, "Ryder, your jacket."

His tone was husky. "Bring it here."

Instead she tossed it from the bottom of the steps. Standing by the Datsun, Ryder caught it, then laughed. She saw the white flash of his teeth in the darkness; it was the smile she had wanted for her sketch of him, and despite her best intentions she felt her heart ache.

"Oh, Laurel," he said softly, "you still think it isn't going to happen again?"

# ❋ *CHAPTER 15* ❋

NEVER, SHE THOUGHT. It seemed the key word, if any, to her life.

With a sigh, Maria Cruz left the late-model station wagon to survey the broad lawns that formed a quadrangle among sandstone buildings covered with ivy.

For a moment she stood, confused. Then she saw the school's low stables beyond a gentle rise of land in the distance, and hurried toward them. It was already half past the hour; daily lessons began "promptly at two," the headmaster's secretary had informed her.

Telephoning the school on Monday after Dan's weekend with her, Maria had been shaking. What would her mother, staunch Catholic and firm believer in truth, have thought of her daughter, lying? "This is Mrs. Daniel Benedict. I would like my son's schedule for Tuesday."

The thought of Ned, Dan's son, made her pulse increase its speed. What would he look like? Maria grazed a hand over her flat abdomen, feeling a faint twinge as she touched one of two short scars through the twill cloth.

Edwin Eliot Frasier Benedict. He'd live up to the string of famous names, to the surname that soon would be. She imagined him: tall and lithe with steel blue eyes, like

Dan's. And of course that same formality to be overcome at first. She anticipated that, too. Dan had said as much.

Still, her heart drummed at the first nickers from the stable, then an answering whinny. A voice called out, "Canter, gentlemen." Taking a deep breath, Maria made a last assessment of her trim khaki-colored jodhpurs, silk blouse, and hunt jacket. Then she started down the hill, her black riding boots gleaming in the sun.

"You'll come to your senses one day, *niña*," her mother had said. "God will guide you. Away from sin with that man, away—"

"Mama. Please." It was an argument as familiar to Maria as the aroma of saddle leather. She stood in the stable doorway, her eyes adjusting to the change of light, and thinking, ten years. But it seemed forever that she'd loved Dan Benedict, that she'd wanted his child.

Maria gazed through the dimness at the six schoolboys cantering around the indoor ring. She'd always been so sure of Dan, until a few weeks ago.

Getting a job—almost any job—had become an obsession. In Dan's absence with the campaign, she'd put together a resumé. A year with Dobbs, Fairfield, but she'd quit the company when Dan moved her to Shelby. Before that, she'd worked as a receptionist.

"Thirty-six years old." A personnel manager would skim her brief resumé. "You've been out of the labor force some time, Ms. Cruz."

The rest was slow humiliation. No marriage, no family. She tried ill health for an excuse, but certainly it didn't help.

She'd thought of asking Dan to help find her a position somewhere, perhaps in Boston, but his first reaction hadn't encouraged her. Was she wrong to want some independence? He did provide amply for her. And after the election, Dan assured her, they'd . . .

Maria broke off the thought, watching the boys on horseback. He made promises to Ned, and didn't keep them. Her gaze swept the riders in the ring, who were slowing to the trot. Which of them was Dan's son?

The procession, raggedly spaced, jounced past. Then she saw the black gelding. Storm. Why hadn't she realized that she would know the horse she'd picked out for him before she recognized the boy?

He was not what she expected, but smaller, slighter. His thin frame bounced up and down with kidney-shaking jolts.

She silently cursed the instructor, who stood in the center of the ring, obscured by rising clouds of dust and saying little. Ned's newest teacher didn't seem to be doing much; it wasn't the boy's fault he was poor at posting.

Maria waited for the lesson to end, her gaze following the instructor from the ring. The others filed past, laughing among themselves. To her relief, Ned lagged behind. She called to him, softly, and he swung his head around.

"Ned," Maria said again, walking from the shadows. "Come here."

His hesitation confused the horse, and Storm stopped, then broke into a graceless trot. "Pull him in," Maria commanded. "Your hands are too loose. Bring Storm around, to me."

Ned sawed at the reins. The horse's great dark head arched into his chest. "I can't," Ned cried.

"Both hands, not one." She watched him closely. "Now turn him left." She saw the horse balk at the command. "Keep turning him, Ned. Don't let him boss you, he's being naughty. Make a tight circle, as tight as you can. Tighter." The gelding lurched and Maria ordered, "Show him who's in charge. That's right. Now come to me. Slower. Don't let him out, that's too much. Good, good."

When he reached her, Ned was beaming.

Answering the smile, Maria stroked a hand along the black's neck. "He's magnificent, but a touch headstrong."

"He makes my arms tired."

"He's a handful now, but intelligent, and you can learn together. I thought so when I . . ."

"Who are you?"

Maria paused, looking up into alert hazel eyes, not blue. "I'm—a teacher."

"I've never seen you here before."

"I don't work at Dawson, Ned."

"Do you teach horses?"

She relaxed slightly. He wouldn't run away; for a second, she'd feared he might. "Yes, I guess I do teach horses. I have one of my own."

"What's his name?"

"Fool's Gold. He's a chestnut, quite large."

"Bigger than Storm?" Ned patted the horse.

"Yes. About sixteen hands."

He pursed his lips, trying to whistle. He had Dan's dark hair, his chin. The clear eyes would be Laurel's. And the smile? It was tentative, but when it broke through completely, all his own, Maria felt captivated. "That's awfully big," Ned murmured. "Do you need a ladder to get on him?"

She laughed. "Sometimes I feel that I do."

Lately, all the time. Depression, her doctor said; it would go away. Like a postpartum malaise, she thought, though he hadn't said that. He had urged her to keep busy.

"I noticed some trouble with your posting during the class," she told Ned.

"I can't post," he said in self-disgust. "If Storm's going up, I'm always coming back down again." To illustrate, he rubbed at the seat of his navy jodhpurs.

Maria smiled. "A common problem. I've had it myself."

"Nobody else does. Nobody here." Ned glanced toward the stables and the sound of boyish laughter.

"It only looks easier for the rest of them. I saw some pretty terrible displays out there a while ago."

"You did? Honest?"

"Honest." Taking hold of Storm's bridle, Maria led the horse to the center of the ring again. She ordered Ned to urge the black into a slow trot. "Try to feel his rhythm first, Ned. Every horse has a different one, just as every person has a different walk. Gold's is long and rolling, which makes my job easier. I don't have to rise and fall as often as you will with the shorter stride. But feel it."

Ned stood in the stirrups, then plunked onto the saddle again. Once, twice. A dozen times. "Knees in, heels down, hands even on the reins. Rhythm, Ned. No, you don't have to stand, just lift a little. Not so much. There," Maria cried at the first perfect melding of horse and boy. "There, Ned!"

He trotted back to her, sweating, his face full of joy. Maria could have hugged him. He was a beautiful child, and in that moment she could have turned her back on Dan forever for neglecting him. "I can do it!" he yelled. "Lady, I can do it!"

They were grinning at each other when Maria realized the instructor was watching her from the entry to the ring. Then he started toward them.

"I have to go, Ned," she said quickly.

"Will you come back? Will you help me again?"

"Yes. I'll try."

"Hello . . . Mrs. Benedict? I'm—" the instructor began, but Maria ducked her head and, with a quick squeeze of Ned's right hand where it gripped the reins, hurried from the dark hall into the sun.

"What the—? Wasn't that your mother?"

Shaking his head, Ned gazed forlornly toward the open

doorway, squinting into the light. Storm danced under him, but he kept careful control. Until today, he'd never enjoyed being on Storm half so much. Ned imagined the woman as Dawson's new riding master.

The instructor looked up at him, the smile fading. "Who was she, then?"

"I don't know," Ned answered.

Sitting next to Dan the next morning, Laurel smiled as the Audi flew along the turnpike, eating up miles.

"What are you grinning at?" he asked.

"Surprises. I love surprises, and so does Ned." Laurel touched the back of Dan's hand on the steering wheel. It was Wednesday morning, with only a few clouds drifting overhead, and other than one brief qualm about last night, she had a new lease on life. "Thank you for changing your mind."

"I shouldn't have. Teague's still cursing over the Lions' Club speech in Plymouth tonight."

"He likes something to curse about. Even this morning."

Last night she had watched the primary returns with Dan, Teague Michaels, the senator, and half a dozen aides at the house on Beacon Hill. "Damn close," the senator kept saying. "Closer than a hair." Though he loved campaigning, he'd always been a nervous wreck from the minute the polls opened.

Voter turnout had been heavy on a sunny autumn day, and heaviest in the industrial areas where Jack Sommers seemed unbeatable.

But at midnight the screen had flashed Dan's narrow victory. Dan Benedict would carry the party standard in November against the Republican, Jay Heron.

Laurel had stood watching the television, not knowing how she felt. Elated, because she had helped him to win and was glad for him? Depressed, at what this first victory meant for their lives, hers and Dan's and Ned's?

"Congratulations, Laurel. You've got a winner."

"Dan's our man!"

"Listen, little lady, you and I need some conference time. Starting tomorrow I'll step up your commitments so that—"

Dan interrupted Teague, who was holding an open notebook and jotting down appointments. "Let me kiss my wife before you drag her off to Concord or somewhere in the middle of the night."

Laurel felt herself enfolded in a sweaty embrace. Dan had discarded his suit jacket hours before, and his dark hair lay plastered to his skull. "Congratulations, darling," she whispered.

"Large credit to you." He drew her to one side of the room. "Laurel, I know you didn't want to pound pavement for me as hard as you have."

"I'm proud of you, Dan. I wanted to help."

He looked taken aback by the statement. "No, you didn't. But thanks." Then grinning, he stunned her by saying, "I think we should take a day to ourselves before things get really crazy. After I make my speech tonight, let's—"

"Oh Dan, could we drive to Dawson tomorrow? It wouldn't be a long day, but it means so much."

"That's not quite what I . . . oh well, sure." He'd turned his head. "Teague, free us up for tomorrow, I don't care how, double book us on Thursday if you want. Laurel and I are going to visit Ned. Call the headmaster and make sure nobody spills the good news, if possible, until we get there."

Pulling her toward the stairs, he'd taken Laurel to their bedroom, where the peaceful silence was like a welcome caress. "We'll have to go downtown," Dan said. "I'm going to have a quick shower. Why not fix your makeup and hair?"

Laurel's spirits sank. She'd supposed he meant to have an amorous interlude. When Dan came from the bathroom and began to dress, talking amiably to her as they so rarely had a chance to do, Laurel told herself how much she appreciated this quiet marital time, even without the hugs and kisses she'd expected. Then the quiet ended.

"Laurel, what is this?"

He bent to pick up a pad of paper from the floor. Her heart began thumping. It was the sketch of Ryder that she hadn't finished in Gloucester, and she couldn't think why she'd left it in her handbag, which had fallen over, except that she'd had no time since Gloucester to unpack.

"Nothing," she tried to tell him, "just . . . doodling, during a long-winded speech somewhere. I can't remember."

"This is hardly doodling, Laurel. You took your time with this."

Not long enough, she thought. The smile still wasn't right. On Monday, and even this afternoon, she'd wanted to work on it. Then, she'd been careless. The memories of Gloucester flooded back. Thank God the smile wasn't right.

He handed her the pad, then went to his closet for his suit coat. "I can see that Teague's right. You need more work from now on." He held the door for her. "I don't want you getting bored and restless. Shall we go?"

Campaign headquarters had been jammed with volunteer workers, Dan's secretarial staff, and hordes of press. Long before they reached the podium for his victory speech, Laurel was blinded by cameras. But the worst moment had come when they were leaving the party. As Dan's aides shouldered through the cheering crowd, a few reporters broke through. Then to her horror, Laurel's gaze met familiar gray eyes.

"Congratulations, Counselor."

Dan replied, "Thank you. It's a great start."

Ryder's favorite Nikon came up. "Mrs. Benedict, how do you feel about your husband's triumph tonight?"

"Very happy. Proud." Except that I've betrayed him, and he knows it.

"Are you going to keep hitting the trail until November? Some would find the pace too exhausting, the rhetoric—"

"I do what's necessary. I always have," Laurel stated flatly. "I was a political daughter." She smiled stiffly into the cameras before moving on. "And I am a political wife."

"Well done," the senator had proclaimed. Then he'd pointed a finger at her. "I want you in Washington next weekend. Your mother's got some gala in the works. Kennedy Center, Saturday night. Great chance to pump a few hands, make some friends. Let the old ones remember you."

"Good idea, Laurel," Dan echoed. "I'll have Teague make arrangements."

She'd been railroaded, but hadn't minded as much as she might have. She'd made it through the primaries with a surprising sense of usefulness. She'd fortified herself against Ryder McKendrick, because if she didn't, wouldn't she only be running from this change in her life with Dan? I've lived up to my obligations, she thought, and Dan's grateful. Or he was, until he found that sketch, which he hadn't mentioned again.

Perhaps she'd reassured him at campaign headquarters.

On the road to Dawson, she leaned into the Audi's plush upholstery and removed her sunglasses, telling herself that the darker clouds moving across the sun wouldn't matter.

Things were getting better. Starting now.

Watching Dan park the Audi, Laurel felt tension rise in her. Odd, that the only other time she'd been to Dawson, except last Sunday by herself, had been with Ryder. Now, Dan's smile had disappeared, like the blue sky, before they'd reached the gate. She had wanted today to be perfect. She wanted them to be a family.

Why did Dan's frown seem to deepen with every step he took? Up the broad front steps, into the cool lobby smelling of books and chalk and little boys. Until she couldn't keep from asking, "Are you sorry we've come?"

"Why should I be sorry?"

Laurel shrugged, unable to put her apprehension into words. "His room is on the second floor, Dan," she said, because he'd walked past the staircase.

"The headmaster promised to keep Ned with the resident counselor until we arrived." He walked along the main floor corridor to a door near the underside of the stairs. Before Dan knocked, it flew open and Ned flung himself into the hall.

"Mommy, I've been waiting since breakfast!" He threw his arms around Laurel's neck. "I got to stay here as a special treat last night, then—"

"Ned, stop strangling your mother and say hello."

She felt the thin arms slip from her, the small frame tense.

"Hello, Dad. I'm glad you could come to see me."

"We've brought good news, Ned."

"Congratulations, Mr. Benedict." A bony young man appeared in the doorway. "I'm Ned's dorm adviser."

Suddenly Dan was the candidate again, shaking hands with the older boy, flashing his winner's smile and talking carefully around the issues. When he finally said, "We'll take Ned off your hands, and get outdoors before it rains," Laurel could have shouted her relief. "He's excused from classes this morning?"

"Yes, sir. As long as you'd like."

"What's he talking about, Dad? Why did he say con— congra—"

"Wait until we've a proper place for the announcement, will you? Don't be so impatient."

Laurel's heart sank. She found herself standing off to one side, observing, as Dan sat Ned down on a wooden bench overlooking the quadrangle, and told him, as if giving a statement to the press, that he'd won the primary last night, if not by a comfortable margin. The figures went right over Ned's boyish head. "But what does it mean?" he asked when Dan paused.

"What does it mean? That I'm in the race to become senator from Massachusetts. My name's going on the ballot in November against the Republican challenger, a man called Heron from Brockton, and—"

"Will you go to Washington?"

"I hope so, yes."

Laurel saw patience begin to ebb from Dan's features. Her stomach tightened as it always did when that expression formed on his face—jawline hardening and lips drawing tight, the steel blue eyes so bleak only when he looked at Ned.

"Do we have to move?"

"We would. Is that a problem for you?"

"Dan," Laurel started to say.

"I don't want to move. Pirate doesn't either."

"Oh, for Christ's sake."

Dan walked away from them, his shoulders stiff. Laurel sat with Ned on the bench. When she took his hand, it was cold. "Why is he mad—angry, I mean?"

"He isn't angry, Ned. He's disappointed. Last night, the primary, was important. It wasn't an easy fight for him—"

"Why was he fighting?"

Laurel closed her eyes at his literalness. "He wasn't really fighting. Not physically. It was a political battle, a small election. Like Grandpa's." Laurel tried again. "Daddy was . . . competing against another man from his own party. . . ." She trailed off at the confused look in his eyes. "Darling, it's like Kip's father getting a raise at work or a new job."

"What should I say, Mommy?"

Laurel whispered in his ear, then added aloud, "A kiss would be nice, too."

Ned slid from the bench, walking to his father, who turned around at his approach, Dan's eyes still with that angry sadness she saw only around Ned.

"Con-grat-u-lations, Dad. I'm glad you won last night."

"Thank you, Ned."

She saw the slight arms lift and the delicate face tipped back to look into his father's eyes. Pick him up, dammit, she thought. Hold him. Let him love you. Then she heard Dan say gruffly, "None of that. You're a big boy now. Men don't kiss each other, Ned. They shake hands."

Her vision blurred. Laurel sprang from the bench and began walking. Look at the turning leaves, their colors. Watch the darkening sky. Even pray for it not to rain. Anything, but don't cry.

"Mommy, wait!"

Ned caught up to her, not noticing that Laurel was blinking back tears. "Dad says, are you hungry? We can get something to eat, then ice cream afterward." Ned lowered his voice. "And I'll show you my present from Aunt Hilary."

"What present?"

"It's a secret." Then he whispered, "A wonderful one."

Oh Lord, Laurel thought. They were off to a terrible start. What would Dan say? She'd cautioned Hilary not to send Ned anything more than a box of crayons and a coloring book. Laurel cast a baleful look at the leaden skies, wondering why she had to play the peacemaker between her husband and her son. She thought of Lexa, always getting into trouble; and Laurel, always getting her out.

"Hey," Dan said behind them, "aren't you two going to wait for me?"

With Ned's formal congratulations, his mood lifted again until Ned took them to view his surprise. "Who sent you this?" Dan asked.

"Aunt Hilary."

"Hilary Chapin," Dan said with a frown. "She's not your aunt." He took the Nikon from Ned's outstretched hand. "It's a damned expensive camera, Laurel. Single lens reflex, 35mm, automatic flash. What the hell's wrong with that woman?"

"You know Hilary. Money isn't an issue with her. It never has been."

"And that gives her the right to spoil someone else's child?"

"I hardly think Ned's going to be permanently damaged by one costly gift."

"One?" He raised the camera. "She has been shipping stuff like this to him since he was a week old. Trains, motorized model cars, room-sized stuffed animals, a jungle gym, for God's sake, when we live in the middle of Boston. Well, it's going to stop."

"Dan, please."

"I could take your picture," Ned suggested. "If you showed me how to use it—"

"I've had my picture taken, Ned. And I don't know how to work the blasted camera!"

Laurel pushed Ned gently toward the door, her pulse racing. "Darling, run down to the car, will you, and get my jacket? It's on the rear seat." Shutting the door behind him, she turned to Dan. "I thought we were going to give ourselves a day off."

"I thought so, too."

"Then why is it that the instant you set eyes on that child you start tearing him apart?"

"Don't generalize. Or change the subject. It upsets me when Hilary Chapin makes parental decisions for me. I don't want him growing up with the wrong idea of his place in the world. I don't want a precious little brat whose every whimsy gets thrust at him—"

"You're exaggerating."

"Am I? That list of 'presents' was far from complete, Laurel."

"Ned isn't spoiled."

"He isn't a lot of things."

Her heart constricted. "Why do you resent him so? I thought that today we . . . my God, what has he done to you?"

"Nothing. I don't resent him. What a ridiculous statement. How could I resent my . . . own son?"

"You sent him away, here to Dawson, because—"

"I want him to have advantages, the right kind. Not outrageous toys." It was his standard explanation. "And once the campaign got underway, you agreed with me."

Laurel hugged her arms to her middle as Dan tossed the Nikon onto the bed. "Yes. I want just as much for him as you do," she said, "not expensive things, of course not. Including this school, which I prayed he'd like but he doesn't—"

"Because he won't make friends!"

She raised imploring eyes. "I'm not sure what's wrong, and I didn't want to worry you. But when he fell from his horse, Ned told me that it wasn't an accident. Dan, he said . . . he said that another boy whipped Storm so that Ned would fall off or run into that tree branch."

"What boy?"

Laurel frowned. "I'm not sure. I think he said Tom, I didn't hear a last name."

Dan came to her, putting his hands on her shoulders. "I know you don't understand my methods with Ned. I can't expect you to. We grew up differently, Laurel, but part of what I learned as a boy in . . . straitened circumstances should apply, just as part of the senator's training ought to."

"I know you think I baby him, but he needs a little mothering still." She placed her hands over his. "And he needs you. Watch his face sometime. He only wants you to love him, Dan."

That painful sadness came into his eyes again, and he released her. "Let's meet Ned outside and avoid the camera issue, shall we?" He held the door for her. "I'd like to go to the stables, see Storm, and while Ned's showing off what he's learned here, I'll have a word with the riding master about that boy, what's his name, Tom."

"But I don't understand," Dan said. "Ned, why would you invent a boy named Tom? Simply to have someone to blame for an accident that was your fault? Carelessness made you catch that limb in the face. Why wouldn't you own up to it?"

"Perhaps he was afraid of compounding the situation, Mr. Benedict," the riding master suggested. "Ned was already upset that he'd lost his horse after falling—"

"I'm addressing my son."

"Yes, sir. Sorry."

"That was a lie, Ned. And disappointing to me that you'd tell your mother a bald lie to gain her sympathy. I'll expect you to apologize."

"I'm sorry, Dad."

"Apologize to your mother."

His heart thudding in fury, Dan stared at the boy's back as he wheeled the black gelding and trotted toward Laurel, who was at the rail outside the ring. When he shifted his gaze, Dan saw disapproval plainly written on the riding master's face. "I suppose you think I was harsh with him."

"I'm not here to make judgments, Mr. Benedict. I'm here to teach your child how to sit a horse properly." The man smiled as Ned leaned down to kiss his mother, then balanced himself in the saddle and began trotting Storm around the ring. "He's made some tremendous gains, and quite recently."

Following the man's gaze, Dan knew that the astonishment showed on his face. "He has, indeed. My thanks, you've done the impossible."

"I wish I could take credit." The smile gathered into a frown. "But I think I should mention that Ned had a visitor yesterday. I saw the woman working with him after class. I came from the stable to see what was keeping Ned when the other boys had already rubbed down their mounts, and there he was, posting as if he'd been born in the saddle."

"Woman?" His pulse jumped.

"At first I assumed she was Mrs. Benedict, but when I—"

"Ned, come here." There was silence except for the soft blowing through the horse's nostrils and the creak of saddle leather between Ned's thighs. "Who was here yesterday, helping you to ride?"

"A nice lady."

"Hilary?" Dan asked.

"No."

"I won't be angry if it was."

"It wasn't Aunt . . . I mean, Hilary."

"Did she give you her name?"

Ned shook his head, looking from Dan to the riding master as if for a clue as to what he should say.

"Well, had you ever seen her before?"

"I don't think so. No."

"What did the woman look like?"

Ned thought for a moment. "Pretty, like Mommy, and she had black hair, too. But her eyes were brown."

Dan felt a trickle of sweat between his shoulder blades.

"She liked horses," Ned offered after a pause. "She liked Storm. But her horse was bigger."

"She brought a horse here?"

"No, she left him at home."

"Where?"

"I don't know, Dad." Ned's hands jerked on the reins, causing Storm to toss his head.

"What else? Is there anything else?"

Ned frowned. "It isn't a lie."

"No one thinks you're lying," the riding master intervened. "I saw her, too, remember. I know you liked the lady yesterday, but we need to be certain that she ought to be allowed to visit."

"She said she would again."

"My God," Dan whispered. His skin felt clammy, and he wondered if there was any color in his face. The riding master was staring at him. "I—I'm rather concerned. A political campaign, my being constantly in the public eye. . . ."

"I understand, Mr. Benedict." He looked up at the boy. "You're sure there's nothing more you remember?"

Ned's face cleared. "She told me her horse's name."

"What was it?" Dan saw Laurel start toward them. "Tell me."

Dark lashes swept down over hazel eyes as Ned studied his hands, white-knuckled on the leather reins. "Fool Gold?" he murmured.

Dan shut his eyes, and swore.

## CHAPTER 16

DAN BENEDICT WAS the perfect example, Ryder had decided, of a man rising to the occasion. In the weeks he'd been covering the campaign, and in these few intense days after the primary, he had come to admire the candidate. Reluctantly, he added.

As he loosened his tie, Ryder kept a firm grip on the steering wheel with the other hand, threading his compact sedan through the maze of rush hour traffic. Boston sizzled in a mid-September heat wave, provoking even hotter tempers. Ryder swore as a silver van with murals on the rear window cut in front of him, obscuring his quarry.

Not wanting to be seen tailgating the candidate and his wife, Ryder didn't try to maneuver around the van between his car and theirs. He ran a hand through his hair, which he hadn't combed since nine o'clock that morning. Christ, it was hot. Unbuttoning his blue dress shirt halfway down, he wondered where the Benedicts were going for the weekend. He'd followed Benedict all over Boston yesterday, grateful for the day's respite on Wednesday when Laurel had disappeared with her husband. Thursday had included a labor union speech, four television interviews, a luncheon at Pier Four, suburban whistle-stopping, then dinner with the lions of the Boston press, including Dan's informal debate with the managing editor of the *Globe*. Today hadn't proved less busy, only hotter.

After breakfast, on the way to south Boston for a street rally, Dan, the senator, and campaign aides discussed strategy for November. Ryder had wedged himself at the last minute into Benedict's limo, notepad and pencil ready.

The first issue to come up had been Laurel's "unfortunate" outspokenness in Framingham.

"The pleasures of crowd manipulation," the senator remarked with a smile. "The harm done was minimal, thanks to that statement you issued, Daniel, appearing to soften your Medicare stand."

"I did soften it."

"Well I, for one, am glad to see Laurel taking an interest."

Dan turned to Teague. "What about the organizer you mentioned before we left the hotel? The one who'd called."

Michaels named the man. "He's done a superb job in the western part of the state."

"And will expect a suitable reward," the senator put in.

It had been the first time Ryder saw irritation on Dan Benedict's smooth features where his father-in-law was concerned. "You just polish up your smile for the rally, sir. I'll deal with him, the rest of my people, too. You needn't contact him."

Ryder was surprised by the rift over political back-scratching. Edwin Frasier had built his career on favor traded for favor; Dan Benedict apparently intended to grease the machinery enough to keep it running, but no more. "When I reach Washington in January, I'll be a free agent for my constituents. No tied hands, senator, no campaign patronage promises."

"One man, one vote, Daniel?" the senator scoffed. "That's a nice notion, but naive—and impractical."

"We'll see."

Ryder felt that the truth lay somewhere between. But at the street rally in south Boston, Dan had charmed a hostile crowd, surprising Ryder even more. He'd given a swift, concise rendering of his platform, emphasizing his commitment to more jobs, better housing, quality education, opportunity.

Thinking about the rest of the day, Ryder couldn't fault Dan Benedict. He'd been running on all cylinders, from the morning rally to the last radio interview at three o'clock. He ran an apparently honest organization, and his politics were surprisingly liberal in an era dominated by conservatism. Astoundingly liberal when you considered his father-in-law. The only trouble was that his new, and reluctant, approval of the candidate left Ryder without a story.

But where was Benedict headed now, on Friday afternoon? Refocusing his attention on the car ahead of the van, Ryder spun the wheel of his Datsun, narrowly missing the cutoff. Logan Airport. He eyed the temperature gauge on his dashboard, helplessly watching it rise into the danger zone. He ran an index finger around his shirt collar, thinking of Laurel and Benedict, twined together for the weekend. He'd tried to find out where.

"None of your business, McKendrick." An hour ago Michaels had snapped his notebook shut, giving Ryder a malicious smile. "The candidate's plans don't include you. You got the weekend off, newsman. Enjoy yourself. Get a little sun." He'd walked away, adding over his shoulder, "Get laid."

He should take the advice, not that Michaels had given it for his benefit. He'd only been obscuring the truth, like the other time Benedict had left the campaign last weekend. Ryder kept the limousine in sight; he could see them talking, Laurel's dark head inclined toward Benedict. Then to his amazement, the car drew to a halt at the terminal and Laurel alighted, leaning inside to kiss Dan good-bye.

Separate weekends.

Ryder's pulse accelerated. He was on the trail of a story again, his vague suspicions beginning to jell. At the charter terminal next, he was out of the car before Benedict emerged from the limousine just in front of him. "Hey, Counselor, you forgot to give me your itinerary."

Dan's surprised gaze met his. "I won't be needing you. Michaels should have—"

"He told me. I decided he was withholding information from the press." Ryder smiled into Benedict's now angry expression. "Business?" he asked. "Or—"

"I'm trying to get elected."

Visions of smoke-filled rooms, shirtsleeves, stale bologna sandwiches, beer and coffee, the whir of political machinery danced in his brain. Ryder could hear deals being hatched; but the fear he saw on Benedict's face didn't go with them, or with Ryder's earlier impressions. "I'm the eyes and ears of this campaign, remember? In your own words, 'No secrets from the voters.'"

Grabbing his overnight bag from the chauffeur, Dan said, "See that Mr. McKendrick gets back to his car," then strode toward a gate that led directly onto the tarmac. Ryder found himself pinned against the side of the limousine, the chauffeur's big hands holding him to the hot metal.

"Private charter." Ryder peered around the other man's body, and the hold tightened. Waiting in the distance amid waves of heat was a crisp-looking Cessna, engine running. He wished he'd had time to grab his camera. "Where to?" he asked.

"Straight to hell for you if you don't—"

"Look, pal, it's my job. Just tell me this much, then. Where's Mrs. Benedict going?"

"Washington, but—"

He'd caught the man off guard, only for a second. It was enough. Then Ryder was lifted by his shirtfront and turned toward his car. "Get in," the chauffeur ordered, his face red, "and start driving."

Ryder jammed his foot to the floor, the sedan weaving along narrow access roads through the airport complex. He was suddenly glad of the longtime habit of carrying an overnight bag in his trunk. Six o'clock shuttle, he thought. Goddammit. If he could find a parking place.

Laurel gazed out the plane window as other passengers boarded. Why couldn't Dan shake all those hands, make the new friends, in Washington? It was his career at stake, not hers—she, the professed political wife—and yet he was in the air, on his way to . . . Laurel frowned as the thought dead-ended. She didn't know where, and to her frustration, it wasn't the first time.

But why did Teague Michaels always know where to find her husband? It seemed more than his being campaign manager. Laurel rested her chin on her hand. Along with Dan's mysterious disappearance, the visit with Ned kept racing through her mind.

In the car as they were leaving Dawson after tearful good-byes, Dan had said, "He was fine until you gave him that look of sympathy, as if we were abandoning him to some Devil's Island. Laurel, I wish you'd learn to control yourself."

"And I wish you'd let go once in a while." She watched

him concentrate on his driving. "Dan, he's lonely. He's trying to fit in because he knows how anxious we are—"

"Trying?" He glanced from the road. "The only thing I see him trying very hard at is to get home again where you can coddle him."

He had told her then about the fictitious Tom who'd been blamed for Ned's fall from Storm. It had shocked her, but in a different way from Dan. The story had struck her as possibly false before, and she'd even asked Ryder's opinion. But Laurel didn't think of Ned as a liar, only as a little boy afraid of his father's wrath. A little boy needing his mother's sympathy. What was it Ryder had said once? Someone to hold him when he's failed an exam, struck out at bat? Ryder, who didn't even like children. Why couldn't Dan understand at least as well? Why was he so unfeeling?

Laurel's gaze shifted from the plane window to the last stragglers making their way up the aisle. She glanced at her watch, then down at her lap. They'd be late taking off, and the senator's car would have to wait for her at National Airport.

"Excuse me. May I put your briefcase overhead?"

Laurel merely nodded. She didn't want company, but . . . She looked up, belatedly recognizing the male voice. "Dear God, what are you doing here?"

"Buying you a drink." Ryder eased down beside her after snapping the overhead compartment shut.

"You're always buying me a drink."

"Trying to." He grinned at her skeptical expression. "All right. Would you believe conducting an interview? I'm sure you would," he answered himself. "The candidate's wife, in depth, firsthand, up close."

Laurel's senses scrambled at the intimate tone of voice but she sighed. "You've followed me again."

He stopped smiling. "I'm a reporter. It's a habit of mine."

Laurel gave up as the engines revved for takeoff. Their flight would be short. She wouldn't even ask him why he was flying to Washington.

"Where's the candidate this weekend?" he said. "Stumping in the hinterlands?"

"Wouldn't you like to know?"

"Yes."

"So would I," she said.

There was a short silence during which he studied her profile while the big plane hurtled down the runway. Then Ryder said, "We're off. Let's try to get that drink. If we hurry, we'll even have time for a refill."

"I hope you realize," he commented moments later, touching his glass of scotch to Laurel's iced Perrier, "that you've turned me into a desperate man."

"We're all too busy to be desperate."

"Still. How do you think I like spending my nights ogling contact prints of you as if they were the latest find from *Penthouse*, trying every trick in the book short of tying myself to the bedframe in some strange hotel so I won't break down the door of your suite?"

He'd tried that, too, she pointed out. "If staying with the campaign's so difficult," she said, "then why do you?"

"I thought that was obvious from my ill-tempered mood." He would have reached for her hand under cover of their snack trays, but she hunted for a tissue in her handbag. "Christ," Ryder murmured, "it's like having Benedict dangle a carrot in front of my nose."

She couldn't have agreed more. Laurel, without intending to, found herself repeating the quote Dan had given her the night of the fund-raiser, courtesy of the senator.

Ryder sifted the words. "Keeping his enemy close, and

staying sharp. And here I've been, respecting the guy."
He paused. "Is that why you've been avoiding me for
three days?"

"He's my husband. And Teague tells him everything.
Well, not quite everything," she corrected, remembering
the aftermath of her speech the day Ryder had driven her
to Gloucester. "Teague's been telling himself he and I are
star-crossed for some time now."

"Neither of us is having much success. By the time this
campaign ends . . ."

Hearing the edge in his tone, Laurel changed the subject. "How's your series coming along? I missed the last
installment with all the primary furor."

"You didn't miss much." Ryder frowned. "I meant
what I said a while ago. I admire Benedict. Which makes
my job tougher, and my articles damn boring."

"I'd be surprised if they were boring."

"Blunt facts about anyone's daily routine usually are."

"Spoken like a true yellow journalist."

Ryder caught her smile. "Well, I only meant that I
can't make much of them, which is what I've usually done.
Made a statement, enlightened somebody. Sara Hennessey's going to chew my ass sooner or later. She had . . .
something more earthshaking in mind."

Laurel straightened. "She wanted you to go after Dan?"

"The Supreme Court frowns on preconceived notions
from the press," Ryder observed. "A couple of years back,
for instance, they handed down a decision against the
*Washington Post*, my *alma mater*, and Sara's, for 'malice
with ill will' in an investigative series on one of the oil
corporations."

Muckraking, she thought.

"What does Sara have against my husband?"

"Nothing that I know of, or maybe a feeling."

"Of long standing?"

"I think so."

"The senator," Laurel said. "She's not the first to make comparisons between him and Dan." She gazed at Ryder thoughtfully. "She hired you because of the stand you'd taken against him years ago during the war."

"I'd be indicted for those articles now."

Laurel smiled. "The senator would have gladly seen you in court then."

"Well, it's his day. Too bad he retired."

She turned toward Ryder. "Would you really slant your writing to hurt Dan in the election?"

He briefly closed his eyes. "I'm not after your husband, Laurel. If he makes the cut in November, he's going to be a damn fine senator."

"He'll make it."

"I thought that wouldn't please you any more than it will Sara," he said. "And I thought, with that talk in Framingham about Medicare, you'd overcome your automatic compliance. Then you tossed off the 'political wife and daughter' speech to me the night of the primary."

"At this point I can't deny what I am."

"Oh, come on."

"It's true." She looked into her glass, not wanting to say too much when he might be interviewing her even now. "I grew up in a rarefied atmosphere with the senator and Judith . . . and Lexa. Our parents traveled a lot and, like Ned, we went away to school. My only real regret is that Ned hasn't anyone like Hilary or Lexa—we were always called The Twins, in capital letters, a force of our own against the world."

"That's not your only regret, Laurel."

Why was he pressing her? Because she'd rejected him in Gloucester again? Turned away from an affair and back to her husband, her child? Her real life?

"But your sister's death must have been tough on you," he added.

"Hilary always said we were too close. In those days twins even dressed alike. Judith bought us each the same clothes, the same toys, and later, the same makeup. I always thought that, getting beyond outer appearances, we rounded each other out. She was outgoing, I was shy. She got into scrapes, I pulled her out."

Laurel looked out the window at a mile-high pile of clouds. "She used to think that the old wives' tales were fact, that one twin could feel the other's pain. Or pleasure, I suppose. I called it nonsense, until the night she died." Until Gloucester, she added silently. "I don't believe in ESP or any of that, but I felt this terrible rush of emptiness then . . . at the exact instant she . . ."

"You think a part of you died then, don't you, that it's still missing?"

"Do I sound crazy?"

"No," he said. "I think Hilary feels the same way about her Navy flier." He set her empty glass on the snack table and took her hand. "So you married Benedict and became a political wife." He paused. "Why did you do it, Laurel, when you dreaded Dan's future in the public eye? And don't tell me it was because you were Frasier's daughter."

Why indeed? she thought. Wednesday's disappointing visit with Ned had further confused her feelings for Dan. Could she love a man she couldn't seem to please? A man who couldn't love their son?

"I think you married him—because she couldn't—for Lexa."

Heart drumming, Laurel didn't answer. The reporter was talking, not the man, or so she wanted to think because it seemed, ironically, safer.

"I think," Ryder continued, "you've spent the last fourteen years playing out someone else's life. Isn't it time you stopped?"

"I'm not playing at anything!" She snatched her hand from his. "Though it's true that I don't have everything I'd hoped for—closeness with my husband, more children—who does? Did you?"

"For a while." From the look in his eyes, she doubted he meant Maggie.

"For one day of my life, I pretended—just one. I was a good wife," Laurel insisted, "until Gloucester."

"I remember Gloucester, too, Laurel, but I remember it differently." His gaze held hers. "It was two days, and I wish the rain had never stopped."

"That wasn't really me," she murmured.

"Don't give me that crap about trading places. That wasn't Lexa. Laurel, you were searching for something there, for yourself and—"

"You think I found that with you?" She shook her head. "You're wrong."

"Maybe."

"But perhaps you are right, that I'm looking for completion, separateness." She remembered the program cover design, her speech about Medicare. Small steps, she thought. "Other than that—"

"Laurel, I care about you. Whether in Gloucester—" his voice lowered "—in bed, or seeing you stand up for yourself with voters, with Teague, or right here, talking about the pain you still feel over Lexa, I care." His gaze was somber. "I don't know that I'm good for you, even if you wanted me, but I only want for you what anyone needs, to be the best person you can be."

Would Dan be able to say that? she wondered.

"You sound very noble."

"Not really." He looked embarrassed by the outpouring of words. "Just concerned."

She realized that she'd been holding him off not only romantically—because she had to—but as a friend. And that Dan was wrong. Their concern for each other was genuine. If they could no longer be lovers, she and Ryder had become friends. In these few moments she'd finally stopped worrying that he meant to interview her, and he'd learned the deepest secret of her heart. Lexa's death had shattered it to pieces.

She touched his cheek, shadowed by the day's beard.

"Thank you," she said and he smiled. "May I tell you something?"

"Anything."

"I've had an idea, just for me." It had occurred to her during the drive by herself to see Ned last Sunday, after Gloucester. She'd been thinking about her sketch of Ryder, and then of Sebastian's car catalogue. "You said you had needed some daytime snapshots of Sebastian's cars, but Hilary wouldn't help him with that. I was wondering..."

"What?" He urged her to go on.

"If he couldn't do a different sort of presentation. He has only half a dozen or so cars ready for sale, and I was thinking..."

"Laurel."

"Thinking that I might do some drawings instead, pastels or watercolors."

Ryder's face lit up.

"They'd be, you know, delicate and classic, which would suit his cars very well, don't you think?"

He grinned. "Sounds great."

Laurel grinned back, feeling excitement pour through her veins. She rattled on about her ideas for a few more minutes, then breathlessly asked, "Should I call Sebastian before he's made other arrangements for his catalogue? Or just make a preliminary sketch or two to send—"

Ryder leaned toward her, his tone conspiratorial. "You don't want to be obligated to me, remember?"

"Well, I did say that, but your opinion—"

"No good, Laurel." He was very close to her. "You're right. What Dan or the senator thinks—or me—doesn't matter. What do you think you should do?"

Smiling, she used his words. "Go for it."

His mouth grazed hers, and his husky laugh sent a shiver of pleasure down her spine that Laurel—as friend—tried to suppress. "Call him tonight."

The whine of jet engines told her they were beginning the descent over the nation's capital. The flight had seemed shorter than ever before. But the nearer the plane came to the ground, the farther away the pleasant interlude with Ryder seemed to become. How many times had she made this trip? How many times had she dreaded it?

Laurel thought of Dan's change of heart on the way home from Dawson, and realized that this time she'd at least have Ned. She'd puzzled over Dan's anger at Ned's lying about the fall from Storm, then giving him the treat of this trip to see his grandparents. No wonder the child was confused, just as she was. Punishment had been followed by reward. Twice.

"I get to keep the camera?" Ned had asked. "I don't have to send it back?"

"Maybe your father can help with it," Dan said to Laurel.

"The senator knows a camera from the same side of the lens you do, and that's all." But she'd been grateful for his second concession.

"Then who will teach me?" Ned had asked.

Glancing at the man beside her now, Laurel sighed. Ryder could teach Ned, she thought as the big plane glided toward the runway. If he liked children. If she let him into her life. She touched the lips he had just kissed and willed them not to feel so soft, so sensitized.

Yes, they could be friends, she thought, and maybe that would be enough.

After touchdown Ryder busied himself getting his camera bag from the overhead rack, then Laurel's briefcase. "Writing a speech for Monday?"

"No, Wednesday. But I doubt I'll have time to review Teague's notes. My parents are hosting a gala at the Kennedy Center tomorrow night."

"Command performance."

Her smile faded as Ryder handed over her case. She wondered whether he would be there, if that was really why he'd come, and they'd just happened to be on the same plane. Wondered if he was goading her for slipping back into her role as political wife/daughter. When she eased from her seat and stood, her body brushed his, then drew away. Ryder grasped her arm, pulling her forward again. "Watch your head, you nearly knocked it on the overhang."

While they waited for someone to pass in the aisle, she let herself be drawn into the half circle of his arm. "How about sharing a cab into Washington?" he said. "You'll be going that direction to Chevy Chase anyway."

"The senator's car is meeting us."

"Us?"

Laurel glanced into his eyes. "My son. He's coming in on the campaign plane from school with his grandfather." She looked down at her watch. "A half hour ago."

Ryder stepped into the aisle. "I should have known there'd be a limousine."

She couldn't offer him the ride, and they both knew it.

"Well." He held out his hand. "Thanks for sharing that drink at last. Enjoy your weekend, if you can. I hope you and your boy will have the chance to get away together for an afternoon."

"Tomorrow, possibly."

"Try the zoo," he suggested. It surprised her that he'd even think of Ned's pleasure. Holding her gaze, Ryder said, "The pandas are a rare treat, even to the natives here, like yourself." Then he was gone, striding the short aisle to the exit before Laurel took a step.

It never occurred to her that he'd been making a date.

In Chevy Chase, cool and quiet as evening descended, the rosy brick Georgian-style mansion looked empty. Urging Ned along, Laurel walked from the entry hall to the last door on their right. Ned let her go first into the room, and a well-modulated voice greeted them.

"I'd nearly given you up."

Judith Frasier rose from a damask-covered sofa. As always when she came home, Laurel was struck again by her mother's looks: her ageless skin, still soft and unlined made a cameo-perfect setting for cornflower blue eyes and dark lashes, the sleek chignon of blond hair skillfully kept that shade by one of Washington's talented stylists. Taller than Laurel, graceful in a celadon green dress, she offered her cheek for a brushing kiss at the air. Then gave her hand to Ned, who pressed his lips to it.

"Hi, Grandma Judith."

"Mother," Laurel said.

The answer was a smile that moved few muscles in Judith's handsome face. "Come, sit down. I've told Cook to fix us something fresh. The roast dried up so—"

"Mother, really."

"I expected you by eight o'clock." She glanced, needlessly, Laurel felt certain, at a slim gold watch. "It's past eight-thirty."

"The car was tied up in traffic. Presidential motorcade.

A dinner at one of the embassies, the senator said."

Judith turned to her grandson. "Tell me, Edwin. How did you like the news of your father's primary victory?"

Ned squirmed on the sofa. "Okay," he said at last.

"What kind of answer is that, dear?" Judith arranged her skirt not to touch his knee. "Suppose a reporter asked you?"

Laurel's teeth clenched. "You will be watched," her mother had always said. "Watched and quoted and criticized. You must be careful, we must all be careful, not to embarrass the senator in any way." The advice applied now, for Dan, to Ned.

"Mother, he doesn't talk to the press."

"By the time you and Lexa were six years old, you were both able to conduct press conferences if necessary— never mind that you paled at the notion."

"Fighting already?"

The senator entered the room, smiling at Ned and walking toward Judith, who stood, as if she were a stylish puppet pulled upright, for his embrace.

Releasing her, the senator headed for the bar, which was housed in an antique cabinet. "Edwin, how about a fruit drink? You look as if you need it with these women going at each other."

"Senator," Judith said, "you're as bad as the child's mother. I can see I'll have to take a hand in his upbringing. As soon as Dan and Laurel move—"

With a grin, the senator handed Ned a glass. "Your grandmother counts votes faster than a computer. What are you having, Laurel? The usual?" Nodding, she watched him pour twice the amount of white wine she wanted into a Steuben glass. "Edwin, why don't you find the kitchen, and ask Cook what she's planning? Tell her we want fried chicken," the senator suggested. "Southern style."

"My favorite!" Ned skipped from the room, yanking at his school tie.

"Edwin Eliot Frasier Benedict," Judith called after him. "Walk, don't run."

Laurel groaned inwardly. Her parents had called him Edwin even when he was a baby, weighing little more than six pounds; the name suited the wiry little boy no better. For a second, she wondered how Lexa had ever been granted a nickname, defying family tradition.

"Now, then." Judith leaned forward. "I thought we'd start looking for a house tomorrow."

I wish *I* were eight years old, Laurel thought; I'd hide in my tree house, dark and cool, with a flashlight and a good, preferably forbidden, book. And a sketchpad.

"A house?"

"Well, of course you'll need a house."

"Mother, can't this wait at least until the election's over?"

"Judy, take it easy."

Softly spoken, the senator's words had, nevertheless, been a command. He rose to fix himself a second drink, the bourbon and branch water that Laurel considered more appropriate to a Western movie hero. "The polls give Daniel forty-three percent today. Lexington's solid."

"After your trip there," Judith pointed out.

"Well, they seemed to like my speech." He had told Laurel about it, coming from the airport. "And Edwin, too. I brought him with me, thought the experience would be good for him."

Vindicated, her mother smiled. "You see, Laurel. You can't begin too early. Dan's a young man with a long career ahead. Edwin will be an asset to him, just as you—"

"If Lexa were alive, Mother, would you be giving her the same browbeating?"

Judith looked stricken. The mention of Laurel's sister was rare enough; in late September, nearing the anniversary of her death, it would be even more unwelcome. "Your sister would understand without my telling her."

The senator laughed. "With Lexa you wouldn't dare."

Laurel saw tears and realized that since Lexa's death, Judith had become more brittle, less resilient. "Mother, I'm sorry."

"I wonder what's keeping Edwin," she murmured.

As always, dinner was a working affair. Ned, intent upon his meal, had his hands full cutting the succulent fried chicken from the bone and missed much of the conversation. The senator expounded campaign strategy, then analyzed Dan's strengths ("People do like him, there's a surprising warmth that's come out in public") and weaknesses ("But he's got to be tougher, make his policies stick with the party regulars, and realize there's more to politics than shaking hands with the voters") while Laurel tried not to fidget at Ned's eating. Finally, she told him to use his fingers.

"Laurel, make him eat properly," her mother said.

"Fried chicken, especially Cook's, is meant to be eaten with your hands. The best etiquette books approve." She picked up the breast portion she'd been pushing around her plate.

"Barbaric." Judith reached across to Ned, on her right. "This is how you do it, Edwin." With sharp motions of the knife, she sliced the meat from the bones, in time with a monologue on table manners.

Laurel averted her eyes. *He's just a little boy. I won't watch, I won't listen.* But the force of her own anger stunned her.

Anger at Judith and the senator, who said nothing; anger at Dan for disappearing all weekend. Anger at herself for compliance. When she had to march in Dan's parade on Monday, Laurel thought, she'd pay attention to the orders. Though she would hardly need to.

Her Frasier lessons had been drilled into her long before Dan's campaign, before she'd ever heard of Ryder McKendrick.

*Why did you do it, Laurel?*

## ❋  *CHAPTER 17*  ❋

❋

LAUREL TRAILED NED through the gates of Washington's National Zoo under a cold, gray sky. Overnight, Indian summer had vanished, and she wore navy wool slacks against the midday chill, a blue cashmere sweater under a herringbone blazer. Pushing her tortoiseshell glasses up the bridge of her nose, she watched Ned skip along the red stripe of Olmsted Walk, the zoo's main thoroughfare to which everything else connected. Dressed in jeans and a blue polo shirt, he'd been bubbling over with excitement since they'd left Chevy Chase in the limousine, and until Henry returned for them, Laurel wanted to feel as free as Ned seemed to.

"Mommy, Mommy!"

Ned waited impatiently by the doors to the panda house. The new Nikon, which he'd insisted on bringing, was still in motion, swinging against the zipper of his yellow windbreaker. Trying not to think about her mother's thwarted plans for househunting that day, she hurried toward him.

That morning, as if the evening before had never happened, Judith had wanted to call the realtor. Laurel had objected that she couldn't disappoint Ned about the zoo.

When Judith insisted that Henry could take Ned to see the pandas, Laurel had dug her heels in. "I'm taking him, Mother."

Laurel allowed herself a smile as Ned held open the heavy door into the animal house. The victory had been small but, like her speech in Framingham, or her idea for Sebastian's catalogue, all her own. If she had to pinch herself every five minutes for reminder, this one afternoon she would forget her mother's expectations, her own duties, unhappiness. And Dan.

"Take my hand, Ned. It's crowded," she began, but he'd jumped ahead of her again, finding a place at the rail close to the glass that separated the rare pandas from their visitors. She started to follow.

Then Laurel saw Ryder.

Steps faltering, she fought the surge of joy that quickly became dismay. He leaned, arms folded over his chest, against the outer wall, surveying the crowd. His gaze found Ned as she watched, and recognition came into his eyes. He was pushing away from the wall when she reached him. Laurel spoke under her breath.

"Are you crazy?"

"Absolutely." A lazy smile made his eyes gleam. Around his neck, the leather strap's color nearly matching his sun-browned skin, was a single, obviously expensive Pentax fitted with an even more costly looking lens. "You decided to take my suggestion, I see. That's Ned, isn't it? The trial-size kid in the jeans and blue shirt?"

"You've seen his picture."

"Why don't you introduce us?"

Laurel stared. "You didn't want to meet him, remember?"

"I want to now."

"Why? So you can shoot pictures of him, draw attention to me in a public place? Then go home and write up the story? That ought to keep Sara Halloran off your back for a while."

"Hennessey," Ryder corrected.

"Does it occur to you that Teague Michaels or one of his hired hands could be spying on us?"

"Laurel, give me a break. I just want to spend the day with you."

"In front of my eight-year-old son."

"With both of you." He smiled at her. "It's going to be all right."

Though he wasn't that sure, Ryder thought. He'd spent the night wondering if she'd understood his message on the plane, doubting himself for giving it, then wondering if she'd come. Wondering whether he could handle seeing the boy. Well, there was only one way to find out, he'd decided. She was here, and so was Ned.

Still, he remembered Sara's tone of voice when Ryder had telephoned after checking into his hotel. "I was trailing Benedict," he explained, "but he lost me." Briefly, they speculated on his whereabouts. Then Ryder said, "I'm in Washington now. I'll be back Monday." He'd given Sara the number in case she needed him.

"What's in Washington?"

"The candidate's wife."

Now he ignored the fact that although, like his mother, Sara urged him to find someone he could care about, she wouldn't be pleased by this particular woman. Ryder said again, "It's going to be all right, Laurel. It has to be."

"God, *I* must be crazy," she murmured, but it was said to herself as he walked toward Ned. Ryder squatted at the rail beside the boy, who was toying with the strap of his Nikon and staring intently at the black-and-white panda eating inside one of the glass cages.

Ryder's heart pounded like a jackhammer. "He's got quite an appetite, hasn't he?"

Ned's gaze didn't shift. "He's the daddy. His name's Hsing-Hsing."

"And the other?" He gestured toward the second enclosure.

"Ling-Ling. They had a baby. But it died," Ned reported.

Ryder didn't know how to take the statement. Sensing Laurel behind them, he watched what Ned was watching: the efficient stripping of a succulent bamboo shoot that disappeared inch by inch into the rotund panda's mouth, as if into a machine. Round dark eyes stared back at them, unblinking. After a while, Ryder ventured, "That's quite a camera you've got there."

"I don't know how to work it. I wanted to take his picture."

"Let me see." Ryder held out his hand, but Ned only shook his head, looking around for Laurel as if he'd belatedly realized he shouldn't talk to strangers.

"It's okay, love. He's not a thief."

Ryder threw her a look. "Thanks a lot." He fingered the strap of his own, more elaborate, Pentax. "I'm a photographer, Ned."

"How did you know my name?"

"I'm a . . . friend of your mother's."

We're in it now, Laurel told herself as Ned watched for her nod of confirmation. Yet she had to bite her lip against a smile, seeing Ryder take the empty camera from her son and examine it as she had wanted Dan to do. He fumbled in a pocket, coming out with a small metal cylinder.

"This is Tri-X, Ned. Newsmen swear by it. Black and white," he said, "perfect for pandas," as his fingers deftly fit the film into the case. Laurel sensed he could have done it, had probably loaded many times, by feel in total darkness. With bullets, and God knew what else, flying overhead.

Handing back the Nikon, Ryder met Ned's eyes. It was a first collision of glances, head-on. He felt the impact like a hard blow to the base of his spine. The photograph in Benedict's library had shaken him. Hazel eyes, not black, but with the same innocence, the same solemnity and lack of trust. Ryder tried to see things differently: Ned had his mother's love, if not his father's, to rely on; Hoa had had nothing at all, no one. Or only him. Which hadn't been enough.

He came to his feet, wondering whether Laurel could see the beads of sweat on his upper lip, his forehead.

"Will you show me how to take his picture now?" Ned asked.

"Well, I, uh . . ."

"Ryder, would you?" Laurel bent to Ned. "Darling, this is Mr. McKendrick. He's been working with Daddy's campaign. He's very good."

"Flatterer."

His heart racing, Ryder forced himself to stay. Dragging air into his lungs, he began to explain.

"This is a simple camera to work. Mostly automatic. Come here, Ned. Stand up against the rail, you can rest the camera on it when you shoot." He hunkered next to the boy again, willing his hands not to shake. It would be all right, just keep talking. About the aperture, no, call it opening. And the viewfinder. "Okay. Now see how these lines are separate when you look through the lens? They've made it easy for you. Turn this ring until they come together—that means your picture's in focus."

Together, they checked the flash for readiness, then Ryder put Ned's index finger on the shutter release and taught him how to press it. "Hold steady and ease it down all the way." He tried not to tremble when they touched. He couldn't stop thinking, remembering, about Hoa. "All yours, Ned. Take more than one, and remember to advance between shots."

"I did it! Mommy, I did it!"

"Oh, Ned, that's wonderful." Moments later, Laurel turned to Ryder, her eyes speaking volumes as they stepped from the panda house into a still-gray afternoon. Ned scampered ahead, the Nikon swinging like a pendulum. "Thank you," she said. "I know you don't like . . ." She shook her head. "No, just thank you for helping him."

He gave her an off-center smile. "The way to a woman's heart."

You louse, she wanted to say. But what could have won her more thoroughly than to see a man treat her son with tenderness and care? It hadn't been easy for him; she sensed that as she had sensed his proficiency in darkness with a camera. How could simple kindness be so arousing?

She gave her imagination free rein, seeing them as a family on a happy outing: herself and Ned and Ryder McKendrick. The fantasy was bittersweet, and dangerous. "I am grateful," Laurel said after a moment. She inhaled the aroma of hot dogs, popcorn, and Ned's favorite, cotton candy. "It isn't often that anyone . . . a man . . . takes time with him."

"Dan?" he said.

"Or the senator, though he's reasonably indulgent, as long as the plaything they're admiring is his, not Ned's." Then she remembered that she had reason to be grateful herself, and she couldn't stop grinning. "Ryder, I called Sebastian."

"And?"

"He loved the idea!" Still amazed, she had a strong desire to throw her arms around Ryder's neck. "But I don't even know what to charge him. What if I can't do the work, what if—"

"You can, and you will. Haven't I been telling you that you need a little more Tower of Power in your life? End of pep talk." He glanced at her. "Who bought Ned the Nikon?"

"Hilary."

Ryder smiled. "She might have tried an Instamatic or a disc camera for starters."

"Hilary doesn't do things by halves."

"I wonder," he murmured and Laurel guessed that he was thinking of Gloucester last Friday. "I think she's hedging about more than Africa. Which is none of my business," he added, "any more than Benedict's neglect of his kid. You don't have to tell me that."

They walked on, both appearing to concentrate on Ned's progress along one of the six trails, his stops to shoot yet another picture. "Wait a second." Ryder reminded Ned to use the camera's built-in meter before he snapped the shot. "Light's your most important tool as a photographer, Ned. Play with it, experiment. Here, try this setting. You'll get a better depth of field for that tiger and her cubs."

Turning back to Laurel, he wore a different expression, one she hadn't seen before and couldn't read. He fell into step beside her, not touching. "Overseas," he said, "in Nam and Laos, nothing was the same as here. Light. Such colors, such depths. They say Ireland's got more shades of green than any place on earth, but it's not true."

"You've been to Ireland, too?"

"Belfast a couple of times. There wasn't much green there at all. But yes, I've seen the country."

They walked in silence, Laurel listening to the trill of birdsong, the cries of animals and once, the scream of a peacock. At last Ryder said, "I couldn't ever make Maggie see about the colors, or the light . . . sure as hell not about the Vietnamese people."

"Anyway," he went on, "Sara Hennessey thought I could make a name for myself overseas—Nixon had just sent troops into Cambodia—instead of reporting the protest at home against the war.

"What did your wife say?"

"She reminded me that we'd been talking about a family." At Laurel's look of surprise, he said, "Yeah, we wanted kids then, both of us. Sara and her husband tried to convince Maggie that we had lots of time." Ryder's mouth thinned. "I guess it's no one's fault that we didn't, unless it's mine."

"I'm sorry." Laurel frowned. He'd implied guilt before. "You'd have made a lovely father. Even in this crazy world. But why would you think—"

"So, I shipped out," he cut her off, his eyes looking far ahead down the path and finding Ned. "And I took a carload of film in those dirty months. Rain, mud, heat, insects, fungus . . . death. So many dead."

He shook his head. "I met another journalist over there, a guy named Hamilton Channing. The book of photographs I did is as much his as mine. It was Ham who convinced me that the pictures to be taken weren't those from battle, but the faces of the people affected by it. The native population . . . running, hiding, mourning. All of that, and a lot more. Laurel, I saw such . . ."

He cast a glance toward the dark sky. "Misery," he finished. "It was Ham's idea, too, that I meet . . . *her*, make a newspaper series for Sara—we didn't think at the time of a book—real gut-level human interest. But by the time I finished, she and Ham—"

As if he'd stumbled on a buried mine along the path, the soft explosion hit his knees. Ryder felt the contact of skin through cloth, of delicate bone and, looking down, met again the liquid, fearful gaze. He went rigid with shock.

His hands grasped thin shoulders, and he found them full of child. The words roared in his ears. "*Don't ever do that again, you hear me?*"

"Mommy!"

"Ryder, let him go!"

He heard the panicked voice of a woman, the rising shriek of a frightened child. But she didn't have a mother; Hoa had no one but him, only he couldn't hold tightly enough to—

"You're hurting him!"

He was trembling, cold and hot and sick. If he didn't tighten his grip, she'd—

"*Ryder!*"

"What?" The air around him seemed to buzz. "What?"

And then, there was nothing in his hands. His fingers went slack, and he was staring into space. Holding emptiness. The rush of his breathing a firestorm. He'd heard of flashbacks, of course; but he'd never had one of his own before. It wasn't Hoa, he realized.

"Oh Christ. God. *Jesus Christ.*"

Shaking, Laurel shielded Ned. Ryder's eyes were glazed, sightless. Then suddenly he was gone. A small crowd had gathered around them, but he pushed his way through, with no apologies. For another moment she stood watching, her body damp with panic. "Don't worry," she crooned, as much to herself as to Ned, who was whimpering. "Don't worry, you're all right."

"I just wanted to show Mr. 'Kendrick the zebras, Mommy."

Her pulse pounded. What was she to do? Instinct told her to run; maternal protectiveness made her do the opposite. Laurel fumbled in her pocket for some change, thrusting it into Ned's hand. "Buy yourself a cotton candy, and stay right here. I'll be back in a minute."

"Why is he so angry with me, Mommy? What did I do?"

"Nothing, love. Do as I tell you."

She pursued Ryder along the path. He was staring down at the painted animal footprints that marked each trail, and walking fast.

"Are you crazy?" she said, and this time meant it.

Her hand clamped over Ryder's forearm, wrenching him around with surprising ease. She knew that part of her anger was for Dan, from the day at Dawson, and thus misplaced; but why would Ryder engineer this meeting only to reveal a side of himself that frightened her as much as it had Ned? "He's just a little boy! What kind of man are you? He's only a child—"

Then she looked into his face and all her anger died. Even on that awful night in the campus clinic, could she have looked as tormented as Ryder did now? I'll never forget his eyes, she thought. In them, Laurel saw pain, and shame. She saw vulnerability. And tears.

"What happened, Ryder?" Laurel whispered. "It wasn't Ned, was it?"

"No. Oh, God," he said, "I'm sorry."

"Mommy, they're all out of cotton candy so I—"

Ned shrank against her as Ryder went down on one knee on the path, his eyes at a level with the boy's.

"Mommy?"

"Please, Laurel." Ryder glanced at her. "I won't hurt him."

"Don't be afraid, darling."

Ryder cleared his throat. "I didn't mean to scare you, Ned. I'm sorry," he said hoarsely. "But do you know— have you ever had a nightmare?"

Ned studied him. "Yes."

"Well, it was like that for me a few moments ago. You

see, I, well, something happened—not then, but in the past—and I was reminded of it when you tumbled into me." He swallowed, a gulp of dry air. "It wasn't your fault. I never would have hurt you, Ned."

Silence.

"It was like having a nightmare," Ryder repeated.

Ned looked thoughtful. "I get awful scared when I wake up from a bad dream. My heart pounds, and I can't breathe right."

"Yeah. Me, too." Ryder rose to his feet. "Listen, Ned. I wonder if you'd give me a few minutes with your mother. Why don't you take the Nikon—" he lifted it from around Ned's neck to turn it over with shaking fingers "—and snap off the rest of the roll. According to your counter, there should be five shots left."

"All by myself?"

"All by yourself."

Ryder touched Ned's tousled hair before the boy seemed to leap out from under his hand; he bounded away for the next animal enclosure. Laurel turned toward Ryder, meeting his eyes for the first time since she'd seen tears in them. She didn't reach out. She knew by instinct that his skin would feel cold and clammy as it had before, as Ned's did when he woke screaming in the night.

"Won't you tell me what that was about?" Laurel asked. "I'm not as simple as Ned, or as eager to trust."

"I don't think he trusts me, either. I think he's just distracted by the camera." Ryder passed a hand over his eyes. "I've got to get out of here, Laurel. Come with me, back to the hotel. We can talk there."

"That's impossible. Ned—"

"Can't you put him in a cab to Chevy Chase?"

"I can tell you don't have children."

"You could call your parents to expect him. He'd be all right."

"The senator's car is picking us up—" she consulted her watch "—in half an hour. My mother's out for the day, my father's at his law office, and the house staff is off. Tonight's the gala in honor of Justice Hulme and his wife."

"Laurel, I need you." Even his eyes pleaded with her.

She was beginning to be frightened again. "I don't know what it is you need exactly."

"You," he said. "I just need you, Laurel, *please*."

When he caught her arm, she shrank from his touch as Ned would have. "I can't, my God, you know I can't."

Ryder's hand dropped to his side. "I'm staying at the Greystone. It's a converted townhouse on N Street in Georgetown. European-style, kind of a bed-and-breakfast place. If you get the urge to go slumming, that is. Which you probably won't."

And leaving Laurel to stare at the place on her arm where his fingers had so briefly been, he was gone.

Ned wasted no time in violating Laurel's commandment to him as soon as they had settled—Ned in a heap of arms and legs and camera, Laurel in weary relief—into the senator's limousine. Facing Edwin Frasier from his place on the jumpseat, Ned grinned.

"Guess who we saw today, Grandpa?"

## ❋ CHAPTER 18 ❋

"RYDER MCKENDRICK."

Judith Frasier had whispered the name. And Laurel, sweeping through the great foyer of the Kennedy Center that evening beneath the sparkle of thousands of pounds of Orrefors crystal chandeliers, felt her heartbeat pause with her footsteps. She saw immediately that the senator, between them, had also heard. "McKendrick?" he echoed. "Where?"

"Across the lobby."

"Dammit, what can he want?"

The question wasn't in the senator's mind only. It seemed that Ryder's name, or the possibility of its being mentioned, had threatened her all day, like a storm. Laurel smoothed nervous fingers over the skirt of her white silk jersey gown, strapless and fitted to the waist, draping in soft, loose curves to the crimson carpet at her feet. But surely Ned's prattle about their afternoon at the zoo hadn't made the senator suspicious.

No, it was Laurel who'd clutched at the limousine seat, her pulse thready with alarm over Ned's question, "Guess who we saw today?" The answer, of course, had been, "Two panda bears, Grandpa."

Looking away from the senator now, Laurel watched Ryder, his sport jacket contrasting with tuxedo-clad gala attendees, then Justice Hulme himself, just entering the lobby with his wife. Both were long-valued friends—the distinguished Everett was her godfather and Myra, of course, was Hilary's mother—but Laurel couldn't return their smiles.

She still hadn't sorted out her feelings from the afternoon, she realized as Ryder's eyes met hers above the crowd; she saw shadows beneath them, intensifying their gray to charcoal, dark smudges in his pale face.

He'd had a tan ever since she'd known him, the result of prior weeks in Beirut, then the end of summer in the States. Tonight, his skin had the underlying bluish-gray cast of illness. He was walking toward them, the ever-present camera around his neck.

"Let me take care of this." The senator put a delaying hand on Laurel's bare forearm.

"Senator, Mrs. Frasier." Not three feet from her, he stopped, raising the Pentax. "Mrs. Benedict, you look lovely, a cool confection tonight, like powdered sugar and rock crystal candy."

Her hand went to her throat, fingering the antique diamond necklace there. It had been her grandmother's, and with its platinum settings it matched the earrings she'd also worn tonight. He took a single shot before the senator moved, ruining the composition. With a gasp, Judith stepped back. Laurel saw several heads turn toward them, including the Hulmes's. Belatedly, she noticed the reckless glint in Ryder's eye.

The senator's voice was deadly as his gaze skimmed Ryder's lean frame. "This gala is hardly occasion for a journalist of your world-class caliber to come all the way to Washington, McKendrick."

"It's still a free country, Senator. Unless you've got an update for me."

"Free country, yes." The senator managed to smile as the house lights dimmed, then brightened again—a signal for the audience to be seated. "But this wasn't a photo opportunity, or anything else, for you tonight with my daughter."

"Your daughter doesn't enjoy a private life these days. I'm surprised that escaped your notice, Senator." His eyes narrowed. "But then, the public arena's exactly what you've always wanted for her, isn't it? Even if she'd have it otherwise."

"Ryder," Laurel began, then a blaze of camera flashes captured their image just as Ryder caught her arm. Blinking, she saw in his eyes the same need of that afternoon, the need she couldn't answer or fully comprehend.

"Laurel, I—"

"Laurel, Justice Hulme is waiting."

The choice was none at all. She turned from Ryder's grasp.

Fury emanating from him in waves, the senator steered his wife and daughter into the crowd, at least half of which, Laurel discovered to her embarrassment, had stopped to watch.

Seated beside Justice Hulme, in whose honor the gala was being given—a seventieth birthday party for the Supreme Court justice, a gift from Washington's power elite—Laurel struggled to pay attention. She pressed her spine into the brocade upholstery of the deep armchair in the Opera House's private box, trying for the hundredth time to make sense of the juggling act onstage.

Ryder's assault on them in the lobby had been followed by a dozen others from the press, scenting a good story, or preferably, trouble, which often meant the same thing. Washington hadn't forgotten the Hawk and the Dove of years ago. God, why had he come here?

Today, tonight, he'd needed Laurel, and she had refused him. Twice. She gnawed gently at her lower lip. What else could she have done?

Good sense had always ordered her life. The senator counted on her to do the right thing, the responsible thing, and her husband expected no less. But refusing Ryder nagged at her. What kind of friend was she?

"Is something wrong?" Justice Hulme whispered in her ear.

"No, nothing."

"Intermission's coming," Myra soothed. "I'm eager for news. I haven't spoken to Hilary in a month."

Laurel thought of her friend, hobbling about the house in Gloucester, and couldn't help smiling. Of course she wouldn't have told her mother; Myra would have gone up to nurse her. "She's been busy. With Sebastian Noble."

"Sebastian?" Myra's animated features lit up. "I knew they'd get on well. Sebastian will be good for Hilary. He won't allow her her delusions."

Before Laurel could comment on Chip Brewster or Sebastian, the music rose, making conversation impossible. As soon as the house lights came up, Justice Hulme and his wife were swamped by well-wishers. Laurel, trying to slip unobtrusively into the hall, was pulled herself into a rough embrace.

"Darlin', that husband of yours should keep a closer watch. You get prettier by the day."

She looked up into small dark eyes and a wet smile. "Thank you, Langford." Senator Martin smacked his lips, one hand finding its unerring way to the clinging silk that covered Laurel's bottom.

"Though I can't say I'm sorry he isn't here." He drew her closer.

"Dan's campaigning."

Laurel's hands were wedged between their bodies, and she couldn't free herself. They had been jostled into the wide hallway that wrapped around the mezzanine like a scarlet ribbon. She cast a pleading glance around, hoping for rescue. The senator was noted, and had been for thirty years, for his caresses in public, usually aimed at women who didn't want them.

"Well, then," Martin drawled. "Why don't we just disappear from this gatherin', find ourselves the back seat of mah limousine, and open a bottle of cold champagne?"

"Very tempting, but I don't think Dan would like the morning papers."

"He isn't goin' to like those other pictures either, darlin'. The damage has been done."

Laurel feigned ignorance. "What pictures?"

"You, the senator—your father, that is—the lovely Judith, whom I have admired from afar these many years, and Rydah McKendrick." Laurel noted that the southerner's accent thickened with irritation. "You yourself, with the enemy press."

She could see it already: Ryder's hand on her wrist, the quick eye contact between them, the pleading in his eyes. Dan wouldn't like it any more than the senator had. But she said, "I think my husband's a better campaigner than that, Langford. He understands the more dubious aspects of publicity."

To her relief, Laurel spied Myra Hulme approaching, eyes sparkling with amusement; obviously, she'd been the recipient of Langford Martin's caresses herself. "Here we are," she announced, handing Laurel a plastic tumbler of white wine and a paper napkin. "Senator Martin." Myra lifted her cheek for his kiss.

"Are you plannin' to spoil mah fun?" Langford asked without his smile. He glanced at Laurel as she put space between them. "Still think that's an interestin' shot of you, darlin', and Rydah. Candid camera, don't ya know. Downright interestin'."

"If I knew what you were getting at, Langford."

"The word *fraternization* comes to mind. McKendrick's got mighty feverish eyes tonight, not only when he looks at the senator."

Her pulse lurched, but Myra intervened. "You naughty politician, stop gossip-mongering or I'll get Everett after you." With a laugh, she began edging away. "Laurel's got to mingle. It's good for business, as you well know." Myra's silvery hair, worn in a sleek knot at the nape of her neck, shone as she shook her head. "Don't be surprised to find the imprint of Langford's palm on the seat of your dress later," she whispered.

"One of Washington's more harmless nuisances."

"Don't be too sure."

Laurel took a sip of wine. "I suppose someone else was bound to unearth that old feud between the senator and . . ." She wouldn't say his name, fearing that saying it might give her away.

"Ryder McKendrick," Myra said for her. She looked along the gallery jammed with people, as if searching for him. "Well, it won't be anything new for either of them, will it? Ryder's had his picture in the papers before."

At Laurel's blank look, the justice's wife smiled. "I forget how young you still are, and how much younger then. You would have been involved at school. The photo with the child," she said. "It made all the wire services around the world. Look it up sometime, in that book he published."

Laurel only nodded, her pulse rate thick and heavy.

"It's a heartbreaker, that's for sure. When I first saw it, him with that little girl . . ." Myra stopped as Everett Hulme approached, his jowls wobbling and his throat pinched a bright pink by his evening tie. He gave her a private smile, then Laurel one of more fatherly affection.

"Ladies, the senator and I have had enough handshakes and kisses. We're planning to bolt ourselves into the box momentarily. Will you join us? Your mother's been wondering where you'd gone, Laurel."

"We were waylaid by Langford Martin," Myra explained.

"That deserves another glass of wine."

But Laurel couldn't appreciate the justice's quip. Her mind raced, and her mouth went dry. She remembered the look in Ryder's eyes when he'd turned on the path after scolding Ned. *Don't ever do that again.* What longago misery couldn't he forget? She had to find out about the little girl.

"Coming, Laurel?" Myra asked as Everett Hulme walked away.

"I'm not going back. Will you tell the others?"

The older woman frowned. "What shall I tell them?"

"That I . . . I've got a headache. No, make that a migraine." Without compunction, she borrowed Dan's malady. She looked around, smiling weakly at several people who lifted their hands in greeting. She couldn't see Ryder anywhere.

"He left, Laurel," Myra said. "He was out the main doors before we reached the stairs to the theater. I don't think he liked the photo session either. I saw angry words being exchanged with another reporter." She paused. "Of course I've heard Hilary's assessment of Dan, many times, and I don't mean to pry, but . . . What's happening, Laurel?"

"I really don't know." She hesitated, not wanting to ask. "Myra, please, may I borrow some money."

"Myra," the justice called out halfway to the box entrance.

"I'm coming, Everett."

"It isn't what you think," Laurel said as several bills were pressed into her hand.

"No? Now you sound like Hilary. Obfuscating. Well, whatever it is, take care." She smiled, touching Laurel's flushed cheek. "Interesting, indeed," Myra murmured, then hurried after her husband and the others.

"N Street, please. The Greystone Hotel."

Laurel subsided against the cab's rear seat, carefully folding her evening cloak, which she'd barely remembered to retrieve from the coat room, around her. The taxi was none too clean, but then neither was its driver, who seemed to have difficulty understanding both English, and directions.

"N Street? You say, missus?"

"Georgetown, yes. Do you know where it is?"

"Yes, I try."

"Wonderful."

Laurel pulled the cloak closer, not only away from the dirt, but to shut out the chill. Both front-door windows were wide open, and the night was cold and damp after the long, gray day. She relished the soft luxury of cream-colored satin lined in sable, a Christmas gift the year before from Judith and the senator. She'd never worn it until tonight; now, she was glad of its ostentatious warmth.

The trip, lurching and headlong by turn, seemed to take forever. Huddled into the cozy fur, Laurel was beginning to wonder whether she'd arrive intact, during this century, when the cab rattled to a halt. "Greystone, missus."

"Thank you. It's been an adventure."

She was feeling peevish by now. Ashamed of herself, Laurel handed the driver a tip, then hurried across the sidewalk to the hotel's entrance.

As Ryder had indicated, the place had its charms: the molded ceiling, the ancient but beautifully faded Isfahan carpet over a once-gleaming floor of white marble. Gilt edged the fireplace mantel, and an ornate white marble stairway with curlicues of black wrought iron flowed upward toward the second floor, a royal blue runner worn to threads along the front edge of each tread.

There was no one in the small lobby. Laurel was glad. She'd been wondering how to ask for Ryder's room.

Perhaps she could simply wait here until he passed through. But if he didn't, she'd be sitting downstairs half the night, making herself conspicuous—she looked down at the elegant cloak—while upstairs, Ryder slept. Or paced. Or drank himself, if he were so inclined, into some sort of peace.

"Help you, ma'am?"

Laurel started. A thin man, all gaunt cheeks and hollow shoulders, stood in the entry from a back hall. "I . . . yes, I'm looking for Mr. McKendrick, who's staying here."

"First right at the top of the steps."

"Thank you." She felt his eyes on her all the way to the staircase. "Thank you very much," she said again.

At the room Laurel knocked, but there was no answer. "Ryder," she called through the door and waited, wondering what to do. She had turned to go when bony fingers reached past her to fit an old-fashioned key into the lock. "You can wait inside," the clerk told her. "No sense sitting on the steps. I've turned off the heat, you'd be cold downstairs." Then he disappeared, leaving Laurel to push open the door.

The room was dark, and she didn't bother with the lights. She wasn't sure how long she'd stay. She didn't know what to say when—if—Ryder came back to the room. She sat down in the nearest chair, which had a lumpy seat, and leaned her head back, feeling weary and tense and frightened.

Her head thumped. It would serve her right if she did develop a migraine. Getting up, Laurel groped her way into the adjoining bathroom, where she turned on a light at the mirror. There was an old clawfoot tub big enough for two, nearly big enough, she thought, to swim in, and a pedestal sink with brass fittings. She fished in Ryder's shaving kit, which he'd left on the edge of the sink.

Looking for aspirin, she felt like a thief. She found a half bottle of Aramis, musky and male, but no aspirin. Tucking everything neatly back into place, she heard the scratch of a door key in the lock.

Caught, she was standing in the bathroom doorway, hugging her arms to her waist, when he saw her. "I didn't think I'd left the light on." At his glance, she felt cold, despite the warmth of sable against silk. "A royal visit," he murmured, turning away. "Why, Laurel?"

"I'm not sure, entirely." She heard the click of his cigarette lighter, then saw a curl of smoke rise into the air. He shrugged out of his camel-colored suede jacket, tossing it on the foot of the bed before he faced her again. It occurred to her that he wasn't wearing a camera, such basic apparel for him that he looked naked. "What would you think if I said that I'd taken your suggestion—" her voice faltered "—to come slumming."

Ryder gave a mirthless laugh as he surveyed the room. "Not much, is it, compared to sable?"

He drew on the cigarette, then crushed it out.

"Ryder, why did you come to the gala?" Laurel asked. "You knew there'd be onlookers, speculation. And the pictures—"

"I'm sorry about that. I wasn't thinking very clearly."

"Is that why you provoked the senator?"

"So I did. Is that why you turned your back on me?"

She kept silent, not knowing what to say. She felt the tension between them, like sparks.

"After the zoo I couldn't stay in this room," Ryder confessed. "So I went out, had a couple of drinks that didn't help . . ." His hands trembled as he lighted a second cigarette, then immediately snuffed it out. "I wanted to see you again. This afternoon was unforgivable of me. I apologize. I can't blame you for leaving then, or for turning away from me tonight, which doesn't explain why you're here now."

"I've been worried about you."

"Have you?"

On the plane to Washington she'd decided they could be friends, if nothing else; at the zoo she'd been glad to see him, eager to tell him that Sebastian would let her do his catalogue drawings. She had let Ryder learn her innermost secret, the feeling that part of herself had died with Lexa. But he was hurting, too. And what had she given Ryder McKendrick as a friend?

He stood watching her with the haunting in his eyes that she'd first seen that afternoon, and again at the Kennedy Center. Thanks to Myra, perhaps she knew a hint of why. Hoping to learn the rest, Laurel took one deep breath before she spoke.

"Ryder, there was a child once, wasn't there, who—"

He tensed. "Where did you hear that?"

"From someone, another friend."

"At the gala," he said. "Are we friends, Laurel?"

"I hope so. I want to be. I couldn't stop thinking about you, about—"

"Laurel, I thought I could talk about it, but I can't."

She took the sable cloak off. "Then I'll stay until you can."

For an instant, she wondered whether she'd been wise. His look was suddenly different, dark and basic. Feverish.

"All I can think about is your being here," he said. "I can't think about anything else and if you stay, so help me God, I'm going to make love to you." He wouldn't let her look away. "To you, Laurel, not Lexa."

Her pulse quickened, her limbs felt heavy.

"I want you so damn much," he murmured, holding her gaze.

"But I'm not free to—"

"Tell me something I don't know." He walked toward her. His voice was shaky. "Tell me—whether it's right or wrong—tell me you want me, too."

How could she deny him? How could she keep lying to herself? This was partly why she'd come, Laurel realized—*he* was why, not only some terrible problem in his past. As his gaze searched hers, looking deep into her heart, her soul, she had a quick remembrance of rain, and loving. Laurel couldn't think about the consequences of what they were about to do now. Yes, he was a friend, but she loved Ryder McKendrick, too, not for Lexa but for herself.

"Yes," she said at last.

Then one of them moved, or both, and with a groan he had her in his arms, and she was giving what she'd kept hidden for too long, giving him her soft embrace of silk and warm, smooth skin. When his mouth had finished its slow, anticipatory descent, Laurel tasted whiskey, tobacco, autumn cold—and Ryder.

"Yes," she repeated, her lips whispering on his, "I want you. Oh yes, please."

## ❋  CHAPTER 19  ❋

❋

"COME ON, SWEETHEART." The bed springs creaked in rhythm, the sound of harsh breathing filled the room. Ryder's taut features told Laurel he was getting closer and closer to the edge. "Relax, please."

"I can't—!"

"God, I can't keep from—"

Just before he lost control Ryder slipped from her body onto his back. When Laurel touched him, he jerked away, gasping. "Don't."

"I'm sorry," she said after a moment, "but it was no use. I couldn't—"

"Give me a minute. It's all right. There's no clock running, Laurel."

But mortified, she glanced over to find him staring at a crack in the ceiling. The blankets had been crumpled at the foot of the bed, his suede jacket tangled in them, and Laurel shivered, suddenly chilled. With Dan, there was always a clock.

"Are you cold?"

"A little," she said.

A lot, she thought. She'd risked censure in Chevy Chase, her mother's silent—and the senator's more vocal—condemnation, and for what? To invade Ryder McKendrick's room after weeks of telling him she wouldn't have an affair, on the pretext of concern as a friend, only to end up making a fool of herself in bed, and hurting him again?

Careful not to touch her, Ryder pulled the covers over them. "Is it something I didn't do that I should have? Or something I did do that you didn't like?"

"No, of course not."

Not meeting her eyes, he raised up on an elbow. "What about ... when you're with Dan?" His voice was uncertain. "Do you turn off like this? Or—"

"No," she said, shocked. "No, because ..."

Ryder reached for his corduroys, pulling them on in a soft ripple of sound. "Sometimes blunt honesty isn't the best policy, Laurel. As the daughter of one politician and the wife of another, you ought to know that." He flicked his lighter at the tip of a cigarette, then stood at the window, smoking. "But then, neither is asking questions I won't like the answers to."

Laurel sat up and tucked the sheets beneath her armpits. What had she hoped to find here? A refuge, a few hours to herself? But Laurel Frasier Benedict made a poor adulteress, apparently able to perform only when she pretended to be someone else.

"I've hurt you," she said. "I'm—"

"Don't say any more, all right? It's my fault. In the six years Maggie's been dead, there hasn't really been anyone else. So maybe I tried to make a connection again all by myself. My mother's Sunday phone calls," he said. "They're like subliminal advertising." He glanced at her. "Only Sara's right. I've been playing it safe. Hell, you told me enough times to back off." He blew a stream of smoke into the air. "Of course, you also told me you weren't happy with your husband."

Laurel passed a hand over her tangled hair. "I won't let you take the blame for this—" she looked at the bed between them "—when it's mine. I don't 'turn off' with Dan because . . . because I rarely respond in the first place."

Turning, Ryder stared at her.

"I . . . that is, I let him think, sometimes, that I . . ."

"You mean you fake it."

She nodded, more ashamed than she'd been before.

"Were you faking in Gloucester?"

"No, but . . . no! Only tonight . . . isn't the same, don't you see? It wasn't Lexa with you that weekend, Ryder, but it *was* Lexa's courage. I had to borrow that part of her, just as we used to switch places when we were children. Lexa was always braver than I. She would have loved you then, with no guilt afterward."

Ryder raised an eyebrow. "That must have set Dan back on his heels. You know, Laurel, a little selfishness isn't a bad thing now and then." He let his gaze rest on her shoulders as he stubbed out the cigarette. "But it's not always good, either. Like bare honesty."

"What are you saying?"

"That I'm not sure I would have liked your sister." He turned briefly to the window. "Not that I have to. She's dead, and, sure, that was difficult for you to face. But fourteen years, Laurel—why do you torture yourself?"

She answered obliquely. "Lexa and I were mirror image twins. Do you know what that means?"

"I'm not sure. No."

"It happens when the mother's egg splits into two, between ten and thirteen days after fertilization. After birth, the twins are exactly like seeing one person in a looking glass. Lexa's hair grew in a counterclockwise whorl, while mine's the opposite. I read somewhere that, in rare instances, even internal organs can be reversed."

"I think your heart's in the right place," Ryder said.

She forced the smile he had wanted. "I hope so. But for nineteen years," she said, "I had met myself in the hall every morning, run into myself coming around corners. When, suddenly, she was gone . . ."

"You were still here, and you're still alive," he insisted. "Nothing's missing, Laurel. You and Lexa were twins, but even mirror image twins are separate people. I doubt very much that she was ever prettier than you or braver or smarter or more talented. I'm not the only one who thinks so. Sebastian Noble liked the drawings you made so much that he took one home with him and has hired you to do his catalogue. Hilary thinks you've wasted yourself for years."

"When did she tell you that?"

"In the kitchen, in Gloucester. We weren't only talking about camera angles that night, or about your talent, either."

He must mean her marriage, and Laurel felt fear closing in again.

"Perhaps you're both right." She thought of Dan's absence this weekend. "But even if you are, there's still Ned to think about."

Ryder went very still. He sat on the other side of the bed from her, his elbows on his spread thighs, and let his head drop into the cradle of his hands. "I should have known before," he said. "Dan's the obvious answer. A quick macho response on my part. Sex isn't the issue here, is it, Laurel? Or your sister? Talk about phony courage. I screwed up my nerve to meet Ned, then I really blew it this afternoon, didn't I?" He shook his head. "I went berserk, and picked your kid to do it with. Christ," he muttered, "no wonder you marched over here tonight. And what do I do? Come on with a cheap seduction, or try to. . . ."

"No, Ryder. I came because . . ." She couldn't say it. *I feared for you, wanted you. I still do, only I'm afraid.* "Because I wanted to help."

He raised his head to look at her. "Social work? Well, I can't blame you for that, either. If I could make sense of today, I sure as hell would." He was silent. Then, "I don't know why I had that flashback when I did, after all this time. Maybe it was just walking along with you, talking at the zoo. But I could feel the jungle again, see the colors. Then, all at once, there was Ned and he looked, he felt so much like . . ." He stopped, taking a gulp of air.

Laurel saw him fighting emotion. She'd seen Dan do it, though he kept his feelings so well buried most of the time that she often thought he didn't have any. Ryder's were closer to the surface.

The only light came from the bathroom. Laurel watched him light another cigarette, which he'd torn from the crumpled package on the bedstand. "I try not to think about her. It hurts too much. Even more than Maggie."

"Tell me. Please."

He murmured, "Snake oil," in a tone that said he didn't believe in miracle cures. "But hell, maybe you're right, though I doubt it." Then after a long pause, he began to talk. "I told you before about this guy, Ham Channing, who'd suggested the series for Sara Hennessey on the war's effect on civilian populations? Well, he'd help me out now and then, give me tips on likely subjects. One day he stumbled on this Catholic orphanage, smack in the middle of nowhere, but only five or ten minutes from the base camp we were using then."

Ryder contemplated the glowing tip of his cigarette. "'You've got to see these kids,' he told me. 'You like kids, Mac. You're crazy about kids, wait till you see 'em.'"

"How many were there?" Laurel asked.

"Over a hundred. All ages, all victims of war. Their families gone, their lives, even their own bodies, blown apart. Sara always calls me her tough war correspondent, but the day I first saw those kids, I turned to mush inside." Then he smiled faintly. "I should say one kid, because when I laid eyes on her, I was gone." He glanced at Laurel. "She went straight to my heart."

"What was her name?"

"Ngoc Hoa. She looked like one of those Oriental dolls . . . everything so fine and delicate, handcrafted. She was three years old, maybe a little more. I never knew for sure. She had big dark eyes and black hair like heavy silk, and she just looked at you, without saying a word."

Ryder crushed the cigarette he'd barely drawn on, then immediately lit another. "The nuns told me she'd been that way for six months, since they'd taken her in after her parents were killed." He grimaced. "They'd been shot to death in a raid by ARVN forces who burned their village, suspecting it as being sympathetic to the VC."

She shivered. "How horrible."

"I decided to win her over, so I took to making visits whenever I could. Two, three times a week unless we were out in the bush somewhere, following patrols, or back in Saigon. Other than a few piasters, I brought her the standard GI luxuries—chewing gum, T-shirts, candy bars." He smiled at the memory. "She was crazy for Hersheys with almonds."

As a mother Laurel found herself making a tremendous identification with a child she'd never seen. "Ned loves them, too."

"He would have liked our routine, then. I'd come in from assignment, jump into a jeep, and rattle my bones over to the orphanage, hold out the latest lure. She'd take it in these fragile hands, a miniature, and then—after weeks of this—she finally gave me that smile. Slow, brilliant. Hoa's smile," he murmured. "It was like a sunrise."

"Did she talk again?"

"Eventually. Another month or so. We taught each other words, but we didn't really need speech. We had a running joke. Her name in Vietnamese means 'Precious Flower,' but I called her Cherry Blossom, no imagination at all and really Japanese, because it made her giggle. That was worth just about anything it cost. She called me Papa-san."

He dragged on the cigarette. "So I wrote Maggie, started all the paperwork without even waiting for her answer. I knew the red tape would take a year at best before Hoa could have an exit visa. The Vietnamese are a proud people, devoted to their children. Until the war the term *orphan* was an alien concept, but by the time I was over there, it was the unofficial estimate that 100,000 children were separated from their extended families. Adoption by foreigners—Westerners—wasn't common, or easy."

He shook his head. "Hell, the government wouldn't make it easy. Verification was required that her parents were dead, or written permission needed from a relative for her to leave the country." Ryder frowned. "Of course, in Hoa's case, the village records had been burned in the raid, too, and her relatives had disappeared. Most kids didn't qualify. Many who did died of hunger before their papers came through. But I wanted desperately to bring Hoa back to the States, to give her a home and a future. We talked about that a lot."

He said it so hopelessly that Laurel couldn't speak.

"For months," he said, and propped the burning cigarette in the ashtray. "Our visits kept me sane, too. The rest was madness. Sometimes I'd lie awake all night with rocket attacks in the distance or mortar poundings, listening to the manmade thunder, thinking about the torn lives, torn bodies . . . some seventeen-year-old kid with both legs ground meat because he'd stepped the wrong way on a path. But then, like some miracle, the sky would start to lighten and the sun would come up. Sunrise. God's in his heaven. Ngoc Hoa's smile," he said, "for all the world to see."

His voice had dropped to a whisper, and Laurel held her breath.

"What happened, Ryder?"

"One morning the sun didn't rise."

He said it matter-of-factly, but with his eyes closed against the memory. After that, there was silence. Laurel felt very cold. She saw him tremble as Ryder reached again for the cigarette. Then he muttered, "Jesus. I smoke too damn much," and went into the bathroom with it. The toilet flushed, then Laurel heard more running water. When he came back, Ryder's face had been scrubbed until it shone and his eyes were bright. Without speaking, she drew him down beside her.

"I can't talk any more, Laurel. My God, it still hurts."

She brushed damp hair from his forehead. "You've talked enough for now."

"Christ, I didn't want to ruin things with Ned, with you." He took a shuddering breath. "It's just that today he reminded me so clearly of her."

"I know," she murmured soothingly, "I know."

"And then Maggie died, and everything that looked so bright, every . . . fucking thing . . . was gone." Ryder passed a hand over his eyes. "Goddamn, *goddammit*. What made me think I was going to get another chance? Laurel, I wonder if anybody does."

Her throat tightened. She put one arm around his shoulders and kept stroking his hair, as she might have comforted Ned after a nightmare. And tried to tell herself that she'd risked too much tonight. That her life, imperfect as it was, was still her life, which had to stay that way. Hadn't she proved that with her frigidity not twenty minutes ago in the arms of a man who'd been only good to her? A man who was now at the outer limit of his control?

Yet she leaned closer to whisper, "We can try, Ryder. Even if it's wrong for both of us, I want to try."

When he lifted his head, her mouth sought his. The kiss was long and complicated, a mix of tenderness and need and passion.

He eased her back onto the bed without her being aware of the motion.

"You won't pretend this time?" His tone was urgent, and she knew he didn't mean only these few hours in his room.

"I never have, with you. I swear it, Ryder."

"Then you don't need to borrow Lexa now," he murmured. "Because the one thing that was true, and completely honest, between us from the start was Gloucester." His gaze faltered. "Wasn't it, Laurel?"

"Yes."

He drew the sheet from her, exposing her nakedness. "I want you so much I ache. But I don't want you to fake it."

"I couldn't, not with you." It was why she'd given up before, unable to relax, or to go on with only the pretense, for his sake, of pleasure. Tonight, they'd gone beyond the fragile closeness of the afternoon. In his grief for Hoa, she saw her own, for Lexa. In the devastation of his marriage to Maggie, she glimpsed the life she had with Dan—and was no longer certain she wanted. But she was certain of now, of this. "I won't, Ryder. I won't."

He reached up, turning on the light. "I want to see you."

Laurel saw, by the alarm clock, that it was eleven

o'clock. The senator and Judith were hosting an after-gala dinner party at an area restaurant, and wouldn't be home yet. Not yet. . . .

"Laurel, let me love you. Just like Gloucester, in the morning, in the rain."

The words sent an arrow of desire streaking through them both. On a groan he took her mouth, his tongue sliding inside, and his arms clasped her tightly to him. Laurel whimpered in response, in surrender. After that, except for her sweet yielding, there was nothing.

"You know something?"

Amusement in his tone, Ryder spoke into the darkness. He'd finally shut off the light, which had only intensified their lovemaking a second time. Now Laurel nuzzled just beneath his jawline, pressing closer for warmth of more than one sort. The room was cold, not merely cool, but in the last hour or so she'd felt bathed in fire, by Ryder's careful lovemaking, by the tenderness they'd shared.

The senator would be frantic by now.

But she didn't want to let these feelings go. She tucked her hands between their bodies. She felt so close to him, as if sometime in the night they'd twinned themselves, to drive out Alexandra. "Tell me," she said.

"Self-pity shits."

Laurel's fingers warmed with her smile. "Good lead. What's the rest of the article going to say?"

He grinned. "I think I'll shoot for the op-ed page."

They were silent, Ryder's hands stroking her back until she almost forgot that the bedside clock now read twelve-fifteen.

"I have to leave," she said. "Maybe I can catch the senator's party at Germaine's." The restaurant wasn't that far away.

"In a minute."

She purred at his slow, silky touch. Then Ryder said, "Laurel?"

"Mmmm."

His tone had sobered. "Thanks. For coming here, and staying, for caring—and listening."

Had he repressed again those nightmarish months in Vietnam, and the untold ending to Ngoc Hoa's story? She wondered whether she would ever hear it.

"I couldn't stay away."

"And thanks for this." His arms came around her in the dark. After a moment he said again, "Laurel? Are you still cold?"

"We could use another blanket. Just for a minute."

Slipping from bed, he left her to freeze, coming back with something sleek and soft. He draped its sinuous heat around them. Laurel imagined the feeling was that of being held by a very large, extremely furry bear. Remembering the pandas, she smiled.

"What is this?"

"Your cloak." Lifting a corner, Ryder brushed the dense pelt of the lining across her cheek, her throat, her lips, bruised now from his kisses. She trembled with resurgent pleasure as he added, "I hope you don't mind."

"What else is sable for?"

Ryder laughed, low in his throat. "Let's find out." His hands began to work their magic. And then once more he said, "Laurel?"

"Yes?" At his continued stroking, the word was a barely audible gasp.

"I love you."

Nothing could have warmed her more, not even sable. She closed her eyes, and said, "I love you, too."

Laurel jerked from a dozing sleep, her heart pounding. She leaned across Ryder to squint at the clock. One A.M.!

With a groan, she bolted from the bed and began throwing on her rumpled white silk evening dress. Wakened by the thump of her shoes as they fell from its folds, Ryder sat up and dragged a hand through his hair. Laurel looked at him beseechingly.

"My God, what will I tell them? They'll have the police out looking for me by now. I didn't mean to fall asleep. The senator . . ." Then she stopped, one hand clutched around her pantyhose, the other holding a shoe. "Tell me not to go. I don't want to leave you."

"Bravery," Ryder muttered, "just when neither of us needs it." Then he said obligingly, "Don't go."

But they both knew he didn't mean it. While Laurel finished dressing and straightened her hair, he pulled on his pants and shirt and shoes. He didn't bother with socks and left the shirt unbuttoned.

Smiling, she slipped into his arms for a hug. "You're half asleep still. Go back to bed."

"Come with me and I will."

With a regretful shake of her head, Laurel eased away to search her small evening bag for money.

Ryder took the purse from her and snapped it shut. "I don't want you to go, but I'll get you a cab."

"No, you stay here."

"Laurel, this is Washington. At one in the morning, not the safest neighborhood in town." He picked up the phone. "And you standing outside alone, wearing a fur-lined coat? Let me call. Then I'll walk you downstairs." Feeling boneless from fatigue and lovemaking, Laurel slid the sable-lined cloak around her shoulders and hesitated.

Ryder pulled her into his arms in the open doorway. "Vacate the premises, lady," he whispered, "before there's trouble."

Together, stealing kisses on the way, they crept down to the lobby.

When the cab arrived, Ryder said reluctantly, "Here you go."

She shouldn't let him put an arm around her shoulders in public, but—

"It's freezing," Laurel said as he held the cab's rear door for her. "You'll catch your death." The interior light cast a golden glow over Ryder's features, and Laurel stared up into his eyes for a moment, transfixed by the love she saw there.

"I hate sending you back to him," he said. His hands burrowed through the opening of the cloak and the sable lining to Laurel's warmly silk-clad waist. She could sense his frustration, his need. Ignoring the cabbie's muttered, "Make the good-byes fast, I ain't got all night," he dragged her closer.

Knowing they were being foolish, certainly indiscreet, Laurel couldn't make herself push him away. A kiss on the cheek couldn't hurt, even if they were seen. Then she couldn't refuse him as Ryder arched her body like a bow, at the same time leaning into her so that she could feel his hardness again through the silk of her dress. Arousal flared in Laurel as he kissed her, open-mouthed. "I love you," he whispered, the words joining his tongue inside her mouth.

"Come on, pal. Take her back upstairs if you want more—"

"Shut up," Ryder told the man, releasing her.

Embarrassed, Laurel turned her back. She'd better go. As she eased into the cab's rear seat, her gaze focused on a limousine parked across the street. Her heart lurched. A uniformed chauffeur sat toying with the steering wheel. The motion struck her as falsely idle; his gaze had focused intently on her cab, on the two people who'd been embracing seconds before.

She wouldn't call Ryder's attention to it, though. Perhaps she was being paranoid, perhaps seeing things.

"Good night," she murmured as Ryder gave the cabbie money for the trip to Chevy Chase.

"See that she gets home safe, *pal*," Ryder said. Before she could stop him, he'd leaned inside and kissed her again, lightly. "Good morning."

When morning did come, Ryder realized that he'd been half expecting the phone call. Like Laurel, he'd seen the limousine parked across from his hotel. Unlike her, he'd memorized the license plate and now knew to whom it belonged.

His worst fears became reality when Sara Hennessey's voice, not as roughly affectionate as usual, said without greeting, "I hope she was worth it."

Ryder could have groaned. "Who was worth what?"

"In your own words, 'the candidate's wife.' And your ass, McKendrick."

She didn't need to say anything else. Ryder strangled the receiver, and remembered their conversation on Friday when he'd checked in at the hotel.

"The senator just called," she said, "loaded for bear."

"Meaning me, I suppose." But what had made him call Sara?

"He seemed very sure of himself, dropping important names whose information he trusts absolutely. Langford Martin, for one." Ryder did groan. It was Martin's limousine, his chauffeur, that had been parked across from the Greystone. What he didn't know was why. "It seems," Sara went on, "that Laurel Benedict left the justice's gala last evening and came home, much the worse for wear, at two A.M.!"

Dammit. Ryder stayed silent. Dammit to hell.

"She was with you, I assume."

"Don't worry about it."

"Don't worry? This isn't just you on the razor's edge, but my newspaper. When Edwin Frasier starts screaming libel, defamation of character, and a dozen other charges he'll throw at you—at us—in court, most of which I've never even heard before, dammit I worry. If you write about his daughter—"

"He can't do a thing. I'm not writing a story. It's a private matter."

Sara made a sound of disgust. "No such animal in this business, Mac. You know that.

"What did you tell Frasier?"

"He told me." The tone of her voice indicated that Sara Hennessey was as furious with herself for being manipulated by the powerful politician as she was with Ryder for being indiscreet. "Of course that was after Teague Michaels got me out of bed last night to ask where you were."

"You told him?" Ryder was incredulous.

"He took me by surprise, from a sound sleep. I thought it had to do with Dan Benedict's campaign. Which," Sara muttered, "in a way it does. Go ahead, blame me. But if I were you, I'd check out in the next sixty seconds."

He felt a wave of despair followed by guilt. "She's a grown woman, Sara. What right does Frasier have to—"

"She's his daughter, the only one he's got."

"I'll see you tomorrow, then." He was already looking toward the frosted glass doors that led to the street.

"Make it this afternoon, Mac."

What had seemed a miracle the night before, lying next to Laurel in a warm bed with the undreamt-of luxury of loving her again, now seemed folly. His, Ryder acknowledged, but dangerous to them both.

Knowing what could happen, he'd been careless of her

reputation, of her position, and of his own standing as a journalist.

"Sara, I really love her." It was the only excuse he had.

He wondered whether the tremor in his voice had carried over the wires. A long silence followed before Sara Hennessey sighed in resignation.

"Then I'm happy for you. At least until Frasier pulls the trapdoor under the gallows."

**❋**

**❋ CHAPTER 20 ❋**

**❋**

ON THE SUNDAY morning after his primary win, Dan Benedict realized he could be living on borrowed time. He stood in the kitchen of the adobe-style house he shared with Maria, focusing miserably on the coffee in his cup. It was cold, but he didn't notice. After the telephone call from Teague, his entire being felt cold. One disaster, Dan thought, had been piled on another, from this morning's news about Laurel, back to his arrival in Shelby on Friday night, still furious over Maria's visit to Dawson. Now, he thought, that was the least of his problems.

"You're not to go to Dawson again," he'd said. "The boy knows the name of that horse you keep here, and God knows what else! I won't have my son's privacy intruded upon, his—"

"Safety?"

His pulse jumped. "Why would you say that?"

"A crazed, unhappy woman, grieving for the babies she'll never have . . . what else would anyone expect? At the very least, a kidnapping. You're a prominent public figure now—"

"Don't you talk to me that way, like a cunning black-mailer!"

"Mistress," Maria corrected softly. "That's what you're really afraid of, Dan. That I'll compromise the 'legitimate' interests of your life, jeopardize that sterling future in government, approach your wife and child—"

"Stay away from them!" he shouted. "Do you hear? Stay the hell away from both of them!"

He'd only been this frightened as a child, and he'd never felt such anger toward Maria. Her shocked face scared him even more. He had to get out before the last of his control slipped, before he hurt Maria as his father had battered him.

"I'm going for a walk," Dan said.

He'd returned hours later, emptied of anything but the need to sleep. Maria lay in bed, their room dark and silent except for the soft sound of crying.

He went down beside the bed, putting his face next to hers and running a hand over her hair. "I shouldn't have yelled. It isn't you, I swear. The campaign, the pace ... I do worry, in general, about Ned being a target."

She spoke into the pillow. "He's a lovely little boy, Danny. I'd never hurt him. I think ... he's been hurt enough." The silken hair slipped against the sheets as she rolled over to look at him. "Can't you try to love him?"

"Of course I love him. He's my son."

But fathers weren't for loving, Dan knew. Fathers were for hating, and leaving, and never, never going back. If he lost this chance, the past would close in on him again, and if he lost her, too ...

"God, Maria. Don't go away from me, don't."

In answer, she eased the first button open on his shirt, her fingers gentle and welcoming as he'd always known them to be until the campaign began.

"I love you, Danny. God help me."

They had made love off and on through the night with a strange bittersweetness that hadn't been there before. On Saturday Dan had wakened with the sun, oddly refreshed after so little sleep.

"I'll buy you a co-op in Washington," he told her. "Then we can see each other nearly every day. How will that be?"

"Competitive." She said it smiling, and, his Maria again, went into his arms.

Then this morning the telephone had rung. "Six o'clock on a Sunday," he'd grumbled, lifting the receiver. Teague Michaels was at the other end. And now Dan was staring into his cold coffee, with the barely mended weekend in tatters. He knew he should have left ten minutes ago.

"Are you ready?"

As Maria spoke he set the cup on the counter. "I'd better be." He wanted to tell Maria why he'd been called back to Boston, but something stopped him. "Come on, let's get going. That charter pilot will charge me by the second if I'm late."

They drove in silence to the small airstrip outside Shelby where he'd landed on Friday, half an hour after seeing McKendrick at Logan Airport. Dan's gut tightened. That wasn't all; in a second, Saturday talk by phone with Ned's riding master about Maria, he'd learned that she hadn't been the only visitor at Dawson. A tall man, he'd remembered, with gray eyes and dark blond hair. He'd helped the stable boy locate Ned's missing horse the day he'd fallen.

"What's wrong, Dan?" Maria finally asked. "I can't remember Teague's calling you here more than twice in ten years."

"Campaign bullshit," he muttered.

It was shit, all right. The kind the papers loved. This close, this goddamn close. What if the story came out?

He'd kill Laurel first. McKendrick, too.

God, he still couldn't believe it. Laurel, and another man. So he hadn't imagined the looks between them, the emotion in her sketch of McKendrick. Or the danger for himself. Well, she wasn't going to ruin him, not now. Nobody was. With a grim smile, Dan traced a finger down Maria's cheek. "I'm sorry about the weekend."

The apology wasn't enough; she'd been grieving too long for something he couldn't quite understand. It wasn't only the children she couldn't have. She wouldn't get to Ned again, he'd already established that; but he wasn't going to lose her, either. By God, he wouldn't. As they parked at the airfield, he offered the small gift of his confidence after all, and watched shock take over her smile.

"It seems," Dan told Maria, "that my wife has taken a lover."

Late that afternoon, Laurel faced Dan across his desk in the den on Beacon Hill. It seemed that one moment she'd been a woman wrapped in love and sable. The next she'd been whisked back to Chevy Chase and the morning newspapers had her picture, and Ryder's.

Her mother had, predictably, wept. "With Lexa, I expected such behavior, but of you, Laurel, never."

The senator rounded on his daughter. "Laurel, what in hell were you thinking of? A married woman. When Myra Hulme told me you'd left the gala with a headache, we were concerned." He took a breath. "Then, when your mother telephoned home from Germaine's just after we'd started dinner for thirty people, I learned that you had never showed up here." He swigged at his bourbon. "Then Langford Martin started talking about McKendrick's feverish looks at you."

Laurel groaned inwardly. "Langford Martin made a

pathetic pass at me, Senator. Which I refused. He was trying to make trouble. You can ask Myra."

"I've heard what Hilary's mother had to say. I'm more interested in your explanation." He finished the drink and poured another. Judith was already helping herself. "Can you imagine how I felt when I called Teague Michaels, thinking perhaps he had sent McKendrick down here to cover the gala for the campaign, only to learn he didn't know anything about McKendrick's trip to Washington? He called me back after talking to Sara Hennessey, who knew where McKendrick was staying—and thus, where you might be."

"I'm sorry I didn't call you."

"It's too late for that. There I was, and your mother, with a roomful of guests—important people—and Dan's campaign in potential shreds. The room was buzzing. If it hadn't been for Langford's discreet offer to send his car and driver to the Greystone . . ."

"How convenient. And did you promise Senator Martin something wonderful for his help?"

"Don't talk to me like that."

But Laurel knew that Martin would be well compensated for the favor. He'd been courting the senator and his power base for months over an upcoming Defense bill. She wished her father would attend to her as closely.

"You were seen by Langford's chauffeur coming out of McKendrick's hotel, and kissing him good-bye, which you may be sure is the operative word here." The senator lowered his voice. "Would you mind telling me what your attraction is to this man, because—"

Laurel hedged a little. "He needed me."

"He needed you all right. How long after your little tryst in that flophouse do you think it would have been before the scandal sheets printed the story?"

"Ryder McKendrick is a respectable journalist."

"Respectable," the senator repeated, too softly. "That man tried years ago to ruin me in this town. It wasn't he who was respectable then and it sure as hell isn't now!"

She swallowed, shutting her ears to her mother's continued sobs, shutting her heart to the fury she saw in the senator's face. And much worse, the disappointment. "That was your fight, not mine."

"Well, you may be sure that it still is."

"Edwin, what will we do? With the election this close—"

The senator turned to his wife. "Judith, not a word of scandal will be heard. I promise you."

"But Langford—"

"I know you don't like the man, but in this case he can be trusted." He faced his daughter again, as if pointing out the opposite. "I must have been a fool, 'keeping my enemy close.' I didn't make many misjudgments in thirty-four years in politics—but that was one. I will assume that this flagrant lapse of conduct on your part was a whim of the moment—a one-time temptation—because the man can be charming when he chooses. You've always been a good girl, Laurel. You have a future with Daniel. And you're going home now to discuss it."

Laurel had been on the plane to Boston within the hour.

"Well?" Dan prompted now.

But what could she say?

"Dammit, this is the life you were born to, groomed for. If Judith hammered into you and Lexa anything, it would have been—"

"Somebody else's life, not mine." Laurel's breath caught. "No one ever asked whether that's what *I* wanted."

"How the hell should I know what you want when

you don't tell me a damn thing, unless it's something to do with Ned, *Christ*—"

He was out of the desk chair.

"Don't shout at me, Dan!"

"After those newspaper pictures? I'll damn well shout when my wife behaves like a common prostitute, and with a man who could destroy us all—"

"He won't, Dan. I know him. He won't."

"That's a fact." His voice dropped. "Accomplished fact."

Laurel's pulse sped. "What have you done?"

"That's my question, isn't it? I'm only sorry to know the answer."

She saw the hurt in his eyes just as she often saw the strange regret that he couldn't quite hide about Ned. Now she couldn't remember things ever being different, better, between them; but their marriage had been good, hadn't it, once? Always, she clung to that.

"One other question." His eyes met hers. "How did you reach Ned's school the day he fell from his horse?"

"By car, of course."

"But you dislike turnpike driving, and you'd have come back during rush hour, the traffic—"

"My son was injured."

Laurel's heart hammered. Why now, when he had never asked before?

"That maternal instinct of yours," Dan said. "It's rather like a wild animal's, isn't it? I envy Ned that, you know. I'd have given a great deal as a child to have my mother's protection. Fierce, and . . . to the death, if necessary."

"Dan—"

"McKendrick drove you to Dawson, didn't he? Don't bother to deny it, Laurel. You were seen, so was he."

At the stables, she thought.

She made a dismissing gesture. "He had come to the

house here because of Teague's threats after the announcement. He was angry. You weren't home. He was still here when the headmaster at Dawson phoned that Ned was hurt. Dan, I kept remembering Lexa that day in the clinic, and—"

"He kindly pulled you together again and offered to drive you."

"Yes, that's exactly what happened."

"In my car?"

"Yes, I'm afraid so." There was no sense in lying now.

"You could have called Teague."

"You know I don't like him."

"I don't care for your friend Hilary, either, but if I needed help in regard to you, I would probably call her, not rely on a stranger."

"Teague was with you, in Chicago. Ryder drove me to the school, Dan, that's all. I know it looks more sordid than that after yesterday, but—"

"Sordid? That's not a word I like particularly, with the election at our backs." He came around the desk. "I'm still going to win, Laurel. I'm going to win," he repeated, "and you agreed to help me."

"I've been helping."

He gave a harsh laugh. "Until recently. It is recent, isn't it? And as . . . innocent as the day at Dawson?"

She didn't know what he was getting at.

"I've got a brutal week coming up," he went on. "I won't spend any part of it dwelling on fantasies of my wife with a man I happen to dislike." He paused. "They are just fantasies, aren't they?"

Laurel tensed. She had seen that look once before, in their bedroom, after the fund-raising banquet. Pulling her to her feet, Dan grasped her shoulders. "Tell me you didn't sleep with McKendrick."

"But I—"

"Tell me." His grip was hard, his voice very soft. "Like this." Bending, he whispered crude Anglo-Saxon in her ear. The four-letter word made her wince. "I don't give a damn whether or not it's true, just say it."

"I . . . I didn't . . . sleep with him."

"Who?"

"With Ryder McKendrick!"

"Tell me the other way," he commanded. "And look at me when you do."

"Dan, I can't."

"Say it! Tell me exactly what McKendrick didn't do to you!"

Laurel bowed her head. Shamed, she said the ugly words he wanted to hear. And still he wasn't satisfied. He made her say them a second time, a third, until she trembled with humiliation. "I hate you! I hate you!"

"I'd think twice about that. You're in this by yourself, you know."

"In what?"

"He's not a part of my campaign any longer. The senator and I agree it's best. I'm sure McKendrick has already joined us, in that at least. If he wants to work anywhere, he doesn't have much choice—and neither do you."

She began to feel sick. "I have the choice of leaving you. What would happen to your flawless campaign then, Dan?"

"What would happen to you? Laurel Frasier Benedict doesn't fit into any other world except the one she's known for the last thirty-three years. Where would you go? To a man who lives out of a suitcase, who hasn't the money to support you? And you, without a job, having to give up Ned, when there'd be no need to if you simply stay—"

"Money isn't important to me."

"That proves how spoiled you are, Laurel." He smiled.

"Money is unimportant only when you have plenty of it."

He had a point. Laurel turned her back. She stared fixedly at a small Degas painting of a ballerina stretching at the barre; she'd always loved its grace, its delicacy. Now she couldn't even see it; unshed tears made an impressionistic blur that exceeded the original.

"What did you mean about Ned?"

Dan sat at his desk. "We can put this unpleasant episode behind us, Laurel. There won't be any story, from McKendrick or Martin or anyone else. It's forgotten, erased."

Laurel's nerves snapped. "What about Ned?"

"Ned is my responsibility, not McKendrick's, who wouldn't have him anyway, from what I've heard. But if you leave me, Laurel, for him or on your own, Ned stays. However," Dan continued, "should you decide to remain, and to go on assisting with the campaign, I'm prepared to be generous." The words fell flatly, as if he'd tired of goading her at last. "You wanted Ned at home, so we'll bargain. You don't see McKendrick again, and I'll take Ned out of that school you never wanted him to go to."

Stunned, Laurel circled from the painting. When she'd put him on the plane to Dawson, moments before boarding her own shuttle to Boston, Ned, oblivious of her late-night disappearance in Washington, had cried. "I don't want to go back there!"

He could be with her again, every day and every night, no more tearful partings.

I love you, Ryder had said. But they hadn't talked about a future. And she wasn't sure he really wanted one. Could she abandon her life here, and Ned, when last night had raised as many questions as it answered?

"I'm waiting, Laurel."

"You know my answer." She bent her head, not certain she could keep from crying.

"May I hear it, please?"

There would be no more shouting. Dan was as civilized now as the senator would be in victory. There would be no more nights like last night, Laurel thought. She remembered Ryder's hands, his mouth, his weight, and when he'd driven her to the very margins of the world she'd always known, he had whispered in her ear, his voice raw silk, and she'd leapt gladly into the void, pleasure exploding around them like a galaxy just being born. No more, she thought, no more.

"Laurel?"

"I want you to bring Ned home."

"I'll just call the school then."

The telephone buttons clicked one by one, and their chiming set her senses screaming. Stop, don't, she should have cried, because it seemed music to end the world by.

What else could she do? Ryder had memories of Ngoc Hoa to contend with, and she had Ned, who was alive, who needed her. Maybe Ryder would never forget, and even if he did, could he want the little boy she loved? The child who made her life worth living?

She didn't take her eyes from Dan's, but caught only part of what he was saying. ". . . mother and I feel that his presence at home . . . a binding time for us as a family . . . election." She clasped her elbows, wanting to rock with grief and joy. The rest was lost, but Ned was coming home.

Forgive me, she thought. I only have one child, Ryder. And then, I'll only have my son.

"That sonofabitch!" Hilary's furious tone carried through the telephone wires from New York to Boston. "Have you spoken to Ryder since you left his hotel? The man must be frantic, not wanting to risk phoning you."

"He didn't make me any promises, Hil."

"Laurel, that man makes you promises every time he looks in your eyes."

Laurel dismissed the gladness that swept through her. "Maybe. But I don't want to make things worse for him than they are."

"The senator tapping phones these days?"

She didn't answer.

"Well, do you want me to call McKendrick for you?"

"No!"

Hilary sighed. "If you change your mind, I'm free until Thursday, when the foreign auto show opens at the Coliseum."

Laurel was distracted from her problems by the announcement. Typical of Hilary, she thought; dropping bombs into the middle of a conversation. "What does a car show have to do with America's top fashion model?"

"I'm part of one of the big Italian manufacturer's sales pitches. Remind me to murder the person whose fault that is." She mentioned a famous fashion photographer. "Six changes of slinky evening wear that I have to drape, along with my body, across the highly polished chassis of the godlike DeNobili's newest inspiration."

"The X7?"

"How do you know about that?"

"I listen well. Remember Gloucester, and your sparring match with Sebastian?"

"God, don't remind me. I've only just recovered from the company of that madman." Skillfully, she changed the subject. "When does Ned come home?"

"Tomorrow."

"What about the campaign?"

"I told Dan I'd continue to help. Afterward, I don't know." Laurel paused. "Whatever happens, has nothing to do with Washington, last weekend, or Ryder."

"All right, maybe he's only a catalyst for change in your life, though I find that hard to believe. But please, love, make the changes. Daniel's been getting his way for too many years."

"We're both getting our way this time. Ned's coming home."

"And Ryder McKendrick's a thing of the past?"

"Oh, Hilary," she said in a breaking voice. "I don't know." Maybe later, if she were willing to sacrifice Ned, which she wasn't, and if Ryder . . . "He has his problems, too, ones I'm not sure I can understand, or that he can overcome."

"Call him."

"I promised Dan I wouldn't."

"Laurel, dammit, call him."

## ✹ **CHAPTER 21** ✹

✹

Squinting into the sun, Ryder surveyed Boston Common, a few blocks south of Laurel's Beacon Hill townhouse. The autumn air, after a steamy September, had cooled, and would apparently remain that way. He'd miss it soon enough.

Now he watched the slender woman in a baggy blue sweatsuit toss a Nerf ball for a large white dog and two little boys. And remembered how she'd looked last Saturday in his room at the Greystone, the sable cloak a luxurious dark sprawl of rich fur. A part of their pleasure that night, when she'd left it had become a symbol of the wealth that separated them, the power. But he didn't want to think about that now, so Ryder noted how the sun struck highlights in her hair as Laurel leaped, ran, spun. The huge dog, undisciplined at best, yelped and darted and tripped the humans in his path. "Pirate, look out!"

"He made me miss the ball, Mommy!"

Ryder's heart turned over at the sound of Laurel's laughter, and Ned's. The game continued, more spirit than technique, a counterpoint to the growing ache inside him. As she shouted at the two boys, he asked himself how long her face would remain carefree if he made his presence known.

"I give up!" Her hands brushed ineffectually at the jumping dog. "I'm done, you three! Have mercy."

Take pity, he'd asked her once. Would she now? With an inward groan, Ryder rose to his feet and began walking slowly toward the children.

Catching her breath, Laurel leaned against the nearest tree, letting her mind drift, taking pleasure in the simple joy of watching Ned and Kip and Pirate frolicking on the green grass.

On Sunday, she'd thought she might die of misery now, four days later, being stuck between the proverbial rock and hard place didn't seem as bad. She'd done what she had to do, even if she didn't have to like it, especially the phone call to Ryder. After that, she'd done her crying. Now, there was this sunny reprieve, perhaps undeserved, but oh, so welcome. She lifted her face to the sun's tepid warmth and briefly closed her eyes.

Opening them again as the dog barked, she felt her pulse trip. Ryder. What was he doing here? Wearing a pair of khakis and a bush shirt she'd never seen before? He approached Ned and Kip, laying a hand on Pirate's head to still the barks of greeting.

She saw him take something from the breast pocket of his shirt, then hold out the package to Ned, who hesitated.

"I can't take it," he said. "I . . . I shouldn't talk to you."

"They're the pictures from the zoo, Ned."

"You may take the pictures," Laurel said. "It's okay."

Ned's expression cleared, and he nearly tore the envelope from Ryder's grip. With Pirate charging behind, Ned and his friend raced for the nearest bench. "Wait till you see the pandas!" he yelled.

Ryder watched them a moment, the dog nudging repeatedly at Ned's hand before he said, "I hope canine saliva's not harmful to Kodak paper."

"You should have sent them."

"I was going to put the pictures in your mail slot at the house. While I was parking the car, I saw you leave with the boys."

"And followed us."

"Old habits die hard," he admitted, then said, "I want to kiss you."

Wanting the kiss, Laurel stepped back. "I left a message on your machine. Didn't you—"

"I got it. I decided not to understand." He tilted her chin with the tip of his index finger, and her skin warmed, sensitized by their Saturday lovemaking to his lightest touch. "What was all that 'Thanks for being my friend'? Past tense. What did they do to you on Sunday, Laurel?"

She could have asked the same question of him. There were dark smudges beneath his eyes, as if she'd looked into her own mirror.

"Bravery seems to have been a passing affliction," Ryder murmured when she didn't answer, "like the twenty-four-hour flu. What's Ned doing out of school? Who's the other boy?"

"His friend, Kip. From Cambridge. They met in nursery school."

She hadn't answered his first question, and, as she might have known, Ryder persisted. "What's the occasion?"

"Yom Kippur."

"You aren't Jewish."

Laurel took a breath. "Kip's school is out for the day." Then she gave it up. "But Ned's at home with us . . . permanently. He isn't at Dawson any longer."

"Why the sudden change of policy? I know Benedict wanted . . ." Breaking off, Ryder assessed her with darkened eyes. "He's brought Ned home to appease you, hasn't he? In exchange for what?"

But of course he knew. "My cooperation, continued, that is."

"And not seeing me."

She nodded, feeling her throat tighten.

"That's emotional blackmail." Ryder touched her arm. "Goddamn him, Laurel."

"I was the one in the wrong," she said. "I was the one caught in Georgetown, in a man's room while my husband . . ."

"What?"

"Worked toward his election."

"I wonder," he said. "Benedict wasn't chasing votes last weekend."

"What was he doing, then?" It had been her fear as well.

"I don't know. But I'd like the chance to find out."

The hardness of his tone made her ask what she'd dreaded asking. "Has Sara Hennessey fired you?"

"Not exactly."

Ryder, his gaze dwelling on Laurel's mouth, recalled his interview with Sara that morning: it had been the postscript, expected and unpleasant, from Sunday afternoon.

"Sara's just fretting about editorial boards, publishers, advertisers." He dragged his gaze now from Laurel's mouth and said, "I'm beginning to think freedom of the press is one of the great myths of our time."

Then he reached for her hand. "Come on, over here." He walked them toward the bench where he'd left his luggage, explaining, "I wanted to say good-bye. That's why I followed you. I'm off on assignment within the hour." Into exile, he thought. "South of the border," Ryder said, already feeling the cramp in his belly. "Not Mexico."

Alarmed, Laurel's eyes met his. "El Salvador?"

"You got it."

"But Ryder, they killed two reporters there yesterday! I saw it on the late news last night."

He shrugged. "One of them a casual friend of mine. A first-rate journalist." He thought of Ham, of Ngoc Hoa.

"Do you have to go?" Laurel asked.

"Yes."

"For how long?"

"A few days, a couple of weeks. Whatever it takes."

"An investigation of the killings?"

"For *Newstrend*," he said. "It's a matter of redemption, mine."

"Is Dan behind this? Or the senator?"

"You don't expect Sara to admit that, do you? Indirectly, I suppose so," Ryder said.

"Will you be in danger?" Foolish question, she chided herself. The streets there were full of armed soldiers, factions; even on TV, hostility to America wavered in the air.

He looked at her unhappily. "The most dangerous moments of my life happened on Sunday. The rest is anticlimax."

He bent to retrieve his overnight bag and bulky leather camera case from the ground beside the bench. Straightening, he cradled Laurel's face in his hands; the heavy leather cases slung over his shoulder ground against her side. "I don't know about you," he added, "but danger makes me rash. It's part of the job."

Laurel looked into his eyes. "We were watched outside the Greystone, you know."

Ryder's gaze sharpened. "By Langford Martin's chauffeur. Why?"

He knew everything but that.

She didn't register surprise that Ryder had also seen the car. "Because the senator's not in office now, but he still has power, and powerful friends. Three of whom," Laurel murmured, "will help push Langford's defense bill through Congress, I'm sure, in the next few weeks."

"You scratch my back," Ryder said softly, "and I'll scratch yours."

"That's the way my father has always worked. I'm sorry you've been dragged into this, too."

"Oh, Laurel, I'm not going to regret Saturday night any more than I can regret Gloucester, certainly not because of the senator or anything he can do to me."

Fear flickered in her eyes. "You'll be careful?"

"I'll try. I'll call you when I get back."

"No. Don't."

Trembling, Laurel set her features in stone. He must have felt the hardness under his fingers. But he hadn't meant just the coming trip to El Salvador; other, more private dangers were in his mind, and Laurel couldn't be responsible for the outcome if he tried to get back at the senator, or Dan. His hands slid away.

"I don't want to hear from you again, Ryder."

He glanced toward Ned, then took a last, hard look at her. "All right, have it your way. Fine. I guess I get the message after all."

She flinched. Didn't he realize that she had to protect him in the only way she could, by giving him up? Feeling like a woman left alone in the wilderness, she watched him walk across the grassy common, to the street. "Good-bye, Ryder." Perhaps she'd only whispered it, but he didn't answer. He lifted his hand, and a yellow taxi hurtled to a stop at the curb.

He didn't look back.

**❋**

**❋  *CHAPTER 22*  ❋**

**❋**

HILARY TRIED TO ease her spine into a more comfortable position, but the required drape of her body against the cold metal side of the low-slung sports car didn't help. A week and a half after returning from Gloucester, she still had a stiff back, and DeNobili's much-touted burgundy X7 felt like a hard hand digging at her bones. Like the memory of Sebastian.

Smiling as her stomach rumbled, she trailed her red manicure over the hood of the automobile. She did this at intervals, the caress meant to attract potential buyers to DeNobili's creation. The smile hid gritted teeth. She was starving, and twice this afternoon the great DeNobili himself had warned her not to scratch the surface of the car with her nails. Or the slinky chain-mail gown she wore, a long envelope of silver, slit to the thigh on both sides and plunging in front halfway to her navel. Another day of this, Hilary thought, and I'll be in a Stryker frame, looking at the floor or the ceiling of some hospital room.

Why the hell had the other model called in late? She was tired of fending off DeNobili's advances and his temper, both of which—

"*Signorina*, please!"

Goddammit, not again. "Yes, Vittorio? Am I blocking the photographers?"

"The paparazzi, no, is their problem." She looked coolly into the jet black eyes of one of Italy's most revered car manufacturers. A handsome man in his way, tall and not too broad in the shoulders so that his Via Condotti suits fit like a glove. She found herself glancing at his hands—immaculate, without a trace of dirt under the nails. DeNobili managed another of his smiles, a generous lower lip drawn back to expose beautiful teeth. "*Cara*, for me, please, not to lean against the lacquer. Twenty-three coats, like a painting by DaVinci, you understand." He gently pulled her off the fender.

"Vittorio!" The photographer's angry tone was lowered so the drifting crowds at the Coliseum's spectacular automobile show wouldn't hear. "I need Hilary exactly where she was. You've already ruined the shoot with the black silk crepe, now the silver lamé's going to hell."

"You go to hell! This is my car, worth more than a hundred pounds of skin and bone wearing a fancy dress."

Hilary stepped between the two men, one of them the fashion photographer who had gotten her into this mess. "It's flattering to have you fighting over me, but—"

"I'll bet it is."

At the third voice, behind her, Hilary's mouth dropped open. What was *he* doing here, when she'd finally gotten through most of the day without dwelling on Gloucester, and that disaster in the car barn? She whirled—straight into Sebastian Noble's smile.

"Don't you punch your card at five o'clock? Or do world-famous fashion models get overtime?"

"You will stay right here, Hilaree, until the other girl arrives."

"Her contract's for eight hours, three days, DeNobili," the photographer reminded him.

"Ah, but the glory that was Rome came about because of slaves. Right, Vittorio?" Sebastian grinned, and Hilary's stomach growled again.

"My replacement's promised to make it by six, and things are slow right now." With a metallic swish of her gown, Hilary turned to smile sweetly at DeNobili. "That should give you time, *caro*, to polish the marks out of your valuable little creation."

"Hilaree, I am sorry, I did not mean to say such a thing about your body. I just see..." Instantly contrite, he shifted his gaze from Sebastian to her. "I mean, I forget myself, how do you say, to lose control...?"

"Incontinent," Sebastian supplied just above a whisper.

Hilary would have laughed, but DeNobili stepped forward, taking her hands. "You are most beautiful, Hilaree. Give me a moment—" he glanced angrily at Sebastian "—then I think we should go together somewhere for a drink and I tell you how very sorry I am for such bad words from my mouth, eh?" He smiled, slow and sensuous.

"Get your hands off her."

Sebastian's cold tone made her jerk free as DeNobili reacted. "*Dio*! You speak to me like that, your own—"

"Don't say it." With the carefully spaced words, she felt herself being spun around, then Sebastian touched the small of her aching back. "Let's get the devil out of here."

"But—"

" 'Tino, wait!"

They were through the downstairs lobby and pushing out the main doors onto the sidewalk before Hilary could speak. She was furious.

"What makes you think I wanted to leave with you?"

"You wanted to leave, didn't you?"

"Yes, but—"

"Well, you've left."

"But I—"

"Hilary, for once in our relationship, will you just shut the hell up?"

Miraculously, Sebastian found a rush-hour cab and gently pushed her inside. Contenting herself with the murmured comment, "We don't have a relationship," she relaxed against the seat, not minding the broken springs beneath the cushion; they felt like foam-rubber heaven after eight hours on cold metal. Damn prima donna Italian genius, she thought of DeNobili. And what was wrong with Sebastian? She'd rarely heard him swear, or seen him angry. Even odder had been Vittorio's strange response to Sebastian's sudden appearance. And why had he shouted after them so plaintively, '*Tino*?

"Sebastian, what happened back there?"

He stared out at the twilight. "Forget it."

"But he called you—"

"I said, forget it, Hilary."

"No. I won't. This is the second time I've heard you go bananas over Vittorio DeNobili. I want to know why."

"Gloucester," Sebastian murmured. "I'd like to know why you vanished the Sunday after Ryder and Laurel came to dinner."

It wasn't easy, but she returned his stare. Hilary had stuck to Laurel like a postage stamp all weekend, but on Sunday morning Laurel had left to visit Ned at Dawson by herself, a welcome show of independence from Dan. On her own again, Hilary had been half insane, fearing that Sebastian would burst through the back door. Determined never to be alone with him again, or if she could help it, even to see him, she'd packed and come back to New York.

"Sebastian, you may find this hard to imagine, but I

have a career, a job, call it what you will." Her heart was pounding. "Why have you shown up in New York all of a sudden?"

"Did you leave Gloucester because I want you?"

Hilary gaped at him. Belatedly, she realized that he'd given the driver her address, and panic raced through her. "Sebastian, you've got to stop."

"Wanting you?"

"Bothering me! It doesn't make sense. I felt better, so I came home. Now you've driven all the way from Cape Ann to—"

"Attend the Coliseum exhibition." He smiled. "It's one of a kind. That's my business, Hilary, remember?"

But he dealt in classic cars, not new ones. "How could I forget the clashing of metal on metal at six A.M.?"

"Aha. I thought you'd learn to like it." Sebastian grinned. "To celebrate, I'll buy you dinner. We can pick up something on the way home. What do you want to eat?"

Home? Her stomach gurgled. "Pizza, but after that, you'll have to—"

"Hilary Chapin. More junk food?"

With an exasperated sigh, she crossed her arms over her chest, ignoring the way Sebastian's eyes followed the motion. "Yes," she muttered. "Anything wrong with that?"

"Tonight? Not a thing." He closed his eyes, and leaned his head against the seat. "Pizza it is."

"You're a cheap date," Sebastian told her, gazing at Hilary across the litter of white cardboard box, tomato sauce, and strings of cheese on the coffee table. "And surprisingly . . . human."

"I'm not your date. But of course it was cheap—I paid."

"You insisted."

Yes, because she hadn't wanted to be obligated to him. Hilary bit the tip off the last doughy triangle, and smiled around it. She didn't know why she felt so relaxed by his teasing; she hadn't felt this relaxed since . . . Gloucester, when Sebastian had tended her injury. Sitting cross-legged on the carpet, she smiled at him again. "If the countess could see you now . . ."

"There isn't any—"

"I know, I know."

"If only," Sebastian murmured into his glass of Coke, "there wasn't Chip Brewster."

He'd done it after all; why be so surprised? "I think it's time for you to leave," she said, beginning to gather the grease-stained cardboard from the table, juggling her glass on it and both their plates.

"Come off it, Hilary. Sit down."

"This is my apartment," she said stiffly, "and you're no longer welcome." She waited by the sofa, mentally tapping her foot while her heart thumped out its own crazy rhythm.

"Why don't you tell me about him?"

"I don't see any reason why I should."

"We'd both feel better," he said, "having the air cleared."

"You might; I wouldn't."

Sebastian smiled. "You might surprise yourself."

"I didn't notice your willingness to confide what occurred at the Coliseum between you and DeNobili."

"Nothing occurred."

Hilary looked victorious at the cold tone. "See? You don't trust me either."

"DeNobili's an old enemy, let's leave it at that."

"You seem too much alike to be enemies," she pointed out.

"We're too much alike to be friends."

Without warning, Sebastian got to his feet and wrested their dinner things from Hilary's grasp. She watched him disappear into the kitchen, and was still watching the doorway when he returned. "Sebastian," she said with a look toward his jacket and tie, thrown over the back of the sofa.

Hilary had changed her clothes while he set out the food and poured their drinks. She was wearing jeans, and a sweatshirt. CARTER COLLEGE, it said in faded blue letters against an ivory ground. Sebastian's gaze went to it, not for the first time. "Is that where you met Brewster? At Carter?" He tossed a damp towel onto the coffee table and sprawled on the sofa cushions, linking his hands behind his head to show that he meant to stay. Hilary sighed.

"Yes, but he wasn't a student. His sister lived on our floor."

Of course Sebastian wasn't satisfied with the scrap of information. Ignoring Hilary's glare toward the front door, he pulled her down onto the sofa.

"When did you meet?"

This time her hesitation was minimal. "During freshman year. When he came to pick his sister up for Thanksgiving."

"So you would have been together, more or less, for just under a year."

"Ten months, yes." As if listening to someone else, she heard herself tell Sebastian, slowly at first, about those few moments in the dorm lounge, casual introductions passing between them while both she and Chip stared, knowing, feeling. When he'd brought his sister back, he'd buzzed Hilary's room to ask her out for coffee. That had been the real beginning of the whirlwind. "Until the following September, neither of us thought of anyone but each other."

If the information pained him, it didn't show on Sebastian's face. "You can't have seen him often," he said.

"He wrote wonderful letters. We talked by phone at least twice a week. We had—he had—several leaves between training programs, and just before he . . ." Her voice trailed away. Hilary tried to ease the lump in her throat, but couldn't seem to.

"Just before he left for Nam," Sebastian finished for her.

"Yes."

He sat up. "You were a virgin when you met him, weren't you, Hilary?"

Startled, she didn't think not to answer. "Yes."

"But not when he shipped out?"

She wasn't taken by surprise this time, but after a silence meant to be defiant, admitted, "No."

He was taking her apart, limb by limb, and she couldn't seem to put up her defenses.

"Have you been in love, Sebastian, like that, I mean?"

"Once," he told her. "Only once."

But he wouldn't describe his own feelings, breaking the moment for her, and Hilary was grateful. Tonight, he wasn't the Sebastian she'd despised and she welcomed his understanding, even his presence now.

"I think I know why Mother let you into the house," she whispered some time later.

They lounged for hours, talking quietly, once even about Laurel and Ryder in Gloucester, and listening to music. Sebastian surprised her again, preferring Bach to Boy George. Then everything changed, as suddenly difficult again as it had been easy before. "It's getting late. I've got DeNobili to deal with in the morning." Stretching, she asked, "Where are you staying tonight?"

"Here."

She jumped to her feet, spewing cushions onto the floor. "Think again."

Sebastian stood up. "I made a spur-of-the-moment decision. I wasn't going to attend the exhibition. The nearest hotels were booked. Frankly, I didn't try any others. Hilary, let's not play hide-and-seek. I've missed you. That kiss in my garage—"

"Was inexcusable, you took advantage."

"Don't try to sound like a Victorian heroine."

Not thinking that she'd made a tactical error, she tore into the bedroom. He was right behind her. "Sebastian, I'm warning you."

She seized the nearest object.

"Don't." He took the hairbrush from her, easily.

She remembered Vittorio DeNobili's eyes that afternoon, so black and enigmatic, like Sebastian's now; soulful, determined. "No, Sebastian." He was holding the silver-framed picture of Chip from her bedside chest. He'd picked it up after setting down the brush. Hilary caught a flash of blue eyes, Navy uniform, blond hair.

"Handsome kid," Sebastian said.

"He's not a kid."

"Then neither am I."

She felt trapped, helpless. The way she'd felt when the news came about Chip.

"Come here," Sebastian ordered softly. "By the bed."

He reached out, offering her the framed photograph, and a thousand memories raced through her mind. "Put his picture in the drawer, Hilary."

"No," she whispered. But he had placed the frame, cool metal and glass, in her hands and was already bending his head.

"Remember when I first kissed you? I'd never felt anything so good. . . ."

"I loathe you, Sebastian." She wanted to pretend she'd felt nothing then. Felt nothing now. But his mouth hovered over hers, at last touched her lips, and she felt the heat again. "Oh, no."

"The picture, Hilary." His mouth moved across hers and back again, light and quick and arousing. "The drawer," Sebastian whispered. "Tonight."

"I . . . I . . ."

Without knowing she had moved, she touched brass with her fingertips, heard the drawer closing. Chip. Then she heard only their breathing in the darkness after he'd extinguished the light, and there was no one with her in the room but Sebastian. Sebastian. Oh dear God, Sebastian.

Hilary looked at him as he slept. Sebastian, with one arm flung across his eyes, his body in a sprawl. Sebastian, to whom she had given herself, freely, during the long night. Her heart accelerated, and she sat up, full of morning regrets.

"Where do you think you're going?"

He had spoken quietly, his voice newly tantalizing, seductive. "To work," she replied, slipping from his reach, and bed.

"Hilary, come back here."

She strode into the bathroom, feeling his eyes upon her, wishing she'd pulled on a robe. False modesty, now. My God. Sebastian. Her body tingled from him. Hilary wrenched the faucets on full, hot, and plunged under the shower, scrubbing at her skin until it glowed; perhaps then she'd be able to tell herself that the soft throbbing of all her parts was simply due to a vigorous cleansing. Which she had certainly needed.

Finished, she wrapped herself in a thick terry robe that had been hanging on the door hook, then went into the bedroom again, shivering against the cooler air. He was still there.

"How long, Hilary?"

Sebastian was sitting on the edge of the bed, clad in the gray trousers he'd worn the day before, and barefoot. The combination of skin and flannel seemed oddly provocative. Hilary looked away from him to rummage in a drawer for fresh lingerie.

"How long what?"

"Since you've spent the night with a man."

She selected plum-colored panties and a skimpy bra. "I thought you'd have the answer. All those wild parties with Rick—"

"But you've never slept with him, have you? Or any of the others."

She tossed the gauzy underwear onto the dresser. "If you had any decency, you'd find the rest of your clothes and leave."

"But I don't have any, so you've always said."

She whirled on him. "Look, Sebastian, last night was an error on my part. I was tired, my back ached, I was hungry...for pizza. That's all, I'm sorry. Now if you'll—"

"Last night, for both of us, was a revelation." He glanced at the bedside chest of drawers where he'd made her place the photograph the night before. "How long has it been since Brewster...disappeared? Fourteen years, didn't you say?" Sebastian's dark eyes held hers. "You think Brewster would expect you to waste all your good years on some slim hope that—"

"He's coming back!"

"There is another possibility."

She ignored the almost gentle tone of voice. "Not for me. Somewhere, half the world away in a prison compound, he's drawing strength from what we have together."

"Had," Sebastian corrected. "For instance, what was it like when you got the news? Think hard. Memory fades."

Well, she'd show him how wrong he was. She took a breath. "His parents called after they'd heard from the military. There was every hope that he'd be found alive. Friendly troops in the area had seen him eject before the plane crashed. So we . . . we waited for the next call." She bit her lower lip, drawing it lightly between her teeth as the memory of those weeks grew stronger. "Every time the phone rang, I jumped. Then gradually, I learned not to jump, not as high anyway. But to this day, I talk to his parents once a month, and still spend a week with them in the summer. The hope's there, Sebastian, alive. Like Chip."

"What you have is an image, an old one. A picture in a frame, not a live human being."

"If I believed that, I'd have nothing to hold onto."

"You've got nothing now." He paused. "Until last night."

She was trembling. "Get out of my house. And don't come back again, not in Gloucester either. If you ever dare open that kitchen door—"

"Hilary, how long are you going to keep waiting for the phone to ring?" He was on his feet now, snatching up his clothes and putting them on. He tied his shoes. "There's an old saying, 'You can run, but you can't hide.' Not from yourself. You've been trying to hide for too many years."

Before she could assess his look, he had moved. Sebastian seized her wrists, pulling her to the full-length mirrors on her closet doors. Hands tight on her shoulders, he forced her to face the glass and said, "What do you see? Tell me."

"An angry woman."

"Well, dammit, I see more. I see an attractive woman, a very appealing woman, a woman who's wasting her life on a dead—"

"He isn't dead!"

"Well, if he isn't, you might as well be. Shrinking from the life that ought to be yours, from the career you'd rather have—you're afraid to risk Africa, not because changing jobs is scary, but because you'd be away from that telephone for a year!" His fingers clutched at her. "And you run from me because another man's arms around you, another man's loving means you have to give up your belief in Chip Brewster, the youthful fantasy that—"

"I love him!" She spun from his grasp, pulling the terry robe more closely around her. "Why can't you understand that?" She clenched her hands into fists. "Oh, but I know why—because love's foreign to you, isn't it? Poor Sebastian Noble, junior high school dropout who ran away from home at the age of fifteen looking for somebody else's money. Rich friends, Sebastian, to make up for all the deprivations? You poor fatherless child!"

"You're acting the child! And I'm going to paddle your behind in a minute. Stop using that age crap on me. There are only six years between us, six years is nothing."

He was coming toward her again. She wouldn't be able to stop him. Nothing stopped him.

"Don't touch me! Don't you ever touch me again, you prying bastard!"

Sebastian came to a halt. For one stunned moment, his dark eyes looked into hers. "Yes," he said, nodding. "You're right, yes."

Without another word he walked past her into the

living room, and out of the apartment. Astonished, Hilary stared at the open doorway through which he'd gone. Her vision blurred. He was crazy, that was all. Crazy. She'd known it from the start, and if Sebastian appeared at the exhibition today, she'd cut him dead.

Sebastian was nowhere to be seen. That she kept looking for him made Hilary furious with herself. But no more so, apparently, than Vittorio DeNobili.

"Hilaree, your attention to the car, please."

He must have said the same thing to her at least a million times after her tardy arrival at the Coliseum.

"I'm sorry, Mr. DeNobili."

"Vittorio. And I think we have a break now."

Was she wearing that mournful an expression? His dark eyes softened fractionally, and he took her hand, walking her from the rich brown sport sedan toward a nearby coffee stand. "You take it black?" he asked.

"Yes, thank you."

He beamed at her. "I invite you to have lunch with me today. To express my gratitude. Three buyers placed their orders for the new X7, thanks to you. I did not mean to bite your head off, *cara*. My temper, is not good sometimes, eh?" He tossed her another grin. A handsome man, Hilary thought again, handsome, but mercurial. And somehow, again, familiar. She tensed as his hand slid down the bare expanse of her back just above the bright yellow gown. "We will be friends, good friends now."

"All right," Hilary agreed reluctantly, noting that the hand was withdrawn as quickly as he'd touched her. But she didn't want friends at the moment; she wanted reprieve from last night, and the look in Sebastian's eyes just before he'd left that morning. "If we're to become better acquainted, I'll ask you a question. Just one. May I?"

"Si, *cara*. Anything."

"Why did you call Sebastian Noble by another name last night? 'Tino,'" she said.

Surprise flickered over his dark features.

"It is a childhood name, for a child I, unfortunately, never see very much. Saw," he corrected himself.

She had supposed they'd done business in the past. "Childhood?"

"But he is a man grown now, is he not? And you went home with him last night."

"He went home with me." Uninvited.

"He is your lover?"

"No!" God, yes. But never again.

He laughed, handing her the cup of coffee. "Do not be afraid to say it. Do you see his auto designs?"

Hilary shook her head, dumbfounded.

"Neither do I, but friends have. They tell me, 'Watch out, Vittorio.' Someday he will, how do you say, pass me by. I would not care. I am proud. Even though he does not like me to be. Yesterday"—his gaze dropped "—he pretends not to know me."

DeNobili, proud of Sebastian? DeNobili, regretful?

"His mother should have done the same, perhaps." He shrugged in the continental manner. "But a long time ago, eh? Such a lovely girl, I like her very much, even now. A difficult choice then, but I could not leave my wife. We had already one child. Still, I am glad for him. I have three daughters, *cara*," Vittorio told her, "but Sebastiano is my only son."

Coffee sloshed over the skirt of Hilary's yellow dress. She heard DeNobili's guttural cry of alarm, then felt his hand wiping at the skirt with a paper napkin, Italian apology flying, with her thoughts, through the air.

My God, he really was a bastard.

If she hadn't hurt Sebastian with that one word, she would have smiled at the irony, which applied as well, apparently, to his father. Instead, it made her cry. And promise herself that she'd never go to Gloucester again.

## ❋ CHAPTER 23 ❋

FROM THE EDGE of the bluff behind Hilary's Gloucester home, Laurel stood watching Ned and Pirate on the flat stretch of beach below. Ned's voice carried to her over the crash of surf hitting rock; Pirate's answering barks as they raced over the sand lifted above the screech of gulls. The sky overhead was thick and gray, the color of—

No, she shook her head to chase away the thought of Ryder's eyes, of Ryder. In the week she'd been here she had found some measure of peace. In the aftermath of his departure for El Salvador, her first real job, for Sebastian, had seemed a godsend; she'd quickly decided to take Ned out of school for a week, that in Gloucester she might escape her memories of the Greystone Hotel and Dan's lasting anger while being able to consult with Sebastian about her catalogue ideas.

Dan wouldn't need her. This week he'd been campaigning for the labor vote in industrial areas where no one cared whether he brought his wife. Until next week, she had few campaign commitments; and for the rest of the year she'd given up all other obligations, including the troublesome charity luncheon scheduled for November, which she'd been planning the day Hilary dragged her to Gloucester . . . and Ryder.

She'd even resigned her chairmanship of the Christmas debutante ball and wouldn't miss that either. Watching Ned and Pirate romp on the beach, she smiled. Judith's disapproval had been strongly stated.

But a little selfishness, Ryder had said, was a good thing. And it seemed that the more Laurel took for herself, the more she needed, wanted, and the easier it became to assert her personal rights.

Perhaps that, as much as the publicity aftermath from the Greystone—the photograph of her with Ryder had appeared everywhere—explained why she and Dan weren't getting along.

Now Laurel arched her spine to ease the stiffness from hours of sitting hunched over Hilary's kitchen table, drawing. She had a dozen good sketches in soft charcoal already. Despite the muscle aches, Laurel realized that she hadn't felt this relaxed in months. Years, she corrected.

"It's good to see you smile."

She turned to find Sebastian approaching from his yard. "I've had a good day."

Sebastian waved a hand as Ned called to him. "Do you suppose they could be persuaded to come inside? I'm ready for a hot chocolate break."

She grinned. "With marshmallows?"

"Wouldn't be cocoa without."

"As long as you're washing the pan," Laurel agreed.

In Hilary's kitchen the air was soon sweet with the smell of sugar and chocolate. Ned devoured two cups, acquiring a white moustache of sticky marshmallow in the process. "Pirate's got one, too," he said with a laugh.

"Why don't you both wash up?" Laurel suggested. "Between the sugar and sand, someone's going to be cleaning house for a week."

"Not me," Ned replied, giggling.

Laurel swatted his bottom as he hauled Pirate toward the bathroom. "Wanta bet?"

Sebastian was leaning back in his chair when she returned to the table. His smile seemed off-center to her, but she guessed that his mood had nothing to do with her, or the catalogue. "Do you want to talk about it?" she said.

Sebastian shook his head. "Have you heard from Ryder since he left the country?"

"No."

She'd caught his byline several times on newspaper dispatches, taut, hard-hitting pieces with that undercurrent of humanity that so distinguished his reporting style. *Are you well?* they made her want to shout across the miles. *Are you safe?* She'd stopped reading the papers, stopped watching the television news. She was too afraid of its being bad.

"Do you think he's all right?" she asked Sebastian.

"I think he's all right." He looked at her. "I hope you won't mind my saying this, but I'm glad this week and our catalogue work have been good for you. We could have done almost as well long distance, but when I first saw you, and the shadows in your eyes, when you told me what had happened, I knew the change would prove beneficial."

"It has. Thank you, Sebastian."

"I'm not looking for thanks. I like both of you. Ryder's a hell of a guy."

Laurel bit her lip. "Yes, he is."

"What are you doing about it?"

Her glance shifted to the refrigerator door, where Ned had taped a picture of his own making, a panorama of beach and sky and Pirate, legs looking six feet long and his eyes the size of plates. She couldn't smile at it now.

"There's nothing I can do. I'm not sure we didn't just use each other to try to cure unhappiness."

"You believe that?"

She smiled. "Not all the time."

And certainly not those first nights, when she had lain in Hilary's bed because she couldn't bear to sleep in the one she'd shared with Ryder that rainy weekend. It made her ache for him again.

Alone, she had found contentment in simple things: a puff of white cloud in a clear sky that became a castle, a dragon; in Ned's open smile and the new freedom she saw when he ran with Pirate; in the sharing of hot chocolate with a friend. Maybe it hadn't been Ryder Mc-Kendrick she needed, Laurel thought, but only a way to find herself. She was at least making a start.

Then why couldn't she forget that night at the Greystone when he'd told her about Ngoc Hoa, and before that, Gloucester?

She held Sebastian's gaze. "I talked to Hilary this morning. I'd thought she might join us for the weekend before Ned and I go back to Boston, but she's got a late shoot today and an early one on Monday."

"I doubt she'll be spending much time here from now on," Sebastian said.

"You haven't had another row?" He'd made light of his last visit to Hilary in New York for the car show and "a few slices of pizza."

"She thinks I'm nothing but a kid, perhaps a fool, I know for certain a . . ." He didn't finish.

"You love her, don't you?"

"I guess that's what you'd call it. I've never been in love before." He gave her a crooked smile. "I thought I'd feel a lot better than I do when it happened."

Laurel touched his shoulder. "You know about her Navy flier?"

Sebastian sighed. "He's a dead man to everyone but her."

He got up from the table, clearing the cups and saucers. Laurel watched him rinse the same plate twice. "Would you like me to call her back? I'm pretty good at getting under her skin."

"So am I, and it didn't help one damn bit."

When Sebastian returned to work, Laurel tried to complete a sketch she'd been making of a rare Chapron Type Six, sleek and elongated like a bullet, its color to be deep bronze when it was finished. But she couldn't get the angles right, and wondered whether the shade she wanted could be mixed at all with the watercolors she had; if any printing process would be able to duplicate it when she did. With a sigh, Laurel threw down her charcoal.

"What's the matter, Mommy?"

She looked at Ned, twisted into an impossible shape at the table. He'd been drawing a portrait of the sleeping Pirate, who had lapped up a pint of hot chocolate himself. Laurel had broken Ned's concentration, too.

"My preliminary sketch isn't working out. I think I'm just feeling rushed right now." She glanced at the kitchen clock as if it were a calendar. "I'm not ready to go home in two more days, but we have to."

"Pirate and I want to stay."

Now she'd worried Ned, who was always sensitive to her mood. "I promised Daddy that I'd attend a speech with him on Monday night, so we have to leave. And you'll have missed enough school. It's fun, though, isn't it, staying at Hilary's?"

"It's a vacation."

Laurel laughed. "A working one. And I've never enjoyed a vacation more."

"Me, too." Ned returned to his picture. But Laurel knew she wouldn't be able to concentrate. For a moment more she stood watching the kitchen light shine on Ned's hair, then, feeling as restless as Sebastian had seemed to, Laurel walked into the other room.

"I think I'll watch the news tonight," she said.

A week later Laurel hurried across the street with rain slashing against her stockinged legs, the dirty water from passing cars splattering her skirt. She hauled open the door to the Cambridge pharmacy and swept inside.

It was not her usual drugstore, but close to Kip's house, where Ned was playing. He had come home from Gloucester with a nasty cold that, in another week, hadn't improved much. Laurel had left him with Kip's mother while she ran to the pharmacy for nose drops, prescribed by Ned's pediatrician.

Leaving the form with the pharmacist, she wandered the aisles. It was a day for Gloucester, she thought; full of wind and rain.

With that thought, Laurel glanced toward the end of the aisle and had to look twice to believe he was real. At the lending library display, Ryder McKendrick stood with his back to her, browsing through a current novel. The set of his shoulders, the stance of his legs, spread slightly apart, the tilt of his head as he read the jacket copy made her heart roll. It couldn't be anyone else.

She walked quickly toward him. The book he held was a spy novel by an author she sometimes read, and always liked. Her pulse pounded like a drum. He was home. He was safe.

"Hello, Ryder," she said, and he looked up.

His knuckles on the book spine went white. "Hi."

Laurel's gaze was suddenly greedy. Did he look thinner? She noted that his hair was longer than usual, more rich honey. She realized what a liar she'd been in Gloucester, thinking she was happier alone.

"When did you get back?" she asked.

"A few days ago."

He hadn't called. She'd told him not to.

"I've been down in bed." He grimaced. "Dysentery." He gestured toward the back of the store. "I'm here for a dose of medicine, just in case. I think I'm over it now."

She smiled. "You need some homemade chicken soup."

"So my mother tells me." He didn't return the smile.

Laurel stared at the front of his trenchcoat: it was damp at the shoulders from the rain. Underneath, she glimpsed a flannel shirt, the green plaid with black and white that he'd worn before in Gloucester. His jeans were snug and faded. "It's an old coat," he said. "My lending library costume, as opposed to my chasing-married-ladies-in-the-park ensemble."

Laurel blushed.

"I'm sorry," he said quickly. "I didn't mean to say that."

What could she answer? She felt as if they were strangers.

"Ned adores the prints you made him. I wanted to thank you." She kept staring at his buttons. "He's determined to make a photographer of himself, though I'm afraid what he mostly does is waste good film."

"Don't be too sure of that. The best pictures are accidents of timing, incident, place. They simply happen with the click of a shutter. No chance to set up or compose the shot. Some call that luck, others opportunity. Being in the right place," Ryder said, "at the right time. Or perhaps," he added, "the wrong place."

Laurel wondered what he meant. Something to do with the end of the story he'd never told her? When she glanced up, he showed her nothing but a barren facial landscape, and blank gray eyes devoid of expression.

"Well, I won't keep you. Ned's waiting a few blocks away at a friend's, the boy you saw with him in the park.

And I think our prescriptions are finished. The pharmacist is waving in this direction."

They walked slowly through the store. Collected their medications, paid for them. He rented the spy novel. She had the feeling she would never see him again. He was off the campaign. She had told him not to call, and he hadn't. After all, he had more sense than she did; more caution. Or bravery, Laurel thought. She hadn't been able to keep from approaching him.

"Where's your car?" Ryder asked.

"I walked. It isn't far, and better than fighting for a parking space."

"I'll get you a cab, you shouldn't get drenched again."

"No, please. You've been ill, and I . . . I'm not quite finished here. I forgot, I need a new lipstick. You go ahead. It was nice to see you."

She lingered, remembering their awkward good-byes. Remembering Ryder's mouth, compressed into a straight line. There'd been so many things she had wanted to ask him, to tell him, so much that had been left unsaid.

She stayed as long as she could. Moments, half an hour? She had no idea. Stepping from the warm pharmacy into cold rain and wind, she realized she'd forgotten the lipstick.

Then a hand caught her wrist and—

"Jesus, Laurel. I can't take this anymore."

She'd been turned into Ryder's arms, against the length of his body, braced against the building. His head was tilted back, eyes closed. Sharp thrusts of feeling went through her. Laurel's arms slipped around his waist beneath the opening of his coat, her cheek over the frantic pounding of his heart. "It feels just like mine," she whispered, "racing so."

His lips moved through her hair, pressed her right temple, then the left before trailing her cheeks, one and then the other, to kiss each corner of her mouth. Breathless, she broke free long enough to say, "I missed you so much. Terribly, terribly."

"I missed you. Too much. Enough to be doing dangerous things now." She felt his warm breath in her ear. "Kissing you in public and not giving a damn. Do you?"

"No." Laurel leaned into him, relishing the closeness. For the first time in her life she was oblivious of the stares of strangers.

"Thank God. I'm too weak right now for battles."

"You poor man, that chicken soup," she murmured. "Have you got one?"

"What?"

"A chicken. In your freezer."

"For you, I think I just might."

"It'll take hours to cook."

"Good." Ryder tipped her chin up, smiling at last into her eyes.

"Oh no," Laurel said, remembering. "Ned . . ."

"Call him when we get home."

Uncertainty darkened his gaze. Ryder paused before entering the stream of passersby, giving her a last chance to pull away, to go back to Dan. Laurel only dropped her head to his shoulder, and heard his relieved sigh.

"One problem we don't have, sweetheart," he said, "and that's, 'your place or mine.'"

"What's wrong, Ryder?"

They were lying in his bed, spent and drowsy. But his muscles were tense, and he shivered. "I just realized that this is the room, the bed, I shared with Maggie." He turned onto his side, facing her. "I've never brought a woman here."

Laurel tried to smile, but couldn't. His words chastised her. Getting up, she began to search for her damp clothes, thinking of Gloucester, and the rain. And how impossible it was to recapture special moments, special times. "I ought to go. Ned's at the whiny stage with his cold, I'm sure Kip's mother will be glad to see me by now."

She had telephoned, making the excuse of a remembered errand in Boston, promising to be back before five o'clock. Already she regretted the call.

Laurel pulled on her gray-green blouse and was reaching for her skirt when Ryder stopped her. "I'm sorry, why should you want to hear that?"

"It doesn't surprise me that you'd miss her." But it shouldn't hurt, either.

"I miss what we should have had," he corrected. "What we had once."

Yes, Laurel thought, but these rooms still held her; not only the bed they'd just tumbled together.

"These are her things, aren't they?" Laurel made a gesture. "The sheets, the towels in the bathroom, the place-mats on your table."

And in the spare bedroom near the front entry, there were cartons stacked full of Maggie's clothes, Maggie's treasures. One of them, she thought, must be Ryder's heart.

She bent to find her shoes under a chair. Slate blue chintz, it was Maggie's chair.

"I don't spend much time here, Laurel. I told you, it's a stopover between trips." Ryder caught her arm, pulling her upright. "Yes, it's full of memories. But you're going home to Benedict's house tonight. And he might even be there."

Their eyes met. He was right. He had his past, but she had her present. Neither was simple, or easy. She'd known in front of the pharmacy that the walk to Ryder's apart-ment would be one-way, a commitment on her part. "Your chicken soup," she said. "It must be ready."

He smiled a little as she drew away. "Smells good. Just the smell's making me stronger." She had taken a step toward the kitchen before he turned her back into his arms. "Not yet."

Ryder cursed himself for having mentioned his wife. Maggie was his problem, not Laurel's. It was a miracle that she'd come home with him today, that he'd seen her in the first place. That she had walked toward him. He'd been fighting himself after that day in the park, fighting the whole time he was in El Salvador, even sick he'd been fighting not to call her again, to see her if he could.

"Stay a while," he begged against her mouth. "Please stay."

"But your soup . . ." She was already opening to him.

"The soup can wait," Ryder said. "I can't."

Hours later Ryder tapped a pencil against his desk, waiting for an answer at the other end of the telephone line.

During the weeks in El Salvador something had been missing: the adrenaline high that kept a journalist going, thriving, in the midst of danger and deprivation. Unlike past field assignments, this one held no excitement; he'd only wanted to get home, alive. He'd had enough of foreign revolution; as Sara had suggested, he was going to fight his own war right here. She wanted a story, and she'd get it. By God, she would.

He waited. Three rings, four. Then someone answered.

Two years ago, he'd pulled some strings, gotten a kid into journalism school at Columbia. The kid's father, an air traffic controller at Logan Airport, owed the favor. Ryder was calling in the markers.

"Yeah. McKendrick. What can I do for you?"

Quickly, he detailed what he knew of Benedict's mysterious weekends. Then waited again through an uncomfortable silence.

"Dan Benedict? Ryder, I don't know. I can't see how the information would prove that helpful, and besides, I could really get my ass waxed for snooping through back files."

"The campaign's coming to a close. Election's three weeks off."

"Well..."

"How's your boy getting along at school?"

More silence. A sigh.

"Reporters," the controller said. "All right, Mc-Kendrick, I'll get back to you."

"Thanks."

Satisfied, Ryder hung up. A little more waiting, that was all. It was a matter of record, and FAA regulations: every pilot had to file a flight plan before leaving the ground.

Anticipation, Laurel thought. For a week and a half she had lived on it, not knowing, or caring, where time would lead them. The rest of the campaign until the election, Dan, Ned: all the realities of life had been put on hold, at least for now. *Now* meant afternoons with Ryder when she wasn't speechmaking somewhere, while Ned was at school. They'd managed several days a week. She didn't want to examine her own guilt until she had to, or to think further than tomorrow.

For now, she was simply a woman in love.

Stretching, Laurel sat up in bed in Ryder's spare room. Except for Maggie's boxes, it was the most neutral spot in the apartment. By tacit agreement, they hadn't used a second time what she privately referred to as his marriage bed. And the sofa wasn't comfortable. She smoothed a hand over the quilt, dusky red and blue—his mother's, he had told her—and wished he'd hurry with his phone call.

In half an hour Ned would be finished at school, a fifteen-minute drive from Ryder's apartment. Getting off the bed, she walked to the chest of drawers, above which hung an oval mirror framed in oak. His mother's, too? She didn't like to think it was Maggie's. Laurel finger-combed her hair into place, then straightened her skirt. She didn't have much time. And today—no, not only today—Ryder seemed preoccupied with something else.

Having left Dan's campaign, he should feel carefree. Instead, he seemed more tense than during the weeks she'd kept him at a distance. His frame of mind didn't make sense to Laurel, when she was taking all the risks.

Walking toward the bed for her wool blazer, she stubbed a toe on one of the cartons that cluttered the floor. "Damn." Why did he leave them here, like stepping stones across the carpet? Laurel's innate sense of order made her begin pushing boxes closer to the closet door.

"What are you doing?"

His voice stopped her, and Laurel turned with a quick smile. "Just organizing. It's a habit of mine."

"Well, leave them. I have my own habits."

The smile faded. "Obviously some die harder than others."

He was scowling, as if she'd trespassed where she didn't belong.

"I have the feeling," Ryder said too quietly, "that I'll come home someday and find all these . . . gone."

Laurel gave him one wounded glance, snatched her purse from the dresser and her coat from the bed, then stalked from the room. "I wouldn't touch them."

"Where are you going?"

"To pick up Ned. To take him home. To make dinner for my son, possibly for my husband. To pick up my life, and stop meddling in yours."

"Laurel, I have my own way of doing things. Hell, I've lived alone here for six years—"

"I don't think you live alone."

Dan didn't come home for dinner that night. And he didn't call. Laurel fed his steak to the dog, and fixed Taco Surprise frozen dinners for herself and Ned. When the phone rang, The Rolling Stones were blasting from the stereo and she was still hoping for a fight.

"Good evening, Benedict residence."

Ryder said hesitantly, "Laurel?"

"What do you want?"

"I want you to come over here and meddle in my life." Silence.

"Hey, I'm sorry," he said. "I'm . . . trailing a hot story, and it got me frustrated today. I was feeling out of control."

"So you took it out on me? I've had enough of that in my life."

"I know. I'm sorry." Pause. "Will I see you tomorrow?"

"I have a speech to make in the morning, then a ladies' luncheon near Salem. Ned has a doctor's appointment at three. There wouldn't be enough time."

"I'll make you a cup of tea. Five minutes, even," he coaxed.

"Later, I'd have Ned with me. I'm not sure that's a good idea." She knew it wasn't but was no longer sure it mattered. "And Pirate's going for his grooming at the vet's. I'd have him, too."

"Bring 'em. I don't care."

"Hi, Ned." The next afternoon Ryder held the door wide. "Come on in, make yourself at home." His gaze became guarded as Pirate pushed past, white plume of a tail flying high, body bumping the walls as he sailed down the hall. "How about a Coke?"

" 'Lo," Ned mumbled without looking at him. "I don't like Coke."

"Orange juice? Spring water? Bourbon?"

He tossed Laurel, the last to enter, an uneasy grin. She gave him a quick, surreptitious kiss on the way by. Ryder followed them inside, wondering if he'd lost his mind, inviting an eight-year-old and a wild animal to Cambridge. Clearly, Ned hadn't forgiven him since the zoo.

"Water will be fine," Laurel said.

"I'm allergic to juice," Ned added.

They made stilted conversation in the living room, with Ned perched on the low-slung sofa, swallowed by its sagging cushions. Pirate prowled the dining area until Ryder thought he would go crazy. "That dog needs obedience training," he said to Laurel.

"He's flunked, twice."

"Three's a charm."

She only smiled. "Ned, tell Ryder about your visit to the doctor."

"I got a shot."

How should he respond? I'm sorry, or did it hurt, or brave boy? He hadn't a clue. Clearing his throat, Ryder invited Ned to see his photographic setup, a privilege, he thought. They trooped down the narrow hall again, Pirate's wet nose poking the backs of Ryder's knees. "He wants to see, too," Ned explained.

Ryder rolled his eyes, not quite amused by Laurel's laugh. He opened the bathroom door, and the four of them crowded in. "Watch him, Ned." The brown glass bottles under the sink contained chemicals; they clinked ominously as Pirate inspected them. "Some of that's poison."

"Is this where you make your pictures?"

"Yes. The prints I gave you, as a matter of fact. See?" Ryder gestured at the line strung along one wall. "I hang them here on these clips to dry."

He indicated the dry area on one side of the room, "for print work," and the wet on the other, "for developing." Ned's eyes widened at the array of equipment: enlarger, trays, stainless steel developing tanks, timers, graduated cylinders, the boxes of photographic paper, the wall rack for dodging and burning tools. Ryder demonstrated the amber safelights, which gave the small room a sci-fi glow he thought a kid would like, and the blackout material that sealed off the window and the door from natural light. He showed Ned the neat files of negatives, all coded and tucked away in glassine. Then Ned maneuvered around the dog to bend down and ask, "What's under here?"

The tub made a base for the raised countertop Ryder had rigged over it; it matched a smaller one over the sink. "Instant darkroom. I built it myself." Under Ned's scrutiny, Ryder began to fidget. He'd expected appreciation, interest at the very least, certainly not complaint.

"It's little in here," Ned remarked. "It's just a bathroom, not a real darkroom."

Laurel reminded him of his manners. "Thank Ryder for the guided tour, Ned, and bring Pirate. I think we'd better be getting home."

Ryder found that he wanted them to go, that he wanted her to stay. "You haven't finished your tea." He'd fixed her favorite, black currant, but she'd barely sipped it. As nervous as he was, then?

Frankly, the kid scared him. He was half afraid to look into Ned's eyes again, afraid of what he'd see. Fear, and Cherry Blossom.

He walked them to the door. Ned and Laurel, anyway. Pirate flung himself against the knob, barking. The walls seemed to shake. "Jesus," Ryder muttered. Then feeling guilty, he told Ned, "Next time we'll develop some prints if you like . . . if you want to come back."

There was no response.

"Ned, wait outside in the hall a minute. Here, put Pirate's leash on, but don't hold it. He might pull you down the steps."

"Dammit, Laurel—"

"We know how to handle him. He's a lamb, really." She turned, with the door at her back. "But I am sorry. You look destroyed."

"They're pretty overwhelming."

"Most children can be. Pirate's only a larger version." She raised on tiptoe to kiss his mouth, soft and quick. He felt the warm shock all the way to his toes. "Oh, God," he said and tried to pull her closer.

Laurel stepped back. "Tomorrow?"

"Tomorrow. Please."

"Alone," she promised.

That night Ryder sat in the dark, knowing what he had to do. The call he'd been hounding the controller at Logan for over the past ten days had come through. Tomorrow morning he'd make the trip north for the stakeout.

Christ, he felt like a cheap private detective. Only *he* was the one cheating with the guy's wife. Where were he and Laurel headed? The whole thing was becoming a nightmare. The miserable, but mercifully brief, visit today with a hostile Ned and that bonecrusher of a dog. His own snapping at Laurel the day before, then not being able to make amends this afternoon. Was this what an affair going nowhere was all about? If so, he was surprised that the statistics on infidelity were so high.

Except he was crazy about her.

Wanted her.

Loved her.

Which scared him to death again.

All the more, because he didn't want to hurt her. He already had Maggie on his conscience—Maggie, and Ngoc Hoa. He should have run like hell when he saw Laurel in the drugstore. Believe that.

Stretching out his legs, he stared at the blackness of the dark wall opposite. But what did he have to give Laurel, except more heartache? Remembering his telephone conversation, he clenched his eyes shut, and swore.

"The same place?" he'd asked in disbelief.

"Every time. There's a whole string of trips. Goes way back, five years. That's when they opened the airstrip up there, anyway. Want me to read 'em to you?"

"Can you send me some copies?"

"Ryder, I don't know. If the boss finds out—"

"It's your civic duty. I promise I won't reveal my source, even under torture."

"With Benedict and, possibly, Frasier, it might come to that."

"Don't remind me."

He heard the sigh again that was becoming familiar. "Yeah, all right. I'll put 'em in the mail. But then we're square, McKendrick."

"Right."

With a heavy sigh of his own, Ryder opened his eyes and got to his feet in the darkness. Another friend lost to journalism. Would Laurel be among them? He went to the sideboard and poured himself a drink. It didn't help, not that he'd expected it would.

Shelby, Ryder thought.

What the hell was in Shelby, Massachusetts?

✻ *CHAPTER 24* ✻

✻

Town hall. Ten miles from Shelby.

"Sorry for the delay." The Register of Deeds' secretary came back into the office where Ryder had been waiting. "We're the repository for this area, so it took time to find the right books."

"Thanks for your trouble."

She was in her early twenties, with lank brown hair and a smile that showed crooked teeth. But she was female. "Oh, it's no trouble—though I shouldn't be doing this." Her eyelashes fluttered at Ryder, who leaned over the counter, smiling. "If my boss were here . . ."

"But he's not," Ryder said, his gaze meeting hers.

She flushed. "I mean, why would a reporter want—"

He let the smile grow. "Reporter, not a private detective," he said. "Why not just put those down on the counter and get back to that letter you were typing? I won't be long."

It took him three hours, and most of his charm. Ryder pored over the ledgers until sweat ran down his face. If he only knew what he was looking for . . . but he didn't. He gave thanks to fate that Shelby was a village with fewer than 2,000 homeowners. He hoped he'd recognize the name he wanted when he saw it on the deed.

When he did see it, Ryder drew his breath in sharply enough to make the secretary turn from her filing cabinet. "Success?" she asked, obviously hoping he'd let her in on the mystery.

"Success." And an even greater puzzle, Ryder thought. He copied down the information, and showing the girl the ledger sheet, asked, "Where is this?"

"Not far. A five-minute drive once you get to the green at Shelby. It's the best address in town if you want space and privacy, and can afford it."

"I'm sure money's not the object," Ryder murmured. "Thanks for the help."

Leaving the office, he suffered only a momentary pang of conscience that he'd spent his morning flirting with a secretary. Long ago he'd earned the label "ruthless," probably from Edwin Frasier, and he wasn't ashamed of living up to it in his work.

The Shelby map showed him a weaving course through the exclusive neighborhood. Glen Forest Road itself was a cul-de-sac, with only four houses, one of which looked like a transplant from New Mexico. It was 123, the number he wanted.

Ryder parked his car along the deserted road, not too close to the sprawling adobe-style house. There was a blue Chevrolet station wagon in the drive, and after half an hour someone emerged from inside and walked out through the garage, toward the car.

Ryder straightened in his seat. His heart began to thump as it always did when he closed in on a story. Who was she? A not-quite-slender woman, generously endowed, but with slim, straight legs encased in black jodhpurs. She wore a hunt jacket, and a jaunty cap over blue-black hair. Attractive, he could tell, and, like the design of her house, vaguely Spanish-looking. Reaching for a camera on the seat beside him, Ryder snapped off a quick dozen shots with the telephoto.

She had started the car and was backing out of the drive. Ryder slid down in his seat until she passed by. After she'd been gone a quarter of an hour, he flung open the door and strode toward her mailbox.

Inside, he found a collection of bills, two letters, and a postcard from someone enjoying a holiday in the Caribbean. Everything was addressed to the same person. He jammed it back in place, having committed the federal offense of tampering with the U.S. mail.

He compounded the crime by taking a slow walking tour of the grounds. At the rear of the house, Ryder pressed his face to the windows, looking into a sunny breakfast room floored in Spanish tile and a large, well-equipped kitchen with countertops to match. Maria Cruz, Ryder repeated to himself half a dozen times. Back in the car, he started the engine and drove slowly out of the cul-de-sac without being arrested.

His thoughts were troubled as he accelerated up the on-ramp to Interstate 90, heading south to Boston. According to the property ledgers he'd seen, Teague Michaels owned the house on Glen Forest Road. But the name was only a front, and Michaels would do anything to reach Washington himself. Lending his name wouldn't be that high on the list. Weekends in Shelby, Massachusetts, Ryder thought. Maria Cruz. And Dan Benedict.

That cheating son of a bitch. He didn't have proof yet, but that's the way it shaped up. He pushed his foot to the floor and the car shot forward. Oh, Laurel. He was an hour late meeting her at his apartment, and he wished to hell he'd never heard of Shelby.

After waiting at Ryder's apartment door for nearly two hours, Laurel began to gather up packages from the floor where she'd dumped them. She'd drive home to Beacon Hill, drop off the shopping bags so Ned wouldn't ask questions she didn't want to answer, then meet him after school. She had an hour yet.

"Sweetheart, I didn't mean to keep you waiting." Ryder bounded up the last stairs of the four-flight climb. "I had an assignment, out of town. Then traffic was heavy."

He held the door with one hand high on the frame, letting Laurel duck underneath. She inhaled the fresh scent of outdoors, of tobacco.

"You've been smoking again."

"Perfect score," he admitted. "Tried to quit a dozen times, and stopped trying just that many."

"I've spoiled a record myself today." Setting her packages in the hall, Laurel shrugged out of her coat. Ryder hung it in the foyer closet with his battered duffel coat, which seemed to be part of a collection of disreputable clothing. "I've never been stood up before."

"Never stood up, huh?" All at once, she was pressed against the wall, Ryder's body holding her in place. Laurel laughed as he brushed aside a thick strand of hair to nuzzle her neck. "Want to try a new experience?"

"You're shameless."

"I'm horny."

Remembering the thwarted visit yesterday with Ned and Pirate, Laurel smiled.

"Later," she said. "You've got a drafty hallway."

"The apartment's not much better, courtesy of the cheap management." He wandered past the pile of bags from Filene's and several expensive boutiques into the living room. "I'll light the fire first. Come get warm."

They were sharing a plate of oatmeal cookies and drinking black currant tea in front of the cheery blaze before Ryder asked, "What's in the shopping bags?"

Remembering his reaction to her moving cartons

around, she wasn't sure he'd like this intrusion any better.

"I . . . I wanted to buy you a few things," she said, and dropped them onto the sofa.

Staring at the bounty from which every price tag seemed to stand out like another sign of possession, she watched Ryder rub one hand over the front of his shirt, plain white with the third button hanging by a thread. His jeans had a worn spot just above the knee, paler as he hunkered down. "It looks like you've bought out the store," he said at last. "Stores. What's this?"

"Sheets." Heart pounding, Laurel tore the plastic from a package, and waves of blue undulated toward them. The design reminded her of the sea at Gloucester when the sun was on it. In the store she had closed her eyes, imagining Ryder's still-tanned skin against the ocean blue cotton.

"Nice," he said, watching the sheets drape themselves over Laurel's thighs. Next she gave him a natural-colored wicker shelf with a small cabinet for the bathroom wall, and a matching plant basket. Then a bright green tablecloth of fine linen and a set of navy napkins trimmed in emerald fringe.

Laurel's pulse slowed. He didn't seem to mind her largess. Grinning, he held up a fan of color, cranberry and turquoise and gold. They were low-cut, hip-hugging briefs of soft cotton knit, and for good measure she'd added a pair in pure silk for him to try as well, French blue. "Where am I supposed to wear these?"

"Right here. Only here."

Laughing softly, he tossed the underwear back onto the growing pile of unwrapped packages, pulling out a more innocent set of thick, thirsty-looking towels. The pattern was striped, black with taupe and one contrasting band of scarlet. "Not as sexy," he murmured, "but maybe on you . . ."

"I get the bath sheet."

Huge and densely piled, it was pure burnt orange.

"Laurel, you shouldn't have."

"I wanted to. Please don't tell me you won't take all this."

"Not if it means you can stay," he said. "I'm glad you're here."

Her spirits soared. He didn't seem to care what her motives might be: buying him linens simply because she felt generous, or because what was already here belonged to Maggie.

"You're very dear," she whispered.

"No," he said fiercely, "no, I'm not. And soon, Laurel, we have to talk. About us. But I'm grateful, and I love you. I don't think you know how much."

She felt her bones begin to melt as his mouth covered hers, Ryder leaning across the pile of presents on the sofa. "Come on, let's try out the sheets. Pick them up."

He rose with her in his arms. The soft wash of blue trailed over them, behind them. "The towels, too."

Ryder sidestepped the jewel-toned gifts falling from the sofa cushions onto the carpet. Wine red and yellow, gem green and delft blue, a blush of peach and cream silk that she hadn't been able to bypass in Jordan Marsh.

"Too much." Then he carried her through the apartment to his bed. His bed this time, Laurel thought, and this time it was all right. As he lowered her, Ryder's lips were at her throat, his whisper brushing delicate skin. "I had no idea I was to become your favorite charity."

Laurel stared again at the check, at Sebastian's signature underneath the dollar figures. "This is the first money I've ever earned," she told Hilary. "All mine, not accountable to anyone else. Not even to Dan." With a grin, she glanced across the table. "What am I going to do with all this cash?"

"I'm too stunned by Sebastian's generosity to respond."

Laurel shook her head, then looked down at her plate. She'd met Hilary, in Boston for a fashion photo layout against the backdrop of Faneuil Hall, for lunch. But she was too excited to eat. And Hilary had been giving her odd looks.

"That check isn't the only reason you've got a terrific glow today." Hilary grinned. "It's Ryder, isn't it?"

A short silence. Then Laurel admitted, "I surrendered."

"And Dan?"

"Campaigning, of course. He hardly knows I'm alive at this point. Less than a week until the election. He's on the trail twenty hours a day."

"I meant the marriage, Laurel."

"There hardly is a marriage," she confessed, looking down at the tablecloth. "Dan and I aren't, uh, sharing a bed just now."

"Where does he sleep?"

"The nights he's at home, which aren't that many with the campaign, Dan uses the third-floor guest room." She was both miserable and relieved. Guilt on the one hand, covert afternoons with Ryder on the other.

"Laurel, you can't mean to keep living in limbo. That's not fair to yourself, or to anyone else. Ryder included."

"I know." What she didn't know was the solution.

"Dan's not doing much to save what's left, is he?"

"We have our differences. Serious ones, I know that. But so do Ryder and I." Laurel pressed a hand to her forehead. "I think he feels it, too. I'm not exactly unencumbered."

"He likes Ned, doesn't he?"

"I think so, or he's trying to, but after that performance at the zoo, Ned's not quite as ready to like him. Years ago, there was a little girl in Vietnam, I don't know the whole story, but enough to know that she broke Ryder's heart and he's not crazy about kids as a result."

"Talk to him."

"I think we're both afraid to." She sighed again. "Good Lord, Hilary, I can't believe this—" she waved the check in the air before stuffing it back into her bag "—but I would never, in a hundred years, have seen myself conducting an affair."

"Serious, too."

"I wouldn't be in it if it weren't."

"Quite the virtuoso, is he?"

Laurel flushed. "You're outlandish."

"So was this morning's paper." At Laurel's blank stare, Hilary opened her own handbag. "I thought you were too calm. You haven't seen this?"

It was the morning's *Herald*, with a clipping from a popular column. "No, I left home without glancing at the papers." Laurel didn't admit that she'd been avoiding them, just as she had ignored the television news in Gloucester for a different reason. Except for her own commitments she didn't want to follow the campaign; it was an ever-present specter in her life without encouragement, invading what little privacy she had with Ryder.

Only they had no privacy.

"God," Laurel muttered, skimming the paragraphs with a practiced eye. "... few appearances lately at the candidate's side:... trouble in political paradise... estrangement in mid-campaign...." She groaned at the rest. "Washington buzzes with rumor ... Mrs. Benedict's disappearance from the Hulme gala ... after an intriguing picture with journalist Ryder McKendrick."

The photo had been reprinted with the piece. Laurel stared at the picture of Ryder, holding onto her arm that night, and saw the same baffled intensity she'd seen then, responded to. Her own face reflected compassion, and love. Or could anyone else read into the expression something that intimate? She hadn't recognized it then herself.

She lifted her gaze to Hilary's. "I'm surprised. This writer's usually the least vicious columnist I know." Laurel leaned back in her chair. "Now I know why Dan's so insistent that I attend that dinner with him tonight."

He'd issued the command last night by telephone to "wear something smashing. And the look of a contented wife." But had his call been advance warning about today's column? Someone at the *Herald* might have tipped him off.

Hilary cursed Dan with her usual enthusiasm. "He never stops using you, does he?" When Laurel refused to answer, she said, "All right. If we were in New York I could lend you my Galanos, if you really intend to go."

"I have to go. And I'm wearing the Nina Ricci."

"That gorgeous satin the color of pomegranates?"

"High visibility," Laurel said. She refolded the newspaper, handing it back. "Well, it looks like a busy week for me after all. Teague will run me from one end of the state to the other. God, I'll be glad when the votes are counted." She couldn't think beyond that, what Dan's victory—or defeat—would mean for them. "I guess Sebastian will have to wait for the last sketches."

At Hilary's jaundiced look she said, "What else can I do? Dan's still my husband. I feel guilty enough." She pushed both hands through her hair, not caring that she'd hopelessly mussed the style. "This next week is necessary, that's all. I can't expect you to understand how complex everything is when your life's so much simpler."

It was hateful condescension, and Laurel could see that it had hurt, but she couldn't bear talking about Dan or Ryder another minute. "You might be surprised," Hilary said at last. "Lately, I've made a rather complicated stew myself."

The shift of topic made Laurel grateful, and aware of how strong their friendship was. She knew that talking about Sebastian didn't appeal to Hilary at the moment either. Yet as she told Laurel in short, tight sentences about the automobile exhibition, about meeting Vittorio DeNobili and taking Sebastian home, the pain seemed to tumble out.

". . . his father?" Laurel echoed when Hilary finished. "But are you sure?"

"DeNobili told me himself, and there'd be no reason for him to lie." Hilary looked at her with darkened eyes. "I actually called Sebastian a bastard."

Laurel said gently, "And you haven't seen him since?"

"You know I haven't. You were in Gloucester."

"With a very unhappy man. Hilary, he's in love with you. Why haven't you called him? It was a misunderstanding, not difficult to remedy. You hurt him, and that's not like you. The only person I've ever seen you be so rough on is Dan."

"*He* deserves it, anyway." Then her smile faded. "I did think of going up to close my mother's house. But I can't face him. I may have hurt him, and I'm sorry, though he wouldn't believe my saying it, but he isn't right about Chip."

Laurel asked carefully, "What about Chip?"

"Sebastian doesn't think he's alive."

"Oh, Hilary. Chip Brewster has been out of your life for fourteen years. It's time you made other arrangements before you end up old, and alone, and looking out the window all day for some man who'd be a stranger to you if he—"

"I won't forget him, Laurel."

"Of course you won't." She gentled her tone. "But—"

"You're wrong, and so is Sebastian. Chip's coming back. Someday." Snatching her hand away, Hilary stood up. "He's coming back."

"Hilary—"

"I'm not messing up my life with Sebastian Noble in the meantime. I don't want a hole-in-the-corner affair!"

"Are you talking about me, with Ryder?" Laurel's tone was hard. There were going to be hurts on both sides today, she thought.

"Yes. Yes, I am. One of these days, Laurel, you're going to have to make some choices. And not for Lexa. Choices that work for you. I've already made mine."

"Again?" Laurel murmured.

"Therapy."

Ryder's arms tightened around her, pulling Laurel back onto the bed. She'd arrived early from her luncheon— and argument—with Hilary, needing to talk, to be loved. Yet two hours later the quarrel continued to break into her thoughts. The quarrel, and tonight's political dinner with Dan in Brockton.

"I have to leave soon."

"Someday you're not going to say that."

The dark silk of her hair slid back and forth against his chest. "I wish I didn't have to now."

"Do you, Laurel?"

"I love you," she reminded him.

"Where does that leave Dan?"

She raised her head, looking into his eyes. "Let's not spoil today."

Ryder knew she was right. With the election next Tuesday, he probably wouldn't see her at all after Friday. And when it was over. . . . He pulled her close, and they kissed.

"If this is all we've got," he told her, "then by God, let's have it." Their lovemaking was fierce and tender at the same time. But afterward he still felt uneasy. The threat of Shelby goaded him. He said, "That newspaper column really bugged you, didn't it, with the picture of us? I was hoping you hadn't seen it."

"If I hadn't, Teague would have supplied a copy. And Dan—"

"What did he say?"

"Just to be in Brockton by six-thirty."

"No comment on the piece?"

"Dan's too busy vote-getting. By tonight, he'll be hysterical for Tuesday to arrive."

"Even so, I can't believe he's keeping quiet."

But maybe Benedict had stopped caring that his wife might be with another man, stopped because he too had a secret. When Laurel let it slip that Dan wasn't staying in Boston for the weekend, Ryder's heart lurched. "Where's he headed?"

Framingham, he hoped she'd say. Lexington, Springfield.

"I don't know. And you've asked me that before."

On the plane to Washington, he remembered, and softened his attack. "Probably planning a few days of last-second stumping, driving from town to town, shaking hands and kissing babies."

"He's good at that." She gave him a grateful smile.

"When's he leaving?"

"Tomorrow at noon."

"When will he be back?" Ryder persisted.

"I'm not sure. Sunday night, I think he said."

Dan hadn't said anything, but Ryder was playing reporter again, though he'd been off the campaign for more than a month. If Laurel could have told him, she wasn't sure she would have.

It was on the tip of her tongue to ask if he were still following Dan when he excused himself, hurriedly she thought, to fix them sandwiches. From the kitchen as he clattered about, she heard the telephone ring.

"McKendrick." He laughed a little. "I know I ought to say hello first. I'm in a rush. Got your phone bill under control, huh? I didn't hear from you last Sunday."

Laurel, smiling at his affectionate tone, wandered to the kitchen where Ryder opened the mayonnaise, holding the receiver tucked between his chin and shoulder. "My mother," he mouthed.

She blew him a kiss and went back into the living room, taking a dust rag with her from the cabinet by the sink. His books were in need of cleaning, she'd noticed yesterday; most everything was.

Odd, but she'd nearly stopped thinking of Beacon Hill as home. It seemed to her like Chevy Chase now, cool and remote and perfect. If she hadn't had Ned there to bless the rooms with noise and sticky handprints, she would have felt as if she were living in a hotel.

"Not at the moment," she heard Ryder say. "I'm entertaining."

Laurel smiled, knowing he was baiting his mother.

"Fantastic," he said. "Slim, curvy, smart, and talented. She's an artist—" Breaking off, he laughed. "Yeah, Mom, she's crazy about kids."

Wondering how much more he'd confide of their relationship, Laurel tensed. But Ryder changed the subject, and the teasing became private, sprinkled with family references. Laurel turned to the bookshelves, wiping the clean rag carefully over each one. Then her fingers stilled.

The dark red spine of the book was oversized, and he had shelved it on the long edge. Slowly she drew it from the shelf, some sixth sense telling her what it was. *Images of Destruction*.

"Sorry," he called from the kitchen. "That was Mission Control. I'll be in with the food as soon as I pour the coffee."

Laurel carried the book to the sofa and sat down, balancing it on her knees. Not bothering with the narrative, she focused on the photographs: page after page of humanity as only Ryder's camera knew how to capture it; old, young, and in between; infants in arms and wizened women with bent shoulders and stooped spines, their eyes hollowed by suffering. Pain, and despair. Laurel found it difficult to look at the faces, the bodies.

An old man sitting on a path, refugees drifting past the cart that carried him, legless. A child, perhaps three years old, dark-haired and dark-eyed, small and somber. Laurel shivered. They were civilians mostly. Little men in black pajamas. A pregnant woman, her belly stretching the buttons of a too-small shirt. The same solemn, fragile child again.

Laurel's heart beat harder. Instinctively, she knew. She flipped the pages back, then forward, coming face to face a dozen times with the child who had ruined Ryder's heart.

A child clothed in rags, with the matchstick legs and arms, the swollen stomach caused by malnutrition; and yet, she was beautiful, wearing innocence like a party dress.

Laurel raced through the book, not knowing whether she wanted to keep looking or to shut it, and turn away. The series of photographs broke her own heart. Ngoc Hoa, he had said; Hoa, sad and frail. Ngoc Hoa, still somber but with a bit more weight, and clean clothes. Hoa, grasping a candy bar and almost smiling. Hoa, laughing in the sun. The pictures had been interspersed throughout the book as a unifying theme. Smiling at the carefree child riding high on a younger Ryder's shoulders, she wanted, unreasonably, to close the book again.

She turned another page, another, and then—Oh God, oh God. Laurel didn't know how long she'd held the page open before Ryder spoke. "You ever fix sandwiches with one hand while talking on the phone? I didn't know it could be done, but..."

She stared with sightless eyes at Ngoc Hoa, and Ryder. It was the last photograph in the book, and it chilled her to the bone. So did his voice when he saw what she was holding.

"Where'd you get that?"

"From the shelf," she managed to say. "It was in plain sight."

"Would you put it back, please?"

"No." Her heart was drumming, her body full of nerves. But Laurel sensed that obeying him, as she'd done with Maggie's cartons, would be the worst thing she could do; it would allow him to close the door again on understanding. "I want you to tell me."

"You've seen the rest!"

Suddenly torn from her grasp, the book was flung against the wall of shelves. She heard the spine crack, saw pages fan across the polished floor. Laurel fell to her knees, gathering the sheets of photographs as if she could comfort that child, as she would hold Ned in her arms.

Ryder knelt beside her. "That's what's known as a grand gesture." He indicated the broken book. "I've got a dozen more somewhere. Contract copies I never gave to anyone."

His hand spread the pages across the floor as if they were cards in a deck. Ngoc Hoa seemed to look at them from every one. "Makes quite a leitmotif, doesn't she?" he said after a moment.

"Yes." She wanted to touch him, but his control was

too finely balanced, and he wouldn't thank her for shattering the last of it.

"Things come back to you," he said. "Funny things, sad things. . . ." He turned over more pages, running a finger over the curve of Hoa's cheek, her printed smile. "Things you don't want to remember." But he went on in a husky tone.

"It was just after dawn that morning, when I told you that the sun didn't come up. It had been raining all night, hard and steady. I couldn't sleep. Finally, I gave up and woke Ham. 'We'll ride out to the orphanage,' I said. 'Surprise the kids at breakfast.' All the way out there, we talked about what to do on a rainy day, remembering games we'd played as children, games we thought Hoa and the others would like.

"We heard the bombers but we never saw them. Ham said it was thunder. When we got closer, we both knew it wasn't. I don't know what happened, Laurel, whether they screwed up the coordinates, or dropped their payload too soon or too late . . . it doesn't matter. In a couple of minutes, they were gone, not even a drone from high overhead. Those guys flew at fifty thousand feet, my God, they couldn't even see the ground."

"Were they—"

"Ours," he said. "There was a cover-up, but actually, that sort of thing happened with fair frequency. And the 'body count' wasn't all that many . . . thirty-five dead, the rest wounded."

Laurel made herself ask. "Ngoc Hoa?"

His shaking fingers moved through the photographs to the last one, which had frozen Laurel's blood. The child lay limp in his arms, as if she were asleep. Her face was still, expressionless.

"There wasn't a mark on her," he whispered. "Not a cut, not a bruise, not a burn. The whole goddamn orphanage was rubble, fires smoking from a dozen different places, every window shattered...but there wasn't a mark on her. I don't know whether that made it easier or harder to bear."

She glanced at the picture and absorbed the anguish on Ryder's face, raised toward the dull gray sky, the tears streaming down his cheeks indistinguishable from rain, tears illuminated by some trick of side-lighting. The fires, she imagined. Ham Channing had used the reflected glow of hell to get that picture. "You're looking at a Pulitzer, of course. Another irony," Ryder said. "A week later Ham Channing was dead, too, caught in a firefight somewhere in the hills."

Laurel was speechless. His wife, she thought; his friend; the child he had loved. All dead.

"Actually, you're seeing an American tradition." When Laurel looked at him, he said, "A hundred years ago, when the pioneers were moving west in wagon trains with the bare essentials of existence, this kind of portrait—excluding the tears—would have been rather common."

"What do you mean?"

"I've explained the precedent in the text, but in the early 1880s the camera was, of course, largely a curiosity. One employed a photographer to record only the most momentous occasions—weddings, family portraits. In an age of high infant mortality, parents often had their dead children's pictures taken for . . . remembrance. In the same fashion, I suppose," he said, "as previous generations kept death masks of their loved ones. We think of it as macabre now, but there wasn't any other way to have the visual memory. Sketches maybe, an oil painting, but who could afford an artist? Not many, I imagine; not most.

"I've seen photos similar to Channing's." He tapped the page that Laurel had looked away from. "A child in bed, perhaps, covers to its chin . . . a young father, cradling an infant in his arms. Both children not sleeping at all. Those old sepia-tone pictures were treasured by families leaving behind not only their friends and parents, but often parts of themselves, too. A baby, a toddler lost to illness . . . or accident."

When he had finished, they sat in silence. Then Laurel murmured, "I'm so sorry about everything that's made you sad, Ryder."

He lifted his gaze to hers. "Some time ago, I wondered whether you were really soft. I'm sorry I doubted you, Laurel." Ryder touched her cheek lightly. "Like everybody else, I came back from that war feeling bitter and cheated and hopeless. I wish Maggie could have offered help, but she didn't. She couldn't, I guess. We had both changed too much in that single year, and nothing was ever right for us again, not really."

"You didn't want children after that," Laurel surmised.

"No, but maybe time would have changed my mind. I don't know. By then, Maggie and I were at war. She hadn't wanted Hoa, and we'd fought about that by letter. Maybe she was sorry. The idea of having a baby became for her, I think, a means of salvaging us, together. She resented my work more and more, the constant travel, and risk. It got pretty bad toward the end." She saw tears in his eyes. "I picked the last argument. She kept telling me how nature wouldn't cooperate much longer, that if she wanted to deliver a healthy child without fearing for her own safety she'd better get pregnant. I told her, not by me."

"What did Maggie say?"

"That she didn't want to divorce me, but she would." Laurel held her breath for the rest. "She was already halfway out the door. Going for a swim, she said, to cool off, and she hoped I'd find a way to do the same." Ryder's gaze slid away. "She told me I was being selfish, and I told her that—that having a baby was the most egotistical act I could think of."

"You never saw her again."

"Not alive," he said, "no."

Laurel turned slightly, putting her hands on his shoulders. "You don't think, surely you can't think—"

"Suicide?" He shook his head. "She loved life too much. I think it was the next thing to murder, if you want to know the truth."

"Oh, Ryder."

"Hoa, too," he said. "You know, her people believe that if a child is given a particularly pretty name, it brings good fortune to the whole family. 'Precious Flower.' That's quite beautiful, isn't it?"

"Yes."

He blinked. "If I'd filled out the papers sooner, Laurel, convinced Maggie, if I'd pushed harder to get them through all the ridiculous red tape . . . if I'd taken her out of the country a week sooner, a few days—"

"But you didn't. You couldn't."

"I should have done *something*," he said, "something to save her."

"That's a selfish notion, Ryder." Laurel waited until he looked up. "Playing God, thinking you might have changed fate. I've prayed a hundred times since Lexa died that I could have made things turn out differently." She couldn't bring herself to say, because of the senator. "I couldn't. And neither could you."

"But, Christ, all the wrong turns, the lousy things I shouted at Maggie—"

"Being human," she said. "That's all. Don't you think I remember every bad thought I ever had about Lexa? And there were some."

He turned from her, stacking the book pages in a pile;

the smiling photograph of Ngoc Hoa, high on his shoulders, at the top. Laurel heard him clear his throat before Ryder turned back to her again. "Survivor guilt," he muttered. His gray eyes were very bright. "It's not so easy getting left behind, is it? There's so much to clean up."

Without another word, she drew him to her where they both knelt on the floor. Like children, they clung to each other. "Oh God, Laurel," he said, shaking. "The whole world's been on fire. Everything around me seemed to be dying, Maggie, Hoa . . . something in me dying, too." He caught her face between his hands. "I'm beginning to feel alive again, and scared. More scared than before. I've let myself love again, and now I'm afraid of losing you."

Ryder lowered her to the carpet, and the world flamed with a different fire, slow and warm and glowing, one he never wanted to put out. They had decisions to make, but the decisions could wait a little longer. Shelby could wait.

That evening Hilary Chapin received a telephone call from Ryder, who could no longer bear the mental image of Laurel and Dan together in Brockton.

Hilary might have asked how he'd learned her unlisted number in New York and that she'd flown home from Boston as soon as she left Laurel, but she kept quiet. Ryder was persistent; and as a journalist of note, he'd have his sources. She reclined on her bed, and asked him how he was.

"Not so great," he said. "I'm going to do something soon that will hurt Laurel just as much as your argument today. Red, I need some advice."

"I thought you'd quit the campaign."

"Yes, but what makes you think it has to do with Benedict?"

"I know you wouldn't hurt Laurel yourself. So it must involve Dan. What have you got on him, McKendrick?"

"Not enough."

"But something. Something rotten."

"Yeah." She heard him sigh. "There's nothing to tell. Not yet." His tone lightened. "Anyway, you'd scoop me."

"I love her, too, McKendrick. I'd like to see my dearest friend have a happy ending . . . or rather, a beginning."

Ryder grunted in agreement. "So would I. I hope you won't both end up hating me for doing my job."

"I'd more easily hate Dan, even Sebastian, but not you, Ry—"

"Sebastian cares for you. Deeply."

She shifted. So they'd discussed her fight with Laurel in depth.

"Whether he's dead or not, Brewster's gone, Hilary." Ryder's tone was flat, and hard. "Laurel's right, so is Sebastian."

Oh, why had she let Sebastian into her apartment that night? Allowed him to stay and . . . no, she wouldn't think about that. One night of madness and sorcery.

"If he's alive Brewster has spent the past fourteen years of his life," Ryder went on, "most of his adult life, in a foreign country. What do you think he's like by now? The same blond, blue-eyed Wasp you sent off to war?" He took a breath. "No way, Red. And I'm not talking character lines or graying hair or the loss of thirty pounds. Changed appearance would be the least of it. And maybe there is no prison camp, have you considered that? Maybe the man just gave up, and settled."

"Settled?"

"By now, he'd be half-Vietnamese. Living in some little village, in the middle of nowhere, out of sight. With some Mama-san and a batch of cross-breed kids, he probably hasn't spoken English in a dozen years—"

"Stop, stop it."

Automatically her fingers reached for Chip's photograph on the bedside table. It wasn't there. In fourteen years she'd moved it only to dust. Then Sebastian had wandered in, giving orders she should never have obeyed. More than a month ago, and she hadn't got the picture out again? Her heart began to pound.

Blue eyes, she thought; a white smile. That blond crop of hair, cut close for the military. The uniform. Chip, looking...

*I can't remember.*

Ryder's voice cut into her panic. "Or maybe he *was* in prison. And they broke him. Think about that. Maybe nobody, the Vietnamese, the United States government, even Brewster himself wants him to come back now."

Frantic, she hauled the drawer of the table open, scrabbling for the picture. Charles Wellington Brewster. She went weak with relief at the laughter in his eyes. But had he always looked so young? He was thirty-eight now, but she'd last seen Chip just shy of twenty-five—younger than Sebastian.

"I need to know," she said, the words muffled. "I need to know...."

Closing her eyes, she hugged the silver frame to her chest, trying to picture him again. But a clearer image formed, of dark eyes smiling into hers, of a dark head bent above her in the night. Sebastian. He was right, she thought; we were children, Chip and I. She shouldn't have hurt him for telling her the truth. She set the frame on the table, facedown. And thought, What am I going to do now? With that? With him? Sebastian.

Ryder said gently, "I'm sorry. But I saw a lot of bad stuff over there. Maybe it's better left alone, Hilary. Maybe the memories are better after all."

"Maybe. But what does that do for Laurel, for that

story you won't tell me about? What does it do for you?
The best memories are cold comfort."

"I know."

"Laurel's loyalties are strong, and deep. Maybe she
loves too much. She gave Lexa and her parents everything. She's given Dan that, too." Remembering their
years of friendship, Hilary shook her head. She'd loved
Lexa, too, but with exasperation, never taking her seri-
ously; it had always been Laurel who drew her, charmed
her. Laurel, who apparently still thought of herself as one
half of a whole. Would she ever be able to love herself,
for herself? With Ryder, she might have the chance. But
if she didn't find the courage soon . . . "I'm sure she'd give
that loyalty to you if she had time to make her choices.
But if she's hurt, or if they need her, Laurel will turn
from you, right back to the life she's always known. To
her, it would be security. The right thing to do."

"I know that, too," he murmured. "I just don't know
how to stop it."

"Whatever he's done, Ryder, tell her first."

Hilary's advice was still ringing in his ears the next
afternoon when, from behind the steering wheel of his
Datsun overlooking the Shelby airstrip, Ryder watched
Dan Benedict climb from the twin-engine Beechcraft and
walk into Maria Cruz's arms.

## ✳ CHAPTER 25 ✳

✳

TIME HAD RUN out, and Ryder had made his decision: He would ask Laurel to marry him. They'd deal with the problems of Ned and Dan—and Maria Cruz—after she said yes.

Ryder took the stairs to his apartment two at a time. He'd raced from Shelby in a cold, hard rain, then hadn't been able to find a parking spot near his building. The two-block jog from his car had him soaked to the skin. Cursing as he reached the fourth-floor landing, he shivered in his wet trench coat.

Someone nearby was playing what Ryder termed soul/funk at top volume.

Heart pounding when no one answered the bell, he dug in his pocket for his key. He'd prayed that she was here; he had given Laurel a key after the day she'd waited in the drafty hall, but today she hadn't used it. Where was she? He'd called Beacon Hill, but she hadn't been home. He'd nearly panicked before he remembered Laurel saying that Ned would be out of school for the afternoon. Maybe they'd gone shopping, he thought. Maybe she'd had to give a last-minute speech. He wondered how to reach her before Dan did.

Ryder hadn't needed to follow Dan from the airfield; he'd given them an hour, a little more, before ringing the front doorbell of the house on Glen Forest Road.

The woman had answered, darkly sensual, with a tentative smile. Ryder had raised the Nikon, then snapped off a couple of shots, straight into her surprised face.

As Dan appeared at her shoulder he clicked the shutter again, another "grab shot," but it was all he had time for. "Smile, Counselor."

"You son of a bitch."

"Who is he, Dan? Who is this man?"

"Ryder McKendrick," Benedict answered, half to himself. "I should have known you'd take to playing detective. For whose benefit, Laurel's?"

"The public's." Ryder had backed off, nearly losing his balance on the slate front steps. "You're taking quite a chance four days before the election."

Benedict's hand shot out but Ryder tightened his grip, the image in his mind as they struggled for the Nikon that of glossy film spiraling toward the ground like ribbons of black snake. "Don't do it, Counselor. You'd owe me three hundred dollars."

"I owe you nothing." Then a slow smile spread over Dan Benedict's face. "But what are we fighting about? You're not going to print those pictures, McKendrick, not one word about this."

"I'm a reporter. That's my job, to be objective."

"Coming from you, it would be an editorial. You think I don't know where Laurel spends her afternoons?"

There was no reason to pretend he didn't understand. Ryder glanced beyond Benedict at Maria Cruz. "Do you care?"

The smile stayed on his lips. "Just now, I care about only one thing: getting through Tuesday. You're right about that much, McKendrick." His eyes slipped over

Ryder's rumpled trench coat, the white-knuckled grip he had on the camera. "But my wife's an earnest little thing. She always has been. You break this story, and I will care. But so will she—for Ned's sake, if not mine. And let me tell you this much: Laurel *Frasier* Benedict won't take your side when this stuff hits the fan." Dan had turned on his heel, gone into the house, and slammed the door. The deadbolt had rammed home like a gunshot.

Now Ryder swore again as he jammed his key in his own lock. He had the story he'd wanted weeks ago, but what would he do with it? The key turned but nothing happened. The door had already been unlocked and he pushed it open.

A blast from Tower of Power assaulted his eardrums.

The music had been coming from his own apartment, where his stereo's woofers and tweeters were being threatened by Laurel's favorite group.

He sniffed the air, so heavy with sound but also with the unmistakable, acrid scent of paint.

Ryder felt his knees go weak. He'd driven at breakneck speed from Shelby, stopped at every rest area to phone Beacon Hill again, had even left messages on his own machine. Now, without turning down the stereo volume, he sauntered toward his kitchen, where he found her surrounded by paint cans, dropcloths, rolls of masking tape, and edging sponges. In sweat pants and bare feet, she wore a ragged T-shirt he recognized as one of his. Laurel had been here for some time, happily oblivious of the scandal he'd just uncovered about Dan.

Ryder propped a shoulder against the kitchen doorway. "I thought Ned was home today."

Startled, she nearly dropped the paint roller.

"Kip's mother took the boys to the library for story hour." She set the roller in the tray. "I'm piling up quite a debt with her, aren't I?" Laurel brushed back a wisp of hair that had escaped from a rubber-banded ponytail. Her smile was warm. "Hi. I thought you'd be away until evening at least. This was supposed to be a surprise."

"I'm surprised."

"Do you like it?"

He saw the hesitancy in her eyes. Sheets, towels, clothing, he thought. And just now a kitchen like a circus tent—stripes of new, sunny yellow against the older, fading blue. What did it matter how many changes she wrought in his life? She looked so right here that it took his breath away. And as she kept pointing out one way and another, she and Sara, he was long overdue for change. But change, Ryder reminded himself, was the least of their problems now.

"I like it, yeah."

He studied the one finished yellow wall, and felt his heart turn over. The paint wasn't quite dry, but she hadn't been able to resist hanging the picture. Having never seen it before, still he recognized it. Framed in black, the black-and-white sketch of a flapper girl had been Laurel's first attempt at doing something with her talent. Go for it, he'd urged her though the effort had been rejected. "Those people were idiots," he said softly, and broke into a smile. The one splash of yellow at the nape of the girl's neck matched the color of his new wall perfectly. "What an eye you've got. Thank you."

"I wanted you to have this," she said shyly.

"So you had to paint my whole kitchen to go with it?"

Laurel grinned at his teasing. "Your whole apartment," she said as she rinsed her hands at the sink.

Ryder groaned. "That's what I get for being crazy in love with an artist."

But he knew when she frowned that, after Shelby, he hadn't sounded convincing.

"Is something wrong?"

At the sink he turned her, then dipped his head to kiss her mouth. "You've got paint on your nose."

In the background he dimly heard the telephone.

"It's been ringing all day," Laurel said. "I didn't think you'd want me to answer. I shut myself in the kitchen to paint and just let the messages record. You must have quite a tape by now."

Louder than the phone, the stereo pumped out the funky rhythms of a song called "Soul Vaccination," and his pulse, centered low in his body, picked up the beat. He'd been given a reprieve. No one could touch them here. He wouldn't let anyone touch her. At the same time, it struck Ryder again that he was the one most likely to hurt Laurel—if he broke Benedict's story— which Sara would insist he do. Hours, he thought; all we have are a few more hours.

"Nothing that can't wait," he said.

Then Ryder took his mouth along her jawline to the neckband of Laurel's—his—shirt. He pressed soft, open-mouthed kisses on her skin, nudging aside the fabric to expose her collarbone.

In the distance he could just make out his own voice on the tape. Damn, *damn*. His hands slipped beneath the T-shirt. "You know, there's something to be said for borrowing. Roomy," he murmured. "Accessible."

"Ryder, you're soaking wet."

"I'm okay, or I will be." He caressed her from narrow waist to slender ribcage to the soft undersides of her breasts.

"Ohhh . . . but you'd better get out of those clothes into something dry first. And a hot—"

"I want you."

"After your shower."

"No," he said. "Before."

But with a mother's determination, Laurel eased the

sodden trench coat from his shoulders. It landed with a splat on the floor, then her fingers combed the raindrops from his hair. Ryder pressed her against the kitchen counter, terror and desire running through him. She would hate him when she learned about Dan and Maria Cruz. He had to convince her to leave Dan, to marry him before he told her.

Playing for time, his kisses were sweet, then hungry and increasingly desperate until, finally, Laurel whispered, "Yes. Before."

In the bedroom she helped him strip off his wet clothes. She pulled the blue sheets and the comforter over them, and he began to feel warm again, invincible. From the living room came sudden silence as the stereo shut off. From outside he could hear the rain once more, as if they were in Gloucester, and wrapped his arms around her.

"Make the world go away," Ryder pleaded, "again," wondering whether the words, like Laurel, could work magic, or were only futile. Gloucester hadn't ended the way it should, he reminded himself, like Maggie and Ngoc Hoa. And he never wanted to feel such pain again.

He had loved her so tenderly, but why with such . . . despair, Laurel wondered with her eyes still closed. She'd been drowsing, she didn't know for how long, but the light filtering through her eyelids seemed soft and hazy now.

Then the light grew stronger, and she heard a click.

Her eyes snapped open to stare into the lens of one of Ryder's many cameras. Instantly she turned her face away.

"Sweetheart, don't," he said. "I didn't mean to wake you."

Blinking, she pulled the sheets high. "I don't want you to take my picture."

"Don't be shy, Laurel. I wanted to photograph you

just after we'd made love, when you look so happy, relaxed and soft all over." He knelt by the bed with the
camera in his hands.

"My body's not . . . after Ned, I mean—"

"You're wrong, but the camera has a diffusing lens,"
he told her. "It hides all imperfections—" he gave her a
lazy smile "—which, in your case, are none."

She shook her head, but not to say no. His chest was
still bare, and his jeans were unsnapped. Laurel's gaze
drifted to his half-open fly. She came up on an elbow,
and cradled her head in the palm of her hand. Her hair,
long ago loosened from its rubber band, swung free and
caught the hazy light coming through the windows.
"You're crazy."

And the shutter clicked once more.

Before she could protest, or stop smiling, Ryder had
advanced the film through half a dozen shots. "You
should see the warmth in your eyes," he said.

The camera whirred yet again.

Does he love this more, or me? she wondered. She had
seen him work before—at Dan's announcement, at the
fund-raiser, at Justice Hulme's gala. On the campaign
trail. She'd seen him with Ned at the zoo, and she loved
the way Ryder moved to compose his shots. Now he
seemed pure, still concentration, and she ceased feeling
embarrassed or violated and found herself watching him
as he watched her.

When he said, "Let the sheet fall, Laurel," a flash of
heat swept through her.

His voice was thick, like honey.

"No one else is here," he said and gently drew the sheet
from her, down and down and down, an inch at a time.
"No one else will ever see these pictures but you . . . and
me."

"Oh, Ryder." Her breath came faster, lighter.

"God," he said with a groan, "you're so beautiful. The camera doesn't lie." He dropped back on his heels and realigned his settings. "The camera is your friend, too, Laurel. It's another eye, that's all. My eye. Let me love you this way, sweetheart."

And she felt her body melt. Braced on both elbows, Laurel let her head fall back. *Click*, the camera whispered, *click*.

"With my eyes. And my hands," Ryder murmured. He paused between shots now, posing her where he wanted, stroking her. "You make me so damn . . ." The last word of his arousal was breathed into her ear.

Laurel cried out as his touch brushed over her from shoulder to breast to hip to the tender insides of her thighs.

"With my mouth," Ryder whispered, "and my. . . ."

The camera fell with a muffled thud to the carpet.

"It was only one roll of film."

Ryder had wakened her the second time by dropping a sheaf of eight-by-ten still-damp glossies over her chest and stomach as Laurel soundly slept.

"Come on," he said when she still hadn't opened her eyes, "look at them."

"I've seen myself before."

The bed creaked as he sat down by her hip. He'd spent her hour's nap in his darkroom, but Laurel wouldn't look at the results.

"No, you haven't." Ryder's voice was taut, and Laurel opened her eyes. "When you look in a mirror, you never see yourself." He held her sleepy gaze with his. "When you look in a mirror, you see Lexa."

Stunned, she couldn't say a word.

Ryder's look softened. He spread the pictures in a pattern as he'd done with the broken pages of his book, and

Hoa, but one that pleased him more. "Lexa isn't here now either. Just you and me." He picked a photograph, and held it out to her. "Look, see how beautiful you are. Look," he said, "at Laurel."

Not Laurel Frasier Benedict, she thought, as the senator and Dan and Teague Michaels would say, but simply Laurel.

The pictures were beautiful. She was beautiful.

The camera wouldn't lie, he'd said; and Ryder was, in his own way, an artist too. But like the pictures of Ngoc Hoa, these—no matter how softly focused through his diffusing lens—reminded her of harsh reality. Of Dan and the campaign yet unfinished. Of Ned who needed her, who needed a loving father. Of Ryder's guilt and sorrow over that little girl, over Maggie. He had seen Laurel through the camera eye, and she was beautiful, but he had seen her with the eyes of a man in love again. Perhaps that image was only illusion that couldn't last. If he had been afraid of losing again, so was she.

"Yes," she murmured, "they are beautiful."

He moved closer on the bed, bracketing her head between his braced arms. He looked down into her face, and she saw something in his eyes that she had never seen before. It seemed to be peace, but at the same time, war. Still troubled by her own conflicts and by his desperate loving, she chose to see the latter.

"What's wrong, Ryder?"

"I have something to ask you." He bent down and softly kissed her mouth. "Something important." His smile was crooked. "The answer—your answer—is supposed to be yes."

She smiled a little. "Thanks for the clue. But what's the question?"

"Laurel, I want . . ." He stopped. "I want you to—oh, hell."

He swung off the bed. Laurel realized that someone was pounding at the front door, and had been for some time.

"The damn phone, now the damn door." Ryder zipped his fly as he went. "Laurel, you stay there."

Ryder's instinct was to keep swearing. He'd been that close to asking Laurel to marry him. If he hadn't tripped over his own tongue . . . . He opened the door to Teague Michaels's nasty grin.

"I thought you might be home. Tried to rouse you on the telephone but . . ." Suspicious eyes ran over him, mussed hair to bare chest to unshod feet. " 'Love in the afternoon?' Are you hiding someone, McKendrick?"

Ryder realized his jeans weren't buttoned. "In my own house? What do you want, Michaels?"

"Dan tells me you've been jumping to conclusions."

"You mean Shelby?" Ryder lowered his voice. "I have evidence, I'll get more. I never file a story without confirming it."

"I know about your photos." Michaels took a step into the foyer. "But you know Dan's clean politically. Let me tell you what's at stake for you if the senator—"

"The senator's a father first and Benedict's mentor second, so—"

"Ah yes," Teague said, "Laurel."

Ryder's heartbeat altered. She had come out of the bedroom at the end of the hall with a clear view of the foyer. Teague Michaels was looking past Ryder's shoulder at her.

"Well, little lady. There are pots and there are kettles, I see. All black." He glanced at Ryder. "Have you told her yet?"

"Told me what?"

She was just behind him now. If he turned, he'd see

the first hurt in her eyes. Ryder glared at Teague Michaels. "Get the hell out of this apartment, down those stairs, and out the front door. If I ever even see you on this *block* again, I'll—"

"I don't think you're going to tell her. She'd be no use to you then."

"Get the fuck out!" Ryder shoved as hard as he could.

Teague reeled back. "That's assault, McKendrick."

"You better believe it."

"And you'd better know you're dead meat in this business unless you keep your mouth shut—goddamn tight!"

Breathing hard, Teague lurched down the steps to the next landing. Ryder leaned over the rail.

"Don't come back. Don't call. And leave Sara Hennessey the hell alone, you hear me?" Turning, he avoided Laurel's gaze but thanked God she had put on her sweat pants and top. "I wonder where he buys his suits," he muttered.

"Ryder, what's going on?"

He closed the door and leaned against it as if to keep her inside. He hadn't stopped the madness after all.

"I told you to stay in the bedroom."

"I've taken enough orders from the senator and Dan. I won't take them from you." Her voice was suddenly angry. "I recognized Teague's voice and I want to know what's happened. What did he mean about Dan and some photographs?" She came toward him. "Teague said you were using me."

"Laurel, I'm not. Trust me."

"Where were you today? Have you been following Dan on those mysterious trips out of town?"

He tensed. What should he say? He didn't think she'd heard them mention Shelby, but she was so close to it, she must smell the truth.

"Why, Ryder? Is it Sara's need for blood? Or rather,

my husband's blood—and therefore mine? What have you learned about Dan?"

When he didn't answer, she walked quickly toward the bedroom.

"Laurel, I haven't used you. But dammit, I don't want to hurt you."

He turned her around, grasping her shoulders. If he told her, she would blame him—as Benedict, and Hilary, had said—not Dan. She already blamed him, and he'd hardly said a word. She had always accused him of playing reporter with her, playing on her fears of publicity. What little trust she gave him had come hard, and slowly. Even if she could accept Dan's infidelity, would she forgive Ryder for exposing it?

Why couldn't he have waited until next week to learn about Benedict in Shelby? The wish went against his very nature as a journalist always hoping for the hot story, but why did it have to break now, so near the election that exposure could cost Dan the Senate seat? When at last he held the power to hurt Edwin Frasier through his son-in-law, instead he wanted to throw away his notes, the photographs, all the records going back five years and maybe more; he wanted to forget he'd ever needed revenge for Ngoc Hoa, for Maggie. Moments ago Laurel had almost been his. He couldn't risk her turning him out now, taking all the light from his life again. By God, he couldn't.

But suspicious, vengeful, half in love with her himself, Teague Michaels had forced the betrayal. With Dan's help, Ryder thought.

"Don't ask more questions," he begged her. "Please. It's going to be all right, sweetheart. I love you. It's going to be okay."

She only stared at him. "If you won't tell me, maybe Dan will."

Pulling away, she picked up his paint-spattered T-shirt and tossed it at the hamper in his closet. She gathered her totebag, an array of color swatches poking out the top.

"Dan's not home," he said. "I can tell you that much. Desperate situation, desperate measures." He took a steadying breath. "Laurel, I want you to go to Beacon Hill and pack. Then I want you to come back here. To stay," he finished.

"Leave Dan? With the election four days off?" She shook her head. "I thought you wouldn't push, that you understood I'm not free to make decisions until after Tuesday, when the votes are counted. What are you asking? That I come to live with you?"

Ryder groaned. Tuesday would be too late; if she left this house without choosing between them, he didn't have a chance.

"Marry me," he said. "I'm asking—I was trying to before—asking you to marry me."

She looked stunned. "Dan would fight for Ned. Then there's Pirate—"

"Bring the dog, too. We'll worry about Ned's custody later."

She shook her head again. "This is all too fast. You're making me dizzy."

"Listen, I know this is a bad time for a clumsy proposal, but these decisions have been coming ever since we met," he said. "I know I'm not always easy to be around, and Ned and I have our problems. The dog's a handful. But all of that's workable, Laurel. I know journalists have lousy track records in relationships, and I'm no exception, and I know I screwed up with Maggie. Maybe I've even been hedging because of that, with you, but if we both really want it to work . . ." He paused, staring at the bedroom carpet. It was wearing badly, and he'd never seen that stain before.

"Ryder, I . . ."

He lifted his gaze. "You can fix the house all you want. It needs fixing. If it's money you're unsure about, well, I make a decent living. I've got some put by, and a few investments, nothing close to what you're used to, married to a lawyer, or as the senator's daughter but—"

"I don't need money."

She knew he'd always been sensitive to her background, to the sable evening cloak and limousines, and the house on Beacon Hill. "I need time, Ryder," she said softly. "If you won't give me your trust and tell me what's happened with Dan before he does, at least I need time to think."

"I told you about Ngoc Hoa," he said. "That was trust."

"Yes."

But he knew by her tone that she wasn't sure his past wouldn't poison Ned's future; that Maggie's memory wouldn't eventually destroy Laurel's marriage to him. "I can't just walk out on Dan," she said, "not now. I don't know whether I can at all." She raised tortured eyes to his, and fear made him angry.

"What do you want me to say? That I'll sit here waiting until you decide that marriage to Benedict isn't what you need after all? That ten years ago in Lexa's place you married a man you didn't love? Well, I won't wait—"

"Don't give me ultimatums, Ryder. Not today."

"Dammit to hell, there isn't any more time!"

Laurel's eyes flashed. "You're expecting me to turn my back on everything I've believed in—my marriage, my home, my family, obligation and duty—on a moment's notice when you won't level with me about Teague Michaels just now and Dan. If I make the wrong choice, there would be no turning back. And a wrong choice would affect you, too." She looked away. "Ryder, I don't want us to be a mistake."

"God, I don't either." But if she just loved him enough to . . . "Say you'll marry me, now or next year, I don't care," he begged. "I'll tell you if you do."

"I can't make a decision that affects the rest of my life and Ned's unless I have the same information to work with that you do."

She was right. But so was he.

"Goddammit, then go!" Fear, and male pride, got the best of him as Ryder waved a hand toward the hall and the foyer. "Go back to Beacon Hill. Stay there and be miserable. But don't worry, Laurel." She started for the door. "He won't leave you, that's for goddamn sure, they never do, and with the senator for a father-in-law—"

"Oh, I'll go," she said, her voice thick. "And you can go to hell."

Hating himself, he pursued her along the hall. "Run home, Laurel. Be a good girl, and wonder for the rest of your life if it's you Dan Benedict loves, or M—"

At the door he ran into Laurel's back. Jesus, he thought.

"Or whom?" she asked coldly.

". . . your dead sister," Ryder said.

"God." He felt her shoulders shake, but when he touched them she flinched, flattening herself against the door. "God, I don't believe you said that."

Before he could reach out, she had wrenched the door open and was halfway down the stairs. Christ, he thought, he had almost said the name, but what he'd said instead had been as deeply wounding to her as the story he owed Sara. And too soon, because of him, there'd be not only Lexa for brutal comparison in Laurel's mind but Maria Cruz.

Looking down the stairwell, Ryder felt as he had with

Maggie and Ngoc Hoa. Cursing as the exit door four floors below slammed shut, he smashed a fist into his apartment door panel. He welcomed the pain. Sharp and hot, it matched the other feeling he had: that of the world, caught on fire again. Only this time nothing could put it out, except the love of the woman he had just lost. And this time the pain was worse.

※

## ※ *CHAPTER 26* ※

※

His face a mask of anguish, Dan turned Maria around as she went into the hallway that led to their bedroom suite, but she freed herself from his grasp.

"I mean it, Dan. Go home."

"I am home, dammit." All afternoon, since she'd opened the door to McKendrick, he'd been defending himself. "And what would I be going back to?" Dan demanded. "An angry wife because that bastard saw—"

"It isn't my fault about the camera, about his showing up here."

"You shouldn't have met me at the airstrip."

"So you've said, a dozen times. Well, I'd seen you twice in six weeks. If it offends you that I happen to miss your 'visits,' I'm sorry. I can't help how I feel."

One of those visits, Dan remembered, had been in Teague's company, just a ninety-minute stopover between speeches.

"The press is never far away, Dan," Michaels had reminded him, parking down the road from the house where Maria waited. "You'll need a good story if someone spots you."

"Good stories are what I pay you for, Teague."

Eager for Maria, he was once again beyond caution. Then she'd taken his visit the wrong way. And now he was paying for that, too.

"Maria, we waste so much time," Dan said. "Let's not quarrel."

"I waste so much time," she replied. "Years, in fact, being supportive of you, ignoring what I need. I haven't expected you to even wonder what my needs might be, Dan. I've never called Laurel when I felt neglected, though I've thought of it." His face turned pale. "And oh yes, I've stayed away from Ned, except the one time. Heeded your command not to go back to Dawson. Even taken you to bed for an hour while Teague Michaels filled his stomach at the local steakhouse, and I felt like a common slut. But I won't open the door to this house—your house—find your wife's lover on the step, ready to snap my picture, and accept the blame from you because someone's found out about us at last! No, Dan."

"It's your house too," he insisted. "Ours."

"Nothing is really ours. It's only illusion to think this is home, for either of us. I've given up my life, Dan, pretending otherwise. I won't blame you for that, because it was my own choice. I loved you. I probably still do, but one of these days, I promise you I won't. Like giving up my last chance to have a child, I'll let go of you, too— no surgery this time, though I imagine there'll be scars."

"Hang on, Maria, until Tuesday. Please."

"And then what?"

He paused. "We . . . well, we'll be able to make plans."

"You must be the only one on earth who believes that. If you really do."

"Christ in heaven, will you stop gossiping with your mother? She fills you with guilt, she turns you against me."

"She's right, and I've come to agree with her. Women

like me—and oddly enough, like Laurel, I suspect—seem to have an almost infinite capacity for hope. Almost," she repeated.

"Christ," he said again. The dull ache was beginning in his temple, and his stomach felt unsteady. All he needed now was a migraine, and McKendrick's story breaking. Even that he could endure, but not Maria's sending him away. "I love you," he murmured.

Maria ignored the desperate words. "Tell me. Is he her lover? That reporter. Is he the one who pulled you back to Boston that other weekend?"

Except for the short visit while Teague ate dinner, and a Saturday night together two weeks ago, it had been the last time he'd seen Maria.

"Yes, he's the one."

Maria looked thoughtful. "Laurel and I have more in common than I thought. We both have needs that haven't been taken into account. She's been a good wife to you, I'd imagine, a good mother to your son. I doubt her decision to take a lover was lightly made. I think I'd like her if we met."

"Well, you're not going to meet. You're going to stay right here until the election's over."

She turned and walked into the bedroom. When he followed she was standing at his closet. Dan stared at the duplicate suits, the weekend clothes so neatly hanging there. What in hell was happening to the careful organization of his life?

"I'll pack these for you later," she said. "I'm sure they're extras anyway."

"Maria, I love you," he said again. "I need you."

"You don't need me, Daniel." Holding a favorite heather wool sweater of his, she faced him. "You don't need Laurel. I wonder why it's taken me so long to see that you don't need anyone."

The ache in his temple began to pulse. More angry than he'd been over her visit to Dawson, Dan balled his hands into fists at his sides. Then as his past came to mind, the anger mixed with fear, because he wanted to strike out, to hurt back. To hurt her.

Drawing a deep breath, he said, "Be reasonable. You haven't a job, or money of your own. I can take this house away tomorrow, the credit cards in your name, the monthly checks through Teague." A jolt of pain shot through his head. "What will you do then, Maria?"

She waited a long moment before answering.

"What else would you expect, Daniel? I'll live off another man."

Sebastian Noble straightened, arching his back to ease the stiffness that had settled in. He'd been oiling Connolly hides on the vintage Bentley for hours, and the backseat upholstery gleamed the color of fine brandy, though he wondered if he could still walk. Shutting the rear door, he smiled at the reassuringly solid thunk of metal, then glanced toward the open doors to the car barn. His heart began to speed.

There was a sedan in the drive next door at Hilary's house and lights on in the kitchen. The gloomy afternoon seemed brighter for a moment. Then he let out his breath, and turned back into the garage.

Sebastian wiped neat's-foot oil from his hands onto a rag. The car probably belonged to Myra Hulme, and she'd come to close up for the season. He had missed Myra's companionship, but if she was here now, he'd have to visit later—and hope she didn't mention her daughter.

Sometimes he wished there really was a countess. Because he hated to spend one more night thinking about Hilary Chapin. Sebastian threw the rag onto his workbench. Right now what he needed was a thick slice of the smoked turkey he'd bought at the deli yesterday, on rye with sprouts...

But damn, if he didn't hurry, he would be late. Slamming the cabinet doors to the workbench, he sensed he was no longer alone. He heard soft footsteps on the concrete floor. "Sebastian?"

"I haven't made any racket for hours," he said without turning around. "But I did have my head in the backseat of this thing—" he gestured at the car "—so maybe I didn't hear you shouting out the windows."

"I haven't come to complain."

Then why did you come? he thought. To torture me some more?

He spun on his heel, and there she was with a look he hadn't seen before. Hilary, humble. Hilary, uncertain. But my God, as always, Hilary...beautiful. So beautiful that, even though he was angry with her, she made him tremble.

"I came to...shut the house. I...should have come sooner." She gazed at the Bentley. "That's a lovely car."

"It will be," he said. "I can give you a good price."

"I'm not in the market for a car. When I need one, I rent one." It was why he hadn't recognized the sedan next door. "Will Laurel do the drawing of this one for your catalogue?"

"I hope so. If it's finished before we go to press. But then Laurel said nothing's progressing at her end just now except for the election." Sebastian looked at his watch.

"Am I keeping you?" she asked.

"Not yet." He glanced up. "What are you in the market for, Hilary?"

"Actually," she said with a nervous laugh, "I'm divesting. If I can rid myself of all commitments by then, I'm going away the first of the year."

"To Africa," he guessed, knowing that he already missed her.

"You won't have to look at my face on those magazine covers anymore."

"The public's loss," he said.

It was the most he would give her. Sebastian put his left shoulder toward her, and moved tools around on the workbench top.

"I really hurt you, didn't I?" Her tone became urgent. "I didn't mean to hurt you, especially not about your father. But I've been in love with Chip Brewster for half my life, Sebastian, and I expected to always love him. You made me see the truth and it scared me. Then after you . . . we . . . that night, I mean—"

"Hilary, I've heard all I want to hear about Brewster. You'll have to excuse me." He slammed a Phillips head screwdriver into its slot on the pegboard above the bench, then started for the door. He'd be damned if he'd apologize for making love to her. His heart felt as if he'd turned it in a vise.

"Where are you going?"

"Where do you think? To have dinner with the coun—" Sebastian stopped, his shoulders slumping. "Oh hell, have your fun. Sebastian Noble, kid from the Baltimore docks, junior high school dropout, bastard—" Facing her, he saw Hilary's uncertain features begin to crumple. "Don't fall down yet," he said. "You'll laugh yourself silly in a minute." Taking a breath, he admitted, "I'm a literacy volunteer. I have a student waiting."

"A what?"

"At the community center," he explained. "Do you know that one in five people can't read well enough to decide which movie listing in the newspaper to choose, or what road signs mean, or how to follow simple directions on a package."

"Are you making this up?"

He wanted to smile at the suspicion in her eyes. "The statistics aren't classified information. Check them out yourself, if you want."

"How did you become a volunteer?"

"When I first got to Gloucester, I borrowed a wrench from this young mechanic in town. When I took it back, he asked me for a favor in return. Couldn't understand the manual for a car he was working on." Sebastian shook his head. "I realized he couldn't read basic information about something he could probably fix blindfolded. I signed up with the community center, and offered to make the kid my first project."

He watched her eyes mist. "And how is he doing?"

"Better by the session. Which reminds me, I'm late."

"Sebastian?"

Halfway to the door, he paused again.

"I could have dinner waiting when you get back, if you're coming back." The phrase seemed to have more meaning than she wanted it to, and she added quickly, "You wouldn't even have to knock."

His heart stood still. "Oh, Hilary." Sebastian gave her a half smile. "What am I going to do with you?"

"Don't you dare laugh when I'm trying to—"

"I wasn't going to laugh," he said.

She looked at him more closely, and he could almost see her thoughts: again, she had misjudged him. They had a lot of talking to do, Sebastian knew, later; for now, this would be enough. "Go ahead," he urged. "Say what you came to say."

"I'm sorry, Sebastian. I'm sorry."

"So am I, Hilary." He felt every muscle in his body relax. "So am I."

\*         \*         \*

Ryder strode along the corridor of *Newstrend* into Sara Hennessey's office and tossed a manila file folder onto her desk. The editor, who had been turned in her chair staring out the window at a gloomy Monday morning, swiveled back again. Neither of them bothered with greetings. "What's this?" she asked.

"A couple of photographs. My notes on the Benedict story."

"You've cracked it?"

"See for yourself."

They were candids, Ryder thought. Paparazzi stuff. The quality was only fair, and the subject matter turned his stomach. He'd fought himself all weekend, thinking it best to burn the film, but developing the negatives in his darkroom even as he thought it. Sara's gaze widened at the pictures of Dan Benedict with Maria. "This isn't the story I expected—" Sara looked up "—but my God, won't it sell copies?"

His heart sank. "I knew you'd say that."

"It's news, McKendrick."

"Trash," he said. "If the election wasn't tomorrow, this story would be gossip column stuff, not front page. That's exactly where it belongs, if not in the garbage." He ran a hand through his hair. "What do you want, Sara? For Benedict to lose the election on personal misconduct?"

"How would you have him lose it?"

"I'm biased."

"Yes," she agreed.

"He's still the better candidate. I didn't expect to think so, only the campaign taught me different. Benedict's not my favorite human being by a long shot, but he's a good politician, a viable contender, and with some seasoning he'll make a fine senator. I hope he wins."

Sara made a business of lighting one of her thin black cigars. "Applause," she said after a silence.

"Lord, I don't want applause." He slumped down into a chair and pulled a cigarette from a crumpled package in his shirt pocket. "I want to kill the story."

Sara took a close look at him, probably seeing the growth of beard he hadn't bothered to shave, seeing the effects of another sleepless night. Three since Laurel had left his apartment, and climbing. When he flicked the lighter at his cigarette, his hand shook. "It's a scoop, Mac, whether it hurts Laurel Benedict or not."

He lowered his gaze. He knew that. God, he knew that. It was the only reason he was here, because his job as a journalist was to record, on paper and on film, whatever he saw. And he had seen Dan Benedict standing in that doorway with Maria Cruz. "I can't do it, Sara."

"It's your story," she pointed out.

"I can't do it."

"Mac, I brought you back—or I've tried to—from some messy little wars that were tearing your guts apart. I brought you back to do this piece, and the pieces before, on Dan Benedict's campaign. You gave me good things. Maybe not what you hoped to learn, which is disappointing to me personally, but you wrote those articles, took the pictures, stuck it out almost to the end."

"Halfway," Ryder corrected.

"It would have been all the way without Laurel Benedict. The fact that you made a costly private error in Washington has been an embarrassment to this newspaper. You owe me this story, sharp and thorough. This isn't a matter of a man and a woman."

"Sara, I don't know how this happened. God knows, I didn't mean it to." He ran a hand through his hair again. "With Maggie, there were never thunderclaps, you know? We went together from the time we were sophomores in high school. It was comfortable, maybe even safe. And I did love her. But with Laurel . . ."

"She's another man's wife," Sara pointed out.

"Yeah." He sat motionless, his cigarette curling smoke into the already blue-gray air. "Rub it in, why not? But what I want to know is, what's in this for you? Personally? You've wanted a stiletto in the senator's back, through his son-in-law, ever since you called me. Why? What did he do to you?" Ryder stubbed out his cigarette. "What was it, Hennessey? A quick affair when you were young and foolish?"

"With the senator? Oh no, I was never one of his 'embassy girls.' That's a cheap, very obvious, assumption, Ryder. I was happily married. You surprise me."

"I'm feeling nasty today."

"You look it." Sara smiled thinly. "Edwin Frasier and me?"

"What, then?" he pressed. "Fifteen years back I'd have liked to see Frasier squirm myself. Hell, I don't like him this minute. Frasier's powerful and petty at the same time, but—"

"He lost you your job, remember." Sara blew acrid smoke into the air. "But then, he found me mine."

With the cigar, she gestured at the office. "All this. Oh, not right away. That wouldn't have looked proper, but has it never occurred to you, Mac, that six months after you were fired from *National in the News*—or rather, asked to leave—I became senior editor here at *Newstrend*?"

"He promised you the job if you'd let me go?" Ryder was stunned. "I just thought you were moving up again." If he'd thought at all; by then, he'd been scrambling for assignments, and he and Maggie were tearing each other to pieces.

"I was moving up. Then up again, into the managing editorship within another year. And here I stay."

"Not because of Ed Frasier, Sara. I won't believe that."

"True, I stay because I work hard. Because like you, Mac, I'm good at what I do. But I'd never, as a woman, have got the chance then for this job if it hadn't been for Edwin Frasier pulling strings because I'd done him the favor of firing you. We've spoken of influence peddling, haven't we? But see how close to home." She wouldn't look at him.

He felt sick. "My God, Sara."

"You need this story, Mac. So do I. Maybe it won't make either of us proud of ourselves, but it has to be done."

He wasn't going to sleep tonight either, Ryder told himself. Disappointment, disillusionment, twisted in him like dull knives. He had admired Sara Hennessey, had always considered her a model of integrity. Toughest editor he knew. Nothing gullible about her, he'd thought. But she was only human after all, and no more innocent than the rest of the world.

Sara looked at her desktop. "I can find you a computer terminal and a relatively quiet corner."

"I'm not doing it." He stood up and touched the manila folder. "I ruined things with Maggie. I helped kill a little girl, but—"

"Maggie drowned, that was nobody's fault unless it was God's for creating the ocean and undertow currents. That child died in a bombing that shouldn't have happened, but you had nothing to do with it, Ryder. You didn't kill them!"

"Not deliberately," he said. "This time it would be."

He'd tried for three days to tell himself that he hadn't planned to force Laurel's choice last Friday, even that Teague Michaels was to blame. But would her choice, even without the story, have been different any other time? All he could do now was not make it worse.

"I want this story, Mac. If I don't get it, you'll never work for me again."

"If you print it, you'll never see me again."

He began walking toward the door.

Ryder didn't hear her coming. When he felt Sara's hand on his shoulder, hauling him around, anger held him rigid. "You publish what you have to, Sara, but without my help." He nodded toward the folder on the desk. "That's all you'll get from me. Write it yourself. And take my byline off the story. I've handed you the gun, but I'll be damned if I'll pull the trigger for you."

"The story's sound, Ryder. It may hurt people, but lots of stories do. I'm not saying this just because I dislike Frasier's politics, professional and personal."

"He doesn't matter." Ryder met Sara's gaze squarely. "Laurel does."

At the hoarsely uttered words, Sara Hennessey drew back. She put both hands on his shoulders and, strangely close to tears, stood on her toes to kiss him.

"Welcome home, Mac," she whispered. "You've been gone too long."

Ryder blinked in surprise. He had a vision of Maggie, years ago, sitting next to Sara in some restaurant that her husband had insisted they try. Maggie, slim and brown from summer. He imagined Sara too, younger then, not so gray, and probably a great deal more ambitious than now. Briefly Ryder closed his eyes, and saw Laurel crying as she had turned to go down the stairs on Friday.

"Then don't make me kill her, Sara," he said. "Please don't make me."

# ❊ *CHAPTER 27* ❊

❊

## BENEDICT LOVE TRIANGLE THREATENS ELECTION HOPES

LAUREL SCANNED THE garish headline once more, the pit of her stomach churning; Dan was already sick, having taken to his bed in their suite at the Sheraton Boston Hotel. As the words penetrated the self-protective daze in which she'd been reading them, Laurel wanted to groan aloud. Earlier when they'd gone to vote, just before the papers arrived, she'd been solicitous of Dan's health. "Poor man, the worst possible time for one of your migraines." She'd promised to put him in a dark room as soon as they returned from the polls, and to deliver his medication herself with a glass of Perrier on ice. Now, she didn't feel unhappy that Dan was suffering.

So was she.

She had been, Laurel noted silently, since those last moments with Ryder at his apartment, when he'd suggested in anger that Dan didn't love her, but Lexa.

Why had he said it, when he'd already known it wasn't true?

Setting the paper aside, she barely glanced at the article's byline. It might not be Ryder's name and, oddly enough, the paper she'd held wasn't *Newstrend*, but it was still his story. The story he had used her to get.

Maria Cruz. Laurel didn't have to look again at the grainy photographs of her husband with the dark-haired, exotic woman to remember what she looked like. Pain flashed through her. Maria Cruz, not Lexa's memory, had been the rival all these years.

According to the papers, there was a house in Shelby. Cars and furniture and clothes in a shared closet, she supposed. A daily routine that could have been any married couple's. That should have been hers and Dan's.

And now the whole world knew.

"It's the next thing to bigamy!" the senator was saying. A vein stood out in his temple, and his face was red. "Daniel, I ought to flay the political hide from you!"

His outburst was followed by a flurry of voices—chief among them Dan's, which carried from the other room. "Get me McKendrick."

Dropping a telephone receiver into its cradle, Teague Michaels went to the bedroom doorway. "I've been talking to a tape for twenty minutes. Besides, it won't do any good, Dan." Michaels waved his copy of the newspaper. "The first printing of the story came from the Shelby *Gazette* yesterday evening. It's a weekly, mostly local police blotter stuff—"

"I know what it is, dammit. Let me see *Newstrend*."

"Nothing," Michaels murmured. "Silent as the grave."

"You're kidding."

"No. I didn't see a word until the *Gazette* arrived this morning. Apparently the wire services picked the story up out of Shelby, and from there the *Globe*, the *Herald*, every major and minor publication in the state."

"Shit," Dan said, then in the next breath he ordered, "Call Shelby."

Teague disappeared into the bedroom, and a more private phone. "She won't talk to you," he soon reported in an undertone to Dan. Standing near the door, unable to move away, Laurel heard only enough of the conversation to feel shock wash over her again in waves. ". . . told me, though, that the house is under siege."

"The press," Dan said. "What the hell am I paying you for, Michaels?"

"Look, Dan, once McKendrick started asking questions up there, this was a foregone conclusion. In a small town, gossip's the primary pastime. As they say, news travels fast, and nowhere faster than among the fourth estate."

"Goddammit. Then get somebody up there."

The senator cut in, but Laurel couldn't understand what the drifting, angry voices from the bedroom were saying. Why hadn't Ryder's piece appeared in *Newstrend*, she wondered. At first she'd wanted to think it was because the story wasn't true.

She'd wondered late Friday why Dan had said nothing to her. It was as if Teague's appearance at Ryder's apartment had never happened; or Ryder's pressure on her to choose. Laurel couldn't broach the subject without incriminating herself. Instead, she'd spent the weekend in edgy silence, in misery.

Now she felt as if she were holding herself together by sheer force of will, and she wanted to be alone. She'd never needed the security of her old tree house more, not even the day of Lexa's funeral. When the senator came out of the bedroom and spoke to her, Laurel started.

"Hold your head up as a Frasier ought to." He shot a glance at Judith, weeping in the corner. "One thing's sure: You can't walk out on Dan. That would only make things worse on election day."

Oh, couldn't she? Then she remembered her humiliation by the press after Lexa died, and knew she wouldn't put herself, or Ned, through that again. Alone.

Dan's voice, a soft croak, called her to the bedroom. Not knowing what she'd say to him, Laurel left the sitting room full of people: some with their attention glued to the television screen, others milling around with Cokes and coffee and hard liquor in paper cups; her mother, still quietly sobbing at this latest upset to her life; and her father, as always on the telephone. Wielding power, she thought as she entered the darkened bedroom. Making things right.

Dan whispered, "I'm sorry, Laurel."

Had the senator ordered him to apologize?

"McKendrick came after me," Dan went on, probably needing to salve his own conscience. "I told you he was using you to get at me."

"Don't try to blame me for your mistakes. I'm trying to deal with my own." She poured fresh ice water from the carafe on the dresser.

"I'm not blaming you." He sounded offended when he had no right to. "Why do women always think I'm placing blame?"

"Women?"

He groaned softly. "A generalization. I didn't mean M—"

Laurel set the glass beside him with a definite click. "I don't want to hear, Dan. We'll finish today, as the senator advised, and right now that's all that matters."

He eased back onto the pillows with a sigh. "Then get me some early projections, will you?"

At midday Dan appeared at the bedroom door, shaky on his feet and pale as the pillowcase on his bed. Knowing that he wasn't in the clear with the migraine yet, and wouldn't be for at least another day, Laurel thought: it must be painful for him. And for the first time in ten years hadn't a qualm about placing her own needs above his.

She stayed as far away from him as she could, welcoming Ned's arrival from school at one o'clock in the company of a security man. "Darling, come sit with me on the sofa with Grandma Judith." Laurel gestured behind her to Teague for a glass of milk and a sandwich sent up moments before by room service. "You must be starving."

"I missed lunch," Ned confessed. "The headmaster made me sit in his office. There were people outside, he said, with cameras, Mommy. Like Ry—"

"Newsmen, sweetheart." Without thinking, she used Ryder's endearment for her. "This is an important day."

"And they want to take my picture?"

She had to downplay the reason. "Yes, because of Daddy's election. The voting will be over soon, after dinner."

"Look, Mommy. I see him!"

Ned leapt from the sofa, but not to run toward Dan, who was leaning against a wall with his eyes shut, taking tentative swallows from a glass of cola. Ned raced to the cluster of workers around the television set, watching the election day coverage—which, at such an early point, was still mainly airtime filler. On tape they'd viewed before, Laurel saw her face, then Dan's as they had emerged from voting at eight in the morning. It seemed centuries ago. He'd been valiantly smiling against the pain of the migraine, and the reporters' questions.

"That's my dad, on television," Ned announced now, but the small boy soon lost interest, and Laurel guided him into the second bedroom, where a smaller color set had been placed for his use.

"You'll enjoy the cartoons more, won't you?"

She returned to the crowded sitting room over which a thick blue cloud of smoke hung like a portent of doom.

She thought of Ryder, smoking again in recent days just when he'd almost kicked the habit. At least now she knew why.

Laurel wished for some sort of relief for her own tension. She wasn't sure she could get through this day without killing Dan.

Dinner, served in the suite, sat in her stomach like heavy dumplings when she'd only picked at a salad and eaten half a lamb chop. She would have done better with Dan's bowl of soup and soda crackers.

"Mommy, why aren't you hungry?" Ned chewed a bite of meat, then spit it out.

"That was too much, Edwin," Judith scolded. "And don't saw with your knife."

"He's doing the best he can," Laurel said tautly. "He's only eight years old!"

Ned's glass of milk tipped over as he reached for it and Judith's voice sharpened. "Edwin, be careful! Look what you've done—quickly, mop up the spill with your napkin and—"

"Mother."

"Laurel, please," Dan said, but Ned's lip was quivering and her pulse shot up like a rocket.

"We've discussed this before. But I will discipline my son as I choose, Mother." She rose from the table, oblivious of the campaign aides who stared. "Or I won't, if I choose not to."

"Really, Laurel. Control yourself."

At her mother's tone, she glanced at the senator and Dan. Both their mouths were open to protest.

"Leave me alone," she said, "all of you."

"Mommy?"

"Ned, for Christ's sake, not now!" his father shouted.

Laurel plucked Ned from his chair, took him back into the small bedroom and soothed his tears in private, then after he'd settled with a storybook she sailed into the larger bedroom and shut the door. She knew her mother was upset, but she was also wrong about Ned, who wasn't her child. On her last visit to Chevy Chase, Laurel had known she would have to stand up to Judith for him. But why today?

She was peering into the mirror above the dresser when Dan came into the room. "Laurel, that sort of display can't happen again. Your mother's got a point, you know. The only way to survive attack by the press—and they will attack as soon as we leave these rooms tonight—is to be in perfect control." He took a breath. "There'll be a lot of difficult questions about those headlines."

"And you expect me to make that easier for you?" She gave him a flat look, then found she couldn't wait any longer to talk about the scandal, even on election night. "If I'm to face the questions, I need to know. Dan, how much of that story is true?"

"Laurel, we agreed to discuss this later."

"After the votes are in? I've already cast mine—for someone who's lived with me for ten years, fathered my only child . . ." Breaking off, she looked away from him. "Maria Cruz," she said. "That's why you've never had an interest in Ned beyond providing his food and clothing, isn't it? Does she have children?"

He stepped toward her. "She couldn't have children."

"God, oh my God." It was true, then. All of it.

"Well, you're hardly innocent, Laurel."

She clenched her hands into fists. "Maybe not. But I wanted this marriage, Dan. It's been important to me, you and Ned. I tried, and all this time, for how many years, you—"

"The press is going to dig up McKendrick," he pointed out.

"Yes, I know."

"It'll be worse than the *Herald* on Thursday. What will you say to their questions tonight?"

Wearily, she sighed. "No comment. With a smile."

Then she realized that Dan was using an old tactic on her, disguising his guilt by probing at hers. It had always been effective.

"How long, Dan?" she asked again.

A pause. "Ten years."

Their entire marriage. Laurel turned aside. "Ten years?" She whirled to face him. "And I was expected to provide what? The senator? Like Lexa before me? And what else? To keep my mouth shut when you disappeared on Fridays? To stop my ears when you made murmured conversation on the den telephone? Oh God, to watch my little boy grieve for a father who wouldn't love him?"

"I can't, not the way you want me to."

"Why not?" she demanded. "Why not?"

"Because he reminds me too much of what I used to be, small and helpless, weak—"

The snap of the door closing made them both turn too late. The doorway was empty.

"Who the hell was that?"

"I don't know." Then Laurel said, "Oh Dan, it couldn't have been—"

"Dan, the first returns are in!" They were interrupted a second time as Teague Michaels shouted from the sitting room. "Didn't Ned tell you?"

"Where can he have gone? Dear God—"

"Laurel, take it easy."

"Don't you tell me to take it easy!" She pressed a hand to her forehead. "He probably heard us squabbling." But how much had he overheard? Laurel wondered. She'd said terrible things herself, accused Dan of not loving Ned.

"The police are on the way," Teague reported, hanging up the telephone.

"Michaels, Goddammit—" Edwin Frasier began.

"In plainclothes, Senator."

The hotel security force was already searching for Ned. Laurel glanced toward the huge projection television screen that dominated one wall of the sitting room. The digital numbers were rolling over, nearly too fast for the human eye to distinguish. They stopped, and someone groaned. "We've lost it. Trounced in the Second."

People thronged about the color screen, exclaiming over the early numbers from various districts. Laurel looked at her watch. Eight-thirty. When had Ned disappeared? Half an hour ago, an hour, two?

"What if he's been kidnapped?" she asked no one in particular, surprised when she got an answer.

"He probably just wandered off, bored with the grown-ups." A college student who'd been Dan's personal gofer that day gave her a reassuring smile. "Want me to look around the lobby again, Mrs. Benedict? The gift shop?"

"Yes, thank you."

"The hotel security force is searching, too. Don't worry."

Don't worry? The boy meant well, but she felt frantic. But assuming he'd left the suite on his own—hadn't been trussed in an overcoat, bundled into a strange car—where would Ned go?

The soft rap at the door, barely audible above the television blare, made Laurel jump to her feet. Dan was there first, yanking at the knob. "Lord, no," he said with a groan.

Hilary Chapin stepped past him, followed by Sebastian Noble. Laurel couldn't have been more astonished to see them, much less to see them together. They both had that same indefinable glow Hilary had recognized in Laurel's face not long ago. "Hilary," she began, distracted briefly from concern over Ned, and took a step. Dan blocked her.

"I'm not here for you." Hilary sent him a scathing head-to-toe glance. "But I'll say this, Dan. You never disappoint me. You're always the weasel I expect you to be."

"Now see here—"

"The headlines were every bit as sleazy as I anticipated." Her fists clenched at her sides. "Why, you rotten bastard, deceiving my closest friend, for years—"

Sebastian restrained her. "He isn't worth losing your temper." He turned to Laurel. "We heard on the news at five o'clock."

"Sebastian, Hilary, thank you both for coming." Laurel hugged them. "Hilary, I'm so sorry for the argument we had."

"I'm sorry too, pumpkin."

Dan was forced to move back as the three friends clung together. Laurel wouldn't have been more relieved to see anybody—except Ned.

"Missing?" Hilary echoed when Laurel told them of his disappearance. There were tears in Hilary's eyes, too, but little time to indulge them, or Laurel's curiosity about Hilary and Sebastian. The police had arrived, their questions intruding like the press.

"Has the boy been unhappy, Mrs. Benedict?"

"Where would he likely go if he ran away from home, ma'am?"

Panic swept her. Then she thought of Kip. "I'll give you some numbers, friends of his. A family in Cambridge."

"Uh, sergeant." Dan cleared his throat. His face was very pale. "We've had no contact from anyone, but I'm wondering about the possibility of a kidnapping."

"Do you have reason to suspect someone?" the sergeant asked, and Laurel's pulse thumped harder.

"Yes," Dan murmured.

After the two officers left, Laurel sat with Sebastian and Hilary, feeling that she'd go crazy. Maria Cruz had taken too much of her life. Surely the woman wouldn't take Ned. Could he have found his own way home to Beacon Hill?

"We've already sent someone to the house, Laurel." Dan shook his head. "There's nobody there."

Even the dog was in the kennel for the night, because she'd known they would be away until the morning after the election.

"Dan, do something. Something more."

"What? You think I'm not concerned? He's my son, too, Laurel."

"You practically said otherwise."

As they argued a shout rose from the campaign workers around the television.

"We've taken the Third!"

"Hot damn! Will you look at those numbers!"

She saw Dan visibly relax, her words instantly forgotten. "Maybe this newspaper mess won't cost me the seat after all," he said.

"I hope not."

He glanced at her. "Do you?"

"I think everyone should get what he wants."

For a moment they held each other's gaze. Laurel didn't know what she would have said next. Teague Michaels gave a hoot of triumph, and the numbers were racing through the board again. "Three more districts." Laurel looked at her watch but couldn't make sense of the numbers there either. "You've taken Cambridge!" Teague yelled.

Dan squeezed her shoulder, then excused himself to go to the television where he stood at the screen. Laurel watched the tense set of his shoulders in the dark blue suit he'd put on. "Look, Senator," Dan called as the latest totals were tallied at the bottom of the screen.

Edwin Frasier joined him, standing slightly apart. "You're lucky to be on the board," she heard him say.

When the figures locked in place, Dan eased away. Telephones began ringing, making Laurel jump. Pouring himself a fresh Coke with ice at the desk, Dan picked up a receiver and punched a button, his expression instantly changing to anger. "You've got one hell of a nerve, McKendrick."

"Let me have the phone, Dan." She snatched it from him. "Hello?"

"Laurel, I thought you'd want to know right away." He paused while her heart beat crazily. "Ned's with me."

"With you!"

"He showed up, ringing my bell about two hours ago. I couldn't call before."

"But how—"

"He took a cab with his lunch money for the week."

"Oh, God." Covering the mouthpiece, she met Dan's eyes. "He's all right. Ned's safe." She removed her hand from the receiver. "Thank you, Ryder. *Thank you*."

"No problem."

"Is he all right?"

"He was pretty strung out when he arrived, but a couple of sugar cones with heavenly hash ice cream did the trick." There was a commotion in the background at his end of the line, a simultaneous echo in the sitting room of the Sheraton Boston suite. Ryder must also be watching the television coverage—and the digital numbers clicking again. Then they stopped.

"That's it!" someone shouted. "Hallelujah! We're home free!"

The senator pumped her husband's hand as Dan stood

stock-still behind the desk, his eyes on Laurel. Even Judith managed a smile. Campaign staffers flocked around in a tight semicircle.

"Congratulations, Dan!"

"Thank God. We're all safe," he said over their heads to Laurel, and broke into a grin.

Over the noise Laurel spoke into the phone. "I'll come for Ned as soon as I can," she said, wondering if Ryder was still there.

"Don't rush. He's sound asleep in the spare room." A brief silence. "Dan'll be making his acceptance speech shortly. I imagine you'll want to be there." Another pause. "Send someone for Ned, if you like, but I, uh, I could keep him until morning."

Ryder McKendrick, babysitting. The notion would have made Laurel smile, but she felt extremely close to tears. His voice sounded so impersonal that he might have been some telephone interviewer, conducting market research. And so did hers.

"No, I couldn't impose. Though if you wouldn't mind for a little while—" but he didn't let her finish.

"I don't mind." She could barely make out his words. The room around her was full of laughter and shouting. The sudden blowing of a cork from a champagne bottle sounded like gunfire. "What was that?" Ryder raised his voice to be heard.

"Celebration."

She couldn't join in. Except for Ned's being safe in Cambridge, Laurel had never felt less like celebrating in her life.

"I know he won't want this from me," Ryder said, his tone husky, "but tell Dan . . . tell him I said the best man won."

Then quietly, he hung up.

## ❀ CHAPTER 28 ❀

❀

"SENATOR BENEDICT, CONGRATULATIONS."

"Thanks." Dan grinned. "I like the sound of that."

"Laurel, how does it feel to have that fifty-seven percent majority?"

When Laurel and Dan had stepped from the podium after his acceptance speech, the press descended on them and as they both expected, the questions weren't a hundred percent friendly: "Any reaction, Mrs. Benedict, to the story about Maria Cruz?"

Dan's embrace tightened around Laurel's shoulders. "The story is false."

"Ten years with another woman, that's quite a blunder," the man persisted, with a hard look at Laurel.

But she couldn't support Dan as she'd always done before, not even when he squeezed her shoulder warningly. With a steady gaze, she looked at the reporters crowding near; under other circumstances Ryder would have been among them, a friendly face, and with a bittersweet yearning she missed him. Yet Laurel felt none of the heart-pounding anxiety she'd always experienced because of the press.

Calmly she glanced from face to face, and as the cameras

flashed she even smiled. For once the standard reply was exactly what she wanted to say.

"No comment."

Then Laurel pushed her way with dignity through the maze of journalists and well-wishers, the kisses and hugs from strangers, toward the Sheraton ballroom exit. Teague's bulky presence, shoving microphones aside and blocking camera angles, served her well this time. But once inside the elevator, she stepped away from Dan. And kept apart from Judith and the senator.

Even Sebastian and Hilary weren't quite welcome now. Before Dan's speech, Hilary had taken Laurel aside to confide about Sebastian that she'd "never been more frightened of tomorrow—not even when Chip went overseas—but I've never felt such . . ." She had shrugged, pink-cheeked.

"Happiness?" Laurel supplied, giving her a hug.

"Happiness," Hilary agreed. "And what about yourself? You've kept your promise to Dan, who didn't deserve such loyalty. I'd bet money Ryder didn't break that story." She'd related their telephone conversation on the night Laurel had been in Brockton with Dan, the night before she and Ryder had parted. "Go to him," Hilary urged.

Laurel had only drawn away from the slender hand on her arm. Hilary and Sebastian's reconciliation made her feel torn: glad on the one hand that Chip Brewster might yet become part of Hilary's past, and on the other, sorrowful that her own future wouldn't include Ryder.

Back in the hotel suite, Dan tried to put an arm around her waist. "You were wonderful," he said. "A trouper."

"That's our girl," the senator added.

"Lexa couldn't have done better," Judith remarked.

Shrugging off Dan's touch, Laurel marched into the bedroom and shut the door. At the dresser mirror she freshened her makeup, smudging eyeliner to soften its effect now that there would be no more glaring lights. She applied lip gloss over the darker color she'd worn for the television cameras during Dan's speech, then ran a brush through her hair to remove the stiff spray that had held it in place.

An ever-increasing sense of calm pervaded her. Tonight she had faced the media under more difficult circumstances than ever before, including Lexa's funeral. She hadn't panicked. She hadn't given anyone else's speech. And she hadn't flinched when her picture was taken.

After her private session with Ryder at his apartment, Laurel knew she would never shrink from publicity again. Her cheeks warmed at the memory. She would never think in quite the same way of being photographed.

Now, without quickly looking away as she usually would, Laurel gazed at herself. Something wasn't right. Hunting through her makeup kit, she dug out the contact case she always carried. Removing the plastic lenses from her eyes, she slipped on the tortoiseshell glasses she preferred, the ones Ryder found sexy. Now it was her own face, not anyone else's, that she saw. Objectively she studied the attractive, thirtyish woman, the normal, I-can-live-with-this-all-day face not carefully enhanced by cosmetics as it had been during Dan's campaign. It was over. Thank God, it was over now.

And she wasn't looking at a copy of Lexa's face. Or even a softly focused photograph of herself as a woman loved through Ryder's eyes. At last she could really see herself. Laurel.

"Laurel, we're opening champagne," Dan called from the doorway. "Come join the festivities."

She grabbed her coat from the end of the bed. "I'm going to get Ned."

"Don't be silly. I'll send Teague for him." Casting a

worried glance behind him, Dan stepped into the room. "The others are waiting. What's this about? We agreed—"

"That I would see you through this election. I've done that." She walked past him. "I'm not coming back. I'm leaving you, Dan."

"Laurel." He tried a laugh. "Come on, I mean the article must have been a shock, but we're going to talk about that."

"I've decided I don't need to talk about it."

He closed the door and leaned against it. "So you're going to run to McKendrick? You can't be serious."

"I'm not 'running to' anybody." Laurel stopped. She might wish otherwise, but she had to rid herself of all illusions. "Dan, I've been the senator's good girl all my life, my sister's replacement—"

"If you're upset because your mother mentioned Lexa, well, Lexa wouldn't have done half as well in this campaign as you did. Frankly, Lexa and I would have been miserable together. You remember how she was, Laurel. Willful, obstinate. She wouldn't have worked for me in the first place, but if the senator had forced her to, somehow, Lexa would have sabotaged me with the press before the first week was out. I wouldn't have made it through the primary."

She regarded him steadily. "Did you ever love her either?"

For a moment, he didn't answer. "I don't know. I thought so, for a while. What difference does it make? I married you."

"And I've been a good wife, as good as I knew how to be. So why did I have to learn the hard way, Dan— today, from a newspaper—that I was just your weekday substitute for Maria Cruz? I've been a substitute to everybody, haven't I? To you, as Lexa, for the senator. Hilary's right. It's time I started living for myself." And so had Ryder been, she added silently.

"Christ," Dan said, taking a step toward her. "Don't be ridiculous."

"You can have a divorce easily, or with difficulty. Whichever you choose, I'm keeping Ned. Fight me if you want. It's going to take me some time to make up to him for what we both said tonight."

"Divorce?" True to his nature, he had picked out the most self-serving of the things she'd said. "I don't want a divorce. I want my wife beside me when I take the oath of office in Washington in January. I want you picking out a house now and closing up Beacon Hill. I want you selecting Ned's school down there for next term, something suitable, maybe in Virginia. I want—"

"It isn't a matter of what you want any longer, Dan. It's what I need." She met his gaze squarely, with a smile. "And I need a little more Tower of Power in my life."

"What? Laurel, dammit—"

The door opened and the senator appeared with a tulip glass of champagne and the smile she knew so well. It could have been Judith's, she thought, on a different face. A smile that asked for cooperation, and no unpleasantness. The senator jerked his head toward the sitting room. "Everyone's waiting."

Dan murmured, "Laurel thinks she's going after Ned."

"I'll ring for my car and Henry," the Senator began.

"I said *I'm* going." Laurel walked toward him.

His tone hardened. "The lobby's jammed with press, all sniffing for something like that, another of your escapes. After the headlines today that's all we need."

"She wants to divorce me." Dan put a hand on her shoulder to detain her.

"Maria Cruz is no longer an issue that need concern you, Laurel."

Laurel shook her head at the senator's words, so reminiscent of the way he'd dealt with Ryder after the Hulme gala. Duty, obligation, responsibility. They had been catchwords in her life for far too many years, for the wrong people. She walked past them, Dan and her father; her handbag was on the dresser and she needed her wallet for a cab. She carried money now, from Sebastian's check.

The senator looked at his son-in-law. "Give us a moment, Daniel."

Laurel waited until Dan had left the room; he had hesitated before he shut the door. "He's not going to follow your orders quite so readily from now on. He's done what he wanted. What you wanted for him. You've got another U.S. senator in the family, but Dan is his own man."

"And my daughter is his wife."

"I wasn't supposed to be, was I?" Laurel asked. "If Lexa had lived—"

"Lexa's dead," he murmured.

Trembling, she looked away. "Yes, she's dead. I was there, alone with her in that clinic when she died. Waiting for you. If it hadn't been for Dan that night..." She broke off, began again. "That night and afterward. I needed you, but you turned away from me . . . and after her funeral, oh God, I knew why. I've spent years trying to make up for her dying. I can't do it anymore." She raised her gaze to the senator's. "I can't be Lexa for you . . . for you and Mother."

"Laurel, control—"

"I've been in control too long. It was always I who telephoned when Lexa got expelled or picked up by the campus police for swimming in the school president's private pool. Who do you think they reached first when she was dying?" She flinched from his touch on her arm. "What if she hadn't died, Senator—what would you have done today, if it were Lexa who'd seen those newspaper headlines, or Lexa who had made them, not Dan?"

He looked shocked. "Lexa could be difficult," he acknowledged.

"And you and Mother let her stay that way while I picked up the pieces." Strangely, Dan's admission had freed Laurel as much as her own decision. "I even married her fiancé to please you. I married an arrogant, selfish man who loved only his own ambition—and possibly, Maria Cruz."

"That woman doesn't—"

"Matter?" Laurel shook her head again. "No, she doesn't." She had always been shamed by the senator's infidelities, which had been rumored regularly throughout her childhood. "What was I supposed to do? Ignore her as if she never existed?" She lowered her voice. "Is that what Mother's always done?"

"Laurel, I won't have this!"

"You have no choice, Senator. I'm not a child, and I haven't lost my mind. I'll handle this in my own way, because I'm *not* Lexa—and I don't want to be! I feel terrible that I can't make you love me, but I can't."

When she'd finished, voice breaking, there wasn't a sound except for Laurel's breathing. Lifting her chin, the senator looked into her eyes. "You're my daughter, too, Laurel."

"Not as much," she said. "Never as much." She held his gaze. "When she was alive, we had each other. We were parts of each other, but when she died . . . and you wished . . . after the funeral when you said . . ."

"What, Laurel? What did I say?"

"At the house when Mother went upstairs to rest, I stayed to be hostess for all the 'important people' who had come. And I . . . I went out to the garden because I felt so sad without Lexa, and you wouldn't comfort me.

For the first time in my life I was truly alone. When you found me with Dan in the garden you were carrying a glass of liquor, I remember. You looked down into it as if you couldn't bear to look into my eyes . . . and you said . . . you said, 'God, why did it have to be Lexa?' "

The senator stood motionless. "Good God, Laurel," he whispered, "you couldn't possibly have felt that I would wish you dead in Lexa's place?"

I still feel it, she thought, but she didn't answer.

The senator seemed to order his thoughts before he spoke. "When you and Lexa were babies, Judith and I always referred to you as The Twins. Remember?" Laurel nodded. "I'm told that's not accepted theory today, that an immediate separation of personalities is essential. Not to see identical appearance as meaning the same person's in both bodies. I don't know, perhaps we were guilty of that. Until," he said, "you both began to grow and change. It may have surprised us to have one baby that slept through the night, and the other who raised hell until dawn, but when Lexa grew into such a handful, and you developed into such a sweet, caring little girl . . . well, we knew there was no such thing as 'identical.' Laurel, I'm sorry for what I said that afternoon. I was grieving for my child, but I would never have lost you—my other daughter—in her place. That wasn't what I meant."

Laurel's heart constricted.

"As for living out Lexa's life to please us," the senator murmured, "I think you've made a blurry line, as usual, between you and your sister." Then he said, "I think you've even forgotten the slight physical differences: her broader forehead, your finer nose; and Lexa's face was rounder, if you recall. I don't know why Lexa never believed me that I could tell you apart instantly.

"Yes," he said with a faint smile, "we counted on you, Laurel, too much as it turns out. It's easy enough to take someone who's levelheaded and responsible for granted." There was gentleness in his eyes. "Isn't it?"

She tried to smile but couldn't, even though she knew he was becoming uncomfortable at this burst of emotional intimacy.

"I loved her so much," she whispered. "I would have done anything to keep her with us."

He said hoarsely, "I believe you have, Laurel," and lightly squeezed her shoulders. "I wish we'd understood that. You know, I've been a crowd pleaser all my life, and let me tell you, it gets damn lonely out there, which isn't something I want repeated."

Then to her astonishment, the senator drew her close and Laurel's heart warmed. Holding her for a brief moment, he let her go again and walked briskly to the windows. She hadn't basked in his embrace before she felt cooled by its withdrawal. She should have known the interlude wouldn't last. He always conducted personal interviews as he would a political meeting in his Capitol Hill office. In fact, politics came first in his life, and everything—everyone—else after that. She wondered that it had taken her this long to understand the kind of love of which he was capable, the kind he wouldn't express in words because he couldn't. I love you, she had wanted him to say, but she heard only silence.

Laurel went to the bedroom door, then turned. He was standing—the solitary man she had always known, loved, even sometimes feared—with the draperies pulled back. As if he were looking out once more over the fall garden in Chevy Chase, shutting out the important people who had gathered in his house for Lexa.

"Good-bye, Senator," Laurel whispered. She would have left him with a kiss, but his shoulders were moving, shaking; and if he was crying, she couldn't invade his grief. This time, she felt, it wasn't only for her sister.

\*　　　　\*　　　　\*

Ryder stood over the sleeping child, unwilling to leave him. Ned had been tear-streaked and trembling a few hours ago when Ryder answered his door to find, much to his surprise, the boy, and a tough-looking Boston cabbie.

The taxi had taken Ned from the Sheraton Boston to Cambridge and Kip's house, where no one had been at home. "I'm a father myself," the cabbie said. "Couldn't leave a little kid on the steps of a dark house all night, even if he didn't have more cab fare." He had intended to return Ned to the hotel. But only minutes from the house, Ned recognized Ryder's neighborhood, then, after circling a few blocks, his building. The cabbie was suspicious. "You know him?" he asked Ryder. "He says your name's McKendrick."

"Yes. We . . . we're friends." After showing his ID, he'd pressed a ten-dollar bill into the man's hand. "Thanks." Shutting the door, he drew Ned inside, the boy clutching a crumpled newspaper with that morning's ruinous headline. When Ryder headed for the telephone, Ned panicked.

"Don't call Mommy! Don't tell them where I am!"

Shaken, Ryder had finally shown the hysterical little boy into his darkroom in a desperate move to stabilize the situation. The first ice cream cone he'd fixed hadn't seemed to help. "Come on, Ned." They'd closed the door. "You can't become a good photographer unless you learn how to develop your own prints, and get the most out of them. Remember, I said next time, I'd show you."

He heard himself jabbering to combat Ned's stiff silence. Scrabbling in his files, he pulled out the negatives and contact sheet of zoo pictures. "Here." He showed Ned the "saves" he'd marked off earlier with a grease pencil. "Try this one." It was Ned, taken by Ryder at the panda cages, and the exposure had been perfect.

"I don't know how to do it," Ned complained.

"I'll teach you."

It had been an awkward business, Ryder shaking slightly—as if he were trying to make up to Laurel at the same time, with no more idea of how to do it than with Ned—and Ned fumbling every step in the process from enlarger to developing tray.

But as the boy slowly thawed and stopped quivering every time they touched, Ryder stopped guiding Ned's hands. "Keep it facedown, so we don't get too much from the safelight and ruin the print."

"It's like magic." When they inspected the picture, Ned threw him a smile. "Can I keep it?"

"Sure you can keep it. You're the photographer, aren't you?"

"Not that one. You were." Gaining confidence, Ned selected a shot of Laurel that he'd taken: leaves behind her on the path, her eyes alive with laughter. Her mouth, soft and smiling. *That damn story,* Ryder thought. *How badly it must have hurt her.*

He'd been wrong, forcing Laurel to choose, even using the truth as a lure. "Make the choice, then I'll tell you." In Sara's office he'd told himself that Laurel's choice might always be Dan and the life she knew. But what if she had picked him? In a day or a week or a year, would she have wakened one rainy morning, certain that she'd made another mistake, that even after the beginning in Gloucester, he wasn't what she wanted either? Because of Maggie, and Ngoc Hoa?

"Ryder." Ned interrupted his thoughts.

He blinked. Giving himself time, he studied the test print they'd made before he said, "Here, let's try a little darkroom manipulation."

"What's that mean?"

"Fooling around with the truth." He felt another pang of guilt about Laurel. "The exposure wasn't right on this one. Probably because the afternoon was overcast. See how dark your mother's face is, in shadow?" He glanced at Ned, who nodded. "We're gonna do some 'dodging' to correct that."

Not wanting to risk Ned's tenuous concentration, Ryder decided against cutting a cardboard shape for the dark area of Laurel's features. Instead, he held his fist over her image, moving it constantly in front of the lens during exposure just enough so that it wouldn't show as an outline on the finished print. After the chemical processing was finished, the result of his hand's blocking the exposure in that one area was a much better picture of Laurel, her face lighter, clear and sharp.

"Next time I'll teach you how to bracket your shots, Ned. That means go up and down an f-stop for each picture to protect them at the start of the process." He stared at the print, and kept staring. If only he could fix himself, with Laurel, by such simple manipulation.

"Why are you frowning, Ryder? Didn't I do good on the pictures?"

"You did great, buddy."

"Are you feeling sad again?"

"Again?" he echoed.

"At the zoo you were sad."

"Yeah, Ned," he admitted, "I'm feeling a little sad tonight."

"Why?"

"I can't explain." How could he tell an eight-year-old that he was tired of crazy wars in crazy places? Tired of brutal endings. Tired of thinking about Maggie and Ngoc Hoa, knowing there was nothing he could do to make things come out right with them either.

Ned gazed at him with Laurel's hazel eyes. "I was sad

before I found your house tonight." He paused. "Tonight my dad said . . . he said he doesn't love me."

Ryder felt as if he'd been slammed into a wall. So that was why he'd come here. For a moment he simply stood still, listening to his own heartbeat. "Let's finish up, okay? I'll get you another ice cream, how's that?"

When Ned only nodded his agreement, Ryder hung the prints with weighted clips to dry, took Ned into the living room, and lit a cheery fire. What would make a kid say something like that, so forlorn yet certain?

Ryder piled a second cone with rich heavenly hash and settled onto the sofa beside Ned. The boy didn't talk, just licked at the ice cream and watched him with wary eyes. As if he'd committed some sin by confiding in a man who didn't know how to answer.

But like most kids Ned loved a good adventure story. Ryder began talking about some of his experiences overseas, the excitement, the danger, leaving out the gore. Ned asked suddenly, "Do you have a little boy like me?"

"No." The question was completely off the subject of the nighttime raid in Beirut, and the child edged closer to him, obviously wanting reassurance. Ryder might have appeared to ignore his comment about his father, but Ned wouldn't forget. "No, I had . . . a little girl."

"What's her name?"

"She's . . . dead now. She died in a war, long ago, and far away. Her name was Ngoc Hoa. It means 'precious flower.' "

"Did she die in Beirut?" The word came slowly, with deliberation over the syllables.

"Not Beirut, no. Vietnam."

"Where's that?"

"A world away," he whispered. "Farther than you can imagine."

"Did you like her?"

With a sigh Ryder pulled Ned closer, mindless of the soft ice cream that dripped onto his clothes. "Yes, Ned. I loved her. Very much." He felt the tears then, against his shirt and oozing between the buttons. "I loved her."

The words were muffled. "Where's her mommy?"

Ryder's pulse lurched. The room was silent, dim, and all the shadows seemed like ghosts. "She's dead, too."

A greater silence. Then, "In the war?"

"No. She . . . drowned. Swimming in the ocean."

"Didn't you hold her up?" Ned tipped his head back to look into Ryder's face. "My mommy always holds me in the water."

"I wasn't there. I couldn't hold her up. I couldn't . . . save her."

Ned stroked Ryder's cheek, and the sorrow inside began to smoothe away with the touch by Laurel's child. He savored those small fingers on his skin, fingers like Hoa's. As Sara had said, it was true. He couldn't save her. Save them.

"Don't cry, Ryder. Don't cry."

"No," he said, pulling Ned to his chest again. "You either, buddy. We don't have to cry anymore."

When he felt Ned's shuddering sigh as he relaxed into sleep, Ryder tightened his arms, rocking. He felt that, for the first time in many years, he'd done something to bring peace. "No more bombs," Hoa used to say, half question, half conviction. Tonight, Laurel's son had needed him as much; tonight, he was here. The flood of love he felt for this small boy in his arms could push back death, and even quench the fire in his soul.

Ned had been asleep for some time before Ryder shifted to relieve the pressure on his left arm, which was numb. Ned's head rested against it, a dark fan of lashes lay across his slim cheek, and his mouth was half open, with the sweet child's breath whispering between his lips.

Ryder had eased himself up from the sofa and carried Ned into the spare room. Putting him on the bed, he'd covered the boy, then gone to phone Laurel at the Sheraton Boston.

Now Ryder twitched the blankets higher. After he'd hung up he had returned to the bedroom where he'd been standing for a long while, just listening to Ned breathe and watching him sleep. Such an innocent sleep, he thought, and realized that part of the peace he'd brought was Ned's but the rest was his own.

Remembering, Ryder ran a hand over the dark silk of Ned's hair. Without pain he remembered Ngoc Hoa, laughing in the sun, and smiled at her memory. Sleep well, Cherry Blossom. Then, his heart full, he bent to kiss Laurel's son good night and walked out into the lighted living room to watch Dan's acceptance speech—and Laurel.

Perhaps, he told himself, love was the only protection possible, for as long as it was possible. And he didn't need to ponder the rest.

Ryder was watching an election night wrap-up on WNEV when his doorbell rang well after midnight. He was surprised, even stunned, to find Laurel standing there in the dress she'd been wearing on a television replay seconds before.

His heart began to thump. "I was just looking at your husband's acceptance speech again. Humble enough, with the right touch of ego in the right places." His gaze ran over her light wool dress of periwinkle blue, carefully avoiding Laurel's eyes except to note she'd worn her glasses. "You look great." Beautiful, he thought. "That color photographs very well, better than I'd expect on TV."

"Thank you."

"Actually, I was expecting some minion or other. Michaels," Ryder said, shrugging.

"I'm the only minion who wanted to leave the party."

He let his gaze drift at last to hers. "Then come in. Want a drink, or some coffee?" He didn't dare the intimacy implied in the offer of black currant tea.

"No, thanks." They stood crowded together in the hallway, Ryder fighting himself not to drink her in like finest champagne, absorb her through his pores if he could, before he edged back again, toward the living room.

"I made a fire. Are you cold?" He glanced at her unbuttoned coat, which didn't look warm. "As you say, it's drafty in the hall. And as I always say, it's not much better inside. I'll put a log on."

"Don't bother. I'm fine."

Her heart drumming, Laurel inhaled the scents of tobacco and woodsmoke and Ryder's skin. Then she walked by him into the large room, noting that he hadn't thrown away the colorful pillows she'd bought for the plain sofa. She heard him behind her lighting a cigarette after he'd turned off the TV, then blowing out smoke like a sigh.

"You've learned to handle the press well. Tonight you looked thoroughly professional."

Laurel smiled. She'd even run the gauntlet of journalists in the hotel lobby by herself. Now she moved restlessly about the room, seeing the homey clutter as if it were her own—papers on the coffee table, the wadded-up paper towel with ice cream spots, the vague outline of body imprints on the sofa cushions. But after last Friday, she reminded herself, this wasn't her home, borrowed or otherwise; not even close.

Ryder wasn't hers either. Laurel turned, her gaze taking in his wheat-streaked, dark blond hair, his damp shirtfront and rumpled pants, and the shaking hand that held his cigarette. Despite her firm resolve, her heart turned over but she only said, "I'm wondering why Ned came to you tonight. Though he would have had to run to someone."

She picked up the newspaper from the sofa.

"Laurel, I'm not responsible for that," he began.

"May I see Ned now?"

Ryder sighed. As he'd feared, she wasn't about to listen. "Anytime you want. He's your kid."

He tamped out his cigarette, and Laurel followed him back along the narrow entry hall to the door on the right, which was the spare room.

It reeked of chemicals.

"We, uh, that is, I was working when Ned arrived carrying that newspaper with the headline about Dan. The quickest way to calm him seemed to involve my darkroom. I let him slop around in developer for a while." Ryder stood in the doorway, leaning one shoulder against the frame. He jammed both hands into his pants pockets as Laurel crept into the bedroom to stand over her sleeping son.

"Thank you for taking him in tonight. I know that children aren't, I mean, that you don't—"

"I behaved myself," Ryder said tautly. "I didn't freak out on him and ruin Ned's psyche for the rest of his life."

Her back was still toward him and she didn't answer.

"Laurel, we found a connection tonight, Ned and I. He helped me as much as I helped him."

As Ned stirred in his sleep, she said, "We should go now."

"What's your hurry? He must be exhausted, and he looks so peaceful." She came back to the doorway, and Ryder's pulse tripped. Nothing about her told him that she wanted to be in his life again, but if she left now, he knew she'd never come back. "Stay a while. Talk to me."

When she didn't protest, he led her back into the living room and poured them each a shot of Russian vodka.

"I suppose an hour's rest would help him," she finally said.

"What happened tonight, Laurel?"

"Dan won." With a sigh, she glanced up. "And Ned lost. They've never gotten along," she murmured. "I don't know why I couldn't accept that, but I kept thinking things would get better. After Ned learned to talk, I'd tell myself, or after Dan's big case finished trial, after Ned learned to ride his horse or play baseball, after the election . . ."

"He's a lonely kid, Laurel."

"Yes. And I made too many excuses. I know that now." She shivered, moving closer to the fire. Putting the vodka down on the hearthstones, she rubbed her arms through the wool cloth of her dress. "But he won't be lonely from now on. I can promise him that. Tonight he overheard us quarreling. Dan said . . . we both said hurtful things."

Ryder wanted to touch her so badly that he felt pain instead of pleasure. But there was such emotional distance between them that he didn't move.

"I stuck it out through the campaign, and tonight. Until Ned disappeared. After Dan's acceptance I left them all drinking champagne—if they could still drink after the shock I gave them." The firelight gleamed on her hair as Laurel shook her head. "Won't your editor love it? A banner headline. I don't know who was more surprised, my husband or the senator." Laurel sobered. "Or maybe me."

"You've left him? Dan?" Ryder swallowed. Had she made the one choice he had despaired of on her own?

"It's what you said you wanted only a few days ago." He was still standing at the oak sideboard, pouring himself another drink. The first hadn't registered on his system. His heart stopped briefly as she finished, "Before we both . . . well . . ."

"Laurel, I didn't write that damn story."

"No, you had someone else write it for you."

"I had that intention." Carrying his glass, he walked toward her. "Sara and I had a hell of an argument over you, and professional ethics, I guess. I thought I'd lost. I gave her my notes and the photos I'd taken in Shelby, but I didn't want the byline and I warned her that if she insisted on printing the story, our friendship was over and I'd never work for her again. Then at the last minute she pulled it. If it hadn't been for some cub reporter in Shelby who got wind of my asking questions around town . . ." Ryder sighed. "The main chance, he would have thought. Hell, so did I fifteen years ago. He went to see Maria Cruz after one of the locals mentioned her name. . . ."

"And she talked to him?"

"Apparently." Ryder glanced at her. "She seemed like a decent woman, Laurel. She's probably been shattered by this, too. Everything about her life would have become public knowledge no matter what she did or didn't do. She must have been angry. And I suppose she got paid for the interview."

"You didn't?"

"Sara wouldn't dare offer me my fee. But yes, those were my photographs in the Boston papers," Ryder confessed. He had talked to Sara early that morning, he told Laurel, learning that she'd released them, but not his article, because the quality of the pictures from the Shelby *Gazette* was so poor. He looked at Laurel. "She did it for me, out of friendship after all . . . I guess hoping you wouldn't hold me responsible for the story elsewhere."

"It was your story. Everywhere. The story is true. I

guess the best that can be said is that nobody's dead from it, are they?"

His heart sank at her tone. "I hope not."

"But you used me," she said, "and that hurts."

"Laurel, I didn't. Believe me."

"Ryder, using people to get what you want is such second nature to you as a journalist that you don't see it, but you did use me. In Gloucester—"

"Not in Gloucester, for God's sake!" He set his glass aside. "Afterward, I didn't pump you for information about Dan, did I? I never learned anything about his mysterious disappearances from you."

"I didn't know anything."

"Exactly." Ryder felt as if he were pleading.

She whirled around. "He's been living with her for a decade, can you believe that? They met three months after we were married. You should have told me," she finished.

"So Hilary said. I know I should. And I'm sorry that I tried to make you leave Benedict when you weren't prepared, or ready to make the choice. There's only one I would have accepted anyway Friday afternoon. Because I was scared. After Teague Michaels saw us I was trying to avoid exactly what did happen, having you walk out of my life."

Ryder stepped closer. "Laurel, I didn't want to hurt you. I didn't mean what I said about Dan loving Lexa. I was only trying to avoid saying Maria Cruz, so I said the first thing—a stupid, cruel thing—that came into my head."

"Truer than you knew. Dan never loved my sister, or me."

"Maybe he doesn't love Maria Cruz either. Maybe he doesn't love anyone except himself."

She shook her head. "No, that's not true. You've seen him with the voters who've elected him tonight. With the poor, the dispossessed, the elderly, and the little Puerto Rican child who may have rickets from lack of proper diet, he's quite wonderful."

"Then maybe some people aren't meant to have private lives."

"Perhaps the senator, too," she said.

"Quite possibly. That's not what I want." For years he had lived with such personal deprivation. Now he wanted more; he wanted Laurel. "Do you?"

She looked up into his eyes. They were clear and not as sadly wise. For a moment, she saw him as he might have been years ago, as she had seen him in the pictures from his book: younger, of course, but happier, freer. The look, though tinged with tonight's weariness, was there now. Like her, he seemed calm—and at last, peaceful.

But she couldn't answer his question, not yet.

"Ryder, what went on between you and Ned tonight? Was it something to do with Hoa?"

"I'll tell you later. I promise." He touched her hair and then her cheek with whisper-light fingers. "There's no sense in waking Ned. He's had a rough day. Why don't we concentrate for now on your forgiving me."

Her heartbeat accelerated. Suddenly Laurel felt as if she were perched again on her tree house limb, wondering whether she could fly. She hadn't been able to before.

"I . . . Ryder, I think you're right. That we should talk later . . . tomorrow."

"Whenever you're ready," he said, sounding disappointed by her retreat. "I know the last few days, and tonight, have been—"

"Yes." She cleared her throat. "I really should go. . . ."

"Where?"

Good question, Laurel thought. She didn't want to stay on Beacon Hill. The memories there were largely false ones. A hotel for the night, she supposed, until she could find an apartment large enough for Ned, and Pirate...

But how many apartments would take such a large, and unruly, dog?

She might spend time in Chevy Chase.

But during Dan's acceptance speech her mind had wandered to Sebastian's catalogue drawings, and the deadline she had to meet. Eager to resume work that she found fulfilling, Laurel at almost thirty-three hadn't the vaguest desire to end up in Chevy Chase or, figuratively speaking, in her old tree house again.

Stay on the ground, the senator had once told her but Lexa had said Jump, Laurel. The thought made her smile, but the smile was bittersweet. All these years without Lexa she hadn't felt complete within herself.

Being twins, she and Lexa had formed a stronger bond than most siblings; they'd had a total commitment to each other, the kind that needed no words to communicate, that passed between husbands and wives in a good marriage, between lovers. A bond, she realized, that in the normal course of time would have shifted to other people as they fell in love, then married, and left childhood behind. Because of Lexa's death at nineteen, they'd never completed the growth—or separation—process.

Love, Laurel thought; unconditional love. She felt that with Ned, but it was a mother's love for her child, just as strong yet different. She'd never known it with Dan. No, she'd felt unqualified love for a man the first time in Gloucester, one morning in the rain.

That morning she'd seen passion in his stormy gray eyes; now she saw love, and uncertainty.

"I'm not sure where," she said at last, "but for tonight I was wondering whether you might have a spare pillow. And time to talk about forgiveness."

Ryder's eyes came to life. She watched him light a cigarette with shaking hands. Then watched him stub it out in an overflowing ashtray on the sideboard.

"That's it," he said. "No more. That's the last cigarette I'm ever going to smoke." He stood just inches from her. "And if I can stop smoking, you can get that dog through obedience training."

"What are you trying to say?"

"That I've got time on my hands. It's all yours. That I've got a spare pillow and half a double bed and you're not going anywhere else." Cocking his head, he gave her an odd, assessing look. "I think I knew it the minute you rang the bell tonight."

"How?" She hadn't known herself.

Ryder touched the tortoiseshell frames of her glasses, then slowly drew them off. "You never wore these for him," he said, "only with me. Because I like them."

"They're not the only difference in me tonight. It's only fair to warn you. There'll be more."

"I'll like them all. Because I love you."

"Danger, if I remember, makes you rash." Laurel's eyes were sparkling. "Do you really want us to stay? All of us? I am rather a package deal, you know."

"I want you to stay, yeah." Setting the glasses aside, he made a pretense of considering her statement. "Danger or not, I'm pretty sure about the rest."

She studied his face, satisfied with what she saw there. "I love you," she whispered and looped her arms around his neck as Ryder spanned her waist with warm, steady hands.

"Sweetheart, maybe that's all we need—" he pulled her closer "—though I kind of doubt it."

"You photojournalists are all alike. Don't be such a cynic," she said. "The war's over."

"Who are you kidding?" His smile widened as Ryder

looked into her eyes. "Ned, Pirate, you, me. A three-bedroom apartment half painted that already seems too small. We need an artist's studio, a photographer's dark-room. We've got two free-lancers here with no visible means of support." He paused. "And by next year we might even have another mouth to feed."

"A *baby*?"

As he lowered his head, Ryder spoke without regret. "Hey, you never know what you can do till you try." When their mouths met, he was still grinning. "I think the war's just starting."

"I can hardly wait."

# Harper Monogram *By Mail*

## Looking For Love?
## Try HarperMonogram's Bestselling Romances

### TAPESTRY
by Maura Seger
An aristocratic Saxon woman loses her heart to
the Norman man who rules her conquered people.

### DREAM TIME
by Parris Afton Bonds
In the distant outback of Australia, a mother
and daughter are ready to sacrifice everything
for their dreams of love.

### RAIN LILY
by Candace Camp
In the aftermath of the Civil War in Arkansas, a
farmer's wife struggles between duty and passion.

### COMING UP ROSES
by Catherine Anderson
Only buried secrets could stop the love
of a young widow and her new beau
from bloomimg.

### ONE GOOD MAN
by Terri Herrington
When faced with a lucrative offer to seduce
a billionaire industrialist, a young woman
discovers her true desires.

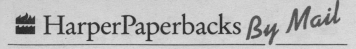